The Murders, The Mosque

Justice in the Golden Age of al-Andalus
Suramarti Saga #2

J. Oestreicher
&
D.R. Oestreicher

Omega Cat Press — California

Omega Cat Press, independent publishing since 1990

Paperback ISBN: 978-1-954225-00-8
Electronic Book ISBN: 978-1-954225-01-5

3 4 5 6 7 8 9

Peace
Salaam – Arabic
Pax – Latin
Shalom – Hebrew

Dedicated to our enthusiastic mystery readers.

Also by J. Oestreicher and D.R. Oestreicher

Pandemic Mysteries #1: Darwin's Paradox
#2: Plague of Equals
#3: The Two Pearls
Suramarti Saga #1: Kitane, Bull Jumper

By Joy Oestreicher

Legends of Azureign #1: Dragon and Oracle
#2: Raka and Secrets

Table of Contents

CHARACTERS

Abbas ibn Firnas — historical polymath, inventor, physician, chemist, engineer, musician, and poet.

The second **Abd al Rahman** — historical emir who ruled al-Andalus 822-852. He loved *Tarub the Learned* so much that he freed her from his hareem and married her. Father of Emir Muhammad.

Abdallah min Alshamal – *Hathus* and *Lylah min Alshamal's* son.

Bhaja — librarian at *Tarub the Learned's* Library. Arabic is her native language. She also speaks and reads Roman Latin and Tamasheq and comprehends the local Latin variations of Galician and Catalan. She is the older sister of *Yusuf.* Their mother is a widow.

Chedar — guard and fighter who freelances. He guards trader caravans and is a friend of *Yusuf.*

Darras of Osuna — manuscript merchant who trades with *Tarub* and *Bhaja* and travels extensively.

Emir Muhammad — historical emir who ruled al-Andalus 852-886.

Ezra – Jewish butcher in Qurtuba who hires *Raviv* as his apprentice.

Gwafa — mercenary fighter.

Hathus min Alshamal — rug merchant. Married to *Lylah.*

Isador — Christian cleric that *Bhaja* hires to do copying and illustration.

Javed — Judge Javan's brother.

Judge Javan the Merciful — compassionate judge.

Judge Kabos, Allah's Protector — hanging judge.

Kaila and **Osora** — illicitly pregnant concubines.

Lylah min Alshamal — married to *Hathus.* Mother of *Abdullah.*

Malik al Jamal – landowner and trader, brother to *Sayyida.*

Naomi – translator, she speaks and reads fluent Hebrew, Roman Latin, Greek, and Persian. She is familiar with but is not fluent in Arabic, Aramaic, and Armenian. Some knowledge of Basque and Tamasheq. Friend of *Darras.*

Qusayma of Osuna – *Darras's* distant cousin, lives in Osuna.

Pai of Qurtuba – mapmaker, shopkeeper, and manufacturer of fine paper.

Pope John VIII – historical Pope, bishop of Rome from 872 to 882.

Raviv – son of *Naomi.*

Sayyida al Jamal – sister to Malik. She lives on the family farm in the valley west of Ronda.

Tarub the Learned – powerful woman whom the second *Abd al-Rahman* freed and married. She sponsors the Library and schools. She holds court at her villa.

Wararni – *Zetian's* fiancé. Member of the Emir's guard.

Yusuf – *Bhaja's* brother. A soldier in training to join the Emir's guard, still living at home.

Wu Zetian, – Chinese woman who works for Pai making paper. Named after an empress by her mother but sold by her father.

Xarq – *Yusuf's* friend, a former guard at the citadel.

Ziryab – historical singer and stylist from Baghdad. He brought new clothing modes, table manners, and other trendy social etiquette to Qurtuba.

GLOSSARY

Abbasid dynasty – seized control of the Caliphate (632) from the *Umayyad.* Ruled over most of the Islamic empire cultivating great intellectual and cultural developments in the Middle East in the Golden Age of Islam. Moved the capital from Damascus to Baghdad.

Allahu Akbar – God is great.

Alhamdulillah – Thank God.

al-Andalus — the southern area of Spain settled by Muslims.

al-Hind — a major section of today's India.

al-Jazair — present day Algeria.

al-Qin — China and the Chinese language.

As-Salaam-Alaikum — the Arabic greeting meaning "Peace be unto you. " Similar to "Peace be with you" used by Christians.

Wa-Alaikum-Assalaam — the Arabic response meaning "And unto you peace." Similar to "And also with you," used by Christians.

Baghdad — the capital of the *Abbasid* dynasty.

Bahr al-Rum — present day Mediterranean Sea.

barjyn — eating implement, two-tined fork.

Bible — the Christian Holy Book, which contains the history of ancient life, and the story of Jesus the Christian prophet and savior, divided into two major sections, the Old Testament and the New.

citadel — the palace-fortress where the Emir lives and conducts business.

diya — in Islamic law is the financial compensation paid to the victim or heirs of a victim in the cases of murder, bodily harm, or property damage. It is an alternative punishment to *qisas* (equal retaliation).

Écija — a small town one day's travel from *Qurtuba* (towards Ronda, southeast), two days west from *Ronda.*

Gades — present day Cádiz.

Galicia – present day Portugal.

Great Mosque – present day Mosque-Cathedral of Córdoba. The first Abd al Rahman began the construction in 785.

hadith — the Prophet's rules for living daily life.

halal – okay to eat.

haram – forbidden, unclean.

House of Wisdom – an immense library and school in Baghdad.

Ifriqa — present day Africa.

Insha'Allah — literally means "If God wills it will happen" in Arabic.

Ishbiliyah — present day Seville.

keffiyeh — traditional men's head covering; usually wrapped, but sometimes left to drape back and shoulders. Sometimes keffiyehs are held on by a band or rope.

Mahgreb —much of northern Africa, including a large portion of the Sahara, but excluding Egypt.

Majus — literally, fire-worshippers (Zoroastrians); used to refer to the Northmen, the Vikings, who attacked several times up the Wadi al-Kabir in the 9th and 10th centuries.

Málaga — the closest port to Ronda.

medina — usually the oldest part of a town or city, typically walled, with many narrow and maze-like streets.

miswak — stick toothbrush, usually of the *Salvadora persica* shrub which has antibacterial properties.

mohreh — a device used to spread the starch to make finished paper smoother and shiny.

muezzin — a man who calls Muslims to prayer from the minaret of a mosque.

Osuna — a small town one day's travel west from *Ronda*, two days from *Qurtuba*.

penner — a leather tube for storing and carrying quill pens.

qibla – obligatory prayer direction in Islam, facing the Kaaba, the massive stone cube in Mecca. If you are west of Mecca you pray facing east, and opposite.

qisas – an Islamic term interpreted to mean "retaliation in kind," "eye for an eye," or retributive justice. In the case of murder, qisas gives the right to take the life of the killer, if the latter is convicted and the court approves.

Qurtuba – present day Cordoba.

Quran – the Muslim Holy Book, which along with the hadiths, pronounces the rules of living, and recounts the Prophet Mohammad's life.

Rumiyyat al-Kubra — Constantinople, now Istanbul.

Sharia – Islamic canonical law based on the Quran and the hadiths.

Shuqunda – village/suburb near *Qurtuba*, with a forest or copses of larch trees.

souk — bazaar, or marketplace.

surah – section of the *Quran*, similar to a chapter in the *Bible*.

Tarub the Learned's Library – library started in Qurtuba with aspirations to eventually compare to the *House of Wisdom* in *Baghdad*.

Tiaret – capital city in *al-Jazair*.

Torah – the Jewish Holy Book, which consists of the first five chapters of the Bible and includes a history and genealogy of the Jewish people. Additional Laws are in the Talmud and rabbinical rulings.

Umayyad dynasty – the first great Muslim dynasty to rule the Caliphate in the Middle East, replaced by the *Abbasid*. Members of the Umayyad dynasty were hunted down and killed, but the first Abd al Rahman escaped and established himself as a Muslim ruler in Spain (756), founding the dynasty of the Umayyads in *Qurtuba*.

Wadi al-Kabir – Great River, present day Guadalquivir, the river flowing past *Qurtuba*.

Wadi al-Laban – River of Milk, present day Guadalevin, the river dividing Ronda.

1. Words and Worries

Bahja felt the presence of someone beside her. She withdrew her head, now covered in cobwebs, from the bottom corner shelves of the Great Mosque's library. She brought with her the single dusty scroll she had ferreted out. Who knew how long it had been lost down there?

As she turned and straightened up, she recognized the visitor. Tarub the Learned. One of the wealthiest and most influential women in the city.

Hastily wiping cobwebs from her hair and hands, Bhaja gave a small half-bow of acknowledgment. The lady was an important woman in Qurtuba, perhaps one of the most influential in all al-Andalus. What could she want with Bhaja?

"I see you are still engaged in putting this library in order," the woman said.

Bhaja felt filthy and scattered next to the woman's perfect appearance. It wasn't just that Tarub was beautiful. It was that she was also perfectly groomed, perfectly composed, perfectly attired. Despite this, her smile, while also beautiful and perfect, seemed genuine. She reached a delicate hand and pulled off another string of cobweb from Bhaja's hair. "The state of this place was disgraceful until you began working on it," Tarub went on.

"I've almost finished now," Bhaja said, "but it was definitely neglected for a long time." She glanced at the finished sections, clean and neatly stacked. Then she looked back at Tarub. Her eyes were caught again by Tarub's appearance, even as Bhaja's mind admired the lady's thoughtfulness.

She could begin to see that perfect beauty might be a problem.

It must be difficult to bear such a fine mind, constantly unnoticed, behind the lovely appearance. Bhaja thought she herself *might* be a match for the mind, but never for the beauty and grace. "Merely pretty," she'd heard herself described, "but awkward as an overloaded burro."

"You've organized the holdings here into categories, I see," Tarub said, studying the clean shelves. "Ah, and you have even created labels, so readers know where to look." She glanced at Bhaja, then back to the shelves. "That means you *think*, as well as read and write."

Bhaja's estimation of the woman rose again. What a thing to notice! "I do," she mumbled.

Carefully holding the dusty scroll away from the lady and from her own skirts, Bhaja shook the dust off and unrolled it. From the first line, she could see it was a commentary a judge had written, his opinion on a court case. Like others of its kind, it should go to the legal category. "A document arguing Sharia," she said, re-rolling it and placing it on the appropriate shelf.

"Is this work that you enjoy?" Tarub asked, eyeing Bhaja's dusty hands and clothes.

Silent a moment while she let her embarrassment fade and her wits to function, Bhaja said, "I enjoy the sense of discovery. There is a thrill of anticipation, as I open each document and identify it. Though I am not fond of reading the arguments of judges, or listings of taxes collected."

The Learned laughed aloud at this. "I think no one is fond of reading those!" She shook her head. "Well, perhaps the imams and our arithmetically blessed Emir. But it is a different matter entirely when the scrolls are filled with history, or parchments adorned with poetry. Many people enjoy those, both reading and discussing them."

Bhaja thought that might be an exaggeration. *Many* people did not read at all. *Could* not. Even those like her friend Pai who had the ability to read and write well, would not spend their time admiring poetry. They had other things to do. But that was not what things looked like from Tarub's point of view, she guessed. "Yes, I can see that. Just as some folks, like Abbas ibn Firnas, love the science and medicine texts. There are not many of those, here." Bhaja looked along the lengths of shelves. "In fact, I cannot think of any."

"No." Tarub the Learned agreed. "Those belong elsewhere. In fact, I have some in the tiny library space in my home that Abbas enjoys looking at." She turned and walked to the heavy oak table where Bhaja had been copying pages of the Quran. "Do you know the Library I recently had built? A building to hold nothing but folios, scrolls and books—and occasionally the people who read and write them?"

"Yes," Bhaja said. "I've admired the construction for the last several years. Its walls make a hexagon!" Built of dark grey marble, the placement of those walls had fascinated her. Just this week the workers had finished laying the terra cotta roof tiles and had removed the scaffolding. "It is beautiful."

"Thank you. I designed it myself, you know." Fitting the woman's reputation, Tarub's boast was so genteel, it did not sound like bragging. The woman just stated a matter-of-fact truth about herself.

Tarub waved a hand at the pages lying on the oak table. "I assume this is your work?" the lady asked.

"Yes," Bhaja agreed. *Allah reveal, what does this woman want?* It was beginning to sound like an interrogation. *What have I done so wrong, that she should come here and question me?*

Bhaja went across the room to the table where a pitcher of water and bowl stood; she washed her hands and face and dried them on the towel that hung on the end bar. Then she turned back to face the woman that had invaded what she had claimed as her own private space for the last several weeks.

"You have a good hand at Arabic," Tarub said, still studying the Quran pages. "Strong, pleasantly artistic, but above all, readable." She looked up and smiled at Bhaja. Even her eyes smiled, Bhaja realized.

"Thank you," she thought to say. She had never before imagined her handwriting to be anything but prosaic.

After a short silence, Tarub said, "Would you like a position as librarian in my new Library? You would do as you have done here, plus collect new items, and copy and translate old ones."

Bhaja blinked twice, collecting her thoughts, which had shot off in all directions. Her? A librarian? Paid by the distinguished woman who had once been an Emir's favorite concubine? What would Pai think? How would her mother react?

It didn't matter. She *wanted* this. All her thoughts rushed back together and pushed her answer out of her mouth: "Yes," she said, excitement rising. "I would love this!"

"Then let us make it so," The Learned said. "Please meet me at the new building tomorrow, mid-morning. I can tell you my thoughts and plans and hear your ideas."

"Gladly." Bhaja tilted her head in a quick bow. She did not need to be subservient; she was not a slave. But everyone respected Tarub the Learned. If she was to work for the woman, she should surely show her the deference she had long ago earned.

When she finished cleaning the last shelves of the library in the Great Mosque and observed sunset prayers, Bhaja sought out the imam. She gave notice to the man that she would not be back, because the library was now as orderly as she could make it. He surprised her with a low bow, and followed that with profuse verbal thanks. He'd known the job needed doing, but had never found the time among all his other duties.

When Bhaja took on the project, she'd thought of it as thanks to the imam's school that had taught her to read and write. The mosque schools did not always permit girls to attend, so she had been lucky it was run by this Umayyad Muslim. The Abbasids were much more strict in their interpretations of the hadiths and Quran. *They* would have expected her to have married many years ago and to now be home taking care of a house full of children.

As she left the building, she knew at least a few of the local young men returning from prayers watched her. They often watched her, even when she was in the women's gallery of the mosque, though none ever approached.

Was it her work for the imam that was intimidating? Or could it somehow be Bhaja herself? She was not certain she wanted to know. She pulled her headscarf up to cover her hair more completely.

She walked home, pausing at Tarub's Library to admire it again. The courtyard at the front allowed entry from three sides, welcoming visitors to the place. Or it would. Presently it was still a tangle of construction materials, dirt, and tools.

The door to the Library itself was closed. Deciding that tomorrow was soon enough to see the interior, Bhaja continued homeward, deep in thought.

What would she need, to make the Library function as it should? First, she would need paper, or at least parchment and papyrus, and quills and inks. A desk or two for copying. Somewhere to sit and just read or converse.

Maybe there was still time to suggest tables outside in the courtyard for eating, since Bhaja was determined to prohibit food inside. She had *seen* the result of food consumption in a library. A major part of the problems in the Great Mosque library were due to food and its consequences: besides dirt and spills, grease marks and stains left on the documents themselves, the crumbs attracted insects. Insects that went on to eat the library holdings once the food crumbs were gone. They especially enjoyed chewing on the older texts, those written on papyrus. She had found at least one—it was hard to tell from the scraps—that had been eaten to nothing. She couldn't even tell what that ancient treasure had been about from the few shreds that remained.

Yes. She would definitely demand that no food be allowed.

She wondered what Tarub would think of that.

Well, that was a topic for tomorrow.

Bhaja entered the portico of her parents' home and kicked off her sandals. Her father was given the house for his part in leading the Emir Muhammad's battle with some Berbers who had revolted against his rule. But Father had only enjoyed their new home for two years before being killed in yet another fight. The Emir might consider them squabbles, not wars, but good men died no matter what he called them.

She could still remember the house they'd had in her childhood. The roof leaked, wind swept through the boards of the upper walls, and the foundation along one wall collapsed from a flood that washed away the mud beneath, making the house unstable. Worse, it had been outside the city walls, making them vulnerable to those Berber attacks.

Their new home, bought with Father's blood, lay well within the medina. Bhaja always remembered to honor his sacrifice with her thanks.

As she came into the kitchen, her mother looked up and smiled from the table where she had been chopping vegetables.

"Mama," Bhaja said, removing her headscarf and over robe, "I have a new job!"

Already sitting at the table, her younger brother Yusuf snorted with disbelief. "You didn't have an *old* job," he said.

"Do you think working at the Great Mosque is not a proper job?" their mother said, frowning at Yusuf.

"Do you think work *without pay* is a proper job?" Yusuf argued. "At least I bring in a little money."

Oh, that was what bothered Yusuf. *He* did not have a regular job; he got work as he could, and while he was well-paid for it—guard work was dangerous—the money he brought into the household was too erratic to be counted on. If not for his irregular contributions, they would have gone hungry several times over the last year. Yusuf had been so proud to bring home satchels of food.

Bhaja's potential income threatened him and his status in their little family.

"What is this 'job?'" he asked.

"I will again be a librarian," Bhaja said. "But I will be paid for my work."

"That is wonderful news," Mother said. She was careful to smile at Yusuf, too, so he would not feel belittled.

"Where is there such a library?" Yusuf asked.

"The new one, near the Great Mosque."

Yusuf scowled. "That is the Library of Tarub the concubine!"

"That's ridiculous, Yusuf. She has not been a concubine for decades! She is a wealthy patron of education and literature."

Her brother's scowl deepened. "She is an enemy of the Emir. You know, the Emir I seek to hire me once my training is complete!" His tone was ugly.

Did he really think that where his sister worked was going to affect his chances with the Emir's guard?

Their mother caught the friction and deflected it. She said, "Your father's honor will buy you that place, Yusuf, so long as you are a capable fighter."

"Besides," Bhaja added, "the extra income will help pay for your battle horse and armor." *You know, the horse and armor you must have before the Emir will hire you,* she did not say. Certainly his old mare was laughable; the only battle she'd had lately was snuffling out fallen oats in her stall.

Yusuf grunted, only somewhat mollified.

Bhaja sighed. "What can I do to help with dinner, Mama?"

"Stir these while I shell the almonds," she said, indicating the pan half-filled with sizzling vegetables. "And Yusuf could bring in some more wood for the fire."

The next morning Bhaja's walk to the Library was filled with anticipation.

Would Tarub want or like her categories for sorting the texts? She'd added Science, Medicine, History, and Poetry, in addition to law commentaries.

The woman was waiting for her at the Library doorway. Behind Tarub, Bhaja could see one of the woman's eunuch guards. While his features were rounded and appeared soft, the man's posture told a different story. Like Yusuf, his muscles and weapons and a ready stance made him a threat. It was sad Tarub needed a guard, but enmity with the current Emir probably made it a sensible precaution.

"Let me first show you the puzzle lock I devised with the help of my woodworkers." Tarub demonstrated how to lock and unlock the big Library door. Bhaja wondered if even the several steps required for the unlocking were going to be sufficient to keep out a determined robber—or an ax-wielding strongman. But she did have to pay close attention to memorize the procedure. Curiosity lit her mind. *How does the cunning thing work?*

That done, they moved inside the building, and Bhaja had to abandon her fascination with the lock for later.

They discussed open shelves versus closed cabinets, and decided on a mixture of both: cabinets below, shelves above.

Tarub wanted discussions to happen in her Library. "I have ordered carpets and pillows and three small couches for this purpose."

"I must insist that no food can be brought inside."

Tarub turned to her, eyebrows raised. "That will limit the ease and length of discourse," she said, a puzzled tone to her voice.

"Food means crumbs, crumbs mean insects, insects mean holes in manuscripts."

An elegant finger tapped bow-curved lips. "I see," Tarub said.

"I think the emphasis should be on the Library holdings, not on festivities." After saying it, Bhaja bit her lip. She hadn't meant to sound critical, just to make her point.

Tarub's eyelashes fluttered, then she said, "I agree the texts are most important. I suppose if a discussion continues through a mealtime, it could be moved to my villa."

"Or perhaps to tables out in the courtyard, here."

"Oh! Excellent!" Tarub's smile was radiant. "I will order a pavilion for shade, and several clusters of tables amongst the plantings and fountains I planned." She met Bhaja's eyes. "Good. An excellent, careful thought, with the emphasis on the importance of the Library holdings." She waved slender, be-ringed fingers at the outdoor courtyard area. "It will be cleared, cleaned, and paved in some sections, with plants and trees in others. Good thing it was planned to be large; your thought on food indoors hadn't occurred to me, but outdoors would be a nice venue for longer talks. Already, people flow from inside my villa out to my gardens and back, so this will be similar."

"It might be limited access in winter—" Bhaja began.

"The pavilion will be oiled cloth, which will fend off at least gentle rains. And in the event of bad storms, the people can then repair to my villa, to continue their discussion."

They spent a few more moments inside Tarub's Library, discussing the small toilet facilities, buying the pitchers, bowls, and towels for washing, what implements Bhaja would need for cleaning and preserving manuscripts, and whether or not they needed a housekeeper.

Then Tarub flicked a hand at the eunuch guard, who removed from his belt pocket a heavy bag. He gave this to Tarub without speaking. In fact, Bhaja realized, he had said not a word the entire time they'd been there.

"This," Tarub said, recapturing Bhaja's attention, "is some coin to pay for things you might need, among them translators and copyists, and your personal requirements.

"I've ordered a beginning supply of paper," she went on, "and some parchment, also a variety of inks, and I have put in a standing order for quills from the finest makers in Qurtuba. The slanted desks I've commissioned will arrive next week. Also there will be two flat tables—oh, and a ladder system for accessing higher shelves! If you decide you need more furnishings, let me know. This," she jingled the bag of coins, "is primarily for you personally, and for small payments to your staff. The general Library necessities will be ordered and paid for through my offices."

Having said all that, Tarub revealed the first sign of discomfort Bhaja had seen. The lady rubbed her hip, a pained expression crossing her face.

Bhaja realized they'd been standing for several hours. The woman must be more than fifty years old, perhaps even in her sixties, and that was a long time for an older lady to be on her feet without a break, if her own mother was any example.

"I will send my collection of documents and texts as soon as the shelves have been installed, which should take only two or three days." Tarub glanced around the empty Library and smiled. "It would be little enough to be embarrassing, except that I also have in storage the scrolls, tablets, and books the first Emir al Rahman managed to bring with him when he fled Baghdad so long ago." She shook her head, displeasure quirking her mouth. "The Emir Muhammad was going to sell them away, the idiot."

Bhaja blurted, "Why? Al Rahman was his ancestor too, wasn't he?"

"Of course. But Muhammad, for all his love of discourse, is not particularly fond of reading, and he is always looking for more gold." She shook her head. "He'd rather make war than read, rather talk to erudite men than spend the energy to read their words, and would always rather visit his hareem than—you understand the matter, I'm sure."

"Oh," Bhaja said. Of course, as one of the elite of the city, and once a popular resident of the citadel herself, Tarub would have intimate knowledge of the Emirs.

"I suspect you will want a full-time translator to bring all the Greek texts into Arabic. Perhaps a copyist or two to make at least one reading copy of each translation, particularly the older things. Medical studies and the like—those could have many readers."

"Yes, I see," Bhaja said. "Of course I can begin working on any Latin translations immediately myself. But the Greek will have to be put aside until someone is found."

How *was* someone to be found? Before she could ask for suggestions, Tarub went on, speaking rapidly now, as if to finish things quickly.

"I have plans to include a locked cabinet for the truly rare finds we may acquire, and it would be a safe place for your coins, as well, Bhaja."

Bhaja nodded her understanding.

"Until that arrives, you should keep the coins locked inside the building when you are not here. They should be safe enough, since everyone knows there's nothing much of value in the building yet."

"Of course."

"I will come by next week and see how you are doing, but if you need something meanwhile, send a runner to my villa."

"I will do so," Bhaja said.

"Check the Library every day starting the day after tomorrow. Once the shelves are installed and most of the cabinets are built-in, your supplies will arrive, and it will be up to you to arrange them as you find useful. Thus you will begin work as soon as there is something to do."

Tarub turned to leave, but abruptly stopped. "Bhaja, I may need your help tomorrow, if you don't mind."

"Of course," Bhaja said.

"I will send a runner to say when and where."

Bhaja nodded, "I will see you then."

2. Precious Paper

A young girl with two long braids held out her hand. "Can you draw me a kitty cat?" Her little brother stood on one leg, presenting his knee, just washed this morning and several shades lighter than the rest of him. "An eagle please." Pai sketched the requests with a few strokes of his quill, making time for the other children that surrounded him.

The drawings would only last for a short while before they were blurred by sweat or faded by dirt, but the morning ritual brought joy to Pai and to the children on their way to school. He greeted each child with "Blessing upon you," "Study hard," or "See you tomorrow."

Later their mothers came to the market and stopped at Pai's blanket to say, "My children get ready quickly, so they have time for a picture," or "They wake up without a struggle." Pai felt the same. Each morning he anticipated the hands, arms, and legs offered for decoration.

Once the school day began, he displayed his maps. *The Roman roads of al-Andalus. The paths and alleys of Qurtuba. The way to Ishbiliyah.* And many others. While he sat in the main Qurtuba market waiting for customers, he alternated his time between copying maps and gossiping with the women. He had the best job, visiting and drawing all day. He was so glad to have left the sleepy village of Ronda for the excitement of Qurtuba.

On a clean piece of parchment, he began *The way to Ronda* with a long blue line representing the Wadi al-Kabir that flowed past the walled medina of Qurtuba. He held the result up for the ink to dry and to admire his artwork. He changed colors to black to draw the route from Ronda at the top of the map to Qurtuba at the bottom. This time his eagle feather quill caught on a rough spot and sprayed a cloud of ink around the road from Osuna to Écija. "Peace be with you," he muttered, meaning the opposite. Parchment was cheaper than papyrus, but still too dear to discard. One way or another, he'd fix it. He always had.

He waved the page to dry the ink and then opened a sack of powdery sand from a deep pool of the Wadi al-Laban. He sprinkled it on his mistake and rubbed the paper with his fingertip. When he blew it away, the cloud of ink remained. He didn't worry. He had other tricks. That stretch of road went through a woods, so he added more stippling and lettered *Osuna Forest* beside it. *Fixed.*

When the muezzin called for noon prayers, Pai rolled up his maps and returned to the home of Abbas ibn Firnas where he swept floors and tended the garden in exchange for a small room and meals. Sometimes he'd help Abbas to illustrate his inventions.

Ibn Firnas had lived in Ronda when Pai was a child. Pai had learned more from the old man than from his teachers. Abbas had taught him, *Do something new every day*. As emigrants from the same village, they became friends when they met again in the city.

When Pai returned to Abbas's house, he was happy to see they had guests, his favorite guests. Tarub sat on a silk pillow in Abbas ibn Firnas's front room dressed in fine robes of silk with wide borders of geometric stitching. Her headscarf was plain white with white embroidery. Soft leather sandals peeked out from under her robes. Bhaja stood beside her patron. While her clothes were plainer, Pai still thought she was more beautiful, especially her dark gold eyes.

He mused, *I'd never have met Bhaja if I hadn't escaped to the capital city of Qurtuba from small-town Ronda, isolated on its mesa.*

Pai listened to Tarub speaking with Abbas. "I offered the paper-making secret to the citadel and the mosque. They have so many scholars and scribes, but they prefer to collect taxes and donations rather than set up manufacturing."

Abbas stroked his long white beard. "You would have better luck with the Emir's council and businessmen like Hathus, the rug merchant."

Tarub scoffed. "They too refused. Travelers report the Baghdad paper market has over a hundred merchants, but Qurtuba has none."

Pai listened intently to this talk of paper.

Bhaja added, "Once your library is open, it will also need fine paper, something better than the parchment, papyrus, and rough paper available today."

Pai nodded his head in support of Bhaja. He knew she would have thought of everything and if she said they needed this paper, he believed her.

He saw Tarub also agreed. Nodding, she said, "You are right. That is why I have acquired a shop to house the secret and make the paper. Now I need someone to supervise the paper production and do the marketing.

Pai forgot about the smiling faces on their way to school each morning. Making paper would be magical. He jumped up. "I'll do it!"

Everyone turned around in surprise.

Abbas spoke first. “Tarub, do you recall my young compatriot from Ronda? He makes maps.”

“Yes, I know him. He is a friend of my librarian.”

Bhaja smiled and her eyes sparkled.

Tarub addressed Pai, “This is a lot of work.”

Bhaja suggested, “Wouldn’t you like to know some more before you decide?”

Pai said, “An eaglet doesn’t ask how high it is before it leaves the nest. I’ll do it.”

Tarub handed Pai a small piece of fine paper. “This is what you’ll be making.”

His fingertips glided across the surface, smooth as a polished stone. He’d never seen anything like it. He held the page against his cheek. *Is this made by djinnis?* Holding it up to the sun, he exclaimed, “See how the light shines through! Finer than a butterfly’s wing.”

He ran to get his pen and inks. “Oh please, can I draw on this?”

Tarub laughed, “Certainly.”

Recalling the splatter on the map to Ronda, he inked his quill and drew a long flowing line. “Praise God. Look at this!” He displayed it to Abbas. “Notice how evenly the ink is accepted. No bumps. No blobs.” *A miracle!* He brought the line close to his face for examination. The ink had followed his pen without a single smudge. With anxious anticipation, he checked the reverse side. “Look at this! Such fine paper and not a bit of ink soaked through.”

Tarub announced, “You will pay me half of everything you collect.”

Pai considered Tarub’s offer. He had no idea how much he could sell the fine paper for, but Bhaja had told him that Tarub had a reputation for fair dealing. Besides, it didn’t matter. He just wanted to make this paper. The alchemists wanted to make gold, but Pai preferred this. “I agree.”

“Meet me following the afternoon prayers where the river wall meets the sunrise wall.”

“I know the place. That is where the fancy shops are.”

Pai thought of Bhaja's question. Should he have learned something more before he agreed? He had given Tarub his answer and he was committed. *Abbas must be proud of me. I’ve embarked on something new today!*

Pai was waiting in the alley when Tarub turned the corner accompanied by Bhaja and followed by a wagon, and a crowd of servants.

"Follow me," Tarub said to Pai. She opened the door to a small room that Pai immediately thought of as his shop. *No more sitting on a blanket in the souk.* She exited the entry area to an atrium.

Pai's eyes grew big taking in the luxury of his own atrium. He could hardly listen to Tarub as his eyes flitted around the rest of the building. It was not a villa, but it was far more than the small room he had with Abbas.

The back wall presented two doorways. A sleeping room and a storeroom he decided. He smelled the odors of animals and looked to his left. Through a narrow opening on the side of the atrium, he saw an earthen floor covered with straw. A stable. A place to house his donkey and horse on cold nights. No longer would they be crowded in the communal paddock.

Pai focused back on Tarub who had been speaking the entire time. He hoped that he hadn't missed anything important.

"First you'll need kettles to boil the cloth," Tarub pronounced and signaled Bhaja.

Bhaja stepped out and called. Pai hopped out of the way when six men paraded through *his shop* and into the atrium carrying three kettles that just fit through the doorway. Suddenly the atrium seemed smaller. The men dropped the kettles and returned delivering wooden paddles, trays, and other constructions that reminded Pai of Ibn Firnas's wondrous inventions.

Fine paper seemed more complex than Pai had expected, but he didn't worry. He tapped his knuckles on the three kettles in succession making an impromptu tune. "Look at me. Yesterday I didn't have even the smallest pot to boil water for tea, and now I have three enormous kettles."

Still no teapot, he laughed to himself.

Tarub turned to Bhaja, "Now the rags."

Four women in simple homespun robes each carried a bundle of old clothes on their backs. They dumped them in a corner where Bhaja pointed.

Pai moved behind the kettles to avoid standing too close to the six women that crowded the space.

What have I gotten myself into? Pai pondered, and *What about the secret?* Kettles, mysterious machines, and rags packed the space, but there was no paper. What alchemy would combine this all to make paper?

Tarub addressed Pai. “This is just a start. You’ll need many more rags. You must find a way to get them.”

Rags, Pai thought. *Collecting rags is easier than conjuring fine paper.*

He looked over to Bhaja. She gave him her quirky smile that simultaneously said, *“I warned you,”* and, *“You can do it.”*

When the old-clothes ladies had left, he walked around examining the paddles and boxes, trying to imagine if fine paper was like cheese or wine. “The secret?” he asked.

Tarub called, “Wu Zetian! You can come in now.”

Pai looked to the door and a short woman in a plain silk robe entered his shop. He’d seen pictures of people from al-Qin with long, straight, black hair and almond-shaped eyes, but this was the first time he’d shared a room with one. Was she the djinni that called forth paper from old rags?

But where will she live?

Tarub said, “Let me know when the first paper is ready,” and headed for the door.

Pai gasped. “What am I supposed to do with this girl?”

Tarub turned. “She is now your responsibility. Take good care of her. She is the secret.”

Pai blurted out, “I can’t have a woman living with me!”

Tarub laughed. “Yes you can. She is my slave. I rescued her from the Emir’s hareem.” Tarub left.

The Emir’s hareem? The hareem was somewhere inside the citadel. A hidden place guarded by eunuchs and mystery. The girl now seemed different, older, a young woman, chin against her chest, slumped shoulders, scared. She reminded him of a young girl who came to the souk each morning but never asked for a drawing.

“Zetian,” he said softly, but she didn’t respond or even look up.

Pai looked to Bhaja.

Bhaja addressed the woman. “Do you speak Arabic?”

Now she stood taller and clearly replied, “Of course. I also speak the language of al-Qin. I am educated. I can read and write.”

“I am Bhaja. I live with my mother.” She pointed to Pai. “This is Pai. He makes maps.”

Pai didn’t interrupt the two women but inwardly exclaimed, *Maps AND fine paper!* He’d call his shop, “Pai’s fine paper and maps.” He’d add his shop to the *The paths and alleys of Qurtuba* map which already had labels for the Great Mosque and the Emir’s citadel. While he was at it, he’d also add Tarub’s Library—now that it was almost complete.

The exotic woman put down the small sack she was carrying. "I am Zetian."

Everyone looked around. In front was a small room that Pai had decided would be his shop. In the back were two rooms separated from the atrium by woolen curtains.

Bhaja pointed to the smaller room. "Zetian, this one is yours."

Pai was happy for Bhaja to take charge of this delicate decision.

Zetian put her sack in the room. "Thank you, but it is still summer. Could I sleep out here under the stars?"

Pai blushed.

Bhaja laughed. "Certainly. I can vouch for Pai. You will be safe."

Pai finally spoke. "This has been a busy day. Let's start making paper tomorrow."

Zetian offered, "I can go to the souk and make the evening meal. I noticed that peas, carrots, peppers, and onions are fresh. I can chop those." She reached into her sack and showed him a knife from al-Qin with a square blade. "I can fry them with some lamb and spices. I can also make rice." She turned to Bhaja, "Will you join us for the first dinner?"

"Yes, and I can bring you some old, but still useful pans, from my mother's house."

Zetian laughed. "Pans. Yes. I forgot there were no pans."

Fine paper and fine dining. Pai smiled and thought about an eaglet soaring over the Ronda valley. *I will also soar.*

3. VISIONS AND VERSATILITY

A week later, after prayers, Bhaja shook out her prayer mat and rolled up her blanket and sleeping mat and hid them in a lower cabinet. Morning light slanted down through the tall skinny windows Tarub had placed high on the walls, so as to never directly strike the shelves and their contents.

Bhaja went and got the new broom that had arrived the day before along with the pitchers, bowl, and oil for cleaning. She swept the entire Library floor, sending the sand and dust out the doorway into the still-unfinished courtyard.

She poured the remaining wash water from her basin over the flat stones that now lay just outside the entrance, so that area was also clean. Then people would not track the dirt back in. She left the arched door propped open as a welcoming gesture.

After a week by herself in the empty Library, she knew enough not to expect visitors. But they would come, someday. The Library was new and contained few volumes as yet, not much of an enticement.

Most scholars would travel to Baghdad to study, where it was said that thousands of scrolls and bound books were available. Of course, the Abbasid rulers there were the ones bragging about the size of their collection, so some exaggeration was probably involved.

Or, perhaps scholars might prefer to go to Rumiyyat al-Kubra—the city of many names, most recently Constantinopolis. The books there were mostly in Latin, while those in Baghdad were written primarily in Persian and Arabic.

Thus language, as much as his or her political affiliation, might affect a scholar's destination.

Here, Tarub the Learned was determined to make Qurtuba such a destination. That would take a while yet, though Bhaja held a secret hope her small progress in obtaining and sorting items for the Library would please the woman already. *She* was due to visit today, regardless of whoever else might show up.

Meanwhile, Bhaja finished the set of labels she had begun writing the evening before. Already they had a dozen histories, some commentaries, and a couple of Greek plays—at least she *thought* they were plays—that had to be translated.

She was still searching for a translator. She had asked her many friends, but no one had been able to suggest anyone. She was reluctant to visit the slave market, preferring instead to hire someone.

She planned to try the schools, but it seemed if a viable candidate was there, Tarub would have suggested it.

And where should she search for more manuscripts? A few had been hiding at the Mosque. Where else could she look? What would she find? Her search was as exciting as a treasure hunt.

As they'd previously agreed, Bhaja met Pai beside the kabob vendor. Pai paid for their lunch, which they carried to the new tables in the Library courtyard.

Still barren piles of dirt surrounded areas of laid stone and packed sand in the courtyard, but the Ashlar-built wall provided them some privacy.

"Did you bring the barjyn?" Pai asked.

"Here they are," Bhaja lifted the sack she had tied to her belt and drew out the two brand new eating implements.

Handles of bone, double tines of brass, the barjyn had been made to the design of Ziryab the Singer, who had brought from the East his fine table manners and modern etiquette when he had arrived in Qurtuba a half-century before. So far, only the elite of the city had taught themselves how to use the tools and adopted the manners, but Bhaja and Pai had decided they should learn. If they ever had to eat in the presence of their mutual patron, Tarub the Learned and her friends, they would not look like complete country clods.

Bhaja managed to slide the meat off her skewer using the barjyn, but then was confused about how to cut the meat into small enough portions. If she put the bigger pieces in her mouth, she would choke before she chewed them small enough to swallow.

Watching her, Pai suggested, "Do you suppose you hold the barjyn in one hand and the knife in the other?" They were accustomed to holding meat in their fingers or inside a pita. They would take bites of it, if the piece was too big to eat in one go. The barjyn introduced another step into the process.

"This is awkward," Bhaja said, trying to manipulate both her eating knife and the barjyn.

Pai stabbed a small piece of meat with the barjyn and popped it into his mouth. "Perhaps the cook is supposed to cut it smaller before it is served?"

Bhaja almost flung a piece of her food onto the table as her barjyn slipped. She laughed, making Pai laugh, and then they got silly, not really trying to use their new implements properly.

Of course, it was at that moment that their long-time acquaintances Hathus and Lylah walked into the courtyard and saw them in their silliness.

Immediately, Bhaja became solemn. “Blessings of the day, Hathus, Lylah,” she said, setting down her barjyn and wiping her mouth with her napkin.

Pai decided to play out their foolish endeavor, flourishing his own barjyn upon which he had speared a piece of zucchini. “Prepare to fight!” he cried, thrusting the points of the tines at Hathus, who dutifully smiled.

“Oh, the barjyn are so difficult to learn to use,” Lylah said, as though she commiserated with them. “We practiced at home for weeks until we could manage them properly.”

Bhaja made the effort to smile at the woman. Since Hathus min Alshamal and Lylah were a Christian and Muslim pair, Bhaja had tried to befriend them, hoping the couple’s experience might give her and Pai insight into the success of such a mixed marriage: Christian man, Muslim wife.

But Lylah always acted superior, as if they were better than Bhaja or Pai, simply because Hathus’s family had always been wealthy.

“We’re on our way to Tarub’s villa for one of her gatherings,” Hathus said. “I understand you work for Tarub now, Bhaja.”

“Yes, that is so,” Bhaja murmured.

Even Pai seemed able to sense the couple was looking down on them. “Have a pleasant afternoon,” he said coolly, and turned back to his food.

Hathus nodded, Lylah waved, and then they were gone.

Bhaja gave up and used her pita to finish her meal. They wiped off the barjyn, and she put them back in the sack.

“Where do we dispose of this?” Pai asked holding up the greasy plane tree leaves their food had been wrapped in. “I know you don’t want it in the Library.”

“Oh,” Bhaja said, frowning. “The gardener is supposed to bring a waste can he can empty, but it isn’t here yet.” She glanced around the courtyard. “Just leave it on the table, I guess.”

The call to prayer sounded, and Bhaja hurried inside the Library to wash and pray. Pai followed her and washed also. When she finished and had stowed her prayer rug, she showed him her slanted writing table.

“I was thinking you would find a similar table helpful when you are drawing your maps. It puts the work at a better angle than a flat surface.”

“It’s a clever idea.”

"Tarub's design," Bhaja said.

Then Pai's arms were around her, and she expected a kiss.

Abruptly, she was transported to a room with fat round columns painted red. She *was* kissing...Pai...that part was right. Then just as abruptly, they were in Tarub's hexagonal Library again, still in the middle of a kiss.

After Pai left, Bhaja again thought through the bizarre transposition she had experienced. Or imagined. As a child, her imagination had taken her daydreaming to foreign places, like those told of in stories. But she was no longer a child. And that was no story, she and Pai really had kissed.

Still feeling a sense of awe, Bhaja rubbed the hair down on her arms and shivered. However real it might have felt, it *must* have been some sort of daydream. She decided to ignore it. She had too much to do to spend her time in fantasies.

Despite her determination to ignore them, Bhaja had two more vision episodes. It was as if their simple kiss had ignited a bonfire, and there was no stopping it. Could she believe anything about the visions? Was Pai in love with her, or was it mere passion, which would fade when he discovered her deep dedication to her religion? There would be nothing more than a kiss between them until they married.

With a deep sigh, she returned to her worktable and immersed herself in translating a land grant written in an old-style Galician.

4. Trash or Treasure

Pai traversed the narrow alleyways of the Christian enclave. He'd solved the challenge of collecting rags. "Coppers for scraps! Sell me your rags!" The women knew him and soon he had all his donkey could carry. In addition to selling him their old clothes, the ones with marriageable daughters invited him to dinner, but his heart belonged to the lady he dreamt of nightly.

His cloth collection complete, he crossed the Wadi al-Kabir entering the walled medina of Qurtuba. His donkey turned to head home with its heavy load, but Pai wanted to visit Bhaja. He tugged on the reins to follow the wide road between the Great Mosque and the Emir's citadel.

Bhaja would be there. From that fateful day when she'd purchased a Qurtuba map in the souk, he recognized her as the woman from his dreams, not her body, but her soul. He was not daunted that she was Muslim, and he was Christian. After all, it was 880 and Christians and Muslims could marry.

While he declared his love in his dreams, he hadn't spoken his feelings to Bhaja. They'd kissed, but that was like another dream. He was no coward. He'd left his small village to seek his fortune in the big city. He'd started a paper business when all others shied away. Nothing could stop him, except Bhaja's golden eyes. They slowed him and stole his voice.

Today would be different. He left his donkey in the Library courtyard and walked to the entry arch. Through the open door, he spied her leaning over her desk.

He rubbed his sandals on the stone threshold making a gentle noise to signal his arrival.

She looked up from her work. "Pai. I didn't expect you. I'm in the middle of a tricky translation." He sensed frustration in her voice when she added, "What do you want?"

She was busy. He wouldn't declare his love today. Maybe tomorrow. There was a broom nearby. He picked it up and swept his sandy tracks from the Library. "Sorry. I didn't mean to dirty your floor."

He replaced the broom and imagined how many times someone tracked in sand from the courtyard. *There had to be a better way.* "I'm going to get you a small rug from Hathus so people can clean their feet before entering."

She quirked her mouth and he imagined she was holding back a laugh. "The floor is fine. Have you come with a paper delivery?"

"No. I'm just returning from collecting rags. My donkey is hitched to a tree in the courtyard."

"Well, it's a hot day. Why don't you give him a drink at the fountain and take him home?"

He was measuring the size of the threshold with his feet when she added, "I expect some new scrolls. You can come by next week and we can see if there are any maps."

He gave her his biggest smile. "I'll do that," he happily shouted, before he left to water his ever-patient donkey.

Friday morning, after dreaming of a stormy sea voyage in the arms of his love, he promised himself, *Today I will speak to Bhaja.* He opened his shop. No more sitting under the hot sun in the market square for Pai. This was his proper shop for his proper customers. The atrium might have a dirt floor, but the room where he welcomed his patrons was paved with a lovely mosaic of red, brown, and black triangles. He washed the glazed tiles until they sparkled in the sunlight. Satisfied with the result, he dumped the water out the front door.

Someone shouted, "Don't do that!"

Pai looked up to see a well-dressed man with wet feet. *Why was this man standing in front of his shop, and so early in the morning?* He scrutinized the man who wore robes of fine cotton, bordered with embroidery, and cinched around his ample waist with a silver belt. The keffiyeh on his head displayed a gaudy pin. He'd never seen this man. *He's a rich visitor,* thought Pai, adding, *and not bright enough to avoid a puddle.*

Pai decided the man wanted to buy a map. *Why else would he be here?* "Welcome to Pai's Fine Paper and Maps," Pai said, and the men stepped inside marking the floor with wet footprints. Pai picked up his broom and bucket and hid them in the atrium. He called, "Zetian! We have a visitor. Please bring us tea."

With a shallow bow, the man introduced himself, "I am Darras of Osuna."

Zetian entered the shop with three cups on a wooden tray. She no longer appeared as an exotic concubine destined for the Emir's hareem. Her plain loose pants tied with a hemp drawstring and a collarless shirt with long sleeves, similar to what Pai wore, blended in with the others in Qurtuba. A headscarf covered the straight black hair that marked her as someone from al-Qin. Only her black, almond-shaped eyes revealed her origins.

She handed each man a cup of fragrant jasmine tea sweetened with sugar. Darras held his cup up to the sunlight and then tapped it with one of his rings. The result was a pleasant tone. He took a sip of tea and ran his tongue around the rim. After a soft whistle, he addressed Zetian, “This beautiful cup, the color of Jade, is from al-Qin!”

She nodded in agreement.

He then addressed her in the language of al-Qin. Pai didn’t understand, but he heard her full name, “Wu Zetian.”

She turned to him and translated, “Your friend has been to al-Qin and wondered if I was named for the Tang Empress. I explained that my mother gave me that honored name, but that didn’t prevent my father from selling me to the grand Byzantine market in Rumiyyat al-Kubra.”

Darras interrupted, “That market is so far away. How did you get to al-Andalus?”

“Malik al Jamal, Emir Muhammad’s agent, purchased me to be an exotic addition to the hareem,” she answered matter-of-factly.

Darras slowly repeated, “Malik al Jamal,” and took a swallow of tea like he was washing an unpleasant taste from his mouth. “But this isn’t the Emir’s hareem.”

She put down the tray and sipped her tea. “I know the al-Qin secret of fine paper. When Tarub the Learned, one of the most powerful women in Qurtuba—”

Darras interrupted, “I know her, she is the patron of Bhaja’s library.” He laughed at himself. “I guess it is really her library—Tarub’s Library.”

“Yes,” she continued, “The Learned decided that fine al-Qin paper was more important than the Emir, so you are in the only fine paper shop in al-Andalus.” She pointed to the atrium. “We make it right here.”

“I am honored to be here, but this shop is also famous for another reason.” He addressed Pai, “Bhaja says you have the best maps in al-Andalus. I need a map to guide my visit to Ronda.”

Pai’s heart beat stronger hearing that Bhaja spoke of him. He asked, “Ronda is such a small town, three-days travel on a fast horse. Why would you want to go there?” He remembered the man’s name: Darras of Osuna. “It is even farther than Osuna.”

The man finished his tea, sat down on a pillow, and began what sounded like a long story. “I have just returned from an expedition east and an audience with Pope John VIII. He has sent me on a mission to Ronda.”

Pai doubted this astonishing story, but he let the man continue. Travelers were rare and always brought welcome news. Besides, he was here to buy a map. Pai waved a hand toward the wall where his maps were displayed. He pointed to one with Ronda on the top and Qurtuba at the bottom. "This one has the most detail. I surveyed the route myself."

Darras stood up to study the map and scowled. "That is such hot, dirty work. I always *purchase* my maps."

Pai ignored his snub. "Would you like to buy this one?"

Darras didn't answer but began to remove the map from the wall.

Pai sized up the haughty man, imagining how many silver coins he could charge. "No, don't take that one. I will get you a pristine one."

When he looked into the atrium, he could see that Zetian was boiling a copper vat of cotton rags to make paper pulp. In a gentle voice, he requested, "Zetian, please fetch a new Ronda map for this gentleman."

He watched her wipe her hands with a cotton rag from the scrap pile. She fetched the map from the storeroom behind the atrium that also served as her sleeping room and presented it to Darras holding it in both hands to signify something of great value, as Pai had taught her. He smiled when he noticed it was the map with the ink splatter now labeled as *Osuna Woods*.

Darras looked from the map to Pai and back. "That is excellent." He handed Pai a gold dinar coin and reached for the map. "Do not try to cheat me. I pay fair and do not haggle."

Zetian looked him in the eye. These maps normally sold for a single silver coin, something she was well aware of.

Pai bowed to Darras. "You have been fair."

Zetian smiled.

While Darras rolled up his purchase, he talked about his travels. "The Pope confided in me the secret of a Christian treasure. I'm going to retrieve it from Ronda."

Pai knew Ronda well and couldn't imagine where anyone would find treasure, especially this Darras of Osuna who was a stranger. "Do you have any friends there?" he pondered aloud.

Darras shook his bag of gold coins. "No, but I'm sure my money and the promise of treasure will make me some." He then rambled on about his many distinguished travel companions.

Pai concluded Darras needed help. "My childhood friend Sayyida lives in Ronda. Would you like me to introduce you?" he offered, expecting to write a note.

"That would be excellent. Can you be ready to go tomorrow morning?"

Pai considered this surprise invitation. He thought about his earlier promise to speak to Bhaja, but he couldn't pass up the chance for an adventure. He replied. "I will meet you at the Bridge Gate."

After Darras departed, Pai went into the atrium where Zetian had returned to boiling paper pulp. She didn't look up. She just stared at the red coals beneath the copper pot. Her reserved behavior concerned him, so he asked, "Is something wrong?"

She banged the kettle with her stirring stick. When the ringing stopped, she sobbed, "Nothing is wrong."

Pai asked again, "I am your friend. You are my djinni. You can tell me."

Tears ran down her cheeks as she lamented, "Wararni has run away."

She was going to marry the tall Berber, one of the Emir's guards. He wondered if the problem was that she wasn't Muslim. Whatever the difficulty, it could be solved. *Hadn't Abbas said something like that?*

"Are you sure? Might he be back tomorrow?" He gently inquired looking for an easy resolution.

She ululated. After she calmed, she said,"He left by the Bridge gate. He is returning to Ifriqa." With a long sigh, she added, "And...I'm with baby."

Pai loved children but didn't know what to say to an expectant mother when the father ran away. He wished Bhaja had been there, but, in her absence, he devised a plan. "If he is headed for Ifriqa, I am traveling the same path. I will find him and bring him back."

Zetian brightened. "Can you do that?"

Pai didn't know the answer, but he knew he'd try. "Sure. He's walking and I'll be on a good horse. I'll catch up to him."

She held her belly and became quiet. *That had been the right thing to say,* he thought proudly, and hopefully, he'd find the errant father.

After four days of travel, Pai and Darras arrived in Ronda without seeing Wararni along the way. Abbas ibn Firnas welcomed them. "We don't have a stable, but you can pasture your horses behind the house."

They walked their horses to the corral which already contained two others. A servant helped them unsaddle and unbridle them. Darras shook the rough fence to test its strength.

"Don't worry about the fence. I give them some barley after the last prayers. As long as they have that they don't stray," she assured him.

Darras still seemed concerned, "Do you have dogs to protect the horses?"

"No, but you have nothing to worry about. These animals are too big for our wild cats, and the wolves never come into the village," she assured him.

Ibn Firnas had waited for them in the atrium. He modestly wore unbleached cotton robes with a plain keffiyeh of similar material. His dress contrasted with the elegant atrium, with a pond, palm trees, and a mosaic floor. "You can leave your satchels in that corner. They'll be safe."

Pai dropped his roughly constructed bag next to the one Darras carried. He noticed the fine embroidery, soft leather handles, and silver buckles. He'd never seen one like it.

Ibn Firnas showed off his famous water clock. This building, atop the cliffs with an impressive view of the valley below, had been Abbas's childhood home.

A servant handed everyone glasses of sweet apple cider.

When Sayyida al Jamal arrived, Pai made introductions. "Darras, this is my friend Sayyida. As small children, we scampered up and down the gorge between her home in the valley and mine up here on the plateau.

She dressed similar to Pai, like other young adults, with loose trousers, and a collarless shirt. He noticed that in recognition of her position as a landowner, she wore silver bangles on both wrists. Pai wore white to honor the Umayyad court in Qurtuba, but living in Ronda, Sayyida allowed herself a wider color palette. She wore orange with a matching headscarf.

"Sayyida, this is Darras who has just come from a meeting with the Pope. He is going to tell us about a treasure."

The portly Darras assumed the role of the patriarch and waved his now empty glass in the air. Once the servant had refilled it, he took a long swallow and began, "Pope John VIII personally walked me around his city walls. I commented favorably on the recent construction. After our tour, he invited me back to his apartments. That was when I knew he had something to give me."

Pai demanded, "Show it to us."

"Not so fast. I had to listen to his concerns about the eastern church in Rumiyyat al-Kubra and the glory of translating the Holy Bible into Slavonian. I'm sure Pope John would expect me to recount this."

Pai questioned the Pope's intentions but listened politely to Darras's tales of his adventures at the Vatican for a second time. Abbas's eyes closed. Only Sayyida seemed engaged in the story of treasure. The news of Rome concluded with, "Then he gave it to me." Darras reached into his robe and withdrew a scroll.

Finally, he's done. Pai enquired hopefully, "Is that a map to the treasure?"

Darras smugly replied, "Better than that. It's a letter from Pope John VIII."

Pai disagreed. *I'd rather have a map.*

Darras unrolled the scroll on the mosaic floor and held it in place with empty drinking glasses.

Pai leaned over the scroll. "Latin script. Who can read Latin letters?"

Abbas ibn Firnas had said little. Everyone in al-Andalus recognized his high forehead and long white beard. His reputation as an inventor, engineer, musician, and poet afforded him more attention than he desired. He had one cloudy eye, a sign of age and wisdom. He closed it and moved so close to the scroll that his nose almost touched the floor, "Latin alphabet for sure, but too fine a hand for my old eyes."

"Then, how will we find the treasure?" Sayyida lamented.

Ibn Firnas laughed. "Let me show you what I have discovered." He raised a glass, itself one of his accomplishments. Before Ibn Firnas, people drank from ceramic, metal, or colored glass containers. After his experiments, crystal clear glass was possible.

"Observe!" He placed the cup atop the tiny writing. "Look inside!"

Each, in turn, peered through the thick bottom and saw the writing magnified. Sayyida exclaimed, "Praise Allah. How is that possible?"

Ibn Firnas ignored the question. Pai wondered if the great scientist didn't have an answer. Instead, Abbas slid the glass across the document and began reading. "Christian treasure buried west of Ronda." He mumbled a bit but then continued. "Half the treasure shall be the reward for locating it."

Pai was still upset by the lack of a map, "West of Ronda is a vast area!"

Darras explained, "The treasure was buried when the previous Emir forced the Christian landowners to forfeit their estate. I've heard that the offense was abuse of Muslim renters, most likely unruly Berbers from Ifriqa."

Pai remembered Wararni, another Berber. He hoped the absent father had stopped in Ronda, affording him a chance to fulfill his promise to Zetian.

Darras sneered, "However, an Emir's justice occasionally—" He stopped, unwilling to criticize the office of the Emir.

Sayyida looked at him and seemed to continue his thought. "Prophet Muhammad decreed, *Stand firmly for justice, as witnesses to Allah, even if against yourselves*. The Emir awarded the valley west of Ronda to my family for valor in battle, possibly not strictly following the Prophet." She paused as if embarrassed by her family's good fortune, before adding, "This all happened before I was born."

Pai guessed that she'd said more than she intended when she placed her hand over her mouth.

After an awkward silence, Darras looked directly at the woman and smiled. "So, by Muslim law, the treasure is yours."

"Maybe. When my father died, Malik took the villa in Qurtuba and the business, leaving my mother and I stuck in Ronda."

Darras repeated, "So the treasure is yours."

"Not exactly. The judge found that Malik deserved even more. Those judges and the Quran always favor the male heirs." Sayyida frowned. "He received part of the Ronda land, with trees and rocks, olives and almonds. The treasure might be on Malik's portion."

Darras lowered his eyebrows in thought. "So, he only owns a small piece, right? Most likely the treasure isn't on his land." His eyes opened wide, and he repeated for the third time, "The treasure is yours."

This time Sayyida didn't object. "I'll use my treasure to move to Qurtuba. Why should my brother be the only one to escape Ronda?"

This wild talk shocked Pai. "I thought you were happy here."

"Pai, do you think only men want something different?" She frowned and pointed at Abbas. "He left Ronda." Having said that, her mouth got small and her eyes became slits. "You also left."

Pai looked to the other men and back to the angry Sayyida. He hoped one of the older men would know what to say, but no one spoke.

Now tears ran down Sayyida's cheeks. "My mother is always after me to get married, but I know *everyone* in Ronda and *none* of them are suitable. I don't want to spend my life harvesting apples, vegetables, and barley!"

Pai offered her a sympathetic smile, aware that they could have been a happy couple had he not been promised to the lady in his dreams and driven by wanderlust to leave Ronda. He hadn't imagined Sayyida might also have that wanderlust, but he had been wrong.

Pai, wanting to change from the uncomfortable subject, returned to the lack of a map, "How will we find the treasure?"

"I left out one detail," Darras said.

"How is that possible?" Pai asked, thinking about how Darras had stretched out his story.

"Pope John told me that the treasure site had been covered with ashes and salt. Nothing should be growing there."

Pai harrumphed, "The ashes would be a good clue if we were geese and could fly over it."

Ibn Firnas clapped his hands, "While no man-made machine will ever achieve the perfection of a goose's wing, my glider can serve our purpose." He recounted the story of his breathtaking flight from atop a hill near Qurtuba.

Pai had witnessed that demonstration. When Abbas ibn Firnas was launched from his perch, many people fell to the ground to hide their eyes and pray. Pai watched the entire journey and cheered when the scientist safely walked away at the end. He thought: *What a wonderful time to be alive. Science allows man to fly with the birds.*

Ibn Firnas sighed, "In my seventieth year, I am too old to take the flight."

Pai seized the opportunity. He jumped up and excitedly declared, "I'll find the lost treasure." Since his childhood high on the Ronda plateau, he'd imagined flying like a bird. Now he would live that dream. Like the eagles nesting in the cliffs, he would soar over the valley.

They followed Abbas ibn Firnas across the atrium. Pai admired the symmetry of four palm trees, one in each corner. A pond covered with lotus blossoms dominated the center. Ibn Firnas entered a small opening behind one of the palm trees.

By the afternoon sun, Pai surveyed the room. Everywhere he saw piles of bamboo, some bound together, and others just jumbles. He also noticed cloth and shiny ropes, all silk from al-Qin.

"All of this needs to be moved to the edge of the plateau." Ibn Firnas pointed out the door. Pai enthusiastically grabbed the largest structure. "Sayyida, lift the other end. We'll have to tilt it to fit it out the door." Pai and Sayyida made many trips between the storage room and the cliff's edge occasionally hampered by curious horses. Darras of Osuna helped as much as his age and weight allowed, transporting silk ropes and baskets of goose feathers.

With each circuit, the flying machine took shape as Ibn Firnas assembled the pieces, binding them all together with ropes. At last, he completed the construction. Pai marveled at the result, wider than he was tall and three times as long. It seemed like magic that such a large device emerged from the small room and through the narrow door. He looked at Abbas with renewed esteem. *How had he discovered the secret of flight?*

Pai adored the machine that would carry him over the valley below. His eyes cautioned him against jumping off the cliff's edge, but his desire to fly argued that Abbas was a genius and he'd never get another chance. Just then an eaglet fledgling flew from a nearby nest, swooping back and forth and squealing its dominance of the sky. Pai took that as a sign and moved to the edge.

Sayyida spoke to Pai, "Allah protect you." Then she turned to Darras. "Let's head down to my villa. You can stay there until we find the treasure."

Darras gave a conspiratorial laugh. "Our treasure." He mounted his horse—a distinctive stallion of the type raised in al-Andalus, all white. "I must ride to Qurtuba today, but I'll soon return, and we will retrieve our treasure."

She turned to Pai, "I'll take the path through the gorge and meet you in the valley."

Ibn Firnas urged Darras off his horse. "I need everyone's help. After I bind Pai into the cradle, all of us will cast him over the edge."

Pai looked into the distant valley. "It's a long way down there." He turned to the famous engineer. "Any advice?"

"Pull on the steering lines and lean to the sides. Allah will guide you."

As a Christian, Pai did not feel encouraged, but he trusted the scientist more than God.

Sayyida lifted one end of the wing, covered in silk and feathers, and Ibn Firnas and Darras raised the other. Pai hung there while Abbas joked, "Sayyida, you can just have your workers collect the pieces and return them whenever it's convenient."

Pai thought, *Pieces? If the glider is in pieces, will I be whole?*

Ibn Firnas shouted, "GO!" The wing approached the precipice. Soon Pai found himself hanging over the abyss and dropping into the valley. *Too late to change my mind. Why do I always volunteer?*

He looked down—his eyes wide open. He sped across the valley faster than any horse. He struggled to breathe, as the wind seemed to be too vigorous to enter his chest. Or perhaps the thumping in his chest had grown too strong to allow breathing. Then he stopped thinking and just flew like a bird. The experience was exhilarating. He was soaring.

He quickly improvised a prayer. "Though I fly over the valley of death, I fear no evil, for thou art with me." He wondered if God existed so far from the ground. Hadn't Jesus the Christ said, "*Look at the birds of the air, for they neither sow nor reap; yet your heavenly Father feeds them?*" Of course, God was with him. He floated like an angel.

He let the wind push him back and the glider slowed. Leaning right, the glider turned right. Soon, it flew right and left in great circles over the valley. The eaglet soared beside him squealing congratulations. He whistled to the bird and they both flew in big ovals together.

He imagined the map. The path from Sayyida's house onto the adjoining land became a black line. The river through the gorge transformed into a blue line. Everything came together in his mind, but he still didn't see the treasure.

Sailing from cultivated fields of vegetables to rolling hills of almond and olive trees made Pai dizzy. *Looking across the valley, he saw a vast ocean, the Bahr al-Rum, as if he were flying along the coast of an island. The same island where he held hands with the lady from his dream.* He shivered and shook his head. The apparition of the lady and the sea disappeared, and he was back over the valley.

Then he saw it, a square of black ground, devoid of any plants. After his vision of the sea, he didn't trust his eyes. He blinked and shook his head again. But the black plot was still there. "I've found the treasure!" He knew exactly how to draw the map, but the treasure was nestled among a grove of ancient olive trees. *What would Sayyida do if her chance to escape resided on Malik's property? No one could exactly say where Sayyida's holdings ended and Malik's began.*

He turned toward Sayyida's home to deliver the news and sketch the map before he forgot. With each circuit over her apple orchard, the ground approached closer. When he could see the individual apples and the chickens in the yard, he realized he had no idea how to end his flight. In his excitement to start, he'd forgotten to ask how to end!

He shouted, "Abbas! Ibn Firnas! Old man, you forgot to tell me how to stop!" He looked for something soft. Not the house, built of sturdy wattle and thatch. Not the apple trees. The stacks of hay looked tempting, but he remembered how they were more like mounds of dirt than feathers.

Everything got larger and sped by swifter and swifter. With no time left, he crashed into the Wadi al-Laban where it flowed across the al Jamal lands. There he stood covered with water cress, black mud, and a broken glider.

Sure enough, the glider was in pieces, but he was whole. He doubted there was a happier man anywhere in al-Andalus, though he'd be even happier if he could merge his real life with his visions and dreams—if Bhaja had been there, and she and the dream lady were one.

5. MIRACLE OR MUMMERY

Bhaja wasn't certain which had woken her, the dawn call to prayer, or the heat in Qurtuba's summer air. She stretched and got out of her nest in a back corner of Tarub's Library. Using water from the courtyard fountain which now circulated fresh water, she cleansed herself. As she finished brushing her teeth with the *miswak* stick, she felt grit under her feet.

It must be that some sand or dust had drifted in onto the geometric tiles of the floor, so she moved before she laid a prayer mat down facing qibla. She would clean the floor later.

She was beginning to find a daily routine in her work at the Library, and she remembered to thank Allah for that as she finished her prayers.

Later, she was staring at the disintegrating papyrus of an Egyptian historian's work when she heard a disturbance at the entry arch by the open door.

"Excuse me," a woman's voice called in Latin as Bhaja turned toward the sound. "Is this the Library of the lady called Tarub?"

Bhaja's skirts made a swishing sound as she went to greet the woman, whom she noted was accompanied by a muscular young man. The woman's robes, like Bhaja's, were layers of thin fine linen. Unlike her own, the woman's were muted grey and blue. *As if she is trying to fade into the shadows.* Bhaja preferred brighter, more cheerful colors.

"It *is* Tarub's Library," she replied in the same language.

"Forgive my boldness," the woman said as Bhaja studied her. "But I was told by a fellow traveler that you need a translator here?"

The woman was small, shorter and darker than Bhaja. Her dark frizzy hair screened her eyes, which Bhaja later saw were green, unlike her own dark gold or the usual deep brown. This close, Bhaja realized the woman was older than she'd originally thought.

But—a translator just appeared in her doorway? It seemed a miracle.

"Indeed we do," Bhaja stated in Arabic, then noticing the woman's confusion, she repeated in Latin.

Maybe this was not so great a miracle as she'd first thought. How much of a translator could this woman be, if she was not fluent in Arabic?

"We have many scrolls that need translating," she said, "and there will be more. But what languages do you have? I notice not

Arabic," she said more bluntly than she intended, but she was already frustrated that her miracle had been snatched away.

"Hebrew, Latin, Greek, and Persian," the woman said. Her face was now marred by a dark scowl. "My Arabic is quite limited, as you note, though I can read and write a little. But I am also familiar with written Aramaic and Armenian, though I cannot speak them."

"Those are very good. Any of the local languages?"

"Some rough Basque and some Tamasheq—enough to get by when traveling, though I don't read them well, so perhaps they won't be useful to you."

"Who are you?" Bhaja thought to ask.

"My name is Naomi. This is my son, Raviv." The son, almost a man of about 19 or 20 years, was devilishly handsome—but seemed not to realize it. He gave her a shy grin when his mother named him. "We have just returned from Jerusalem, a...a hajj you would say," Naomi continued. "We came by way of al-Jazair, in the Mahgreb, where I met a friend of yours, Darras of Osuna. He is the one who said you might need a translator." She took a deep breath. "To be frank, I am desperate for work and a place to stay, since we have very little money."

Well, in addition to no Arabic, that presents another problem. They had nowhere to live. But she couldn't let them stay here, as she did.

Most of the local young Arabic-speaking men already looked askance at her because of her job: speaking, reading, and writing three languages. And no self-respecting young Muslim woman should be alone in a library, even a private one run by the famous Tarub.

She supposed they thought of her as a weird sort of concubine's concubine. Untouchable, unless they wanted to invite Tarub's wrath. Unmarriageable, because of her association with the famous concubine—never mind that Tarub had been freed and taken as a wife by al Rahman, and was now a leader in the city.

Such a reputation both protected Bhaja and prevented her from finding a good match, to her still-hopeful mother's great despair. Bhaja was well past the age when good Muslim women were traditionally wed.

In a way, the woman Naomi's presence at the Library could be helpful, both as a sort of lady's companion, as well as whatever translation work she could perform.

But the son?

"Does Raviv have work?" she again asked in a direct manner.

"He is to be taken into apprenticeship by the butcher, Ezra, but we have not gone to him yet, so we are not certain of this placement."

"Naomi, I am interested in you for translating. It is possible you could sleep here with me, and guard the Library if I must go out. But I would need further references from you first." Bhaja sighed and met the older woman's eyes before continuing, "And, of course, I cannot have a young man sleep here, at all."

"No, certainly," Naomi said, frustration plain on her face.

What could she do for them? She thought about what the woman had said. She spoke Hebrew, and had returned from a hajj to Jerusalem. As well, Raviv was to work for Ezra the butcher. The kosher and halal butcher.

No Muslim would call a trip to Jerusalem a hajj. No Christian would find work with a kosher butcher.

Making an abrupt decision, she turned and retrieved Tarub's bag of coins from her desktop.

"Here," she said, handing Naomi two dinars from the bag. "This should buy you some food from one of the vendors near the synagogue, as an advance on your pay. I recommend you seek out the local rabbi and ask him for suggestions about housing. I know by reputation that the Qurtuba Jewish community supports its own. I will show you the way, if you need. Then please come back tomorrow when you have a place to stay for Raviv and yourself."

Gratitude now filled Naomi's face. Bhaja had to wonder if the woman had ever trained as a player, since her face was such a direct expression of her feelings. "I know the way to the Jewish quarter, thank you. I will return tomorrow morning, with good news," she said.

The next morning, Bhaja dressed and grabbed the new ceramic water pitcher. She unlocked the Library door, and stepped out to get fresh water from the courtyard fountain. She poured enough water into her basin to wash, taking satisfaction that however odd her occupation and station were, she still carefully followed the Muslim prayer laws and rules of modesty.

Following hard upon that thought, she realized today was Friday, and she should keep the Library closed, but she had asked Naomi to come.

She frowned, thinking they were going to have a complicated schedule to keep, since Naomi was Jewish. The woman's own holy day would begin this evening.

Then she sent the worry away and lost herself in the simplicity of prayer and honor to Allah.

A commotion arose outside as she put away her prayer rug. She stepped through the open door just in time to see a herd of gardeners and burros arrive in the courtyard, despite it being the Muslim holy day.

Then she realized, that of course, these men were not Muslim, nor certainly the burros. She hid her grin behind her hand at the thought of Muslim burros. She watched the commotion unfold into order.

Two tall palm trees and several small fruit trees were on a wagon pulled by big draft horses. Burros, covered in tools, smaller potted plants, and burlap bags of soil, were guided to one side of the courtyard. The head gardener, whom Bhaja had not formally met, directed men and animals with an authoritative air. Then he smiled his gap-toothed smile at her as he approached and asked where she wanted the two bigger trees.

It was her job to choose? Bhaja stepped out into the courtyard and looked around.

Pavement provided a level area for the clusters of tables and benches, stools and chairs scattered throughout the large courtyard. Tarub's pavilion had arrived, and lay in wait to be assembled and raised. The gardener had managed to keep it safe from the burro hooves and the bags of dirt, today.

Bhaja pointed to two spots, one near the northwestern library wall, and one near the central fountain. "Palms there and there."

"Do you not wish to shade the tables?" the gardener wondered.

"The palms don't really help, do they?"

He made a face. "I suggested a row of them, which *would* help, but the lady doesn't much like palms," he said.

'The lady' must be Tarub, of course.

"Are there going to be any shade trees?"

"I have put on order several trees as the lady suggested. But these are all I have today."

She shrugged when he asked about the other plants and trees. He should decide that, she thought, since he was the one with the most plant education. The man smiled and nodded and then went about his business. Bhaja returned inside, closing the door against the noise.

She wanted to go pray in the women's gallery at the Great Mosque for the Friday prayer session, but she must wait for Naomi. Wishing she had specified a more specific time for the woman to return than simply "morning," she pulled out the most recent copy she had made of the first *surah* of the Quran and began reading, checking it for errors.

Eventually someone knocked on the door.

Bhaja placed polished, purified stones on the Quran surah scroll to hold it in place and walked to the door. It was the translator.

They greeted each other, then Naomi blurted, "You will be pleased to know I am stationed at the home of a feeble widow, who is glad to offer me lodging at her home in exchange for my help with meals and housekeeping." Naomi paused for a breath and to smile at Bhaja. "And the rabbi also helped to see that Raviv is settled with Ezra the butcher, who can use the help, if the line of customers out his door is any indication."

"That is well, Naomi."

Noticing Bhaja's bare feet, Naomi removed her shoes at the door. Bhaja made a note to get a mat or a low shelf for the purpose; its presence by the door would remind visitors to leave their shoes outside. The less dirt tracked in, the better.

"Now," Bhaja told her, "I would like to begin by teaching you the Arabic alphabet. We will work on words, sounds, and diacritical marks as we go, but it would be truly helpful if you could learn Arabic quickly and well. Otherwise—"

"I'll have to translate everything Greek or Hebrew into Latin, which then requires you to translate from the Latin to Arabic."

"Exactly," Bhaja agreed. "Double the work, with that extra step."

"Yes. And do we eat inside, or out, or at a vendor? Also, I meant to ask you if there is a toilet here that we can use, or if I must leave the premises."

"No, here it is," Bhaja said pointing to the small room adjacent to the row of lower cabinets. "And we are connected to the wastewater system now, so it is very clean." She also showed Naomi the pitcher of water next to the toilet, and the pitcher and basin on the stand nearby their writing desks. She washed her hands, indicating the translator should, too. "As to food, I eat in the courtyard for the first two meals each day. I visit my mother for the evening meal."

Naomi nodded. "Good. I will bring my noon meal, and eat the others at the widow's house, in that case." She held up the small satchel she had been carrying, and Bhaja showed her an empty cupboard where she could put it. Then they got to work.

Monday promised to be another scorching day. Bhaja could only hope a breeze would spring up along the river, as it sometimes did, but so far it had not. She gave up on sitting out in the courtyard. The sun had risen over the Library and the Emir's citadel far enough to slant brightly into that open space. The slight shade from the new palms wasn't enough to help.

She picked up the scrolls she had been comparing and walked toward the arched doorway, pausing to smell the sweet jasmine that had gone berserk with blossoms, as though it wasn't certain it would ever be permitted to bloom again. She sighed and went into the relative shade of the Library.

Just as she settled down at her writing desk—really just a slanted table—Naomi finally arrived. Bhaja deliberately did not look up from her work until she had finished reading the section she was on. The woman arrived later each day; it was annoying. Worse, it was delaying the overall progress of the Library.

Had both she and Darras been wrong about Naomi?

Perhaps sensing the younger woman's irritation, Naomi moved quickly, getting out the document they had been translating the previous day, and setting up her inks and paper.

"I am ready now, whenever you would like to begin," Naomi said.

Bhaja glanced at the woman, then at the Greek scroll they had been translating for two days, so far. Two days, and only two paragraphs done.

"You do realize that when you arrive mid-morning, we have only a few good hours to work before you then need to leave in the afternoon?"

"I'm sorry. I really am," Naomi said. "The widow is so dependent upon me now, she clings to me like a leech. I had to just walk out on her today, leaving her sitting at her table in tears. She is weak and afraid of everything."

"It sounds like she needs the rabbi, or perhaps a nurse," Bhaja said, not feeling very sympathetic. "You are there for more than three quarters of each day as it is. I cannot continue to pay you for a day's work when you are here for only half."

Naomi stared at the shadows on the wall for a moment, apparently composing herself. Bhaja began to feel bad she had chided the woman so strongly. "I think perhaps you are correct," the translator finally said. "I will talk to the rabbi. He can't have meant for me to spend all the hours of my days caring for the old woman."

"Mmm," Bhaja said. Brightening, she remembered her find from the evening before. "Oh! I found two other places where that word we were stuck on occurred. Perhaps between them, you can decipher the meaning of that obscure passage from Acusilaus of Argos. Maybe we can finish that section of the scroll, now."

Naomi held up the two scrolls Bhaja had put with their work in progress. "These?"

"Yes, about midway down on both of them."

"Good, I will let you know when I have finished reading them."

Bhaja finished comparing her own translation of a Latin parchment with the original. She wrapped a string around the original and her translation and made a note on a scrap of paper describing the two for her catalog. By the time she had properly labeled and shelved the documents, the muezzin was calling for mid-day prayers.

Naomi continued working. After prayers, Bhaja looked over the stack of pages needing translation into Arabic. She still had had no time to make copies of anything.

As if reading her mind, Naomi said, "I've finished practicing my Arabic, and with translating this. Do you want me to spend time making copies, or do these other translations?"

If you were here before mid-morning, we would have much more translated. But she had already said that. Instead, Bhaja said, "Do the translations." Then she nodded and said, "I think the time has come to find and hire a good copyist."

Naomi's eyes darkened and she became sad. "Not a slave, I pray."

"I do not like buying people either," Bhaja said. "But I do believe their life would be considerably better with us than it might be elsewhere."

Naomi's response was a wordless grunt.

"It is rare to find an educated slave in our markets, in any case," Bhaja said. "I was thinking, there are some priests or monks—or whatever the Christians call those men from the Abbey, there are still some of them living there. Most of them can read and write well. That is one thing the Roman Pope has done, is to make sure their clerics are well-trained. I was thinking to hire one of *them*."

"That's a good thought. I wonder how many of them may be adept at Arabic as well as Latin?" Naomi said. "Maybe he could take these things I'm learning to translate and turn them into something beautiful."

Bhaja nodded agreement. "Would you like to come along with me, when I go there to ask? They are rather poorly housed out in the ruins of the old Christian Abbey, outside the west wall."

Naomi looked up from her work, blinking. "We might want to take a guard with us," she said. "I've heard there are still bandits who think there is treasure inside the Abbey, even after all these years."

"My brother could join us, I suppose," Bhaja said. "He's not a real guard yet, but he has some training, and a decent weapon. Are you available tomorrow?"

"Tomorrow would be good for me, if it is for you," Naomi said.

A copyist will help make up for your tardiness, she did not say. Then she could feel the heat flush over her face. Was she turning into one of those old judgmental harridans who sat outside the Great Mosque, criticizing everyone who walked by?

The older woman chuckled, unaware of Bhaja's mixed feelings. "It's going to take a real artist to turn this into something pretty. My Latin and Greek aren't bad, but my Arabic is like a child's. Half the words are missing and the letters are all awry." She waved a hand at her paper. "A stick drawing!"

"Ah, not so bad as that," Bhaja said, trying to be kind. But the Arabic lettering on Naomi's page really was quite ugly. A Christian copyist with a fine hand might improve things a lot. Perhaps one that could add illuminations to the manuscripts. Tarub would be pleased with that.

For a wonder, Naomi was on time. They set out from the Library the following morning, before the heat of the day rose.

As they walked north through the city, they walked past the construction zone the Emir's builders made. They worked on extending the city's wastewater system. Piles of dirt, bricks, and clay pipes lay along the sides of the once paved and now partially deconstructed street.

Soon the work would move well past the Library and the Emir's citadel, and then would go elsewhere in the city. She and Pai had a bet on about where the Emir would extend the system after that. She bet on the square and gardens near the Great Mosque. Pai thought it would be to the northeast, into the rich peoples' neighborhoods.

Once past the construction, they turned west, stopping at Bhaja's mother's home to pick up her brother Yusuf. She introduced him to Naomi, and Bhaja hid her smile at her brother's stiff posture. He was trying so hard to be one of the Emir's guards.

He did *look* a lot like a fighter. He had a leather shield, a short sword, a leather chest piece over his short robes, and a leather cap over his long dark hair which hung down, protecting his neck. He was a half-dozen years younger than she, and it was hard for her to think of him as an adult, much less a fierce warrior. She had no idea how well he could fight if it came to it, but the display might intimidate any possible attackers enough to wait for weaker prey. Besides, this gave her a simple way to acknowledge his skills.

They walked west. As they passed the small square, she saw a face she thought she recognized; it looked like Lylah. The woman ducked behind a tethered horse so quickly, Bhaja began to doubt she'd seen her. When she looked back after a few steps, she did not see the woman at all. Odd.

They exited Qurtuba from the western gate. Bhaja did not see any sign of Lylah after that.

They made their way past the square to the huge wooden doors in the city wall. The doors were left open during the day, as usual—unless there was a war on, or reports of bandit attacks. From there, their path went past the Cemetery of Amir and then split into paths that encircled the olive, apricot, and pistachio orchards, and one that continued straight to the Abbey.

As they approached the ruined buildings, they were confronted by a priest—or what Bhaja assumed was a priest, perhaps he was a monk—in long black and brown robes—the dye work was uneven, she noticed—and no head covering. This man put his palms together at waist level and pointed toward the two women and their guard. He bowed over his hands and smiled at them.

"Allahu Akbar," Bhaja said, tilting her head in a sort of bow or acknowledgment to the man. "I am looking for someone to hire who writes well in Arabic and can copy documents for Tarub's Library," she went on. "I hoped to find such a person here."

"I see," the man said. "There are several such persons I could recommend; however you should know they are all men. If that is acceptable, I can bring them to you to meet, each with a sample of his work, so you might determine which would serve best."

Meaning he wasn't going to invite her group into what remained of the Abbey, Bhaja realized. So, she, her brother, and Naomi were expected to stand and wait out here in the sun? She could feel her forehead rumple as she frowned.

But perhaps his manners were better than that. "Please follow me; there is a small garden where I can bring tea while you wait," he said.

Bhaja nodded. "Thank you."

"I am sorry our accommodations are less than you might expect," he said as he led them under the shade of a grapevine-covered arbor. The dappled shade lay over a small stone table and two heavy wooden stools—more like old log pieces that had been scraped clean of their bark and polished a bit on the seat portion. "We have not had the resources to repair this place since the battle with the *Majus*, the Northmen, many years ago."

It certainly had been many years ago. The raiders had not gotten past Qurtuba's sturdy walls, but of course, anything outside the walls, like the Abbey, had been robbed and razed. Bhaja remembered her mother's stories about the brief siege. Since that raid, nearly forty years ago, the Majus had concentrated their efforts on Ishbiliyah down the river, which had no wall.

One side of the arbor was open to the orchard, and that is where Yusuf took up his guard stance, facing outward.

After a brief wait, another man, in a well-dyed but threadbare brown robe, arrived with a tea service. He offered to pour, but Naomi shook her head and took over that duty. The brown-robed man disappeared before they could thank him.

Bhaja noticed there were three cups, and Naomi filled only two. Was it the Jewish way to not serve their guards? Bhaja handed her cup to Yusuf who had glanced over his shoulder to see who had come. She then poured the third scant cup for herself.

The original man eventually returned with three other black- and brown-robed...priests? Monks? Bhaja could not remember how to tell them apart. The men were all clean-shaven, with short hair and no headscarves, making the shaven bald spot at the top of their heads seem unduly obvious. It seemed so odd to see men this way, as if they were half-naked.

Two had pale skin; the third, in a well-worn brown robe, was darker-skinned. He most resembled a person of Ifriqa. The man who had first greeted them bowed to Bhaja and Naomi in the same way he had met them, then he disappeared back into the wrecked building.

What now? Bhaja wondered, but one of the men stepped boldly forward, gave a half-bow, and introduced himself.

"This humble person is named Riga," he said of himself. "I speak and write Latin and Arabic. This is my work." He held up a parchment with a few lines of Arabic, then he stepped back into the short line and the next man stepped forward, not so close to the two women. He similarly introduced himself and displayed his work. He had Latin and Arabic also. His Arabic had grand arabesques and was much too florid to suit Bhaja. She'd rather it was simple, elegant, and readable.

The third brown-robed man did not step forward. He offered a deep bow. "This one is named Isador," he said. "My skills include reading classic Greek, ecclesiastical Roman and Catalan Latin, and Arabic, and I write these also, though my Greek lettering skills are weak." His scroll was a full page of a strong but elegant Arabic. Bhaja recognized a Psalm, a poetic prayer, from the Christian Bible.

After a brief glance at one another and Naomi's quick nod, Bhaja said, "Isador, are you available two or three days a week to come into the city and work with us in Tarub's Library?

He raised his gaze, which had been on the ground, to meet her eyes. "Yes, lady."

"Do you know where the new library is?" Naomi asked.

"Yes, lady," he said again.

"It is probably best that you come tomorrow, Tuesday," Bhaja said, "and I will tell you at that time if we will need you on Wednesdays as well. If your work is adequate this may become a regular routine."

All three of the men bowed and then walked away, bare feet shushing softly on the stones of the garden.

Naomi met Bhaja's eyes again. "He didn't even want to know how much you would pay him," Naomi observed.

"I suspect the Abbey and its people may be desperate," Bhaja said. "None of them looked over-fed."

"No, they did not," Naomi said.

6. Maps and Mayhem

Pai had seen the square of scorched ground from the glider, just as Darras had described it. So, Darras wasn't a buffoon. The treasure was real. Pai imagined gold and precious stones, relics rescued from the churches in advance of the Berber invasion. *But whose treasure?* The Pope declared it to be Christian. Who were the Christians who lost this land to the Muslim conquerors? Did the riches belong to the family al Jamal? Did his friend Sayyida have a claim? Would the prize allow her to leave Ronda? What about her brother Malik?

Pai struggled to leave the river. The muddy bottom sucked at his feet, twice refusing to release a sandal, and requiring him to submerge into the cold water to retrieve it with his hands. When he finally climbed up the riverbank, he collapsed and fell asleep in the warm sunlight.

The sun had lowered in the sky when three young men, dark and muscular from working in the fields, pulled the glider remains from the muddy shallows of the Wadi al-Laban. They carried the bamboo to Sayyida's house, taking a shortcut through the paddock. Pai followed along the familiar path, leaving a wet trail in his wake.

"Wait here," one of the men instructed.

Water dripped from Pai's clothes. Shortly, Sayyida appeared and offered him dry garments. "You're welcome to stay overnight with the workers."

With the workers? he pondered.

Feeling unwelcome, he waved his arms and shook his head. "Thank you for your hospitality, but I left my drawing kit at Ibn Firnas's house and must rush back there before I forget the map."

A servant came out of the house with a large pitcher of water, several circles of bread, and a bowl filled with eggplant cooked in olive oil with cumin and cinnamon. Pai's mouth watered from the savory smells. He reached for the bowl. "I'll take this with me. I have no time. I must hurry."

He drank all the water, grabbed the food, and ran off.

Sayyida shouted after him. "I can find some parchment for your map. Don't leave so soon. You need to dry off before you slip and fall."

Sayyida now sounded like his old friend, but he thought, *No! Parchment is too coarse for this map and I need my pens!* He continued on his way, but he did heed her warning about slipping.

He'd known since he was little that wet leather was dangerous, especially on this rocky path. He sat down and scoured his sandals with dry dirt until all traces of wet mud had vanished. He checked that the straps were tight before he sped away.

He felt like he could run forever. Bounding up the gorge, springing from boulder to boulder, he followed the Wadi al-Laban that divided the Ronda plateau into two parts.

Most people lived in the larger piece with the souk, the church, and the mosque. The other side contained huts for shepherds and farmworkers, who were mostly Christians, interspersed with the Jewish quarter and their small synagogue. Farthest from the gorge, the town limits were marked by Roman fortifications. Even though they were in ruins, Pai often visited them. He admired the Roman stonework, evidence that Christians had settled al-Andalus before the Umayyad.

Before Pai reached the top of the gorge, the sun had set. The fading light made it difficult to see where his feet were landing. Having made it this far, he stopped for dinner, dipping the bread rounds into the bowl of spicy eggplant. The food was even better than it smelled. When he had scraped the bowl clean with the last piece of bread, his belly was full. He hid Sayyida's bowl in a rabbit hole. He'd retrieve it at another time. By the last rays of light, he carefully wended his way between the boulders until he came to the plateau and the Roman road.

He wished that Ronda had streetlamps, as were being installed in Qurtuba. In the faint moonlight, he followed the road until he reached the marketplace. He cut through the dusty square and soon came to Abbas's house, only to find the door barred for the night. He considered banging on the wall but didn't want to wake up his host.

He'd flown the glider, crashed into the Wadi al-Laban, ran up the gorge, and followed the Roman road by moonlight. His supplies were in Abbas's storeroom, so close, but still out of reach.

The storeroom! He ran around to the horse pasture and found the storeroom door ajar. He grabbed his drawing kit and went out to the atrium, joining two others already asleep.

Pai cleaned his hands in the fountain and wiped them on his pants before taking a piece of paper and positioning it on the smooth mosaic floor. In the light of an olive oil lamp, he sharpened his black quills and quickly sketched the map before being overtaken by exhaustion and nightmares.

His body demanded rest, but his mind refused. He'd forgotten an animal path that meandered from the Wadi al-Laban through some brambles to the ashen treasure site. *How could I have left out such a crucial detail?*

The exhilaration of the flight returned. His tired body suggested that the map was good enough. The well-marked treasure was easy enough to locate. However, his mind protested. The map was his responsibility.

He opened his eyes. By the light of the last quarter moon, he felt along the wall until he found a fire starter. He struck the two stones, careful not to bang his fingers, until a spark set fire to a scrap of cotton. With the flaming cotton, he relit the lamp. The pleasant odor of the olive oil filled his corner of the atrium.

He added the missing trail to his map and returned to sleep, but sleep would not come. No matter how worn out he felt, his mind's eye continually repeated his flight. Again, and again, he scrambled for the fire starter and modified the map. A forgotten hill, two ancient olive trees, and a large sea. *No! Not the sea! That was just a vision, not something to put on the treasure map.* Each time, he covered the lamp, extinguishing its flame.

After the final addition, he stretched out under the stars. But the stars had faded, morning had arrived, confirmed by the muezzin calling the faithful to the dawn prayers. With the sun, the morning chorus of birds sang in rhythm with the chittering squirrels. Soon the streets would echo with wagons and burros clattering on the Roman roads.

Pai gave up on any idea of sleep. If his sleep was this disturbed, he must not need it. Besides, the household had now awakened. He joined Ibn Firnas and his servant around the pond where everyone washed. While they prayed, he admired his map, one of his finest. He opened the penner containing his colored quills and added a few details in costly blue and red ink, the Wadi al-Laban, and the treasure location. The morning light showed off his beautiful illustrations. *Truly a work of art.*

Ibn Firnas waved his hand to the front door. "Come with me. We'll get you some breakfast."

Pai tucked the map into a hidden pocket in his robe.

They walked a short way into the sun before arriving at the dusty square located in the overlap between the Christian and the Muslim quarters. A six-sided fountain marked the Ronda market. Around the edge, women sat on blankets wielding long stalks of sugarcane that were variously to shoo away small children, hungry dogs, or curious cats, depending on what they had for sale.

Ibn Firnas stopped at baskets filled with spices of every color of the rainbow. He handed the lady a small jar and a silver coin. "Yarrow, please." The woman remove the cork seal and filled the jar with a small wooden spoon.

Pai's stomach growled. Abbas laughed. "Let's not delay our breakfast any longer."

Pai nodded in agreement and walked past the row of blankets piled with grains, vegetables, freshly slaughtered lamb, and live chickens. At each blanket, he greeted women who'd known him since he was a child getting swatted away from their tempting goods.

He was greeting old friends when he spied Wararni. Now that he'd promised Zetian to capture the Berber, a race renowned as fighters, he noticed Wararni's muscular arms and broad shoulders. The Wararni standing across the souk was formidable and dangerous. Pai had promised Zetian to return her fiancé and he would. *But how?*

Rather than make a commotion in the crowded market, he grabbed a small dirty arm that had reached into his leather coin bag to pilfer a few. The boy cowered until Pai held out a handful of copper coins. "Do you see that tall Berber?" Pai pointed.

The child grinned displaying a mouthful of sparkling white teeth. "The dark one with the long blue keffiyeh?"

"Yes. That one. Can you follow him and discover where he is living?"

The boy looked at the coins and nodded.

"I am staying with Abbas ibn Firnas. Do you know where that is?"

The boy pointed to Abbas and nodded again.

He handed the boy the coins. "A silver coin for you when you tell me where that man is sleeping."

The boy took the coins and ran off.

Pai continued shopping. He pushed through the noisy crowd of workers eager for breakfast and women purchasing ingredients for the evening meal.

"Good morning, Mother of Fruit." Pai addressed the woman with the nickname used by all the children, having never learned her real name.

The lady who had been old when Pai was a small child chasing Sayyida around the market, smiled. "Welcome back Pai. I've heard good news about your paper shop. They say you are a favorite of Tarub the Learned."

Pai smiled, feeling like a child with a good report on his schoolwork. “Thank you. You are looking well.”

She responded with a wide grin missing several teeth. “What would you like child? I will give you the best fruit for the best prices.”

He signaled by pointing and raising his fingers. The fruit lady reached for a couple of apples and four bananas from neatly stacked triangular mounds. He exchanged the fruit for a silver coin.

He gave Ibn Firnas an apple and two bananas. “In gratitude for your hospitality.”

“Good morning,” Sayyida greeted the two men eating their breakfast while sitting on the fountain wall.

Pai quickly swallowed. “Good morning to you, Sayyida al Jamal.”

She grabbed the wrist of the man standing with her and pulled him forward. “You both know my brother Malik. He’s been away on Hajj.”

Malik added, “And trading exotic goods.”

Abbas ibn Firnas responded, “Allahu Akbar.”

Sayyida addressed Abbas and Pai, “I was hoping I’d see you here. I’m having a big celebration in honor of Malik’s return. You’re both invited.”

Pai quickly accepted. “I’ll be there. I’m sure your brother will be interested in the map I’ve drawn of the treasure hidden among the trees and rocks.”

Malik scowled. “What were you doing on my land?”

Ibn Firnas patted Malik on the shoulder. “Do not worry, he didn’t set even a single foot down. He flew over in my glider.”

Pai thought of Sayyida’s interest and added, “Not necessarily your land. It might be Sayyida’s”

That didn’t improve Malik’s mood. “And why is everyone talking about treasure, my treasure, without asking my permission?”

Sayyida interrupted. “Let’s not get excited. Darras of Osuna learned about the treasure from the Pope. The Pope has declared it to be Christian treasure and Darras as his emissary.”

Her brother shouted. “That charlatan! I forbid him from going anywhere near my territory. He shouldn’t even be in Qurtuba!”

Pai protested. “My friend Bhaja, who is responsible for Tarub’s Library, does business with him. He has every right to be there or here.”

“As Allah wills it. Darras can be in Qurtuba, but never in Ronda.” Malik turned to Pai. “If you have a map of treasure on my land, you must give it to me. It will show the treasure is mine, not Sayyida's, not the Pope's."

"I'll show it to you at Sayyida's dinner, but you can't have it."

Malik grabbed Pai. "I want it now!"

Sayyida pushed him away. "These are our friends. There's no reason to get upset!"

Pai backed away when Malik drew his dagger from his ankle sheath and attacked. Sayyida put out her leg and tripped him. "That's enough brother! Can't we settle this without fighting?"

Sayyida retrieved Malik's weapon and held it for him as he dusted off his robes.

Pai placed his hands on his knees and bowed towards Malik. "Can't we settle this like friends?"

But Malik didn't return Pai's peaceful gesture. He shouted at Sayyida, "Why are you joining with them? I thought you were *my* sister. I'm leaving!"

Pai sighed in relief as Malik walked to his horse.

Sayyida followed her brother. "We are family and shouldn't let this come between us."

Malik turned around and moved his face so close to his sister's that their noses touched. "Yes. Remember that. You and mother must listen to me!" With that outburst, he grabbed his dagger and charged Pai. "You must give me the map!"

Pai followed the flashes of red and white as the jewel-encrusted hilt of Malik's knife swung back and forth. Malik slashed the blade at Pai's arm. Pai felt the cut and the warm blood on his skin. He grabbed Malik's wrist with both hands and fought to keep the weapon from inflicting any more damage.

The two men rolled on the ground where they both lost their keffiyehs. Pai's arm left blood everywhere as he tangled Malik's long hair around the knife. They remained locked together until a mob of women stopped the fight by beating them with their sugarcane stalks.

Pai maintained his stoic silence while Malik covered his head with his arms and cursed the women. Sayyida kicked her brother and shouted, "Silence!" When he obeyed, the women backed away and allowed the shamed Malik to mount his horse with its striking white blaze that looked like the minaret of the Great Mosque.

Before Malik galloped off, he shook his fist at Sayyida. "If you're against me in Ronda, you can forget about moving in with me in Qurtuba!"

Pai gave his friend a quizzical look. "Are you leaving Ronda?"

"He had agreed to make a place for me in his villa."

Abbas smiled, "Let me be the first to welcome you to the city."

"But now he's mad at me," Sayyida looked at Pai as if it was his fault.

Pai offered his palms to her in supplication. "I'm sure this can be fixed. He is still your big brother."

She took his hands and whispered, "That's right! And I know how to do it." Then she raised Pai's arm and cried out, "He's bleeding! Someone help him."

Pai pulled his bloody sleeve up and discovered a deep cut in his forearm. Soon he felt his shirt pulled over his head. Abbas ibn Firnas wrapped the bloody shirt around Pai's arm. The pressure made the pain more intense, but Pai gritted his teeth.

"I showed him, didn't I?" Pai whooped. "I don't think he expected me to be such a good fighter."

"You're a tough one," agreed Sayyida, adding, "for a mapmaker." She grabbed his good arm.

Ibn Firnas applied more pressure to the bleeding and led his patient away.

With one friend on either side and Pai holding his injured arm tight to his chest, they moved back to Ibn Firnas's home. Once in the familiar atrium, Ibn Firnas washed Pai's forearm in a large basin. Sayyida rinsed his shirt in the same water, which turned a violent shade of red.

She examined the wound. "You are fortunate. The cut is clean with no tearing. I've seen much worse."

The scientist, now physician, instructed his servant. "Stoke the cooking fire. Fetch the poppy seedpods. Brew a strong tea."

He turned back to Pai. "I'm leaving you in Sayyida's care while I fetch the honey and yarrow ointment. It is the latest treatment. I read about it in a scroll Bhaja acquired for Tarub's Library."

Pai held his injured arm and listened to Abbas moving jars and complaining, "I am getting old. I can't remember where I put anything." The banging got louder, until Abbas gave a happy shout, "I found it!"

Ibn Firnas tilted the cup of warm poppy tea into Pai's mouth. "I know this is bitter, but you must drink it all."

Pai finished it in three swallows and a burp.

"Sayyida, I need you to hold the wound shut."

She squeezed Pai's arm. "Be still. I've done this before for my ungrateful brother. Abbas works quickly."

Pai watched the needle piercing into his arm and back out, over, and over while Sayyida pinched the two flaps of skin together.

“Don’t be too dainty with those stitches. I want a vicious scar to warn off my next attacker.”

Abbas warned Pai, “This is no time for a joke. This is a deep gash; you could lose your arm.” Ibn Firnas spread the sticky ointment on Pai’s arm. The honey gave it a sweet smell. “All done.”

Pai reached his good arm into his robe and shouted, “My map is gone! Malik stole my map! Fetch my drawing kit. I must draw another one before I forget.”

“Later,” said Abbas in a gentle voice, handing Pai a second cup of bitter tea. “Drink this. There will be time tomorrow.”

That was the last thing he remembered.

“Allahu Akbar! Allahu Akbar!” the muezzin called.

Pai opened his eyes. The atrium was spinning. He closed his eyes. His head ached. His mouth was dry. His arm was sore. He reached his other arm over to investigate the pain and his fingers stuck to the sweet salve.

It all came back to him. *The fight. The dagger. The cut. The map! He must recreate the map!* As well as his parched mouth could manage, he gasped, “Get me my drawing kit!”

No one answered his call, so again he opened his eyes. The sun was directly overhead. The house was empty. *Friday!* Everyone had gone to the Mosque.

Pai ignored his arm and his head. He stumbled into the storeroom for his penner and another piece of precious paper. One more thing he required—a cup. He squinted his eyes and spied one on the edge of the pond. He eagerly drank cup after cup of water. Unquenchable thirst dominated his behavior. The water soothed his throat and spilled on his shirt. Finally, he was satisfied.

Then his stomach clenched, and he had but an instant to turn his head before all the water spewed onto the mosaic floor. He looked around, thankful that his paper was beyond the unexpected flood.

This time he drank just a single cup of water and carried a second one, for later, to his paper. He retrieved a blade from the penner containing his black-ink quills and sharpened them. Soon, he had another map, not as nice as the one Malik had stolen, but it would do. He didn’t put it in his robe but tucked it into the bottom of his drawing kit and hid everything in the storeroom.

With that taken care of and grateful that his stomach had accepted the cup of water, he risked a second drink, and returned to sleep, wishing Bhaja was there. After defeating Malik in battle, he had the courage to tell her of his love.

"Are you feeling better?"

Pai looked up at Abbas ibn Firnas. "Thank you for mending my wound."

His physician examined the arm. "Your injury is angry and swollen, but I am happy with your progress. You won't lose your arm."

"Thank you for your care. I never feared for my arm."

"Be thankful for the honey-yarrow mixture. Previously the medical scrolls recommended covering such a wound with clay. This is an improvement."

Pai relaxed, thinking: *What a wonderful time to be alive. Science is finding better ways to cure.*

"Is it night? I haven't heard the sunset prayer call." Pai's dry mouth formed the words with difficulty.

Abbas replied, "No, my foolish friend. You will know the truth in a moment."

Pai wondered how the sky could be dark when it wasn't night. *A storm must be coming.*

Then the sky flashed bright and rain poured into the atrium.

Ibn Firnas handed Pai a cup of hot tea. "Today is your Christian holy day. You slept through the entire Jewish Sabbath. Now your God has blessed you with rain. Come outside. The rain is good for healing."

Pai sipped the pleasant drink, glad it wasn't the bitter poppy tea he'd had before, as they walked by the horse pasture to the edge of the cliff. The storm moved across the valley. The freshness of the rain cooled and rinsed his arm.

The scientist instructed his student. "Listen to the clouds. You will learn something today."

The sky flashed again. Soon a loud clap of thunder sounded.

An excited Abbas ibn Firnas clapped his hands. "Did you see that? The lightning comes first and the thunder later."

There was another flash. This time the thunder came more quickly. Soon the storm blew over the Roman ruins, and as quickly as it arrived, it was gone, and the sun returned.

Pai turned around to head back to the house. The rain had helped; his arm felt better. He had taken just a couple of steps when Ibn Firnas exclaimed, "Can you see that?"

Pai looked back into the valley. The lightning had started a fire. Far below them, the brambles that grew along the Wadi al-Laban were red and a column of smoke rose into the now clear sky. "The treasure's burning! The black treasure site will be swallowed by the blaze," Pai exclaimed.

"Be cheerful Pai, you are now the only one who knows where the treasure is located."

He replied to Abbas, "Except for Malik who stole my map."

He had no reason to celebrate and no claim on the treasure, but possibly it would benefit Sayyida—if she could wrest it from Darras and Malik. He pondered, *Why do men control everything?*

Not always, he argued with himself. *Tarub the Learned is rich and powerful even though she began as a concubine.*

Abbas urged him, "Once the steep trail down the gorge dries and your arm heals, you must go down and find the treasure."

As much as Pai didn't want to overstay his welcome at Abbas's house, he'd have to stay a few more days. "As God wills it."

7. Charlatans and Chickens

Bhaja glanced up at the doorway as Naomi slid off her sandals and made her way inside. *Late, again.* Bhaja scowled. She was embarrassed to have to tell Tarub how little they had accomplished.

She made a decision: she resolved to tell Naomi she must cut her pay. Yes, she was going to have to do that. It was difficult because she already liked Naomi, and the woman's work was good—when she was there to work. She sighed.

After prayers, Bhaja went to work on one of the new parchments Tarub had recently bought and sent to her. She read then re-read the archaic Latin, putting the translation down in a fine but plain Arabic script.

Naomi exclaimed as she unrolled one of the old Greek scrolls that had been in the Library since the beginning.

"A medical text," she said. "Really, it's a marvelous find."

"We will make a couple copies of the translation when it is finished," Bhaja said. "People will want to refer to it."

The afternoon was broken up by the arrival of Darras of Osuna. The bulk of the man blocked the Library doorway as he stood there, letting his eyes adjust to the relative darkness inside the big hexagonal room.

"Darras!" Bhaja cried, looking up. "I have been wondering when you would turn up!"

Surprising her, Naomi also looked up with a smile. Then Bhaja remembered Darras was the name the translator had cited as a reference when she had first arrived and applied for the job. Somewhere on his travels, Darras had befriended the woman.

Darras stepped into the room, and Bhaja welcomed him with a half-hug, half-bow that felt warm, then awkward and clumsy, rather like her feelings for the aging man. "How are you? Have you brought any treasures to us?"

Then it was Naomi's turn to greet her friend, in a much more subdued but no less heartfelt manner.

"It is good to see you, my friends," Darras said, clasping Naomi's wrists, but smiling at Bhaja.

"May I offer you tea?" Bhaja asked, finally remembering her manners.

"That would be splendid," Darras said.

Bhaja retrieved her teapot from the cupboard. Leaving Darras and Naomi alone for a few minutes, she dashed out the door and across the courtyard and street to the vendor that always set up shop near the Emir's citadel. She passed her empty pot to the wrinkled old woman along with several coppers. With a smile, the vendor filled her pot with fragrant jasmine tea. Steam rose from the pot's spout. The old lady added sugar and milk to the pot, so Bhaja didn't have to carry them separately. "Thank you," Bhaja said. "*Alhamdulillah.*"

"Allahu Akbar," the woman responded automatically.

Back in the Library, Bhaja poured tea into three of the four nice glasses she had and served both Darras and Naomi.

"Naomi was just telling me how your work is going here," Darras said with a smile.

Bhaja considered the old man like an uncle, a little too hearty, a little too greedy for good food, but otherwise generous and kind. She smiled warmly back. "We are adding to the holdings little by little," she said, careful to phrase it not too much in Naomi's favor. She was still disappointed with the translator's working hours. Or lack thereof.

"Speaking of which, I found these items in the souk of Tiaret." Darras pulled a bundle of five scrolls from his pack that he had set on the floor by his feet. "And these," he pulled out a handful of parchments, "from a seller outside the House of Wisdom in Baghdad."

Bhaja took both items and set them on her worktable. She noticed the top parchment in the small stack had been written by the poet Gani Kashmiri and copied by some anonymous cleric in the Abbasid court who had been permitted to use only his—or her—initials, "rk," at the bottom. That was significant only because she had seen "rk" on another document here in the Library. Interesting.

Meanwhile, Darras was showing Naomi another scroll he had brought, and Naomi was exclaiming over it, which was extremely annoying. *She* had not asked for it, nor paid for it, yet here she was acting like it was hers. Bhaja used both hands to rub her forehead. Why was she so disturbed by Naomi today? Was the woman really so bad? Or was Bhaja herself just in a bad mood?

Darras looked up and must have caught her expression.

"Look, Bhaja! Naomi thinks this might be one of the original copies of the *Mahavamsa* in Greek!"

It was nice of Darras to invite her to be part of it, but did he not remember she did not read Greek?

She tilted back her head, watching the bits of dust float in the sunbeams slanting down from the late afternoon sun through the high windows. She was still trying to figure out how to respond without being churlish when another person entered the Library.

Unlike Darras, this man was unknown to Bhaja. Short ashy-blonde hair, with a brown and grey beard. His robes were arranged well, contributing to his overall attractiveness. In fact, he was quite handsome—and he knew it, if his sly smile said anything.

Bhaja physically confronted him and was opening her mouth to ask who the man was and what he wanted, when he blurted, "I am Malik al Jamal. You may know me as an agent for the Emir," and immediately she knew who he was. The family name was important in Qurtuba and the areas around it. And the name Malik al Jamal was quite well known to her, Tarub, and others. He was one of the Emir's advisors and agents. Like Darras, the man traveled a lot. Unlike Darras, he had rather a bad reputation and she was glad she had never happened to meet him before. As one woman—a friend of her mother's—had long ago told her, "The man's devilish good looks make as much trouble for him as Tarub the Learned's great beauty always did for her. Be wary."

She heard Darras clear his throat. She turned toward him and Naomi, leaving the al Jamal man still standing in the doorway.

Naomi seemed distressed. Her face was pale, her eyes wide and frightened. Malik al Jamal moved further into the room, scowling at the other woman. Without a word, Naomi jumped up, knocking over her stool, and ran from the Library, stumbling as she hurried out the door.

What was that about?

Meanwhile, Malik walked over to where Darras was still perched on a stool by Naomi's desk.

"You!" Malik said. It did not sound at all like a friendly greeting.

"What do you want?" Darras said, his whole manner now stiff and cold.

"What rags and waste have you pretended to find this time, you old charlatan?" Malik said, a smirk on his lips and hostility in his eyes.

Bhaja scowled. Weren't there enough interferences to her work today, without this unseemly squabble?

While she did not care for Malik's accusation against Darras, she did know the Emir trusted the man, who had procured several worthy slaves, including the papermaking Zetian, at Pai's shop. But what did Malik mean, calling the documents Darras had brought "waste"?

"If you could even read, you would know these are all authentic," Darras said calmly.

Malik scoffed and flicked the top parchment onto the floor with his forefinger.

With an exclamation, Bhaja ran to pick it up. She met Malik's eyes as she stood back up, parchment in hand. "You are not welcome here, sir. Please leave."

"I have business with you," he said to her.

Then why are you accusing Darras of something, she wanted to say. But that would probably just prolong the interruption. "*What* business?"

"I need to see the city's land records. I am trying to trace back the original ownership of a particular piece of land near Ronda."

Taken aback, Bhaja stared at him for a moment before she responded. "I have nothing like that here! All city records are held at the old governor's palace. Or perhaps at the Mosque."

"Ah. Well then, I will try those places."

Bhaja scowled at him and ushered him to the door, feeling like she needed to grab the broom and sweep him out.

"What do you have here, then?" Malik asked in a scornful tone. "More of Darras's fake histories?"

"This Library contains numerous well-known tracts on philosophy, poems, the nature of man," she said. "Many of which the *Emirs* have personally collected," she finished, letting a little threat enter her tone.

"Of course, those would be genuine," Malik said, nodding. "But you should verify the provenance of anything Darras of Osuna might bring you, and anything the hag provides."

Hag? Did he mean to insult Tarub? Already inclined to dislike him, she now felt absolute animosity toward the man. Who did he think he was?

She tried to get him out the door by taking a step outside, herself, and sweeping her hand outside. Malik did not take the hint. Speaking loudly enough she was certain Darras could hear him, Malik said, "My own experiences with this man have been unpleasant. I simply recommend caution."

"Please leave," Bhaja said curtly. "You are interrupting my work," *and you are rude and a bully,* she did not add.

Malik al Jamal bowed to her, an amused expression on his face as he left the Library and stalked off through the courtyard.

As he walked, she heard him shout at someone out of her view, "What are *you* doing here!" Then Malik al Jamal exited by the east courtyard archway, turning toward the Emir's citadel.

Bhaja leaned out the door, both to make sure the belligerent man was indeed gone, and to see if she could see whom he had yelled at.

She could hear rapid footsteps running along the outside of the courtyard wall. Then a woman ran by the northern exit gate of the courtyard. It was a little hard to see so far away, but the woman looked a lot like Lylah. Why did she keep seeing the woman?

Or was she imagining things?

Allah is wondrous in the world's complexity, but what was that all about? Bhaja went back inside to see a look of uncertainty on Darras's face. Did he think she would trust a complete stranger's disparagement over her own lengthy experience with him?

She smiled. "Now, what were you saying about the vellums?"

Darras cleared his throat and took a deep breath. "Just that the seller claimed they were poems attributed to Gani Kashmiri as well, though the handwriting style seems completely different to me."

"Well, the other parchment *was* copied," she said, examining several pages of vellums. "This one has no copyist's mark; it could be an original."

"Ah, that would explain the differences, then." Darras waved a hand indicating all the vellums. "These were a private sale to me from one of the librarians at the House of Wisdom. The seller is a long-term acquaintance of mine. So they're not all originals, then, but copies by an unnamed cleric, or perhaps a slave."

Bhaja nodded. "I will examine them. But I think our patron Tarub is most interested in having *any* copy, whether it is an original or not, to add to this collection. Originals, while doubtless more accurate, are often prohibitively expensive."

"Quantity over quality, for the beginning years, the lady said to me," Darras agreed. "Later we will focus on rarities."

"These are wonderful, Darras. Thank you so much. And thank you for referring Naomi; she is very well educated."

He must have heard something in her tone. "But...?"

Bhaja sighed, throwing up her hands. "Her work ethic is lacking. She is late almost daily, sometimes by *nearly a half-day.* I can understand that sometimes life intrudes—but I cannot pay her if she is not here, and she is here less and less." She frowned. "And now she is gone altogether, with scant work done today at all."

"I am astonished," Darras said, frowning also.

"The old widow she stays with is her excuse; she says she tries to leave, but the old woman detains her with problem after problem."

Darras tapped his fingertips against his lips. "She told me how to find the widow's house, so I could stop by for a visit and see how things are there."

"Perhaps I should join you," Bhaja said. "A few words to the widow might fix the problem."

"Good." Darras slapped a hand on the desktop decisively. His many rings made the slap more of a clunk. "Can we go *now?*"

"Ah, as soon as I clear all this away. The pens need washing—and prayers are soon. Then I can join you for a brief visit. I need to check on Pai's shop, too, though that is the opposite direction."

"I have seen the paper shop," Darras said. "But I would like to look again." He nodded at her. "Do you mind if I read this while I wait?" He indicated the current translation in progress.

"Yes, certainly." Meanwhile she wondered if the old man could walk that far—to Pai's shop and back, then on to the Jewish quarter? Perhaps they should hire horses. "Would you then join me for dinner with Mother? I know she would enjoy seeing you again."

"Thank you," Darras said. "I will need a good meal before I set out for Osuna and home."

Eventually, she locked the Library and they headed toward Pai's shop. The crescent moon rising did not offer much light; Bhaja again thanked the foresight of the Emir's planners, who were adding streetlights. The major avenues along their route were lit well. Bhaja still did not feel wholly safe, since she had been feeling eyes on her for the last several blocks.

Someone was following them. Or was she imagining things again?

"Don't be concerned about Malik al Jamal," Darras said, making her wonder if he felt a watcher as well. "I believe he is looking for a supposed Christian treasure that he'd like to claim as his. I've run across the man several times over the years, and I can tell you he is far more interested in money than anything else."

"It was odd he would think city records would be in Tarub's Library."

"Well, I have to say I wonder where they would be found, myself. The Emir, at least, must have plans of the city and surrounding suburbs."

"Yes, I should have sent him there."

"He may not have gone to the Emir with this, for a reason," Darras said with a chuckle. "The provenance of the treasure is at issue; whose land was it on? That determines who any riches go to. Does it belong to the Christian family that originally owned that land? Should it go to the Pope if it is a Christian treasure? Is the new Muslim owner entitled to all or some of it? All I know is, if Malik gets his hands on it—whatever it is—the Emir may never get the chance to decide the issue, because it will all disappear."

She had no idea how the Emir could make a decision about treasure without making at least one of the parties involved quite angry. She did not envy the man his job, regardless of how she—and Pai—felt about his ability to do it.

Just past the Great Mosque, Bhaja looked around for a runner in the square they were crossing. Finding one with an orange and green headscarf—meaning he was one of the Emir's paid servants, and trustworthy—she handed him coins for his pay. "Please take this to my mother's house," she handed him a small packet of coins wrapped in a cloth scrap, "and tell her we will have Darras of Osuna to a late supper tonight. She will know what to do."

The runner nodded.

"You know my mother's house?" surprising her, the runner nodded again. "Good. Thank you."

He headed off in the correct direction while Bhaja and Darras turned again the other way.

They did manage to walk all the way to Pai's shop, though Darras's plump face was quite red by the time they arrived. Bhaja greeted Zetian, who was hard at work in the back.

Really, the woman should check the front of the shop now and then, or Pai's valuable paper might all just disappear. It was like leaving jewels unattended; some among the very poor might see it as a gift from Allah meant to help them out of their troubles.

But then, if Zetian kept a close eye on the shop, she wouldn't have time to make the paper in the first place. Bhaja shook her head. Pai should be here, not off doing...whatever it was he was doing.

Beyond that, Zetian was well; Pai had left her money for food, and she had plenty of work to keep her busy. Bhaja suggested bolting the shop door while no one was there to watch it. Potential customers could always ring the bell Pai had put outside his door for that purpose. Zetian nodded as though she had understood. As they left, Bhaja watched and saw the woman indeed lock up the shop and disappear back into the back, presumably to her slurries and paper drying racks outside, or to the *mohreh* table to polish the finished sheets. Bhaja had found the whole process fascinating when Pai had asked Zetian to demonstrate the steps.

Then, from the nearby square, they hired a horse and cart to get from Pai's shop all the way back across the city to the Jewish quarter in the opposite corner of the medina.

They located the widow and Naomi's residence and dismissed the cart. When Naomi opened the door at their knock, she seemed startled, but she recovered quickly.

"Please enter," she said.

Bhaja and Darras kicked off their sandals, wiped their feet on the towel provided for that purpose, then entered the house. Bhaja could hear a non-stop, querulous voice coming from deeper within the cool stucco building, which did not seem to have an atrium. The voice got louder as Naomi led them from the modest entry directly into the main salon.

"This is my patroness—"

"What are you doing bringing strangers into my home?" the woman interrupted, face red, wispy hair damp around her face.

Bhaja realized the woman was not really the frail old lady she had supposed from Naomi's description. Perhaps somewhere between forty and fifty years old. The woman's dark hair was pulled back into a low bun. Wispy curls framed her forehead. Not much grey showed at all; Bhaja adjusted her estimate downward again.

"These are not strangers," Naomi was saying, "these are my friend and my employer."

"Come to beg tea and cakes from a poor old widow, no doubt," the woman said tartly.

The woman's clear un-welcome took Bhaja aback. Then she got angry. "Actually, I came to see why Naomi has been late to work every day, and to ask you if some arrangement could be made to ensure she arrives on time. She spends most of the evening and all night with you as it is! Surely the mornings are available for her paying job." Without meaning to, Bhaja let slip an emphasis on "paying."

"Her job is taking care of me!" the woman said. "For which she receives room and board. How dare you imply I am keeping her late."

"*Not* board," Naomi said, defending herself. "I've bought the food for all our meals since I have been here!"

Bhaja was dumbfounded. "So you are using a *single room* in her house, for which she expects a payment of three-quarters of every day, plus food? This is not right!"

Indignance turned the widow's face a darker, alarming red. "Naomi has a safe house to live in, and my companionship!" She raised her chin, defiant. Her hands were shaking as she tucked a stray lock of hair back into her bun.

Bhaja could not determine if the woman really was ill, but it certainly seemed as if she could take care of herself, shaking or not.

Darras, silent until now, cleared his throat. "The issue is, if Bhaja has to hire another translator to do Naomi's job, she will not be able to also pay Naomi. Then *you* will become Naomi's full-time employer, and *you will be required to pay her!*"

"That is absurd!" the widow cried.

"That is the law," Darras said, voice firm. "You must decide to either give up your malingering or pay this woman to take care of you all the time."

Naomi opened her mouth to speak, but the widow suddenly burst into tears. "I have no money!"

Naomi went and patted the woman's hand.

"Would your rabbi really have expected Naomi to spend all these hours with you, in exchange for the use of *one room*?" Bhaja asked. "She could come sleep in the Library as I do, for free. Then she would be already there in the morning and she would *never* be late."

Darras said, "And it should be observed, Naomi is your companion as much as you are hers. If she is paying for her food as well as yours, you are definitely asking too much for too little. It should be reported to the Emir, who is quite strict about such things."

The widow collapsed back into the chair she had half-risen from. "No," she said, voice now shaky, too. She used an edge of her over robe to dab at her eyes. She heaved a great sigh.

Silence reigned in the room as she gulped several deep breaths.

Then she got to her feet, not in the least bit shaky. She said, "I will be less needy. It has been a long, lonely time for me. Perhaps I have taken advantage of Naomi's presence and good heart." She met Naomi's eyes. "I am sorry."

Biting her lip, Naomi nodded.

Bhaja said, "I will ensure Naomi's Friday evenings and Saturdays are free so that you can attend Temple together or observe your holy day as you see fit. The other days, I will expect Naomi at the Library shortly after the dawn call to prayers."

The widow nodded. Naomi nodded. Darras and Bhaja agreed as well, and with faint smiles all around, the matter was settled.

Bhaja's mother was delighted to have an unmarried guest, even if the man was as old as Darras. She had taken the money the runner brought from Bhaja and bought two chickens. She roasted them, and also served eggplant in garlic, fire-blackened peppers, flatbread, and chickpeas in curry sauce.

Yusuf appreciated their guest as well; it meant he could stuff himself with meat instead of the lighter meals the women usually enjoyed.

Bhaja was proud of her home; its elegant mosaic entry had elicited an excited comment from Darras who had not noticed it the previous time he had come to their house. And he was quite pleased with the food.

"I appreciate a home-cooked meal with friends," Darras said, thanking Bhaja's mother. "I spend many days on the road, never knowing what to expect from my accommodations."

"Darras has brought us several wonderful scrolls and many parchments," Bhaja said.

"And—" Darras raised his cup of coconut milk as a gesture to get their attention— "I wish to tell you, there is much more! I have two entire trunks full at my home in Osuna." He faced Bhaja. "I am sorry I could not bring them on this quick trip; I must return to Osuna as soon as I can and waiting on a wagon full of trunks was too slow."

"Oh," Bhaja said, thinking about how many documents there were to translate and copy already. It was just as well he hadn't brought the whole load at once. It was doubly fortunate she had found Isador.

"I am hoping you will come and meet me in Osuna by Friday, and we will get them packed properly so that you can bring them back to the Library. I suspect Tarub will be especially interested in several of them." He used his flatbread to sop up some chicken juices and popped it into his mouth. "I was waiting for the completion of the Library as well, so there was a place for them."

Bhaja had to wonder how the man could still be eating. Even Yusuf had stopped, hands resting lightly atop his now-plump stomach.

"You will want guards for this shipment," Darras went on. "Another reason I did not bring them with me on this trip." He waved his handmade *barjyn* around—it was pure silver as best as Bhaja could tell by looking at it, lost in his hand.

Bhaja was aware her brother's fingers were as greasy as her own. It was easy to see why the implement was so well-liked. She felt rather like a country bumpkin compared with Darras's fine manners.

"Perhaps Yusuf could be your guard," their mother said, looking fondly at her son. "You could ask a friend to come along, perhaps."

At Yusuf's developing stubborn expression, Bhaja put in, "I can pay you. Two or even three of you. Also, I will pay for the accommodations and meals in Osuna."

"Oh, no, no!" Darras said. "You will all stay at my home. I insist! There is plenty of room, it is built like a villa with guestrooms around the atrium garden!"

Yusuf rolled his eyes. "I have trouble explaining why my sister is paid by the enemy of the Emir, when I wish the Emir to pay me."

"Surely he cannot begrudge you honest work!" their mother said, indignant. "Besides, how would he ever know?"

"There are spies," Yusuf said. "Little butterflies who flutter to him and tell tales."

Darras nodded in agreement. Bhaja remembered the feeling of being followed. Had it been a spy from the Emir?

"He's right, I'm afraid," Darras said. "The Emir would find out."

Bhaja turned and faced Yusuf. "But, I have to ask, if the Emir is so fussy about the work you might do for other people, as part of his consideration of someone he *might someday* hire, do you really want to work for him?"

Yusuf groaned. "My friends are there."

"You might consider making new friends," Darras said. "If you value your life."

"What does that mean?" Yusuf demanded, leaning forward. "The Emir is in the business of *hiring* guards, not killing them!"

"So you say," Darras said. "Others say different."

"You have been told something?" Bhaja asked.

"Those at Tarub's gatherings know the truth of many incidents." He glanced at Bhaja again. "This Malik al Jamal, for example," he finished chewing the last bite of apple tart Mother had made. He swallowed, used his napkin to wipe off the *barjyn*, tucking it in his pockets, and went on, "There are reports of him 'taking care of' the Emir's enemies. People who are never seen again."

"The Emir's enemies include your Tarub!" Yusuf said. "Which is why I would avoid doing business of any kind with her, if I could." He thrust his chin at Bhaja. "Just knowing you is making trouble for me with the Guards!"

Their mother tsked. "How can you reject your own sister?"

Darras smiled at Yusuf, eyebrows raised. "Have you been informed of the new requirement for Emir's Guards?"

Yusuf stared at him; mouth tight. "That's just an ugly rumor."

"I know it for fact," Darras said.

"What requirement?" Mother asked.

"Ahh." Yusuf turned bright red and covered his face with his hands. They all stared at him a moment, but he said nothing further.

"Perhaps it is best left unsaid," Darras said. "Thank you for the lovely meal." He stood up and smiled at Bhaja's mother. "You are very kind to invite me." He cleared his throat and met Bhaja's eyes, as she stood up also. "Then I will see you in Osuna on Friday?"

"Yes," Bhaja said. "Perhaps I can find some other guard, if Yusuf will not take on the job. Two days to Osuna means I will leave on Thursday."

Darras nodded. "I am to stop by Tarub's usual literary gathering for a brief time before I head back to Osuna later tonight. I will see you at my home, in four days."

"I'll join you in leaving now," Bhaja said. "I need to return to the Library."

She kissed her mother and met Yusuf's eyes, as she gathered her over robe and head covering.

Yusuf cleared his throat. "I will be there at your Library early Thursday morning with a friend or two," he said begrudgingly. "Or our mother will never let me rest."

"Thank you," Bhaja said, meaning it sincerely. Then she escorted Darras to the door. "I asked for a carriage to arrive after nighttime prayers, which we skipped tonight being in the middle of our meal. I will join you partway, if you don't mind." He nodded, looking around; the carriage had not yet arrived.

She must inform Naomi of the change in plans. Perhaps she could hire Isador to sleep in the Library until her return from Osuna. She dared not leave it unguarded.

Her heart lifted as she stepped into the carriage and sat beside Darras. It would be an adventure. As close as it was, she had never before been to Osuna.

8. Death and Deception

"I forbid you from that treacherous gorge. It is haram for you, too dangerous with your arm still in a sling," warned Abbas.

Pai conceded, "I promise to stay on the plateau, but I can't be confined to your atrium like some wounded soldier."

Pai retrieved his drawing kit from the storeroom along with a piece of bamboo to use for a walking stick. He anticipated a long walk, so he requested a couple of bread rounds from the servant and filled a waterskin made from a lizard by sewing the leg holes shut. The servant also gave him a handful of dried apricots and a few pieces of meat.

As he walked across the atrium juggling everything with his good arm, he could hear Abbas laughing, "You look like a pack mule."

He let everything drop and looked at the jumble: bread, meat, water, apricots, drawing kit, and walking stick. Now he laughed too.

He packed the food into his drawing kit and tucked it into his sling. He hung the water over his shoulder. Now, with just the walking stick in his good arm, he confidently marched out the front door.

"That's better," Ibn Firnas called after him. "Be back for the evening meal."

The Muslim quarter bustled with activity. Children returned from the souk with fresh fruits and vegetables. The women swept their houses and washed the stones in front of their doors. *I should be in Qurtuba taking care of my shop. Hopefully, Zetian has remembered to clean each morning. And I wonder how Bhaja's doing in the new library.*

The roar of the Wadi al-Laban crashing downhill reiterated Abbas's warning to avoid the gorge trail. Regardless, he didn't let this wisdom stop him from retrieving Sayyida's bowl. The path he'd navigated with care in the dark was as safe as the broad Roman road in the light. With the bowl stowed in his drawing kit, he waded across the river where it was broad and shallow.

A short walk through the Jewish quarter took him to the Roman ruins. Resting on a warm stone block, he drank some water and ate a round of bread. Two stray cats, one black and one striped, both with white feet, rubbed against his legs until he tossed them some bits of bread. They swatted the bread a couple of times before covering it with sand.

"You are fussy kittens." He dug through his food until he found the meat. This they ate while purring loudly.

They slept in the sun while he sketched the Roman wall on a scrap of parchment. As he studied that stonework, he compared it to the palace in his dream. The dream palace used larger stones that were fitted with finer joints. When he closed his eyes, *he could smell seawater. The dream lady approached him across a wide bridge. Just as he asked her how to speak to Bhaja,* the vision faded. No problem, he'd already decided to talk to Bhaja as soon as he returned to Qurtuba.

Always looking for business opportunities, he pondered: *If I make copies of the Roman stonework, I can sell them to Christians who want to remember their former days of glory.* He showed the drawing to the cats sleeping in the sun. One swished her tail and the other blinked. He scratched their ears and chided them, "You remind me of an old married couple, never agreeing on anything."

He removed the map from his drawing kit. He didn't want anyone to steal this one, so he extracted a loose brick and hid the map in the Roman wall. It would be safe there. Before he headed back, he shared another snack with his two feline critics.

"As-Salaam-Alaikum." Someone pulled on Pai's robe. "As-Salaam-Alaikum." Pai stopped and turned around.

"I found him. Follow me."

Pai waited for the boy to lead the way, but the boy stood still with his hand palm up.

"Yes. Of course," Pai laughed while he went through his money for a silver coin.

The enterprising boy grabbed the coin and ran. Pai had lost the boy and his coin. Pai had been a similar child roaming the streets of Ronda. He couldn't be angry, but he wondered, *Had the boy failed to locate Wararni? Was the tall Berber already on his way to Ifriqa? At least the boy's family would eat well tonight.*

What would he say to the unfortunate Zetian?

Just then the boy whistled and signaled Pai to catch up. Pai shouted, "I'm coming."

They wound through the narrow paths of the Muslim quarter. In front of some homes, women sat spinning wool or weaving. Others milled barley into a coarse flour or baked bread on a small brazier. Everywhere small children ran naked, and older ones collected wood or water.

Then suddenly the boy stopped. He pointed to a house with a woman sitting on the front door stone and nursing. Pai pointed also. "That one with the baby?"

The boy nodded.

Pai looked at the dark child. Did Wararni already have a wife and child in Ronda? He asked the mother, "I am looking for Wararni. Is he here?"

She picked up her child and retreated into her home.

It would be impolite to cross the threshold without being invited. But he looked into the comfortable room. No Wararni. "Do you know where he is?"

"Gone."

Had Wararni abandoned two women? "Did he go to Ifriqa?"

"Ifriqa? No. My husband will find that funny," the woman laughed. "My cousin Wararni went in the other direction. Osuna."

Pai apologized to the wayward Wararni who was visiting family, not another girlfriend. He thanked the woman and handed her a silver coin. Looking around her home, he knew she didn't need the coin, but he couldn't think of another way to express his gratitude. *What was Wararni doing in Osuna?*

He'd find Wararni on his way back to Qurtuba. He'd promised Zetian to return her fiancé. He would do it.

A few days later, Pai sat in the sun holding a knife with his bandaged arm and sharpening his quills. He waved to Ibn Firnas. "Look! I'm all better."

"Don't do that! You are going to break the stitches."

Pai had grown tired of waiting. He'd spent too many days dependent on Abbas's hospitality. "I'm going to search for the treasure today. I have to get there before Malik."

"Not today. It's Friday. I can't go with you on Friday. Tomorrow, for sure."

"I can't leave Zetian alone in the shop any longer. I need to talk to Bhaja." Mostly he wanted to see Bhaja. With Abbas still warning him to delay, Pai walked out back where his horse munched on the new grass brought on by the rain. The servant came out to assist Pai with his saddle. She stroked the horse's flank while Pai took care of the bridle.

"Beautiful mare," she said as he set off to the Wadi al-Laban trail eager to go before the sun rose too high and the day got too hot.

He stopped at Sayyida's house to refill his waterskin.

"Welcome, Pai. Please honor my home and come inside for tea."

She was dressed for the mosque, wearing a blue robe and a matching headscarf. The fancy scarf even had a narrow band of embroidery—Arabic calligraphy of surahs from the Quran.

He wanted to keep going, but there was no way to politely refuse. Resigned to accept Sayyida's hospitality, he walked his horse to the familiar paddock enclosed by a stone wall. When Malik was in Ifriqa, Pai had assisted Sayyida's father with the annual repairs. He could still see the stones he'd laid in the wall, the newer mud and hay mortar still paler than the old.

He didn't bother to unsaddle his horse. This would be a short visit as Sayyida had to be on her way, and in the opposite direction.

He was startled when he entered the farmhouse. He even stepped out to be sure it was the same house from his memories. He didn't recognize the inside. When Sayyida's father had been alive, Sayyida and her mother lived with dirt floors and a row of pitchers to fetch water from the river. When her father died, Malik moved to Qurtuba and the two women inherited the farmhouse. Now the floors were paved with mosaics and a fountain had been installed with four storks spraying water.

"Have a seat," Sayyida pointed to several large pillows, also new. "The tea will be here soon."

Pai removed his shoes before stepping on the polished mosaic. He followed Sayyida to the atrium. "Allah be praised, that is a beautiful fountain."

"Thank you. Abbas ibn Firnas designed it. I find the bubbling water very relaxing. Now that we manage our own money, we've made some improvements."

Sayyida's mother joined them elegantly dressed in flowing robes with gold embroidery. Tiny pearls adorned her headscarf—not her everyday clothes. She examined Pai and gave a disapproving frown at his simple shirt and pants. He imagined her thinking, *Nice young man, but not attending mosque today*. Then she turned to Sayyida in a way that spun her robes showing off its fine fabric.

"As-Salaam-Alaikum daughter."

"Wa-Alaikum-Assalaam mother."

Pai was surprised by the formality between the two women. He sensed some tension and regretted accepting the invitation for tea. Some time had passed since he met her mother, so he waited for an introduction.

Sayyida started, "Mother, you remember—"

The older woman interrupted. "Are you going to introduce me? Is this good-looking man here to call on you? At your age, you should be married."

Pai wished he could disappear.

Sayyida responded sharply. "Mother, you must remember Pai, who used to live in Ronda and came here in the summers to help Papa. Now he supplies fine paper to Tarub the Learned and her Library."

Pai gave a head nod in the old woman's direction.

Sayyida continued, "He is not a suitor and you must stop mentioning marriage to every man that accepts our hospitality. I have my own money. I don't need to get married."

"Don't you want to raise a family in our beautiful farmhouse?"

"No! You may love the quiet life here in the valley, but I want to live in Qurtuba, just like my brother."

The mother apologized, "I'm sorry, daughter, but he seemed so much better than the fat, old man who stopped by the other day."

Pai didn't think her mother looked sorry.

After an awkward silence, the tea arrived. Sayyida grabbed the teapot and poured three cups usurping the role of host from her mother. She handed a cup to Pai saying, "Welcome to our home," as if he'd just arrived and the disagreeable behavior of her mother had never happened. "Your arm looks much improved. Please relax and tell us why you've ventured down to our valley?"

"Malik has my map. I want to find the treasure before he does. I don't trust him." Then he remembered that he was talking to Malik's mother, but before he could apologize, the mother nodded in agreement and muttered, "He takes after his father, more interested in money than family."

Thus encouraged, he ventured, "Have either of you seen him?"

Sayyida quickly responded. "No. No one has come by our path. If you're asking about the treasure, our path is the only way to reach it without jumping off the cliff with Abbas ibn Firnas's flying machine. The Roman road passes us high on the plateau. In all other directions, the land is uncivilized, certainly no barrier for the wild boars, but I've never seen people cross it."

Pai puzzled: *What about the visitor your mother mentioned, probably Darras?* He silently answered his own question: *Malik's the important one. No reason to worry about Darras.*

He stood up. "Thank you for the tea. As you surmised, I'm going to search for the treasure."

Sayyida seemed worried. "I'm going with you. So soon after the fire and the rain, that area is dangerous, and this is my land."

Pai looked to her mother, expecting an objection to skipping Friday prayers, but she just squinted her eyes in a disapproving scowl. He didn't want Sayyida to join him. The search would be difficult and lengthy—best accomplished alone.

Still watching her mother, he asked, "Sayyida, aren't you going up to Ronda for Friday prayers?"

She replied, also looking at her mother. "You are injured. Allah tells us to care for the sick. I'm going to change my clothes."

In a short while, Sayyida returned with two workers, a tall one carrying a mattock and a short one with a shovel. The tall one also had a large waterskin over his shoulder, while the short one wore a baldric holding a long sword that dragged along the ground. Pai's simple visit had turned into an expedition.

The tall one kicked the sword. "That weapon's too big for you. How are you going to defend the treasure if your arms are too short to unsheathe your sword?"

The short one surprised Pai by his grace and speed as he thrust the sword at his companion.

"I surrender," squeaked the tall man.

After that, the men just sang. Most of the songs were bawdy, but Pai recognized a hymn: *Te Deum*.

He led the way and made easy progress until they reached the area scorched by the fire. The group went quiet. They had entered an area of death. Dead trees. A dead rabbit. Even the horses were solemn as the soft ground muffled their hoofbeats. The thick layer of ashes formed a grey cloud irritating Pai's mouth and nose.

That animal path that had been so obvious from the glider had disappeared in the black sameness. He looked around for the landmarks he'd seen from the sky. He turned in every direction, but he couldn't find his bearings.

Sayyida pulled on the reins and pointed her horse away from the sound of the river. "I think we should search closer to the cliffs."

Pai had a better idea. "You can look there, but I'm going to go in circles, ever-increasing circles. That way I won't miss anything." While he said that, he wondered if he'd recognize the treasure location even if he stood atop it. He regretted leaving the map in the Roman wall.

Sayyida seemed disappointed but stayed with him as he spiraled. He'd have been happy if she'd gone off on her own. After a few circuits, she again suggested moving closer to the cliffs, but he ignored her.

He sought for some familiar signs, a unique hill, two ancient olive trees, a singular boulder. So much had happened in the last week and everything looked so different from the ground. The treasure was lost.

She was still close by when he saw something. At first, it appeared to be a boulder, but when he looked closer, he spied a silver line gleaming in the sun. He kicked his horse and galloped over to investigate. The others followed.

"It's Darras. I recognize his belt. He must have gotten caught in the fire!"

Pai shuddered. Being burned alive was a terrible way to die. Bhaja would be upset when she learned of his accident. She had known him for years. Pai wanted to hurry back to the city to give her the news. It is always best to hear bad news from a friend, especially someone who has the full story. He owed that to her.

Sayyida jumped off her mount and looked for other clues among Darras's burnt garments. "Look at this." She handed Pai the gaudy pin Darras wore in his keffiyeh.

"Bhaja is going to be unhappy. They were friends," said Pai accepting the pin. He examined it and added, "I will give it to her."

Pai was grateful when Sayyida offered, "My men can take care of the body, and you can return to Qurtuba."

Sayyida held the reins as she directed her men to drape the corpse over the saddle. One man held the legs while the other tugged on the arms. They tried to lift the awkward load but only succeeded in knocking his keffiyeh from his dangling head. Pai almost laughed when one of the men slipped and Darras landed on top of him. The comedy abruptly ended when Pai saw that Darras's hair was matted with blood. He exclaimed, "Look! He hit his head."

Sayyida concurred. "He must have stumbled running for the river to escape the fire."

Pai carefully dismounted, protecting his arm. He moved closer to inspect the head wound.

The two workers raised Darras and heaved him over the saddle. The stir of activity spooked the horse. It humped up and bucked, ridding itself of the body. It pulled away, but Sayyida held tightly to the reins. The frightened animal kicked wildly.

Pai sprang out of the path of the nervous horse's hooves, but Pai's feet slid on the wet ashes and he fell to the ground, landing on his injured arm.

He sat up. His arm felt warm. He thought it was the midday sun, but after checking, he noticed his shirt was red. *Blood, again.* His arm didn't hurt, and a little blood didn't compare to poor Darras. He held his shirt sleeve tight to slow the bleeding and continued to examine Darras's head wound, not certain which damage killed poor Darras and what had been caused by the clumsy handling.

Pai regretted allowing Sayyida and her crew of inept helpers to join him. Nothing had gone right. His arm was bleeding. Darras lay in a disheveled mound on the ground. As much as he wanted to search for the treasure and examine Darras, it wouldn't happen today.

Sayyida sent her men away to get a cart.

"We must wait until they return," Pai properly observed.

Sayyida pulled up Pai's shirt sleeve and examined his arm. She tore a piece of cloth from Darras's robes and used it for a bandage. "You will be fine."

"Thank you," Pai replied, thinking he should have Abbas ibn Firnas look at it.

Oh! Abbas? He didn't look forward to the ordeal of Ibn Firnas stitching his arm again, nor explaining why it was needed. But he felt justified for ignoring the scientist's advice because of the discovery of Darras's body. Once safely mounted, Pai squeezed his legs and his horse set off for the medical science only available up on the plateau.

He passed the men returning with a cart. As much as he wished to continue on his own, he resigned himself to accept that Sayyida would soon catch up to him.

Upon reaching the steep section of the gorge trail, Pai pulled up on the reins. He passed them to his injured arm. Even though the arm was bleeding, his hand could still hold the reins. He'd need his good arm to hold the saddle to maintain his alignment as he stood up in the stirrups. Once comfortable with his balance, he squeezed his legs, and they began their ascent. Sayyida also stood up as she followed him up the narrow trail.

He held the reins loosely to let his horse control her head and pick the route. Surefooted horses were valued in Ronda. Abu Ubaidah had written fifty books about the al-Andalus horses. Pai's horse was one of the best. He sat tall, aligned with the trees while the horse picked her own route.

When he reached the level ground, he expected an easy ride. The horse walked smoothly, but Pai felt like that morning after Ibn Firnas had stitched his injury. He gripped the saddle tightly and it took all the strength of his good arm to keep from falling. He turned to Sayyida and gasped, "I cannot stay in the saddle much longer."

"We are almost there," Sayyida encouraged him.

He didn't have the energy to reply. He held tight and counted on his horse to find the way back to the field of tender grass behind Abbas's house.

Abbas examined the arm. "Allah has blessed you with good health. The stitches are strong. You broke the scab. That is why you are bleeding."

Abbas guided Pai to the pond and washed his arm before covering the gash with a clean bandage. "Tell me what foolish thing you were doing when this happened."

Pai explained how he went looking for the treasure but found Darras instead.

Sayyida added how Darras got caught in the fire and had fallen and hit his head.

Ibn Firnas held his hands behind his back and walked around the atrium. He stopped in front of his servant who waited discreetly in a doorway and whispered something to her.

Ibn Firnas continued pacing until the servant appeared with tea and pieces of cut fruit. He signaled the others to sit and everybody took refreshments.

"First," he pointed to Sayyida. "You must bring the body to the Christian church in Osuna without delay. Surely, they'll know Darras of Osuna, and he must have some family there."

She nodded. "Insha'Allah."

"Second, I do not remember Darras as a person who would wander far from cities and well-traveled roads. He didn't look like someone who took adventures. What was he doing in that wild space?"

Pai was going to say, treasure, but Sayyida said it first.

"Treasure?" pondered the scientist. "I find it hard to believe he'd go alone."

Pai suggested, "Malik?"

Sayyida agreed. "My brother had the map. Maybe they went together."

"That doesn't make any sense. Malik hates Darras," Abbas noted.

Sayyida countered, "My brother could have sneaked up on him and killed him to have the treasure for himself."

Abbas said, "A brief interlude for refreshment will help us think clearly." He passed the bowl of fruit to Pai. "Eat well. You have a long journey ahead of you."

Pai ate some melon and banana. "What long journey?"

"You must immediately return to Qurtuba and report this to the Emir as soon as you arrive."

Pai scoffed, "I doubt he can make sense of this."

Whatever Ibn Firnas thought of the Emir, he didn't let it show. In a stern voice, he repeated his admonition, "You *must* go to Qurtuba and report this to the Emir."

Before Pai packed his drawing kit, he took out Sayyida's bowl and returned it to her. "Thank you for the eggplant. It was delicious."

"Will I see you in Osuna when we bury Darras?" she asked, looking to the Roman road. "Can you see my men bringing the wagon with Darras?"

Osuna! Pai remembered that Wararni was in Osuna and he needed to return him to Zetian. "Yes, I will see you there."

After he packed his drawing kit in his bag, he realized that he hadn't seen Darras's bag with the leather handles and silver buckles. He made a quick survey looking for it. "Just checking to make sure I didn't forget anything," he muttered to cover his search. The bag with the silver buckles was nowhere to be found.

"I'm going now," Pai said.

"Have a safe journey," Abbas replied.

While Sayyida stood in front of the house waiting for the wagon, Pai went out back, strapped his bag to his saddle, and began his quest to find Zetian's fiancé, still curious about the whereabouts of Darras's bag.

Was Darras murdered or did he have an accident escaping the fire? If he was murdered, who did it?

9. ROMANS AND ROADS

Early Tuesday morning, Bhaja rose from dawn prayers to the sound of knocking on the Library door. She was surprised to see not Naomi but Isador standing there, a small satchel in hand.

"I was uncertain what time you wished me to begin."

"It's a little early, but that is good, because we have plenty of work, and will be acquiring more very soon."

She showed Isador where the ink and paper supplies were. He had brought a penner containing his own quills. "These are the best wing feathers molted from our own Abbey geese," he said.

"You use your left hand to write?" Bhaja asked, mostly for confirmation.

"Yes."

"The quills our patron Tarub sends us are stripped of their barbs completely, so you should be able to use them, if you like, and save yours for Abbey work."

Isador smiled and nodded.

"Also, we have a few crow feather quills for extra fine work, and some swan for titles and other large lettering that might be needed."

"Excellent," Isador said, choosing some quills from the tray Bhaja showed him and putting his own back into his satchel.

After waving him to the one tilted and several flat tables that were empty, she left him to choose which he would use while she went and scooped up the small pile of things she'd selected for him to copy.

Naomi arrived—pleasantly early—and greeted them both, and then went to her table.

Bhaja handed Isador the handful of scrolls, "These need to be copied."

"Do you want them on similar stock to the originals? Or all on the good paper?"

Bhaja thought a moment. "I think I will tell you individually. Some items, like the medical reports, should probably go on vellum for longer life and multiple handlings. The rest should go on the good paper, Tarub insists on that.

"However," she went on, "if you could both stop for a moment, I need to inform you of a slight change for the next week or so."

Isador set the scroll he was holding down, and Naomi placed her quill on the ink felt which absorbed spills and drips.

"Darras told me last night," she glanced at Naomi who had fled, and not heard about it, "that he has at least two trunks full of parchments, papyri, and scrolls of writings he has collected. These are at his home in Osuna. So on Thursday morning, I will be leaving for Osuna to pick them up. I imagine I will return right away with the trunks, so I should be gone less than a week."

She smiled at Naomi. "I am going to leave you in charge of the work, and," she turned her gaze to Isador, "I am asking if you can sleep in the Library overnight each night I am gone, since Naomi has other duties at her lodging at night."

At Isador's dubious expression, she hastily added, "If not, do not be concerned, I will make other arrangements."

"Ah, it's just that—I am not much of a guard," Isador said.

"Nor am I," Bhaja laughed. "I've decided that a presence here is a deterrent at least as strong as Tarub's puzzle lock."

"Ah?" Isador turned to study the door.

Naomi said, "Oh, yes. You must show him how it works, if he is to stay."

"It must be set from the outside." Stepping out, Bhaja showed him how to lock and unlock the puzzle mechanism, letting him do it by himself a couple times to be sure he remembered the sequence of movements. Then they moved back inside and she demonstrated sliding the beam that hung in the massive iron brackets, to bar the door from inside.

"If needed, now you know how to open it," Bhaja said, but when I am in town, I will always be sleeping inside and the door will be barred."

Isador nodded his understanding.

"If you need to return to the Abbey before then, Isador, please do so when Naomi is here. I will let Tarub know what is happening, and she may send someone to relieve you, or perhaps a real guard." When she saw dismay on Isador's face, she added, "I expect no trouble, this is just backup protection of the manuscripts in our care."

"I will stay," Isador said, though there was still a slight frown on his face.

Naomi just nodded her acceptance.

"I will leave it to Naomi to choose what gets translated and what we need copies of while I am gone."

"We are going to be busy for a while with this new work," the translator said.

"Yes," Bhaja agreed. "I'm not sure how much there is, but 'trunks full' sounds ominous."

Naomi gave a crooked smile. “We’d best finish up everything that’s here already if we can.”

Bhaja nodded. “Indeed. Is this all acceptable for you, Isador? Obviously I am hoping you are available for these days.”

He nodded, then said, “If I may, I would visit the Abbey for our Holy Day. I would return at day’s end.”

“Of course. Fortunately, Naomi will be here then, if you can be sure to take care of things on Friday evening and Saturday for her own observances.”

“Yes,” Isador said.

“Depending on the actual quantities I return with, it is possible your help will be needed for more than Tuesdays and Wednesdays, Isador.” She raised her eyebrows, asking.

“I am available. Anything extra I can earn will help my brothers. We have been scrimping to buy cows so we can begin to make cheese again. That has been our primary source of income.”

“Even I’ve heard of your cheese,” Naomi said. She glanced at Bhaja. “It’s kosher—a correct food for us to eat.”

Bhaja smiled, then went on to her own day’s work: a note to Tarub telling of her plan and asking for suggestions about transport for the chests from Osuna. Then a note to Pai, to let him know her plans, also. Paying a runner to go all the way to Ronda seemed a ridiculous expense, but it was the only way she knew to tell him.

Finally, she moved on to a ferociously complex legal text in archaic Latin that she hoped to finish translating before Thursday.

Thursday morning, a crowd awaited when she poked her head out the door. Naomi, Isador, Yusuf, and two martial-looking men, along with a cluster of horses, including the loaded wagon Tarub had sent to carry the chests home.

On this leg of their journey, the wagon was filled with things Tarub had traded to Darras in exchange for the books: kegs of beer, bottles of wine, various dainty foods including smoked sardines, clams, and salmon, and she could see big jars of olive oil and a stack of cheeses.

She stood aside as both Naomi and Isador went inside. Her brother dismounted from his elderly black mare.

“These are my friends and fellow guards, Chedar and Xarq.”

Chedar bobbed his head from atop his mount, a white-footed bay.

The other guard, Xarq, who looked very Berber to Bhaja's eyes, smiled down at her from his own big chestnut. Its shapely head suggested Arabian blood. It gave Xarq the look of a professional compared with Yusuf's mount, that was certain.

"I'm informed our wagon driver has no tongue and cannot speak," her brother said. "Your lady Tarub's stablemen said he is just called, "Driver."

Bhaja glanced at the wagon again and studied the driver, an older man who looked a bit...crumpled, as he slumped on the bench of the sturdy wooden wagon.

"He should be able to follow at a walking speed," Xarq said. "Our two days of travel will be long and slow to accommodate the wagon."

"This is what Tarub sent for you to ride," Yusuf said, grinning. He passed to Bhaja the reins of a grey Arabian, with dancing hooves. It was a magnificent-looking beast.

"Goodness," Bhaja said, eyeing the horse. "Good thing I begged father to teach me to ride."

Yusuf laughed. "He was so annoyed that you kept asking, he just gave up and let you learn when I did."

"Oh." She handed the reins back to her brother. "One more important thing, then I'm ready to go."

Bhaja returned inside. She opened the safe, this time without showing either Naomi or Isador how that lock, quite different from the one on the door, worked. She took out Tarub's bag of coins. Adding up expenses in her head, she gave Naomi a stack of the silver coins for her pay in advance. She gave Isador pay for three days, calculated with the standard rate for scribes, plus extra for his food and staying the nights.

"I will have more for you when I return," she said addressing Isador, then she turned to include Naomi. "You know where Tarub's villa is if there is any emergency you feel you are unable to manage."

Naomi nodded, but Isador just stared at her. "Well, you can send a runner to Tarub's, they all know where to go." She set a small stack of copper coins on a shelf. "This is for runners, or for food if you need. Also, if necessary, Naomi knows where my Mother's house is. She can provide you emergency food or help."

Naomi nodded again, and Isador ducked his head.

"Thank you for your patience. Darras sprang this on me rather suddenly, so I've had just a short time to prepare. I hope I've remembered everything."

She then took a goodly number of gold and silver coins for travel expenses and returned the bag to the safe and locked it.

"I will see you within the week!"

"Good journey," Naomi cried as Bhaja went out the door. "And a safe one!"

Back outside, she asked, "Do any of you know the way?" She managed to mount the grey without embarrassing herself. Or Yusuf.

"Yes," the guard introduced as Chedar, said. "I usually run trade caravans and have been to Osuna and Ronda and back a number of times.

"Good," Bhaja said. "Please lead us, then."

Chedar clicked to his mount and led the way out of the courtyard's eastern gate.

The other guard, Xarq, took up the rear, behind the wagon, leaving Bhaja to ride beside her brother.

It was good to be on their way.

"Mother sent bread in case you've not eaten this morning, and she also sent a big meal for mid-day," Yusuf told her.

Bhaja chuckled, meeting his gaze. Mama always made sure there was food. Yusuf smiled back, and then paid attention to his mount as they entered the street to Bridge Gate. People crowded the street, going into and out of Qurtuba. Vendors lined both sides of the road, narrowing it further. Cries offering food made Bhaja's stomach growl.

"I'll take some of that bread, if it's in easy reach," she said.

Yusuf rummaged one-handed in his saddle gear, coming up with a cotton-wrapped package. Bhaja recognized the embroidery on a scrap of an old robe she had worn when she attended the Mosque school, years ago. Mother's bread inside was still warm and fragrant.

They crossed the mighty Wadi al-Kabir on the Gate Bridge, then turned south. Eventually they left the river and their city behind, heading south and a little west to Écija on the old Roman Road.

Eyes wide, Bhaja took in the countryside, and noted each farm and its crops, each ranch and its animals. The sun shone through high hazy clouds, quite hot, but an intermittent breeze helped cool them.

They approached Écija before sunset, having stopped to pray once on the way, while the others watered the horses. Then they ate their midday meal together in the shade of a big oak.

It was difficult to keep proper time without the muezzins' calls to prayer. It had never occurred to her before how much help that was for keeping track of the time left in the day. Water or sand clocks—and certainly sundials—were impractical for travelers. They just had to guess by the sun's position.

Écija, which had been established as a traveler's stop on the Roman Road, still maintained a lodging house that had been established at that long-ago time. This particular building looked quite new, but the owner assured them "It was built atop the ruins of the original." Bhaja paid for a small room for herself, and a shared room for the men.

The men went out and took care of their horses, while Bhaja walked the street, hoping to find a food vendor. She did not, but she did find a housewife picking vegetables. The woman wasn't willing to take coins in payment, so Bhaja gave her her headscarf. In exchange, she received a few carrots, parsnips, and a small not-quite-ripe squash.

The lodging house offered a pot and a fire, and Bhaja prepared the vegetables, with Chedar's help, once he'd finished with his horse. While the food cooked, Bhaja went out for a walk, and to check on their horses and the wagon. The lodging house offered bags of oats for a small fee, and one of the men had gotten enough of those to feed all the animals, even the big draft horse that had pulled the wagon. While she was admiring the draft horse's huge hooves, she heard someone ride into the partly-paved stable yard with a clatter of hooves.

She turned and saw a faintly familiar face. The man did not see her. He dismounted, tossing the reins over a post. Bhaja watched for another minute, verifying her guess.

Indeed it was Malik al Jamal, the man who had disrupted the Library and demeaned Darras.

What was he doing here? He had not noticed her, and she kept it that way, eager to avoid any further confrontations with the belligerent man. She moved behind the big draft horse, then walked away, putting distance between them.

She walked on past the stable into the gardens behind the lodging house. She turned the corner and saw the sunset-lit sky. The sun glowed orange and scattered deepening gold beams of light as it sank behind the low hills in the west. The now-puffy clouds turned pink and orange.

She returned to the lodging house through the back door, carefully checking for Malik's presence as she made her way to the fireplace. There was no sign of the man.

Chedar declared the soup finished and served it up into wooden bowls the various men, including Driver, had brought; apparently that was something Bhaja should have had for herself, too. But Yusuf had thought of that and brought two. She smiled at him gratefully. They shared out the remains of the breakfast bread, and Yusuf pulled another round loaf from his saddlebags.

The men offered to clean up, so Bhaja returned to her room, made her ablutions and tardy sunset prayers, and prepared for sleep. They'd be up and on the road early tomorrow.

She missed Pai, but it had been a good day.

Bhaja was saddle sore by the time they reached Osuna. Her bottom felt numb, and her thighs had been rubbed raw. She would most likely ride the cart home, along with the books. She patted the grey and dismounted, wondering if the horses ever got sore from people riding them.

She approached a group of old women who sat alongside a fence on the outskirts of Osuna in the shade of an ancient oak, and asked them for the way to Darras's house.

Rehearsing the complicated directions, Bhaja rather unwillingly climbed back up on her horse and led the way. None of Osuna's streets ran straight, which seemed odd, since the small town was built on the flattest plain she had ever seen, and there was no particular reason for twisty, turny roads.

After one wrong turn and retreat, they found Darras's house. It was indeed better described as a villa, Bhaja decided. The front wing was wide enough to hold three rooms, which would be matched on the back wall. The long parallel lines of the side walls would hold another three or four rooms each. The place was huge.

An old man creaked his way out of Darras's stable to take their horses.

"Is Darras here?" she asked the ancient stableman.

He gave her an intense look, which she could not interpret. Then she heard Pai's voice calling her, and also Abbas ibn Firnas's inimitable happy laugh. She turned to meet Pai's gaze, which was sad, surprising her. She saw a bandage on his arm.

"What happened to you!?"

He gathered her into his arms for a rather too-public embrace, then stepped back and said, "I am sorry to say, your friend Darras is dead."

"Dead?" she said stupidly. "How can he be dead? I just saw him in Qurtuba." As if that should somehow confirm his aliveness. Bhaja's heart stumbled as the words penetrated.

"I'm fine," Pai said, "though the cut is sore. I'll explain soon. Would you like tea? The housekeeper and cook have been plying us constantly with tea and various foods; I'm sure they'd be delighted to feed you."

"I have lots of people with me," she said. "And lots of food and drink as well, come to think of it, though not exactly a meal."

"Come, sit down," Pai said, eyeing her dusty hair and clothes.

"I would wash," Bhaja protested.

Pai pointed to a table with pitcher, bowl, and towel. Bhaja went and freshened up.

"Who have you brought with you?" Abbas ibn Firnas asked.

"Well, Tarub had a wagonload of goods to bring to Darras, and Darras has a couple of trunks of books and things for me to take back to Qurtuba for the Library. So I brought my brother and two guards along with a driver for the cart."

"Is this a wagon or a cart?" Abbas asked, a twinkle in his eye. "There is a difference, you know."

She managed a faint smile for him as she sat down. "Wagon."

"What is in it?"

"Wine, beer, cheese, other foods. The men are unloading it now." She thought a moment. "Though, I suppose some or all of it should be returned to Tarub."

"Let us get the men inside," Pai suggested. "We can eat and sort out what needs to be done. Soon Sayyida will arrive with Darras's body."

"Tomorrow morning we will examine it to see if there are clues to what happened to Darras," Ibn Firnas said.

Bhaja glanced around the room. A salon, she decided, since it had several divans and pillows scattered around the floor. Pai returned from outside followed by Yusuf and the others.

"If the man is dead, what are we going to do with all that wine?" Chedar said. "Can we drink it?" He glanced around the room, uncertain. "That is, can we who aren't Muslim drink it?" His white-blonde hair seemed to brighten the dim room.

A stout fair-skinned woman wearing a mostly-white apron tied around her ample waist entered the room with a quick bow. "Please come to the dining area for the evening meal. It is ready now."

Everyone washed up except Pai and Bhaja, who went directly to the room following the woman, having already cleansed themselves.

"How will you eat one-handed?" she asked him. "And how in Allah's name did you manage to hurt it in the first place?" She imagined glider crashes—she knew he would have at least tried to fly on Abbas al Firnas's invention—or had it been some other mishap?

As they ate, Pai told his story. Bhaja exclaimed at the fight with Malik, and nodded at Abbas's knowledge of modern healing.

"That is so strange," Bhaja said. She told them about Malik's confrontation with Darras at the Library earlier that week.

Abbas grunted at this. "These two have known each other before."

"And...what's happening with the wagonload of wine?" Chedar wondered again.

Pretty much everyone at the table scowled at him.

"I think it should go to the Christian church here; it will pay for the burial and services they will hold for Darras," Bhaja said.

No one argued with that dispensation, but Bhaja did notice later that one of the cheeses from the wagon was now on a side table along with knives to cut it, and various fruits to eat with it. Darras's staff could use some of the wagon's contents, now he was no longer here to keep them paid for their work.

Bhaja realized she missed Darras already. The big, bluff man had been a friend to her, especially when she had spent her first few days in the Mosque Library feeling lost and overwhelmed, and he had come in to deliver a document the imam had requested.

He had approved of Bhaja's work so eloquently, she had immediately felt much better about it and herself.

"Darras introduced Naomi to me," she told Pai and the others at the table, not remembering if she had mentioned that fact already or not. "Naomi and her son Raviv arrived on my doorstep at his recommendation."

"You are collecting lost souls as well as lost manuscripts," Pai said softly, giving her a quirked grin. He drank the tart lemon juice, smiling at her with his eyes over the rim of his glass.

"Ah, are you lost, then?" she teased, and then was swept by a chill as she felt an overwhelming sense of remembrance—*already seen, already experienced.*

The setting had been different: *She was atop tightly fitted stone walls surrounding a city on a hill. Pai stood next to her, looking far down to a swirling sea, a lost look in his eyes and a quirked smile on his lips.*

"Or is it I who am lost?" she murmured, coming back to the present. She got up from the rug.

They chose their separate rooms, and exhausted, slept until morning.

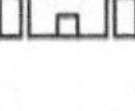

The first thing that happened the next day was the arrival of a woman who named herself Qusayma, saying she was Darras's cousin.

"Darras never said anything about a cousin," Bhaja exclaimed.

Wise old Abbas ibn Firnas agreed. "Darras always claimed he was the last of his family."

The young woman nodded her head. "I also thought *I* was the last; my mother never told me of a cousin named Darras. When the priest here contacted me, I was astonished."

"Priest?"

"He has family lineages kept in the Osuna town Bible since...I don't know how long. A long time. Since Roman days when our family was awarded several estates here." She looked down at the table, where her fingers fiddled with her glass of tea. "Then the holdings at Ronda were taken away, and the priest contacted me about that. By then, I had married and moved to my husband's home near Málaga, you see. I don't know why Father Yusuf didn't tell me about this place, and who lived in it."

"Father Yusuf?" Yusuf asked.

"The priest," Pai explained. "Called Father among Christians. This priest also happens to be named Yusuf." Yusuf the brother grunted and glanced at Bhaja.

"I think we have delayed enough," Abbas ibn Firnas said. "We should learn what we can learn from the body, and then release it to the Father for burial."

As if she'd been listening—and she probably had, Bhaja decided—the apron-wearing housekeeper stepped into the room. "The master's body is in the chilling cellar," she said, pointing outside.

Bhaja, Pai, Abbas, and Qusayma stepped outside through the kitchen door. Trailing behind them came Yusuf, Chedar, and Xarq. No one had invited them, but no one told them to stay away, either.

The cellar contained sacks of root vegetables, nuts, olive oil, and surprisingly, many bottles of wine. Everything had been pushed back against the walls. In the center of the room, upon a low table, was Darras's body, wrapped in a sheet of linen.

"It may have been an accident," Pai said. "Darras was in Malik's fields searching for the treasure. There was a thunderstorm, and lightning struck the fields, setting them ablaze. Darras died in the fire."

"How horrible." Bhaja glanced up, noting Abbas's grim face.

Pai loosened the wrappings, Yusuf stepping forward to assist him. They let the sheet drape down the sides of the table, beneath the now-bared body.

Holding an oil lamp up for extra light, Bhaja examined the body. She noticed Abbas did the same on the other side of the table.

"Pai," she said. "I am sorry to contradict you, but this was not an accident."

He looked up at her, eyes startled.

"What makes you say so?" Abbas ibn Firnas asked, peering at Darras's body, then staring at Bhaja. That direct a stare was rather unnerving, she discovered.

"Look at the blood and skin where the cut is. See, it looks burnt."

"Yes," Pai said. "There was a fire, I told you that."

"Exactly. Darras was dead before the fire; he did not run from the fire and trip and hit his head on a rock; the head wound came first."

Pai chewed his lip. "I don't remember any stones where he was lying, that is true."

"Someone hit him, and he fell, and then he was burned. The cut was already there when the fire burnt the skin and burned away a bit of his hair on that side. The wound was exposed to fire, so the wound had to come first."

Abbas nodded his agreement. "I noted something else."

Bhaja nodded, then continued, "Well, the second clue I could not be certain about until Pai said there were no stones nearby. The wound is on top of the head. If Darras ran and fell and hit his head, the damage would be on the *side* of his head somewhere. He couldn't trip and land on the top of his head, it's just impossible. Falling, he *might* have crashed against a boulder, scraping the top of his head, but—"

"No boulders," Pai finished.

"Third, you made no mention of a puddle of blood around the body when you found him, nor was there one beneath where he had lain after the body was removed."

Pai's eyes went distant as he remembered the scene. "No. There was no puddle of blood where Darras's body lay. Just some blood on his head."

"It could have been burned up!" Chedar suggested.

"But even a burned puddle of blood would be noticeable," Ibn Firnas countered.

Bhaja nodded. "This suggests to me, again, that Darras was dead before he even fell to the ground. Some blood covered his head when he was hit, then he died, and then he fell."

"Bleeding stops when you are dead," Xarq said. "All warriors know this. If a comrade is not bleeding from his wounds, then it is too late to save him."

Abbas ibn Firnas nodded. "Healers know this as well." He combed his fingers down his long, tangled beard.

"So," Pai said, "Darras of Osuna was murdered."

At this pronouncement, Qusayma burst into tears again.

10. SWIRL OF SUSPICIONS

Pai went off on his own to find Wararni. He began his search at Osuna's mosque, a modest structure, even compared to the small one in Ronda. Zetian's missing fiancé had to be somewhere in town, and the mosque was a good place to start. The minaret took advantage of an old Roman foundation, building atop the ancient structure to achieve visibility from anywhere in the city. Once he'd identified the men's entrance, where he'd most likely find Wararni if he were here, he stepped through the archway and removed his sandals.

He'd never been in this mosque, and no one knew him in Osuna, so he was extra careful. He sat by the fountain, and just to be safe, he washed his face, hands, and feet. It wasn't a prayer time and the courtyard appeared empty.

There was only one other person, a thin, young man; Pai guessed he was still in his 20s. The man wore a white robe with a matching cap. He looked pious with his long black beard and bushy eyebrows. His robe was fine cotton and his cap woven with an intricate pattern. *An important person.*

Pai walked up to him and bowed his head. "As-Salaam-Alaikum."

The man responded, "Wa-Alaikum-Assalaam."

"I am Pai of Qurtuba."

The man responded, "I am the imam. I can see you aren't Muslim."

Pai couldn't figure out how the imam knew, but he relaxed with that in the open. "I am looking for someone from Qurtuba. A man called Wararni."

Now the imam gave Pai a broad smile. "Oh yes, I know him. His sister married a man from our village. She is a dutiful wife and has blessed us with five children, three still live."

Pai never knew what to say when children died. It was just too sad. "Insha'Allah," he whispered.

"We are proud of Wararni. He is a member of the Emir's guard. We hoped he'd find a wife in Qurtuba, but not yet."

Pai didn't mention Zetian. When the first thing the imam had said was, *I can see you aren't a Muslim*, he couldn't imagine that the imam would rejoice about Wararni's engagement to a Buddhist from al-Qin. He decided to tell the imam as little as he could get away with. "Have you seen him?" he asked.

"Oh yes. Allahu Akbar. He came to Friday prayers yesterday. We were glad to see him. I imagine he is staying with his sister's family."

Pai thanked his God for such a helpful imam. "Does she live nearby?"

The imam pointed towards the qibla wall. "By the hill."

Pai thanked the holy man and bowed. Using his good arm, he awkwardly put on his sandals. Finding Wararni had turned out to be easier than he expected.

Osuna was crisscrossed with straight Roman roads built to survive for all time. However, the people of Osuna had little respect for those engineers of the past. Two homes might be built adjacent to the roadworks but the next one would usurp the ancient stonework for its foundation, completely blocking the roadway. Thus, the village didn't have a single straight path. Each house chose its own space, like so many dice thrown by a giant.

He would have gotten lost were it not for the hill, the only interruption in the broad plain that contained Osuna. When the flat land ended, he looked for someone to direct him to Wararni's sister. He couldn't believe his good luck. The first person he saw was Wararni himself.

"Wararni! I've been looking for you. Zetian misses you." He almost mentioned that she was pregnant but stopped himself. "I'm here to bring you back to Qurtuba." He reached out his good arm and took Wararni's hand. We need to return."

Wararni raised his sword and knocked Pai away with the flat side of the blade against Pai's injured arm. "That was your warning. Stay away from me. I'm not going back."

Pai held his arm, throbbing with pain, and bleeding again, as Wararni ran past the houses and into the wild brush that covered the hillside. Pai first thought was, *He's afraid of me.*

He briefly considered chasing Wararni but had to accept that he was no match for one of the Emir's guards armed with a sword. On his way back through the Osuna maze, he devised a plan to capture the tall Berber. Zetian would have her fiancé returned.

As soon as he entered Darras's house, Bhaja greeted him, "Peace be with you."

Before he could reply, she noticed his arm. "Pai! Your arm is bleeding." She ran into the villa courtyard.

Pai waited with her brother and the two guards. Yusuf gave him a sympathetic look. "Don't worry. She'll be right back."

Chedar poked at Pai's arm. "Does this hurt?"

Pai flinched. "No, not much."

Xarq slapped Chedar's hand. "Don't torment him."

"What happened this time?" Yusuf inquired.

Pai had begun to tell them about Wararni when Bhaja returned with Abbas carrying a jar of salve and strips of bandages. Abbas examined his wound, "This is healing well, but you must stop reinjuring it."

While Ibn Firnas treated his arm, Pai continued explaining about Wararni and Zetian, how he'd located the missing suitor, and how he intended to return him to Qurtuba.

Bhaja's brother nodded with deliberation. "I doubt you'll capture one of the Emir's guards by yourself."

Yusuf had unwittingly given Pai an opening to implement his plan. "That is something to consider," Pai said feeling confident.

"Do you have a plan?" Bhaja asked. She added, "You usually do."

"Yes." I'd like to take these three fighters away from the noisy house, so we can strategize."

Chedar protested. "I saw someone preparing food. Can we go later, after we eat?"

"No, we need to talk now. I'll buy you some food." *Later we're going to capture Wararni.*

Chedar immediately agreed. "I saw a food vendor with spicy chicken! Can we go there?"

"Let's go. Abbas says a good meal clears the mind." They followed Chedar's nose to find the food vendor.

Pai held up four fingers and a silver coin. The lady reached over her head to raise her ceramic brazier and placed it on the ground. This movement stirred up the hot coals, filling the air with orange embers and the mouth-watering smell of spicy chicken. She picked up four wooden skewers and handed them to Pai and his three companions.

The young men went silent as they enjoyed their juicy chicken alternated with peppers and onions.

Pai began, "Let me tell you how we're going to capture Wararni."

Yusuf finished eating first. He dropped his skewer to the ground where it was stolen by a stray dog. "You should never have gone after Wararni on your own."

Pai didn't welcome a lecture from Bhaja's younger brother, but he needed help and didn't want to argue. "Of course, you're right. With the three of you, we'll easily succeed."

Yusuf looked at his two companions and they both nodded. "I can certainly help you because you are my sister's friend, but Chedar and Xarq have responsibilities. Fighting is how they contribute to their families."

Pai understood. "When we return Wararni to Qurtuba, I will give each of you a silver coin."

That did the trick. Everyone was excited to capture the Emir's wandering guard.

Xarq, the oldest, began, "Approaching him during the day was a mistake. Nighttime is the best for capture."

Blonde Chedar added, "We should surround his house and wait until he comes out for a middle-of-the-night piss."

"We'll jump him while his hands are occupied," Yusuf added.

They all laughed at this.

Xarq thought for a moment. "Tonight is perfect. Waxing crescent moon. Dark enough to hide us, but enough light to see him."

By then they'd all finished their chicken. "We'll meet at Darras's house after nighttime prayers. From there we can go to Wararni's sister's house," Pai directed his soldiers.

Pai felt sure he'd have Wararni in tow before midnight. With that settled, he felt invigorated. He had a straight back and a strong step, as he went to find Bhaja.

The gods smiled on him. He sighted her, alone, in the shade of an ancient olive tree, the symbol of peace and friendship. Many olive trees appeared in his dreams, scattered around the grassy hills of that other time and place. "Bhaja," he called. She waved for him to join her and smiled. The cloud blocking the sun blew away, leaving the afternoon bright and clear.

He held his bandaged arm and hurried to meet her. "Bhaja, I'm so glad to see you. Can we sit a while?"

She gave him another smile and adjusted her headscarf.

Pai felt the thumping in his chest, aware that the time had arrived. He would tell Bhaja of his visions and his love.

Just then the muezzin chanted the mid-afternoon call. Yusuf joined them. "Prayer time, Sister." The rest of the group followed. What had started as a private opportunity abruptly had become a crowd.

Abbas, Bhaja, her brother, and Xarq retreated to a nearby fountain for their ablutions, leaving Pai with Qusayma and the oafish Chedar to wait under the olive tree. The three sat in the shade, where Pai still hoped to seize a moment alone with Bhaja...eventually.

Qusayma sat as close to Pai as modesty allowed. "I must remember to thank everyone for helping with my cousin's funeral," Qusayma said in a soft, but clear, voice.

Pai looked at her dry eyes and thought, *The family doesn't have a moment to mourn until after the body is buried and the crowd departs.* Pai didn't know Darras well but Bhaja thought highly of him. "It is a blessing to do what we can."

Qusayma then asked, "You said he was murdered. What should we do?"

Chedar sat up and replied, "As Abbas ibn Firnas has said over and over, the Emir must be notified without delay."

Qusayma turned to the young fighter as if she'd forgotten his presence. Pai was also surprised. Chedar was ill-mannered to listen to their private talk. Pai promised himself to make sure the man was nowhere nearby when he spoke with Bhaja.

Since Darras had been murdered in Ronda, Pai doubted the Emir in Qurtuba would do much about it. Certainly, if Emir Muhammad learned about the murder in one week or two, it made little difference. Pai replied to the rude Chedar. "We will identify the murderer before reporting to Qurtuba. It is better that way."

Chedar grumbled. "No. The Emir will find the culprit."

Pai didn't want to draw the disrespectful young man into further discussions. He grimaced but said nothing.

After prayers, everyone collected around the ancient tree, and the discussion turned to murder. Abbas spoke first, with his idea about Darras's fate. "I observed Darras of Osuna. He talked too much."

Pai thought back to when the chatty man entered his shop, "You're right! He had just met me and already he told me about the treasure. He spoke loudly enough for Zetian to hear. Surely, anyone walking down the path outside would also have learned his secret."

Abbas went on, "I suspect some highwaymen overheard him bragging and followed him here. They forced him to reveal the treasure, killed him, and are now long gone."

Xarq jumped up and waved his sword in the air. "If I'd been here sooner, I could have tracked them. I'm sure they went to Málaga. They're probably on a ship to Rome or Byzantium by now."

Chedar stood next to him and crossed his sword with Xarq's. "We should leave..." he sheathed his sword, "...immediately. Hey! Maybe they haven't found a ship and are stuck in Málaga."

Yusuf addressed his two brothers-in-arms. "Behave yourselves." They sheepishly sat beside Yusuf, who dramatically sniffed the air. "Have you gotten into the wine that Tarub sent?"

Xarq gave an unconvincing response. "Wine is haram, forbidden." He gave a crooked smile when he added, "I may have had a taste of Chedar's beer."

Yusuf looked to the others and shrugged his shoulders. He put his arms around his two inebriated friends and drew them close. In a loud whisper, he said, “We’re not going anywhere. We promised to help Pai on a secret mission tonight. Remember?”

Observing their drunk behavior, Pai regretted enlisting their help.

After the evening meal, Qusayma’s guests sat around the red coals. She had served a grand menu: whole roast goat, soft wheat bread, spicy barley soup, and a special dessert of pistachios and honey. While the servants removed the large serving bowls that they’d all shared, everyone gathered around the fountain to wash their fingers. The group from Ronda, Osuna, and Qurtuba amazed Pai. People so rarely traveled. Most never left the city of their birth.

Last night he had dreamed of a long journey from the coastal palace, grander than any in al-Andalus, to a mountaintop temple. Just like a line on his map, the route passed through wildlands. As in all his dreams, the same lady accompanied him. Together they met so many others. Soon he’d share his visions with Bhaja.

Pai suspected the murderer was someone they knew. Observing this group of visitors serendipitously collected in the small town of Osuna, brought together for different reasons, he became aware of an important clue. “I am wondering why Malik al Jamal and Darras of Osuna both arrived in Qurtuba at the same time from their distant travels.”

Ibn Firnas stroked his white beard. “I doubt it means anything, but you are right. Al-Andalus is not a crossroads. Qurtuba sees few travelers, and rarely two simultaneously.”

“This is more than just a crazy idea,” Bhaja began. “When Malik saw Darras in the Library, he got angry and accused Darras of fraud. He even threatened to use his influence with the Emir against Darras.”

Qusayma asked, “Had Darras done something to offend Malik?”

“Nothing that I could see. He was just selling some scrolls he’d collected.”

Abbas pondered, “Maybe there is something in those scrolls—”

Bhaja brightened, “Malik did ask about ownership records for his land in Ronda, but I told him I didn’t have anything like that. I sent him to the Mosque and the governor's house. Perhaps I should have sent him to his friend, the Emir.”

Qusayma mused, “When I was young, we all went to Osuna for Easter. While the children picked flowers, the parents talked about the lands they lost when the Berbers sailed over the Bahr al-Rum from Ifriqa. Maybe Malik wanted the scrolls, the ones you are here to collect for your library."

"Scrolls! That is a good clue," Pai added. "When Malik discovered I had a map to the treasure, he attacked me. We fought." Pai pointed to his injured forearm. "He stole the map during the fight."

Bhaja cautioned, "We must find Malik before we go to the Emir. Since he's on Emir Muhammad's council, he will never be considered as a suspect, or as a murderer, unless we present strong evidence."

Xarq liked this theory too. "You're right. They are probably long-lost brothers and argued to disguise this truth. They came to steal the treasure together and Malik killed Darras to get it all!"

Chedar shouted. "He's on his way to Málaga. Let's go after him."

Yusuf shook his head and rested it in his hands.

Bhaja patted her brother on the shoulder. "Your friends need to stop drinking." Then she turned to Abbas. "If you want to consider strange circumstances, listen to this."

Everyone went quiet and turned to Bhaja.

"Qurtuba had three, not two, travelers at the same time. In addition to the two men, a Jewish translator named Naomi recently showed up."

Qusayma gasped, "A Muslim man, and then my cousin a Christian man—" She paused to cross herself. "May God save my cousin's soul." She sighed, "And now a Jewish lady." She crossed herself again.

Chedar turned to Xarq, "Could the Jewish woman have killed Darras?"

Bhaja looked sternly at Yusuf's friends. "Do you think she murdered Darras and is hiding the treasure in Tarub's Library?"

The fighters gave her a quizzical look.

"That's right. She works for me in the Library. Do you still think she is the murderer?"

Yusuf's friends flushed with embarrassment and stayed quiet.

Bhaja answered her own question. "My Naomi isn't a good suspect for murder. I saw her in Qurtuba every day, so she couldn't have been in Ronda, three days away."

"Well then, did you and Naomi kill Darras together?" asked Chedar.

Xarq cuffed Chedar. "Do not talk about Yusuf's sister like that!"

Bhaja came to poor Chedar's defense. "Not me, obviously, but I feel Naomi is involved in some way. When Malik started yelling at

Darras, she got upset and left the Library. I wonder what her part is in all of this?"

Abbas asked, "How did you come to hire her?"

Bhaja responded in a soft voice like she was talking to herself. "Darras recommended her. We must find out more about her, but unfortunately, our best source is dead."

Xarq and Chedar had no further comments and the conversation ended, and the group broke up. Pai knew this wasn't the end of the mystery.

Pai met the three men after nighttime prayers. The group made a few wrong turns on the way to Wararni's sister's home. After the first time they got lost, Pai worried that he'd assembled the wrong people. But by the time they reached their goal, Pai felt confident. Gone were the jokesters he had seen earlier. Yusuf's companions were now proficient soldiers as if the darkness had transformed them.

Chedar silently approached the door left open to allow the cool night air into the crowded building. Just as quietly he returned and held up six fingers.

Pai whispered, "Perfect. Husband, wife, three children, and Wararni. Now we wait."

Xarq spoke up. "I'll take the first watch. You others can rest your eyes."

Chedar agreed. "That way we'll all be alert when the time comes."

Pai was on watch when Wararni appeared and headed for the hill, walking with stiff legs. Pai poked his three sleeping companions with his toe while keeping watch on Wararni's direction. Like experienced troopers, they came to the ready soundlessly.

Xarq naturally took charge. With hand signals, he directed Yusuf to the left and Chedar to the right in a half-circle formation. They were hidden in the dark shadows of the moon, as they followed Wararni.

Wararni wandered up the hill, first stopping at a bush, then finding it unsatisfactory and moving off in a different direction. At every turn, the half-circle adjusted to contain their prey. Finally, Wararni found a tree to his liking where he scrunched his tunic around his chest and squatted down.

Xarq and Chedar exchanged hand signals. Chedar wanted to attack while their target was vulnerable, but Xarq overruled him. Chedar moved behind Wararni and Xarq moved to the right. Pai's confidence increased. The half-circle was now behind Wararni with Chedar in the center.

Wararni grunted and sighed and finally stood up. He took two steps back the way he came and Xarq raised his fist in the air. Two more steps and Xarq lowered his fist. Chedar sprinted forward and crashed into the unsuspecting Wararni who fell to the ground. Chedar placed one foot on his prize to hold him and shouted, “Don’t move!”

Wararni ignored the command, grabbing Chedar’s leg and twisting. As Chedar tumbled, Wararni grabbed the knife Chedar had strapped to his ankle. He raised his arm to stab Chedar, but Chedar blocked the attack. Chedar grabbed the arm that held the knife and the two men rolled down the hill.

“Stop!” Xarq shouted as he moved out of the shadows. Unfortunately, the noise startled Chedar more than Wararni. In that instant, Wararni had one arm around Chedar’s throat and the other held the knife against his belly. “One step closer and I slice open your friend’s guts.”

Xarq moved closer. “There’s three of us. You don’t have a chance.”

The Emir’s guard didn’t look concerned. “Maybe, but I will take one or two of you if you approach any closer.”

Pai felt the threat was real, but he had confidence in Xarq. Pai noted how Xarq had cleverly said three, not four. *He might have not counted Pai because he had an injured arm, or, more likely, he had not counted Yusuf because he hadn’t been seen.*

Xarq yelled at Wararni, moving so close that he could have bitten the Berber’s nose. “This is your last warning!”

While Wararni considered the angry Xarq, the hidden Yusuf ran up behind Wararni and stabbed him in the buttocks. Wararni screamed and by the time he stopped, the three fighters had him under control. Chedar pulled a leather strap from his belt. He bound their captive’s hands.

Pai wanted to dance and cheer at his plan’s victory. He gave each man the silver coin he’d promised them for getting Wararni to Qurtuba. “Good work.”

“What should we do with him?” Yusuf asked.

“Can we just drown him in the river?” Chedar suggested.

“No! He must be kept alive. He is engaged to Wu Zetian. Take him back to Qurtuba and hide him in a stable. I will come for him when I return.”

“We can’t leave now,” Yusuf protested. “We need to escort my sister on her trip home.”

Pai had forgotten about Bhaja in the excitement. “Yes. Yes. You can take him and protect your sister at the same time.”

“No problem!” Chedar yanked on their captive’s bound hands. “You won’t make trouble, right?”

“I can’t return to Qurtuba,” Wararni shouted with a mixture of anger and fear.

Chedar sneered. “Oh, shut up. No one is asking you.”

Pai wondered if he was missing something about Zetian’s reluctant fiancé as the man was led away with tears running down his cheeks having been suddenly transformed from a skilled fighter to a frightened child. He questioned whether his desire for Zetian and Wararni to marry had blinded him to something important. Regardless, they’d all soon return to Qurtuba.

11. PRESENCE AND PRESENTS

Bhaja had not attended a Christian funeral before. She wanted to honor Darras, but was not familiar with the formalities.

She discovered she had to mostly sit and listen, and then stand and listen. Qusayma delivered a short...homily? Not a prayer, for she was familiar enough with those from her own observances to recognize the one said in Latin by the priest, after Qusayma spoke. Qusayma's words were a sort of remembrance of the family, more than Darras specifically, and about general philosophy, such as the meaning of honor and respect.

Then the body and all the people moved out of the church and into the graveyard behind the small but ornate building.

Graveside, another prayer was said, the body was laid in the ground by several strong men, and then Qusayma let go a handful of dirt over the linen-wrapped body, murmuring what Bhaja assumed was, but could not hear, another short prayer. A final moment of silence, then people began drifting away, some talking, some not.

They returned to Darras's villa where Qusayma had prepared a large cold meal, spread across the dining table, which had been pushed against one wall. People took food and stood eating it and talking.

Once they had spent what seemed to be an appropriate amount of time, all those from Qurtuba left the room to pack up their belongings, ready to return home.

Bhaja and Pai, with some little help from Abbas, who was busier talking than helping, carefully went through the trunks filled with things for the Library. They repacked everything and separated the delicate papyri from the rest. Those were placed inside a lightweight wooden crate provided by Darras's housekeeper, to keep them from being broken by heavier parchments and scrolls. The boxes Darras had called trunks turned out to be large leather containers slung from wooden frames, each with a lid that fitted over the frame to cover it. These were not small. Each held a double row of scrolls with room for parchments to be stacked or set on edge, besides.

"There must be five hundred scrolls here!" Abbas interrupted his diatribe about various weaponry and how the guards used them, to notice.

"Three hundred and eighty scrolls, one hundred and ninety parchments of various sizes. I did not think to count the papyri, though," Pai announced.

"Only about thirty," Bhaja said. "I did not count any of Darras's personal papers in that. I need another box or a big bag to bring those along."

"Doesn't Qusayma want them?" Pai wondered.

"It seems she can barely read. But no, she doesn't want them. She thought some might be appropriate to bring to the Emir for the judge, such as this letter from the Pope, which Darras had with him when he died. The...Father—that sounds so strange! Anyway...the priest who prepared the body gave it to me." She added it back to the sprawled stack of Darras's personal letters and other papers. Then she held up a small sack for the others to see. "And his rings."

"Hmm," Pai said. He pointed to a canvas drawstring bag that hung beside some of Darras's garments in a niche in the wall. "What about this?"

"That is plenty big enough," Bhaja said. "Thank you." She glanced through the messy stack on the bed cushion. She began rolling scrolls and stacking parchments—though there were few of those—and packing them into the bag., including the letter from the Pope and the bag of jewelry.

From over her shoulder, she heard her brother say, "Do you think we will leave tonight?"

She turned to him. "I was thinking to spend a last night here, then leave early tomorrow."

Yusuf nodded, frowning. "Chedar is at the wine again. The old stableman and he have been having a fine old time."

"I thought we sent all that stuff to the church," Pai said.

Yusuf nodded again. "All but three or four jugs, which those two seem intent on emptying as soon as possible." He met Bhaja's gaze. "I apologize for bringing Chedar; I had no idea of his fondness for inebriation. You can pay him less, if you like. I don't think he can complain, and it would be more fair for Xarq, who has done his job carefully."

"It will be fine, Yusuf. Just warn him to be sober when we leave tomorrow, or he will have to stay here. I won't have him along reeking of alcohol."

He grunted, looking disgusted. "One can see why the Prophet recommends avoiding the stuff."

"Indeed," Bhaja said.

After a light breakfast of bread and cheese, the trunks and people's various personal items were loaded onto the wagon. Driver, who had been pretty much invisible during their stay, reappeared and hitched up the big draft horse.

When Sayyida's wagon assembled behind Driver, Bhaja asked, "Are you coming to Qurtuba with us?"

Sayyida smiled, "Yes...if you would permit me."

Bhaja enjoyed the woman's company and a larger caravan would discourage trouble along the way. "Certainly. What brings you to Qurtuba?"

"My brother. He has invited me to stay in his villa after all."

Bhaja looked into Sayyida's wagon, packed with boxes and bags. "Do you intend to stay long?"

"Oh yes. I've always wanted to move to the city. This is my chance."

They mounted up, Pai on a borrowed horse from Darras's stable, Bhaja feeling sufficiently recovered again on the pretty grey Arabian. Chedar, sober and morose, led the way out of Osuna to the road.

Pai had elicited a promise from Wararni not to run, so he was allowed to ride in the wagon without being tied up.

They were halfway to Écija, Bhaja estimated, by the time they stopped for midday prayers and food. Abbas Ibn Firnas, who had also been riding the wagon, made some comment about Darras's body.

Bhaja turned to him with a questioning look.

"No one spoke of the evidence of disease," Abbas said again. "Dried blood, diarrhea—either traveler's malaise, which seems unlikely for a man who traveled so much and knew how to avoid it, or else the man was fatally ill of the tumor disease with not much longer to live.

"Oh," Bhaja said, thinking back. "Maybe that's why he was so eager to get things settled," she waved a hand at the wagon and its load, "and get these to the Library. He did want me to come to Osuna right away."

The old man nodded. "For all our science, we have never found a way to deal with tumors. In Egypt, they tried cauterizing them, in Greece there was a sometimes-effective treatment involving cutting them out. But—"

"Perhaps we can discuss something a little less grisly while we eat," Bhaja suggested. Only Yusuf seemed disappointed; he'd always been fascinated by the body, blood, and other excretions.

"Well," Abbas said, swallowing his bite of pear, "the man was an expert at finding hoards of writings. This haul has even a few books, I understand?" He raised his eyebrows at Bhaja, after a quick glance at his audience.

"Books?" Pai said around a mouthful of bread. "I didn't see any! Bound books?"

"There are two leather-bound parchment volumes and two loose-leaf folios with gilt lettering," Bhaja said. "Possibly more in the parchment stacks. I only found one bundle of scrolls that seemed to go together, the rest were only two or three leafs each."

"Tarub will be pleased," Abbas said, reaching for the last pear. Bhaja let a small frown cross her face. She hadn't even had one yet, and this was Abbas's third. Did the man eat nothing else?

"I am to let her know as soon as we arrive; she intends to come look over the collection that Darras has provided."

Abbas nodded. "Good," he said. "She likes to know where her money goes. It isn't endless, like the Emir's."

"Where does it come from?" Chedar asked. "I mean concubines aren't paid, are they? And while she eventually married him, the second Emir al Rahman would not have passed his riches on to his wives: that money belongs to the people, the city by way of the citadel."

"Ah, well that's a story," Abbas said, settling into storyteller mode. "Of course, this all happened while you were yet in swaddling wraps—or maybe before that! —but to me it was a lively time!

"The extraordinarily beautiful Tarub was one of al Rahman's favorites. One day, they had an argument about something, and she locked her door against him. She was stubborn along with her more positive attributes, and refused him again and again.

"Finally, desperate to see her, the Emir had brought to the hareem stacks of sacks filled with gold! These he had piled up against her door so that when she opened it to go out to prayers, the sacks fell into her room and spilled gold coins across her floor." Abbas took a swig of water from his waterskin. "From that time on, her door was open to him. Not long after, realizing how much he desired and appreciated her, he freed her from slavery. Then the Emir and Tarub were married. Tarub the Beautiful was no longer a mere concubine!"

While everyone had finished eating, his audience was so spellbound that no one made a move to leave.

"Tarub has always been canny; she backed several winning horses in the betting on the tribal horse-races. She supported various Berber rug-merchants, in bringing their goods to al-

Andalus, making a good profit. And she was careful about selling the jewelry gifted to her by the Emir. By the time al Rahman died, she had doubled her money. This is how she is able to fund the Library, and the hospice at Shuqunda that I am in charge of." Abbas laughed. "There was a single emerald necklace the Emir had given her, that was much desired by a concubine of the present Emir Muhammad." Abbas drank again. "Now, Muhammad believed that necklace belonged to the citadel, while Tarub believed it was hers, *given* to her by the previous Emir as a wedding gift. She offered to sell it to him, while he insisted she give it back.

"So, the Emir appointed a judge on the matter, who examined the Law and the interpretations of the Law, and who eventually pronounced in favor of Tarub. The necklace was given to the Emir's *wife*, and so was hers."

"That's why the Emir and Tarub are at odds!" Yusuf cried.

"That and another reason, I will relate in a moment," Abbas replied. He smiled. "So she offered to sell the emerald necklace to the Emir again, but now the price was twice what she had asked before, because he hadn't trusted her claim. He was so angry! But he indeed paid the price, so he could give it to his concubine. And Tarub, who cared little for emeralds, after all, had added to her fortune." He stood up and stretched, still smiling.

"So what was the second reason?" Bhaja wondered.

"Ah!" Abbas said. "That was the matter of the heir to the Emirship. Muhammad's mother was Emir al Rahman's first wife. Tarub was his third wife. So there was a slight preference toward the offspring of the first wife, although Tarub fought for her own and al Rahman's son to be appointed. The panel of judges who were to decide the matter argued that her son was more influential and better educated, but the decision eventually went to Muhammad, whose mother was powerful in her own right at that time." Abbas sniffed. "Before she died, she told Muhammad she was glad they had won, but that it had been a very close thing. So, Muhammad has never forgiven Tarub for introducing such a powerful competitor for the title."

"Tarub herself is powerful," Bhaja said. No one argued with that pronouncement. "Well," she said, standing up. "Let's get to Écija, so we can then get home tomorrow." She walked to the grazing, hobbled horses.

"We should remember to throw a blanket over Wararni when we cross the bridge into Qurtuba," Xarq suggested. "The Emir has men out looking for him."

"Good idea," Chedar said. "I can sit on him, too." He and Wararni glared at one another as the rest of the group mounted up.

Tarub was waiting in the Library when they arrived back in Qurtuba late the following day. Bhaja's eyes were drawn to the dragonfly necklace the woman wore. It reminded her of her own lotus blossom necklace with delicate gold and enamel work; a family heirloom, her mother told her it was ancient, and the one item the family had that was probably worth more than all the rest put together, including their house. This dragonfly was of a similar design in the goldwork, tiny balls forming the dragonfly's body, beautiful blues and greens enameled perfectly, coloring the wings, as the pinks and lavenders did Bhaja's lotus blossom.

Tarub seemed to know its value, covering it protectively with a hand when she leaned forward to look at something Naomi was showing her. She watched with interest as the trunks and bags were unloaded, seeming rather overdressed for the event, and Bhaja realized how much her sponsor admired the written word, and had attired herself to honor it. As though it was a form of art in itself, much like the necklaces.

Bhaja reached for a stack of scrolls, but noticed how much dust coated her clothing. Instead, she walked back outside and shook her headcloth and over robe into the courtyard. Dust flew off in a cloud. She went back inside and washed her hands and face, and then began the process of sorting the scrolls.

Meanwhile, Tarub stepped to the doorway and gave Driver an order to "put up her canopy," and the man nodded. Curious, Bhaja paused as she went back past the doorway.

Driver put a vertical pole into a fitting she hadn't noticed at each corner of the wagon bed. Then he lifted, with Yusuf's help, a cloth covering that fit onto the poles. Then Driver unfolded from the floor a second bench, this one fully under cover of the canopy. The wagon had been transformed into a carriage.

As Bhaja turned to go back to her work with the acquisitions, she saw Hathus and Lylah and their son approaching through the courtyard.

"What's all this?" Hathus asked as they neared, eyebrows high, a haughty tilt to his chin. If Tarub was overdressed, Hathus was positively adorned, jewels and embroidered silks covering every bit of him. Bhaja raised her own eyebrows, keeping her face still so that she did not appear to mock his ostentation. His wife and son were much less decorated, and she settled her gaze on Lylah, to keep from laughing.

"Our new writings," Bhaja said, "collected by Darras of Osuna."

"Ah, Darras," Hathus said. "May we look inside?"

Bhaja met Lylah's eyes as she murmured, "Of course." Why did Lylah look frightened?

Hathus saw Tarub sitting at one of the tables piled with scrolls. "So all this is yours, now?"

Tarub looked up and gave him a tight smile. From her face, Bhaja would have guessed she considered Hathus an enemy, but her voice was friendly enough. "These are all items I have commissioned from Darras over the years. He's been collecting them on his travels."

"Indeed? I wonder that he left them sitting so long in Osuna, if they were intended for you."

"We were waiting for the Library to be completed," Tarub said, an edge to her voice as she stood up, moving to one of the sorting tables. Then she addressed Bhaja. "What are these?" meaning the bag of Darras's personal papers.

Bhaja explained. Then, "Oh, I should have given the rings to Qusayma!" She pulled the little bag of jewelry loose and dumped it out onto the table.

"We are not yet certain Qusayma is a blood relative," Tarub said. "That is for the Emir to decide, along with what happens to the family's lands in Osuna. Keep these in the safe for now."

Bhaja nodded. She would do so once Hathus and his family were gone; she did not need to advertise to this narcissistic person that they had a safe that presumably held valuable items. She didn't think he would attempt to rob the Library, but he might try to bully her into selling him some things.

"Who did the al Jamal lands belong to before they were given away?" Pai asked, glancing between Tarub, Hathus, and Abbas ibn Firnas. "Does anyone know?"

"It was much more than forty years ago," Abbas said, and Tarub nodded, seating herself on one of the Library benches. "I recall it was a Christian family. The confiscated land was given to the al Jamals as a reward for all their fighters who helped the second Emir al Rahman with an attack by the last of Roderick's followers."

"Roderick!?" Tarub's astonishment was plain on her lovely face. "Roderick has been dead for a century and a half!"

"Yes, but there were many Christian followers who attempted to hold off the *invaders,* as they saw it."

Hathus nodded his agreement and looked at Abbas, eyebrows raised. Bhaja glanced aside and saw that Lylah was eyeing the jewelry. Bhaja reached forward and scooped it back into the bag. Whoever it belonged to, it wasn't Lylah.

"I think you give Roderick too much credit!" Tarub said.

Abbas grinned, not at all disturbed by Tarub's argument. "Perhaps, but there are still Christians who believe this land is theirs, and are willing to fight for it!"

Tarub shook her head. "Well, it doesn't matter now, though I am fairly certain the land belonged to the Christian family of Darras before it was given away."

"Yes, it used to belong to Darras. It is the al Jamal's now," Hathus said firmly. "I looked it up."

"Oh," Bhaja said. "Where did you find the records, Hathus?"

"The Emir has all the records now from the former governors and from the Mosque histories."

Bhaja blinked and said, "So whatever the treasure is, it is Malik and Sayyida's now." She looked closely at Naomi and then Lylah who both flinched at Malik's name.

"That is correct," Hathus said. "Though the Emir may still try to claim it for the citadel, especially once I make a case for Malik al Jamal to be tried for the murder of Darras."

"You think Malik murdered Darras?" Bhaja couldn't keep the surprise from her voice.

As the venom grew in Hathus's tone, Lylah's face turned paler until she was almost grey, listening to her husband. "He wanted to secure his title to the treasure. Darras was the last of his line, so far as anyone knew, and even if this long-lost cousin has a claim, it is a distant one, so with Darras out of the way, Malik's greed is satisfied."

Bhaja was alarmed at Hathus's whole demeanor, which was cold and angry. The man obviously did not like Malik; Bhaja had to wonder if there was history between them. Which, she supposed, might explain Lylah's reaction, too.

Lylah put a hand on her husband's arm, presumably to calm him, but Hathus ignored her and spoke again. "I will ensure the Emir knows of the matter, and why Malik is the obvious murderer!" It sounded from Hathus's dark tone that he held Malik in the worst regard.

"I wonder if it would not be better for someone else to present the matter, Hathus," Lylah murmured.

"Malik is a friend of the Emir," Abbas said, in agreement. "That's apt to prejudice your case and cause you to lose face with the Emir."

Hathus shook his head. "I hear what you are saying, but—"

"Please, Hathus! Please! Let it be!" Lylah said, sounding like she was going to cry.

Tarub frowned, then looked away from the couple, glancing at Bhaja and Abbas. "Has the Emir been informed of Darras's death, yet, and the cause of it?"

"I believe Pai is going there now, to let the Emir's staff know," Abbas answered, overriding Bhaja's attempt to do so.

"Good," Tarub said. "He gets grouchy if he doesn't have long enough to consider each issue and choose the appropriate judge well before time."

"I know," Abbas said, glancing at Bhaja. "It is why I insisted he be told soon." The old man stood up from the stool he had been sitting on. "What do you think of all this?" He waved a hand, meaning the trunks from Darras. He looked at Tarub from under his brow, glancing from the woman to the acquisitions and back.

"A wonderful addition to the Library," Tarub said. "Bhaja, I would like a listing of the individual items as soon as you can go through them and make such an inventory."

Bhaja nodded. "Naomi and I will need to do that together; many of the items are in Greek."

At her name, Naomi looked up and smiled. Whatever troubled her at Malik's name had now faded from her face.

The same could not be said for Lylah. The woman was speechless and pale, and seemed almost dizzy, clinging to Hathus's arm as the couple made their goodbyes. Hathus and Lylah and their unintroduced son then departed the Library with well-wishes from all, though Abbas was scowling fiercely.

That reduced the crowd somewhat. With a sigh of relief, Bhaja watched Lylah, who looked back once as the family walked away, eyes tight with worry...about *something*. Bhaja wished she knew what it was.

Eventually, the guards Xarq and Chedar were paid and sent on their way with the fugitive Wararni, leaving the Library almost quiet again.

After noon prayers, Tarub also took leave of the Library. "This is not an idle invitation," she said directly to Bhaja, confirming her earlier request. "You and Naomi must come to the party tomorrow and tell my guests about some of the more important things we have acquired through Darras's great effort."

Bhaja nodded, wondering if she would have sufficient time to make an inventory and judge and list the "important" items.

Besides reading through all their new material, she had other errands. She was going to have to go buy new robes; at least an over robe to cover everything beneath. Even the better of her two nicest gowns was becoming worn and colorless. It wouldn't do at all for a party at Tarub's villa.

She glanced at Naomi, wondering if the woman had any fancy garments; certainly the plain cotton robes she wore to the Library every day wouldn't fit in at a fancy party.

But as she exited through the doorway arch, Tarub let Bhaja know she had been thinking about that as well. "I am sending a pile of robes I am tired of, or that I didn't like. You and Naomi can pick through those. Some of them have never been worn." She smiled, eyes sparkling. "Give one or two to your mother, also, Bhaja. I know she seldom has the inclination to shop."

"Thank you, lady," Naomi said.

"Yes, thank you," Bhaja hastily added. "And my mother would be delighted, I'm certain."

"I've already given the most ragged ones to Zetian at Pai's shop, to be used for her paper. Anything you two don't like you can give away." She eyed Isador in his faded and threadbare once-black robe. "Maybe the Abbey can use some of the fabric to make what they need, as well."

Isador's eyes widened as he looked up and nodded an embarrassed thanks.

Tarub swept out the door, two of her silent handmaids following her to where her converted-wagon carriage waited.

Bhaja made a mental note to be sure she held a few things back for Zetian at Pai's shop to *wear,* not to be made into fine paper. Even if the woman found traditional robes unsuitable while she was working, she would want something nice for her wedding day. Then she shifted her focus back to her own problems.

"I guess we'd better get busy if we are to have a list by tomorrow night," Bhaja said eyeing the open trunks and piles of unsorted manuscripts. "Isador, perhaps you can write while Naomi and I examine. It needn't be beautiful, just clear enough for us to read from."

Isador nodded, reaching for a piece of scrap parchment and a fresh quill.

Bhaja smiled fondly at Pai, who had appeared in the Library entrance loaded with food trays a short time after the sunset call to prayer. She hurried across the room to take some of the load and take it back outside to place on the larger of the two tables in the courtyard. Pai had clearly gotten enough food to feed the four of them, and maybe several visitors, as well.

It was as well he had, since shortly after she and Pai, Naomi and Isador had begun eating, Yusuf showed up. Bhaja invited him to sit at the large table with her and Pai. Obviously hungry, Yusuf took a pita and loaded it with roasted lamb. She'd been hoping there would be enough for Isador to take back to the Abbey to add to the monks' meager meal.

There was plenty of food in Qurtuba. But like many cities, the distribution of food among the people was not always as evenhanded as she would like. But tonight Pai had brought so much, Yusuf might well eat all he liked and there would still be leftovers.

"Is Wararni settled?" Yusuf asked Pai.

"For now," Pai said around a mouthful of fruit. Or at least that's what she thought he'd said.

"Hathus intends to accuse Malik al Jamal of murdering Darras."

Yusuf frowned and shook his head. "I don't like the man, but it doesn't seem like much of a motive for murder; did Malik really do it?"

"Well," Pai said, swallowing, "that's partly what the inquest is for, tomorrow, yes?"

Bhaja smiled at him.

As they finished their meal, a clatter of hooves announced an arrival at the courtyard. It was Driver, back again, this time with a wagonload of cloth. He didn't smile to see them, nor did he frown. It was as if his face was frozen in neutrality.

The man got down from the wagon, offered a short bow to Bhaja, and began lifting gowns and robes and scarves from the pile in what was again a wagon bed, and taking them inside the Library. A couple scarves slipped from the stack he carried, and Bhaja realized they must be silk.

Driver, or someone, had placed a large linen sheet underneath to keep things from snagging on the wood of the wagon. It was as well that had been done, Bhaja thought, as more of the items she picked up clearly felt like silk, smooth, slippery, and cool, among the cottons and fine linens. What a bounty!

Once the wagon was empty, Driver bowed again, and just quietly as he had arrived, he left, the only sound of his presence the clop of the horse's hooves.

Seeing the growing pile of goods, Naomi had risen from her meal with an exclamation. She washed her hands as Bhaja did, and then they sorted through the items together.

Naomi set aside the silks for Bhaja, saying, "You are the librarian, I'm just the clerk."

Bhaja did not reply, but she knew she didn't need *three* complete multi-layered silk outfits. How many parties was she ever going to? Well, she could take one to her mother, she supposed.

Startling her, Isador made an exclamation, and stood up, knocking over his stool. "I think—" he broke off and swallowed, holding up several scrolls. "I think," he said again, "these are from Origen of Alexandria's *Hexapla*!"

Bhaja smiled at the man's enthusiasm. "I recognize Origen of Alexandria's name, but not this Hexapla thing," she said.

Isador blinked. "It's a critical discussion of translation differences from the Hebrew into Greek of the books of the Old Testament!" Isador glanced at Naomi, who looked just as puzzled as Bhaja. "The original translators corrupted the meaning of several passages, and changed the emphasis of others!" When the two women still seemed unimpressed, he added, "It's a very important study."

"I am so glad you have understanding of what it is and what it means, Isador," Bhaja said. "I will certainly read it closely once it is in Arabic."

"I will be interested in seeing it as well," Naomi added. "Now that I think of it more, I believe I know who you mean and what his arguments involved."

"I will make several copies," Isador said, holding the scrolls as if they were gold.

"Thank you," Bhaja had the wit to say. She swallowed her smile and turned back to the gowns and robes.

Most were a solid color, but a few had embroidery or were dyed in shifting colors.

"Goodness," Naomi said, swirling a watery blue and green marbled scarf. "What did she *keep*, if she gave this away?"

Bhaja laughed in agreement, picking up a beaded belt and offering it to Naomi. "This can be yours, if you like it," Bhaja said. Naomi accepted with a flourish, eyes sparkling, and Bhaja was glad she had made the offer; it was certainly not something she would seek out for her own self to wear.

Pai's slight smile betrayed his enjoyment of the moment as well, as he'd followed them inside after packing up the leftover food. Yusuf had followed him in to wash up, then brought in a fresh pitcher of water from the fountain. Then he'd left, saying he had errands.

Bhaja looked over the generous contributions of both Darras and Tarub with a feeling of delight.

Tarub not only was thoughtful, wealthy, and kind, but she also had exquisite taste. They'd feel comfortable among the wealthy guests at the party, Bhaja thought. At least they'd *look* like they belonged there.

Pai laughed to see the women making imaginary outfits out of some of the colored robes. "I'm heading back to the shop, Bhaja. See you tomorrow."

She looked up at him and smiled. "Thank you for bringing dinner," she said.

12. Bullies or Buddies

The thunder woke Pai. He wrapped a pillow around his head and rolled over. Another clap of thunder. He sat up and wiped the sleep from his eyes. Starlight filled the atrium. No clouds. No rain. Another loud noise. *It's not thunder.*

Zetian's sleepy voice echoed off the walls. "Someone is banging on our door. Shall I let them in? Do you think someone needs a map in the middle of the night?"

Another sound outside, more urgent this time.

Pai stood up. "I will go. Stay covered. It is not proper for you to greet visitors—" He tilted his head back. Stars and a quarter moon lit the black sky. "—in the dark of night."

A voice demanded, "Hurry, let us in."

Another voice sounded frightened, "The night watch will be here soon."

The first voice, "We can't let them find us."

Pai rushed to the door, opened the bolt, and peeked outside.

Two men pushed into the shop, sealing the entrance behind them.

Even in the dark, Pai recognized them. "Chedar! Wararni!"

Wararni's hands were tied with a leather strap. Chedar held tight, but Wararni pulled like a wild dog.

"What are you doing? Zetian is here. Think of her reputation. You can't be here in the night."

"I told him that," Chedar stated in a voice of reason, once again transformed by the night into a serious soldier.

Pai looked to Wararni. "Why did you drag Chedar here?"

Wararni murmured, "Tell Chedar to let me go. If I remain in Qurtuba, the Emir will make me a eunuch."

Zetian gasped from the atrium, but everyone protected her modesty by not acknowledging her presence.

Pai sighed. This wasn't a dream. "Eunuch? You are a great guard, why would the Emir castrate you?"

Nighttime Chedar tugged at Wararni's bound hands. "He can't help you if he doesn't know everything."

"It started when two concubines showed to be carrying babies. Wararni sighed. "But let me start from the beginning."

His tale started before he became a guard when he was a child, and his parents were poor. Pai prodded him with, "Yes, I see," and, "Of course," but nothing sped the story along.

Pai interrupted. It was time for a break. “Sit down. Do not open the door, and do not enter the atrium where Zetian sleeps.” The men sat on the mosaic floor, politely facing away from the atrium. “I will fetch us some tea.”

By the faint moonlight, Zetian had already prepared tea and handed him the tray. He signaled her to stay out of sight.

Finally, Wararni neared the end, “The concubines were less favored, so the Emir knew they weren’t carrying his children. Someone else had been with them.”

Another gasp from the atrium.

Pai interrupted with, “Did you lay with these two ladies while you had promised yourself to Zetian?” He did his best to control his anger.

“Oh no! Never! I had nothing to do with them. I would never go near the Emir’s hareem. Besides they’re Christian. They avoid Muslim men. Christian men aren’t circumcised.”

Chedar laughed. “Zetian is blessed to have found such an innocent suitor. I’m Christian and I can tell you that at the critical moment, we all look the same.”

Pai did his best not to laugh as the big warrior’s ears turned a bright red. Pai hadn’t ever thought about this but saw no reason to continue the embarrassing discussion.

“Tell him the rest,” Chedar prodded.

“They didn’t want to get their boyfriends in trouble, so they agreed to point their fingers at me.”

Pai wondered aloud, “Didn’t the other guards defend you?”

A sad voice explained, “The other guards don’t like me. They think I’m too proud because I won’t get drunk and visit prostitutes with them.”

Chedar added, “And they knew you couldn’t tell the Emir that you were engaged to a woman from al-Qin.”

Pai nodded, “So with no wife or lover, you were the perfect target, and they could punish you for being so superior.”

Wararni hung his head, “Yes. Untie me. Let me say goodbye to Zetian? If that is impossible, just tell her I love her. I must leave Qurtuba.”

Pai considered telling Wararni he was to be a father, but there was enough to worry about for now.

Dawn prayer announcements echoed across the peaceful city.

“You can’t stay here, but do not give up hope.”

Chedar stood up. “We must leave before the streets fill with people. I’m hiding him in the Emir’s stables.” He smiled as he opened the door. “No one will think of looking for him there.”

Pai stood in the open doorway of his shop. "Do not despair. I will find a way to clear your name so you can marry Zetian." The two men ran off through the dark alley, racing against the rising sun.

Wararni and Zetian had their difficulties, but they had each other. Pai still hadn't spoken to Bhaja. But, when he closed his eyes, *he could see a beam of sunlight shining through the high windows of the Library. It illuminated her as she leaned over her desk, a vision of the woman from his dreams.* He would speak to her today.

When Pai heard the muezzin's noon call, he headed for the citadel. The Emir made pronouncements and accepted petitioners after the prayers. He joined the flow of pious people going to the Great Mosque for congregational prayers. Certainly, a smaller group than would fill the path tomorrow, Friday. Today, most shops stayed open. The noise of men fishing in the Wadi al-Kabir echoed over the city walls. While everyone turned to enter the mosque, he continued to the citadel.

One other person waited there. A smiling Hathus greeted Pai, "Peace be with you."

"And also, with you," Pai responded automatically, but not believing it. "Do you still intend to accuse Malik of murder?"

Hathus's smile vanished. "What does it matter to you?"

Pai hadn't intended to upset the proud man. "I was thinking of your family, your wife Lylah, and young son Abdallah."

The tall man's pale face got red to match his fiery hair. "This has nothing to do with you."

"You know Malik is on the Emir's council, and his father before him, don't you?"

Pai didn't say anymore as the big man shook his fist in Pai's face shouting, "I am also a confidant of the Emir." Hathus lowered his voice. "Besides, no one knows how much longer Malik will be on the council. I hear that he has a big tax bill for the time he was away." Hathus smiled. "He's not as good a trader as his father was. He may be off the council and the Emir might take his properties."

Hathus moved close to Pai. Pai could smell the onion and spices he'd eaten. Hathus hissed, "I don't need your advice, but I'll give you some." Hathus spoke in a calm, but threatening voice, "Emir Muhammad defeated Tarub when she tried to place her son on the throne and will do it again if necessary. You and your librarian girlfriend should tread carefully."

Girlfriend? How did Hathus know about his feelings for Bhaja? If Hathus knew, that might mean Bhaja also knew. He should stop delaying and speak to her from his heart. He promised to do it right after this afternoon's audience.

Pai stepped away from the citadel, avoiding Hathus.

The soft shuffle of sandals on the flagstones signaled the end of noon prayers at the Great Mosque. Judge Kabos, in his fine robes, solemnly traversed the short distance between the two most important buildings in Qurtuba. Everyone recognized Allah's Protector who prayed at the mosque five times a day. No one rushed past him as he led this pious procession up the wide staircase.

At the grand entrance, two men in white robes of fine cotton, the color of the Umayyad, opened the magnificent doors. The judge announced "Allahu Akbar," and the crowd entered.

The ceiling of the Emir's great hall resembled the Great Mosque—supported by beautiful arches of alternating red and white stone. He marveled that each arch was the identical twin of the next. While not as grand as the mosque, there was enough room for Pai to keep a distance from Hathus. In the balcony and behind a wooden screen, the women were permitted to observe, but not participate. He wondered if Tarub, or Bhaja, was there and could see him.

The Emir had covered the back wall of plain stone with oak and juniper panels carved with surahs from the Quran in ornate calligraphy. All the new woodwork gave the room an odor similar to a forest grove. After a short time, one of the wooden panels opened to reveal a secret door, and everyone stopped talking.

"The Emir Muhammad," someone proclaimed.

A short man with a black beard entered the room. Below his purple keffiyeh, grey streaks started from and continued down both sides of his beard to meet at his chin. His most trusted advisors accompanied him as the procession completed one circuit of the great hall. This daily ceremony reminded the crowd of the Emir's power and position. It allowed them to admire his elegance and offer their allegiance.

Upon his return to the front of the room, the Emir climbed up three steps to sit cross-legged on a purple silk cushion with gold tassels on each of the six corners. From his elevated position on the marble dais, he looked down on his advisors who stood on either side facing the audience.

Pai observed that Malik al Jamal stood with the Emir's council while the arrogant Hathus remained in the crowd. Maybe Hathus would reconsider. Even if Malik had murdered Darras, there wasn't enough evidence to accuse the Emir's friend.

The Emir stood. "As-Salaam-Alaikum."

The crowd responded, "Wa-Alaikum-Assalaam."

"First, I regret to announce that one of my guards, named Wararni, has violated my hareem."

The crowd gasped and the men standing around the Emir nodded their heads.

"When I discovered his transgression, I selected Judge Kabos, Allah's Protector, to deal with him. When Wararni didn't show up to defend himself, the Judge sentenced him to castration."

A chorus of ululations emanated from the balcony.

"Wararni's location is unknown and today I offer a bounty of one hundred gold dinar for his apprehension."

Pai would warn Yusuf and his friends to be careful now that everyone knew that Wararni was an outlaw. If they were going to save the father of Zetian's baby, they'd have to work quickly.

The Emir signaled for tea. Two slaves carried in a low wooden table set with a silver tray and cups. They placed it convenient to the Emir's tasseled throne. Another slave poured a long stream from a teapot raised over his head exactly filling each cup without spilling a drop.

The men spoke among themselves while the people in the great hall waited. The Emir talked to Malik al Jamal and Malik pointed to Pai.

Malik stood. "Pai of Qurtuba, the Emir requests that you reveal what you know about the treasure on my lands in Ronda."

Pai had warned Hathus against speaking, but this was different. He stood tall and spoke in a strong, clear voice that would be heard by everyone, even the women in the balcony.

Pai recounted Darras of Osuna's visit to his shop to purchase a map. He then described his glider flight to locate the treasure site. He ended with, "However, a wildfire has obscured the treasure location, and I have lost the map."

Pai congratulated himself for talking at length without mentioning the treasure ownership or Darras's murder.

"Who owns this treasure?" the Emir asked.

"Certainly, that is a question for a judge, not for me," Pai replied confidently.

"I've heard that Darras of Osuna had his own answer."

Pai said, "Darras is dead and has been buried in a Christian ceremony in Osuna where he has family."

The Emir looked at Pai. "You've spoken with him. What did Darras believe? Did Darras think he had a claim on this treasure?"

Pai told the Emir about the Pope's letter and the contention that the treasure belonged to the former Christian owners.

The Emir looked to his council. They circled around him. After a brief conference, the Emir stood. "Pope John VIII, no matter his excellent reputation in the east, has no dominion over al-Andalus!" He looked around at the crowd and they murmured agreement. "However, I am a fair ruler and follower of the Prophet's laws. I will not prejudge this question. I appoint Judge Javan the Merciful to determine the rightful owners."

Pai smiled. Judge Javan had a reputation for being fair. This was good for his friend Sayyida and Darras's cousin Qusayma. They might receive a portion of the treasure.

The Emir took another break, and more tea was served.

Guards moved through the crowd. Two of them escorted Hathus to the front of the room. Someone must have heard of Hathus's rash allegations. Pai had warned him but now it was too late.

Then two other guards grabbed Pai and he found himself standing next to Hathus. The two men looked at each other with apprehension. The Emir was better known for punishments than rewards.

Pai relaxed when the guards brought Abbas ibn Firnas to stand with them. Certainly, nothing bad would happen to the respected scientist. Pai moved closer to Abbas and away from Hathus.

The Emir addressed the three men. "I remind you that the Quran states, *Let not the witnesses refuse when they are called upon*, and *Do not conceal testimony, for whoever conceals it, his heart is indeed sinful*. Let us hear about Darras's murder."

Pai testified about finding Darras's body and thinking his death was an accident. Abbas explained, at length, how he knew that Darras was murdered.

The Emir dismissed Pai and Abbas before turning to Hathus, "Do you *think* you know who killed Darras?"

Hathus didn't take any of the advice he'd received, but instead, he made a fist and his face again turned red. He shouted through clenched teeth, "Yes, I do! Malik al Jamal did it!"

The Emir asked Hathus for his evidence with the reminder, "I know your Muslim wife takes her son to study at the mosque each day. Allahu Akbar. I trust he's told his Christian father that the Quran teaches, *We do not testify except to what we know* and *Avoid false statements*."

As before, Hathus became agitated when he spoke of Malik al Jamal. He stammered, “Mal, Mal, Malik—”

Pai feared for Hathus, a Christian who had married a Muslim woman, now accusing a Muslim member of the Emir’s council. Qurtuba might be a tolerant city, but Hathus had gone too far. Even though his son studied at the mosque, that might not be enough to avoid the Emir’s wrath. Pai was astounded when the Emir softened towards the man with a red face and red beard, asking with a gentle tone, “Did you want to tell us about the property in Ronda?”

Hathus took a deep breath. “Yes. Forty years ago, your father confiscated the land in the valley west of Ronda from Darras’s family. They were powerful landowners of Ronda, but afterward, they were only small traders from Osuna.”

The Emir nodded. “My father the second Abd al Rahman acted justly following the principle of Diya. Darras’s family abused their Berber tenants, so my father awarded their estates to the Berber family al-Jamal. The Quran reminds us, *Allah commands justice and fair dealing*. Surely, you do not doubt my father’s virtue.”

Hathus put his palms on his knees and bowed to the Emir. “Of course not.” He stood up and crossed himself. “Darras had a letter from the Pope asserting a Christian claim to the treasure and the land. As Darras was the last of his line, Malik murdered him to invalidate this claim.” Hathus pushed out his long chin and finally stood silent.

The Emir looked to Malik and the two men nodded. “Hathus, many remember that you and Malik al Jamal fought often as boys. If this testimony is a continuation of your childhood battles, Malik can claim compensation under Diya, and you could forfeit your wealth and position.”

Hathus crossed himself again. “Standing before my God, this is true.”

“Insha'Allah,” Emir Muhammad declared. “Since Judge Javan the Merciful is already hearing the question of the treasure, he will also adjudicate the murder.”

Judge Javan wouldn’t convict Malik without a much better case than Hathus had put forward. Pai had warned Hathus and now looked at him with pity. If he were charged with bearing false witness, he could lose much.

The Emir stood and addressed the crowd, even looking up to the balcony to emphasize that he meant his pronouncement for everyone. “Questions about the treasure and the murder will be decided by Judge Javan the Merciful. The Quran declares *Obey*

Allah and obey those charged with authority among you. No one may participate or interfere without permission from the judge.

On that ominous note, the secret door opened, and the Emir departed.

There was a crowd moving through the great entry doors, so Pai waited off to the side for it to thin out. Behind him, a voice said, "As-Salaam-Alaikum." Pai turned to see who had greeted him. “Malik! And also, with you.” Pai had delivered a slightly different Christian response but Malik didn’t seem to notice or care.

“Pai, I thank you for your fair testimony.”

Malik’s unexpected friendly gesture felt like a betrayal of Sayyida. The brother and sister appeared to be locked in a constant battle. Despite his testimony, Pai still believed Malik had something to do with Darras’s murder and he hoped to discover the truth even after the Emir warned everyone not to interfere. Emir Muhammad was notorious for demanding tax payments, a well-known cause of uprisings in the countryside. Malik might have been desperate for the treasure.

Malik added, “My sister has taken residence in Qurtuba and has requested that you join us for breakfast to make up for the dinner I missed in Ronda.”

Pai didn’t let it show, but he was surprised that Sayyida would attend a meal with her brother after he had so abruptly refused her invitation in Ronda. However, her move to Malik’s villa seemed to indicate the two siblings had reached an understanding. Pai didn’t refuse. “I would be honored. Tell your sister that I look forward to seeing her again.”

“Until tomorrow,” Malik said and exited through the secret door to the Emir’s inner sanctum.

The afternoon heat overwhelmed Pai when he exited the citadel. He went to the fountain in front of the Library to quench his thirst. With the Emir’s audience complete, he was prepared to speak to Bhaja. He stood straight, set his shoulders back, and held his head high. He was ready. Today, he wouldn’t let anything interfere. He’d ask her to show him some of the new scrolls while Naomi and Isador worked. Once in a quiet corner, he’d confess his love.

He entered through the archway. His plan went as dark as an unprotected candle caught in a sudden gust. The Library echoed with loud voices. The tables which normally contained scrolls, inks, and quills were spread with fine clothing.

“Pai! I’m so glad to see you.” She held up a fine robe. “Isn’t it simply perfect?”

Pai wasn’t going to be able to speak with Bhaja in private today. He looked at the robe Bhaja held at her shoulders. She spun around showing off the delicate yellows, greens, and oranges in a beam of sunlight. He said the first thing that jumped into his mouth. “Isn’t it too small for you?” As soon as the words had escaped, she stopped turning and laughed.

“Oh, Pai! It is not for me. It is for Zetian—for her wedding.”

“Zetian is not getting married.” He told her about Wararni being bullied and the Emir’s reward for his capture. In a low voice he added, “Even worse, Zetian is pregnant.”

Bhaja was unshaken. She wrapped up the wedding costume and handed it to Pai. “Take this back to Zetian and I will speak to Tarub.”

“How can Tarub help?”

“She lived in the Emir’s hareem; she’ll know how to save Wararni.”

He thanked Bhaja, took the package, and headed home, eager to tell Zetian the good news. All the way, past the shops, listening to the fishermen, one thought ran through his mind: *I love that woman so much. Bhaja always knows what to do.*

13. People at Parties

Bhaja exclaimed over the papers in Darras's personal amassment. "Oh, my!" she glanced up at Naomi. "I can't believe this! No wonder Malik accused Darras of being a fraud!"

"Why?" Naomi asked, "What do you mean?"

"This 'letter from the Pope' that Darras claimed the Christian Pope had written? It is entirely a fabrication of Darras himself!" She held up three pages from Darras's collection. "These are draft copies he made of the letter, composed by and in Darras's hand. Clearly *not* from the Pope."

Naomi's face was still for a moment. "I wonder that Darras was so intent on claiming a treasure, if he was ill, as you say."

"Yes, he was ill. Abbas confirmed that. Yet, it is possible Darras was ill without thinking he would die soon. I wonder if he knew about his cousin Qusayma, and was trying to provide for her? Still, that doesn't seem enough justification for this—this forgery!"

Bhaja glanced at Isador, who had put on his blankest expression. He would know the seriousness of this forgery, she realized. "How terrible was it?" she asked him.

"A mortal sin is a deliberate turning away from God, especially to seek personal gain. To fake a *chirographa*—a letter from the Pope—for such a purpose, is more than simple forgery. It is avarice compounded with selfishness of a startling degree." Isador bit his lip. "However, I do know Darras was a personal friend of the Pope. It is possible he may have had permission to write a letter in his own hand to then send to Rome, and ask if the Pope would approve it and rewrite it." He shrugged. "Perhaps that was Darras's intention. Anyway, without the Pope's personal seal, it would be meaningless."

Bhaja recalled the appearance of the letter the Father in Osuna had found. There had been no seal upon it, that was certain. She took it out of the safe and put the bag of rings in. She compared the letter to the rough drafts.

Darras did seem to be trying to get the wording just right. Though what his purpose had been would remain forever a secret the man had kept to himself. Since there did not seem to be much for her to do about the whole issue, she simply wrapped the drafts together with the version Darras had had on him when he died and placed the whole bundle into the safe.

She locked the safe, collected the clothes that she wanted for the party together with her mother's nice silk ensemble, and left the rest of the garments for another day. Maybe Yusuf could carry them home sometime, if she got them bundled up and ready for him.

By the time Bhaja left, Naomi had already gone to prepare herself and the widow for her absence that night. Bhaja would pick her up later. She wanted time to go home and bathe and wash and dress her hair, with plenty of time to relax as she did so.

With Isador to look after the Library all night, both she and Naomi could enjoy some extra time to prepare. Thus she was free to spend the early evening with her mother, as they ate a light meal and designed Bhaja's hair for the party.

After brushing out her still-damp hair, Bhaja's mother's fingers brushed, wrapped, and tied off many tiny braids. "I'm going to loop these up and pin them," Mother said, meaning the braids, "then if your headscarf slips or you remove it, your hair will still look lovely."

"Scarves come off entirely, at Tarub's," Bhaja said. "I've heard gossip—"

"I have heard that gossip as well," her mother said, voice a little strained. "I hope you will be sensible."

"Naomi and I plan to stick together. No naughty business for us."

"Good. Now, which over robe did you plan on? I want to use matching pins."

Together, they went through the hairpins Bhaja had bought for the two of them to share. The mixed box she had found at the souk had been surprisingly priced, well within her means. Some were antique, some new. Some had enamel figures from nature, butterflies and flowers and such, while others were metal wrought into interesting geometric shapes placed on long shanks capable of holding up wraps or buns.

"Let's use the more golden colored geometrics," Bhaja decided. "I chose the robe with the Egyptian lotus and papyrus designs."

"Necklace? Earrings?"

"The family necklace would look wonderful with these robes, don't you think? But to go with it, just small gold earrings. Some delicate bangles for my wrist. I do not wish to appear gaudy, just more elegant than I usually do."

"Yes," Mother said. "You will be among the elite tonight, best not to feel too small. I will fetch the necklace."

She had the carriage she'd ordered stop by the Library after picking up Naomi. Bhaja went in and Isador looked up with a smile.

"Just finished," he said, handing her a gilt-illuminated list of the most important and valuable of the new acquisitions to give to Tarub. Bhaja looked it over.

At the top of the list was Origen of Alexandria's *Hexapla*, followed by an excellent medicinal plants folio by Dioscorides, his *De Materia Medica*. Third listed was one by Galen of Pergamon, a Roman of whom even Bhaja had heard. She was certain Abbas knew of the Dioscorides and no doubt the Galen as well.

Besides the medical texts, there were a half-dozen Persian, al-Qin, and al-Hind philosophies, two Greek plays, and two excellent and famous Persian stories. This list should make Tarub very proud as she announced her new holdings, with more perhaps to come as the librarians finished going through all the new materials.

"Thank you Isador, you made it look quite beautiful."

Flushing with embarrassment, he bobbed his head.

"I'll see you tomorrow, best lock the door behind me."

He got up to do that as she went back out and climbed into the creaky wooden carriage. Unlike many she had rented before, this one had no roof to cover them, and Bhaja prayed the rainclouds held off until they arrived at Tarub's villa.

Far from Tarub's original comment about inviting a small group to hear about the Library's acquisition, the villa was packed with the elite of Qurtuba. Mostly they were people Bhaja had never even seen before, much less ones that she actually knew. Thus it was an odd relief to see Lylah and Hathus min Alshamal enter the room.

Bhaja glanced aside to see that Naomi had found some people to talk to, so she left her side and approached Lylah.

"As-Salaam-Alaikum," Bhaja said to her almost-friend.

"Wa-Alaikum-Assalaam," Lylah replied. "What a beautiful necklace!"

"Thank you," Bhaja said, lightly touching the brilliant pink lotus. "A family heirloom," she clarified. Lylah nodded. Bhaja desperately looked for a complementary compliment to return, but she noticed more how tired and worried the other woman looked. Finally she said, "I like your scarf; the fabric is lovely."

Lylah nodded and murmured thanks. She glanced around at the room filled with gossiping people. "There seems to be a certain dread in the air," she observed.

Bhaja nodded. "Though the murder occurred three days travel away, still many of these people knew Darras."

"Many liked him, as well," Lylah said. "A circumstance made all the more ironic by someone choosing to murder him."

Bhaja glanced at her. Was that what concerned Lylah so much? Her husband had accused Malik al Jamal of the deed. While the man wouldn't have been welcome here at a Tarub event, he was well known in the city as a member of the Emir's entourage.

"Do you agree with your husband's assessment of Malik as the killer?" she asked more bluntly than she had intended. Why could she not control her tongue?

Lylah's eyes widened, but she spoke calmly. "I don't know. I knew Malik when we were much younger. I fancied he and I would wed at some point, but then he was sent away for military training. When he came back after those ten years..." she shook her head. "I don't know. He was just *different,* somehow."

"He had grown up?"

Lylah shook her head again. "There was more to it than that, but I have never been able to explain it."

"Perhaps Hathus accuses him because he was once a rival for your affection?"

Lylah's expression cooled. "That seems a facile explanation, don't you think?" With that the woman walked away, leaving Bhaja flushing with embarrassment and confusion. She was saved from any further gaffes by Tarub's call for attention.

Tarub looked around the room, and meeting Bhaja's eyes, waved her forward.

"My friends, we are gathered here to speak of my Library, and my librarian and her workers, and recent acquisitions collected by my good friend Darras of Osuna."

There was instant silence in the room. Bhaja did not think it was for her sake, but rather for the murdered Darras. She felt like there was a coiled spring of tension gathering in her neck, and someone had just turned the crank to tighten it.

She wished Pai was there. His lighthearted and energetic presence would have lightened her mood considerably.

The evening ended when lightning flashed and thunder blasted overhead. Buckets of rain poured into Tarub's gardens and atrium. Guests hastily made their thanks and left. Bhaja could feel her tension release a little more as each batch of guests took their leave, emptying the rooms and outdoor areas.

Fine covered carriages and palanquins stopped under the extended cover of the portico to receive guests and take them safely home. Abbas waited with his carriage to rescue as many walkers as would fit. Lylah and Hathus left in their palanquin with little regard for the soaking received by their carriers. Many of the guests had guards to accompany them, a further sign of the unease that circulated in Qurtuba.

When she thought of leaving herself, she almost cried, remembering the open-topped carriage, and realizing how drenched she and Naomi were going to be by the time they were delivered to their respective homes.

But it turned out to be an empty worry. Their carriage never appeared. After waiting out on the portico for many damp, windy moments, Tarub called them back inside.

"It's as well," she said showing them into a small receiving room off the atrium. "We can have tea and discuss this other problem you had mentioned, Bhaja. That of Zetian of Pai's shop, her pregnancy, and her fiancée, while my maids prepare a room for you."

Naomi began a protest, but Tarub shushed her, so Bhaja simply said, "Thank you. The storm is dreadful, and I am glad not to have to go out in it."

Tarub nodded. The servant delivered a tray of tea and served a glass to each of the three women. Bhaja's fingers found the glass a little too warm, especially after the frigid air outside had chilled her fingers to numbness. She set it on the table beside her to cool.

"Wararni has been accused of possessing two of the Emir's concubines," she began.

Tarub nodded, and Bhaja's eyes were captured by a lock of the woman's hair that escaped the swept-up roll making a crown on the top of Tarub's head. It seemed appropriate, she thought. Even the fallen lock.

"I know the situation," Tarub said. "I had taken concern over the women involved, and how to help them. I confess, I hadn't given thought about the man or men involved."

"Wararni has eyes only for Zetian," Bhaja said, knowing that to be true. "He would never have invaded the hareem."

"Do we have any idea who did?"

Bhaja shook her head. "Wararni said it must be a guard, or with the help of a guard, otherwise—"

"It's impossible to break into the hareem, yes," Tarub said.

Bhaja blinked. Of course this woman would know the exact arrangements of the hareem and its two sets of guards: the eunuchs who guarded and interacted directly with the wives and concubines, and an outer set of whole men who guarded access points into the wing of the citadel that housed the hareem.

The intruders to the hareem would have been among the latter, or had been men from outside the citadel altogether with the help of an insider.

"I intend to speak to the women involved, to encourage them to confess who with and how, they came to be in this position."

That of being pregnant when the Emir had not visited either of them any time in recent memory, she meant. So he certainly was not the father. But who was?

Tarub set down her glass of tea and went on, "While the Emir Muhammad is not a violent or beastly man, he will be forced to display a firm hand or be seen to be ineffectual. I intend to buy the women when they are sent to auction as drudge slaves, which he certainly will do. I have an agent within the citadel who can help me arrange this, hopefully before the women are physically punished."

Naomi's eyes bulged at this. "Physically punished?"

"They could be beaten, burned, disfigured—any number of horrid things are common punishments for this kind of betrayal of the Emir." Tarub sniffed. "Though their sale would bring in more money at the market if they are unmarked."

"The poor things just wanted someone to love," Bhaja murmured. "Especially if they have been ignored by the Emir."

Tarub made a face. "They are also fools to do this and be caught out so easily! But I do try to make allowance for their age. Neither has more than twenty years. They are still too young and foolish to understand what their position could be." She cleared her throat. "Could have *been,*" she corrected.

Meaning what being a wily—and perhaps *very much more beautiful*—concubine could have meant they achieved, as Tarub herself had, Bhaja realized.

But that time, at least, she managed to keep the words inside her head, clenching her teeth to ensure her mouth stayed shut. It would not do to insult their hostess.

At last Bhaja and Naomi were ushered to their room for the night: a boudoir more elegantly furnished than she could have imagined, decorated in rich damask and silks of gold and russet and sand.

Naomi looked at the single but large bed and turned to Bhaja. "I will sleep on the floor, if you prefer," she offered.

"Allah forbid," Bhaja returned. "We will share the bed. It certainly is big enough!"

Tarub had even had nightclothes laid out for them, she noted. Fine cotton so thin it was translucent.

"These would be welcome on a hot summer night, but this storm makes them somewhat impractical," Naomi said, holding up the one Bhaja had not chosen. Even through the double layers of the cotton sleep gown, Bhaja could discern the reds and blues of Naomi's over robe.

Bhaja pulled back the bedcovers, admiring the silky-fine linen sheets and layers of silken throws. "There are plenty of coverings," Bhaja said, displaying the layers.

Naomi bit her lip, but said nothing further as they undressed and put their nightgowns on.

Feeling almost deliriously relaxed now that the social conventions were finished for the day, Bhaja performed her cleansing and prayers and crawled into bed. Where she discovered most of the pins in her hair were going to have to come out before she'd be able to rest.

As she worked, removing them, she could see the other woman's tension in the stiffness of her body, the taut expression on her face.

"What troubles you, Naomi?"

"It's foolish," she said, turning to her back. "I'm afraid of everything, like the widow." She closed her eyes and pretended to sleep. But she kept twitching, various parts of her body displaying how tightly together she was holding herself.

"Fear becomes less challenging when faced directly, I've found," Bhaja said, trying to open a path for the other woman to discuss what troubled her.

At last, with a groan of defeat, Naomi sat up. "I'm keeping you awake, along with myself," she said.

"What troubles you?"

"Darras!" Naomi's mouth curled in a moue. "I keep thinking his murderer knows I was a friend to the man. Darras helped me several times through my troubles in al-Jazair and elsewhere."

"Yes, he seemed a kind man."

"But if even *he* was attacked, what does that say about me and my son and our many fewer friends?"

Bhaja was still confused why this should trouble the woman so. "Darras had many friends, and many people he helped. That you were one of them does not make you less than him in any way."

Naomi's face crumpled. As tears ran down her cheeks, Bhaja attempted to comfort her, rubbing her shoulder, and holding her hand.

This apparent over-concern began to trouble Bhaja now as well. Was there something to the notion of the three travelers' simultaneous arrivals they had discussed in Osuna? Darras, Naomi, Malik al Jamal.

Did Naomi have a suspect for Darras's murder? Did she think Malik had been responsible, as Hathus did?

It felt very much like the woman knew more than she was saying, to the point Bhaja was now uncertain whether Naomi could be trusted.

She frowned. This was not at all how she had imagined this day ending.

14. THE BLOODY BLADE

Pai lived near the river wall. The nice shops, along with the Great Mosque, the Emir's citadel, and Tarub's Library, all resided within the sounds of the river. The boasting of the fishermen in the morning and gossip of the washerwomen in the evening echoed into the medina. On hot days, children could be heard splashing and playing in the shallower pools.

This morning Pai put on his finest white robe and visited the central market. If he closed his eyes, listening to the haggling and smelling the fruits and spices, he'd be transported back to Ronda. With his eyes open, the expanse of blankets piled high with an enormous variety of goods boasted of the size and opulence of Qurtuba. Some said, Ishbiliya, south along the Wadi al-Kabir, was bigger, but Pai didn't know; he'd never been.

He searched the offerings for a special gift to bring to Malik. He rejected some tasty red apples from Ronda as too ordinary, and the fragrant Qurtuba oranges as too bitter. In a lightly traveled corner, he found sweet dates from Ifriqa. He had not expected to find the sticky treat, so he also purchased a small basket to carry them.

With his gift in hand, he followed the well-maintained paths leading to the nicest neighborhood in the medina, the one farthest from the crowds and commotion. Malik's house presented a broad white wall interrupted by just a single door, carved to copy the grand entrance of the citadel.

Pai leaned close and announced through a small opening, "As-Salaam-Alaikum." After waiting a polite interval, he repeated his greeting, louder this time, becoming disturbed at Malik's rude behavior. *And what about Sayyida? Wasn't she now staying at the villa?* When he was still abandoned in the quiet alley, he became concerned.

After one last attempt, he banged his fist against the carved wood. Again, no one greeted him, but the doorway creaked open. He stepped inside and shouted, "Peace be with you," a final time.

He'd never been in Malik's home, grander than any in his experience except, of course, Tarub's villa. It didn't look like someone who couldn't pay their taxes. He admired the mosaic floor, an expanse of black and ochre triangles in a pattern that never repeated. The missing servants had set up for a meal. Pillows surrounded a low table containing a pot of steaming tea on a charcoal brazier and a tray of cut fruit. He placed his basket of dates on the table adjacent to Malik's elegant serving containers.

Since no one had appeared, he followed the smell of burning food. Just off the reception room, he entered the pantry open to the outside. Bread, still in the outdoor oven, had turned black, filling the pantry with smoke. Skewers of lamb had collapsed into the fire and burned with a sooty flame. There had been servants preparing a meal, but they were gone.

Pai rushed back past the breakfast and into the atrium. He marveled at an open space much larger and grander than the one Abbas ibn Firnas had. Looking around, he counted four fountains and ten palm trees, along with a border of colorful blooms around the walls.

He searched the elegant space for a clue to the missing servants until he noticed a sandal behind the farthest fountain. It was an expensive one of fine leather enclosing a dusty foot. He ran over to the sandal and was shocked to find Malik face down with his hands stretched out over his head. He sensed something was wrong. He shook the body, but Malik didn't wake—no breath, no sign of life. To be certain, he picked up Malik's arm to check his pulse.

A knife dropped from the limp hand.

The wrist was cut. Both wrists were cut.

Pai released the cold flesh and grabbed his own injured arm, trying to imagine cutting his wrists. He couldn't. He crossed himself.

The Emir's words echoed in his mind. *No one may participate or interfere without permission from the judge.*

Judge Javan lived nearby, but it was disrespectful to leave the body alone. He asked the empty house, "What about Sayyida? Doesn't she live here?"

As if in answer, he heard "As-Salaam-Alaikum," from the door.

It was Sayyida.

He rushed to stop her before she saw the grisly scene. "Wait here. Do not enter the atrium!"

She looked at him like he was deranged and kept walking. "I'm going to my room. I've been in these clothes all night."

He blocked her path. "All night? Where have you been?"

She gave him a sly smile. "It's none of your concern." When he didn't step aside, she explained, "Abbas gave me a ride home from Tarub's party and I spent the night in your old room in his house."

Pai was glad she missed whatever violence had transpired at the villa. "That was good."

He pointed to the steaming tea and cut fruit on the table. "Please have some breakfast and wait here until I return."

Running into the street, he turned away from the central market to the most exclusive quarter. Guards blocked the lane where the judge lived with other Qurtuba dignitaries.

"Halt!" Two guards barred his way. "Where are you going?"

Pai stopped to catch his breath. "I must see Judge Javan the Merciful."

The guards didn't move.

"Malik al Jamal is dead!"

Now the guards led the way to the judge's home, an even wider expanse of white stucco than Malik's. They prevented Pai from approaching the door. One guard entered while the other unsheathed his sword. Pai waited. Since he entered this well-kept neighborhood, he'd been doing a lot of waiting.

Eventually, the guard returned with the judge's incompetent brother. "I am Javed, Judge Javan has not finished his breakfast and study of the hadiths." The brother looked like a poorly dressed version of the judge, except that his hands showed calluses from hard work, not the hands of a cleric who spent their days in study. His presence demonstrated that Malik wasn't as important as Pai imagined.

Pai knew Javed's reputation, erratic and unpredictable. Sayyida would prefer a real judge. Pai tried to get the real judge. "Malik is on the Emir's council. I could wait for Judge Javan."

Javed scoffed. "The judge often has me take care of small cases like this one."

Pai responded silently. *Yes, and every time, families and friends regret it.*

The men marched to Malik's house without any urgency. Another indication of Malik's status.

Sayyida sat with her brother's head in her lap. She had removed his keffiyeh and was smoothing his hair. She sobbed. "My brother! My beloved brother."

Javed moved the corpse's arms with the toe of his sandal. "Malik slit his wrists, killed himself," he announced in a dismissive tone.

Sayyida became more agitated. "No! Not my brother."

Javed quoted the Quran, "*Slay not yourself. Allah treats you kindly.*" He left the atrium. "I cannot stay with a sinner. The home of a sinner is forbidden, haram."

Pai had expected a more thorough investigation. The judge's brother hadn't even rolled Malik over. He almost shouted, "Search the house!" and "Where are his servants?"

From the entryway, the judge's brother added, "Do not take the body to the mosque. He cannot be buried with the righteous."

With that proclamation, Sayyida began ululating in the manner of new widows.

The doorway closed and the judge's brother disappeared.

"Judge Javan should have been here," Pai yelled.

"You did your best," Sayyida comforted Pai. She'd stopped sobbing. Pai looked at her dry eyes and recalled the funeral in Osuna. *The family doesn't have a moment to mourn until after the body is buried and the crowd departs.*

He offered, "Even if Malik is forbidden from the mosque, we can still clean his body."

"I will do it. Help me carry him to the reception area, away from this scene of sin and death."

They placed him on the mosaic floor with his head on one of the pillows that had been set out for the breakfast.

Sayyida went to fetch a basin of water when the front door slowly opened. Malik's servants had returned.

"We saw the guards leave."

Sayyida looked at them with disdain. "Where were you when your master needed you?"

"We were preparing the meal when we ran out of water in the cistern. I sent the boy to fetch some from the fountains."

A boy, who couldn't have been more than eight or nine, stood with his hands clasped and made a shy smile.

"When he saw the master, we were scared and ran away."

Sayyida sighed. "I'm glad you returned. You must help me wash the body."

The servants stood motionless, staring at her.

She responded to their unasked question, "Malik has no male relatives, so I will wash the body myself."

The elder servant nodded. "Insha'Allah." She cuffed the boy's head. "Hurry. Go fetch water."

Sayyida looked to Pai. "Thank you, friend. This is a time for Muslims only. You can go."

Pai took one last look into the atrium and saw the knife. It was not a dagger. It was a knife for food. He asked the boy if it belonged to his mother. The boy denied any ownership with a silent head shake. That seemed strange. He picked it up, wiped the blood from the blade, and tucked it into his robe. It might be important, so he kept it wondering why there'd been so many deaths. *Why have I been the one to find two dead bodies?*

Pai followed rarely used alleys, turning this way and that until inevitably he entered the central square. His belly growled. *I have not eaten this morning.* Nothing displayed in the market looked right until he saw a neat mound of oranges. He bought two of the bitter fruits and sucked on them as he wandered in the direction of the river.

Before he realized where he was heading, he found himself in front of the Library. He discarded the orange rinds beneath a palm tree and rinsed his hands at the courtyard fountain.

"Peace be with you."

He looked up at the speaker. It was Bhaja. "And also, with you," he responded.

"Where have you been?" she questioned.

He was relieved to be with Bhaja, away from Sayyida, her dead brother, and the uncaring Javed. "I visited Malik al Jamal."

She squinted at him. "Why would you do that?"

Pai didn't recount the story of the unexpected breakfast invitation. He just spat out his news. "Malik is dead."

"Allahu Akbar!" she exclaimed. "What happened?"

He told her about the events of the morning. She listened patiently as he repeated everything except the sweet dates, the bitter oranges, and the bloody blade.

"I am so angry about the judge and his brother." He kicked a rock. "They were supposed to be his friends!"

Bhaja stayed calm. "It seems odd that Malik would kill himself."

This got Pai thinking. He looked at Bhaja with admiration. *I love this woman so much. She always asks the right questions.* "You're right. Do you think someone murdered him?"

"Did Sayyida murder him to inherit his property and the treasure?" Bhaja wondered aloud. "I know she preferred to live at the villa in Qurtuba than on the farm in Ronda." She paused, "But she'd already moved to Qurtuba. We saw the wagonload she brought here from the farm."

Pai countered with, "Hathus seemed so mad with Malik yesterday. Even after the Emir warned him, he risked his power and position to accuse Malik of murder—with no real evidence. I wouldn't be surprised if he murdered Malik himself."

Bhaja gave a little nervous laugh. "I've never met Judge Javan's brother, but from your description, it sounds like the murderer will escape without notice."

Pai had calmed down. "That is not right, but Malik is not my concern. I think I should listen to the Emir and not get mixed up in these legal dealings."

Bhaja shook her head. "No. Instead of just finding the truth of Darras, we must also do the same for Malik."

That was the right answer. He was halfway back to his shop when he realized he'd not asked her about how she and Tarub would save Wararni, and even though he felt his love for her so strongly, he'd not told her.

He laughed. *Next time. He'd speak to her next time. But he then realized, Darras and Malik wouldn't have a next time. He should speak to her while he had his chance.*

Pai and Zetian were busy boiling cotton rags when he heard a crash on the roof. It sounded like a cat jumping from the city wall. The tiles clattered loudly. It must have been a big cat. Then there was a crash in the courtyard.

Zetian exclaimed, "Wararni! What are you doing here?"

Wararni was dripping wet.

There was a loud banging on the shop door.

Wararni rolled up in a ball and hid in a corner behind a pile of old clothes. "Don't let them find me."

Zetian frantically tossed the rags over her boyfriend who looked like a wet dog.

Pai went to the doorway. "Welcome to my shop. Do you need a map?"

Three men pushed their way inside. "We are looking for a fugitive."

Pai stayed calm. "Maps. I have maps, not fugitives."

The men looked around the shop and went out to the atrium.

Zetian stood in front of the pile of old clothes. Pai stared at the fire and the large pot of boiling rags willing the men not to look up and notice the wet footprints on the roof.

The men searched the back rooms, the ones with wet footprints above them. After they found nothing, they returned to the atrium.

Pai distracted the men by adjusting the drying racks. "Please be careful of the paper. It is quite valuable." He knew they would eventually look at the pile of rags.

Zetian stepped away from Wararni's hiding place and stumbled on a long log extending out from the fire. "Oh, clumsy me," she cried out when the moving log tumbled the pot. Hot water and wet rags flooded the atrium, especially her boyfriend's sanctuary.

Pai looked at her and saw a small smile.

"We've seen enough," remarked a disgusted guard. His friend agreed. "He's not here. Let's go check the next house before he gets away."

After the men were gone, Wararni came out.

Pai asked him, "What happened?"

"They found me in the Emir's stable, but I escaped to the river. I had to stay under the water, breathing through a hollow reed until they went to look elsewhere."

Zetian queried, "How did you end up here?"

"I assumed I was safe, but someone saw me come out of the river and raised the alarm."

Pai said, "You can't stay here, but I know where you can hide."

Zetian and Wararni waited for his directions.

"Malik has killed himself, so his house is haram. No one will enter. You can hide there."

Wararni frowned. "I follow the Prophet and cannot enter the home of a sinner."

Zetian patted her belly. "You will soon be a father. You must stay safe my love."

Wararni ran around the atrium, jumped, and clapped. "A father. A father. I will do it. I'll hide in the haram house." He hugged Zetian and said, "This is such a grand joke. They accused me of entering the hareem and now I hide in the haram house.

While Zetian made soup for the evening meal, she sang a song in the language of al-Qin.

Pai repeated the melody in his head. "That is a beautiful song. Where did you learn it?"

"My mother sang it to me when I was little."

"Is it a traditional song of al-Qin?"

Zetian stopped stirring the soup. "Oh no! Bai Juyi wrote this less than a century ago. He is one of the most famous poets of the Tang Dynasty. He wrote it when he was just sixteen."

She spoke the song and Pai appreciated the poem even though he didn't understand the al-Qin words.

"What is it about?" he asked.

"The grass. In al-Qin, there are vast prairies." She outstretched her arms and waved her hand to signify the tall grass waving in the breeze.

"Grass? Do many people of al-Qin write poems about grass?"

"You must learn more about poetry." She stirred the soup filling the atrium with the odors of garlic and onions.

"Please, teach me." If he knew more about poetry, he might be able to speak to Bhaja.

"Few poems about grass, but many about love. Even in this poem, the grass represents love."

Pai thought about Bhaja again.

"Let me translate part of this poem as best as I can, *The blades of grass are burnt but not destroyed by prairie fires. When spring winds blow, they bring it back to life.*"

Pai got excited. He understood. "Even though love might appear to die, it returns. Love is forever." Pai's dream made sense. The love of the lady in his dream had come back to life like the blades of grass destroyed by the prairie fires.

"Yes, Pai of Qurtuba. You have it." With that, she added a handful of rice to the soup and sang the song again.

He silently repeated the translation about grass over and over. One day he would recite it for Bhaja.

15. Gossip and Guilt

Bhaja was appalled at the sheer quantity of people and noise at the slave auction. She had always suspected it was a place she did not want to visit; in fact she had always avoided the whole area on the days when it was announced. Seeing all the commotion made her grateful all over again that Naomi had appeared at her door, and they'd had business with the abbey that had introduced her to Isador, so she had not needed to find a slave to do their work.

While she had known buying slaves at the market would be unpleasant, she had not pictured in her mind what the place would look like, and how people would act. She wanted to believe the best of her fellow Muslims, but.... Perhaps a good owner buying a person would relieve that one slave of the risk of a bad master—but she still did not think placing a person in even a good environment as a slave was going to be an uplifting act, *for either* the buyer or the slave.

It seemed especially hypocritical that most of these people, *good Muslims,* had just come from Friday prayers, as she and Tarub had.

The prayer talk that day had been about the Prophet's views of the nature of man and the admonition that Muslims "should help our fellow human beings." Had the imam been pointing at the slave market, and the treatment of slaves? Bhaja shivered.

The next batch of people to be sold included the two former concubines who had betrayed their Emir. Many people in the audience had inspected the women, even to the point of looking at their teeth and lifting their robes. It was horrible.

Even worse was the party atmosphere surrounding the square. Vendors hawked all sorts of gear, clothes, and materials. Bhaja shuddered when she saw whips being sold alongside translucent silks the vendor claimed were "love" robes.

Foods of all kinds were cooked and sold, giving the air a pungent mix of spice, meat, sweat, and fear, as the slaves huddled together in a pitiable group, even the concubines clinging together in fright.

Yet she and Tarub were there to acquire them, same as the other potential buyers. She gritted her teeth as the bidding began. The auctioneer knew his audience: he appealed to their greed as he announced the first young woman as being pregnant, two for the price of one.

Tarub at first bid modestly, giving a slight raise to her offer as the bidding went back and forth. Then she realized, with a muttered oath, that this was going to keep going, as the other buyers seemed to feel it was a sort of game. She named a fairly large jump in price for her next bid, and the other buyers went silent.

"Well, we have one of them," Tarub said *sotto voce*.

For some reason the auctioneer skipped the other concubine and went on to a very beautiful young Nerubian woman. Those that had bid against Tarub now bid heavily and rapidly, until only two were left, who vied against one another to what Bhaja thought was a ridiculous price. The auctioneer was the only one who was happy with that sale. Then he brought forward the other concubine.

"I hope she remembers what I said to her," Tarub said. Bhaja had not been there for such a conversation, so she raised her eyebrows, but Tarub did not explain.

As she was led to the selling platform, the woman stumbled, revealing a scar on the inside of the leg facing the audience. She had apparently managed to pull her skirts up so it was visible as she fell up the stairs.

"Good," Tarub said.

Bidding for this one was desultory, even though the young woman's pretty face and smooth skin were lovely. Apparently the buyers didn't like scars. Tarub managed to buy her for less than half what the first one had cost.

Unfortunately, Bhaja learned, they had to stay for the rest of the sales before their purchases were released to them.

She cried when she saw a family of four sold off to a hard-faced farmer. Those two children would know only a life of hard work and skimpy food, if the farmer's looks said anything. The law stated slaves must not be treated badly, but that law did not define what "treated well" meant.

After that sale, Bhaja closed her eyes, and tried to not listen to the auctioneer. She tried to remember a better place and time. She succeeded so far as dreaming of a slave market from long ago.

The people's skins were all a golden brown, no blacks, no stark and pale whites or pinks. The odors around the market were different as well, fewer meats, fewer spices. She caught the distinct scent of hot cinnamon tea and honey. Pai, though it was not really Pai, but still it was *him, was beside her.* Then she was jostled and awoke to the end of the Qurtuba slave sale. Tarub tugged her arm, heading to the pickup area.

Bhaja waited with Tarub among a swirl of people picking up their purchases, or just standing around gossiping. Bhaja saw a woman she knew from her work at the mosque and waved. The woman walked over and they shared greetings, then the lady murmured for Bhaja's ears alone, "Have you heard of Malik al Jamal's suicide?"

At Bhaja's nod, the woman went on, "Well I heard he was despondent because Lylah married Hathus, so he and Lylah could never get back together."

Someone else said over the woman's shoulder, "Malik was gone too long! Of course she married someone else!"

"That's why Hathus and Malik are always arguing," the woman's husband speculated. "A love triangle! The wrong man married Lylah!"

As if she had heard her name from across the crowded square, Lylah appeared, walking next to Hathus. Perhaps she had heard what people were saying, because after greeting Bhaja, the first thing she said was, "I am not unfaithful, Bhaja. You know me well enough to know that."

"Explain why Hathus was at Malik's house!"

"I saw him there, too! They were arguing!"

"Arguing about you, Lylah!"

"I once loved Malik, but that was long, long ago," Lylah said, eyes wide.

One of the gossiping women turned and faced Lylah directly. "Then why is there so much speculation that you love him now? Where there is smoke, there is fire!"

Lylah made a face. "Hathus is a good and kind husband. As many of you know, Malik al Jamal bargained with anyone who would deal with him, including many women he met on his travels." She shrugged. "Why should he marry, when he always had a free choice of lovers amongst the unwed ladies?"

This felt like a dig to Bhaja, herself an "unwed lady." Her temper got the better of her, and she snapped, "And you among them once upon a time!"

Lylah nodded, an odd expression crossing her face. "Yes, I loved Malik long ago, when I was still a child. He was a sweet boy, then. But after his parents sent him away—"

"To keep him away from you!" someone called.

"To toughen him up, he was a daisy!" someone else said.

Lylah ignored the interruptions, and went on, "—when he returned from al-Jazair, he was indeed a different man."

"That was what his parents had planned," Bhaja said, "wasn't it?"

"He was tougher, as they had hoped," Lylah said, as the gossipers quieted to listen, "but he wasn't more a man. He was perhaps a bit cruel, and I'm told by ladies who 'knew' him that he was rough. The army training ruined him," she said and shook her head.

"But why would he take his own life?" someone shouted, and many voices joined in asking that question in various ways.

"Everyone knows Malik al Jamal was a proud, selfish man. He would never kill himself!"

Lylah shook her head. "Maybe he felt guilty for killing Darras of Osuna," she offered.

"That's just gossip," one of the gossipers said. "That's not proven!"

"Well, *someone* killed Darras!" Bhaja said.

"I saw Malik yelling at the butcher's assistant!" They meant Raviv, Bhaja realized. Naomi's son. Was Naomi involved with Malik's death?

"Malik yelled at everyone, except the Emir!"

"The Emir had it done! He sent a soldier to kill Darras," someone in the crowd suggested.

"Yeah, maybe that soldier they're searching for. Warni, or whatever his name is."

"The Emir never liked Darras, he was a Malik man!" After saying this, the man ducked down out of sight, perhaps afraid the Emir's guards would hear him and identify someone speaking evil about their leader.

Ignoring Lylah's presence, the first woman repeated her theory, "I saw Hathus and Malik arguing. I think Hathus finally killed his rival!"

Having come full circle, Bhaja shook her head and tried to retreat from the gossips and their speculations. Tarub met her eyes and waved her over to where she had taken possession of the two former concubines.

"Help me get them to my villa," Tarub said to Bhaja and to her guards, who pressed a way through the crowds.

Bhaja felt mostly confused. Who killed Darras? Did Malik really kill himself? Was Hathus involved?

One thing was certain. There was some kind of tangle between Malik, Darras, Hathus, and Lylah.

Bhaja glanced up at the bright sun, wishing the gardener had had time to plant the big mesquite trees he had promised her, "for shade." She had also asked him for a *spinachristi,* which had medical uses as well as the shade it could provide, but he had been unsure if he could get one. In the interim, they'd had to sit in the sun.

Tarub had noticed. She had her servants install a tent-like pavilion, with a roof and loose cloth sides that could be pulled closed for privacy.

"Try it, and see if you like it. If you do, I will have a permanent one installed. Shade trees only provide shade for part of the day, even when they are big enough after years of growth," Tarub had said. "And more, a pavilion will also provide cover for rainy days."

When Bhaja had begun to protest, Tarub waved a hand. "No, I like your prohibition of food from the Library," she gave Bhaja a crooked smile. "This will help you enforce that rule. If people have a nice place to eat outdoors, they will sit there, not try to sneak their meals in with the books."

This time the 'they' sitting there was just herself and Pai.

"This is nice," Pai said of the shade the canvas awning gave them.

"Yes, so much better than being baked by the sun on these hot days of summer," Bhaja said.

Besides bringing food and quietly sitting to eat it with her, he had come on an errand, with something to discuss with her.

"Let's eat first, undistracted by the puzzles that have come into our lives," Bhaja suggested and he agreed. But then he immediately brought up weddings, and Wararni and Zetian.

"You have purchased the concubines? Or rather, Tarub did."

"Yes," Bhaja said.

"And they need to be married to their baby fathers, soon."

"Yes."

"Well, can we make a big wedding for them all?"

"You mean all together?"

"Yes," Pai said.

"That could be fun."

Pai nodded. "That's what I was thinking, too."

"But first we have to rescue Wararni."

"So, what's being done for him?"

Bhaja thought it through. If the Emir had indeed hired the guard Wararni to kill Darras—for some unclear reason—he doubtless would want to keep that a secret. Was that why the Emir's guards were so relentless in their chase of Wararni?

"Well, Tarub had the former concubines dictate statements and sign them, and last I heard those were to be delivered to the citadel for the Emir's consideration."

Pai nodded. "That is good."

"I'm sorry to say one of the fathers is one of the men I hired to guard us to and from Osuna: Chedar."

Pai's expression was disbelief tinged with amusement. "That man has more balls than brains," he muttered, then blushed deep red as he realized Bhaja had heard him.

"Indeed," she said.

"Did Chedar sire both babies?"

"Oh, no. The other was one of the supposed eunuch guards, who had visited Osora. Chedar's wife-to-be is Kaila."

"They will marry?"

"Tarub insists on it. They will work as housemaids at her villa, but will go home to their husbands each night."

"But how can a eunuch sire a child?"

"That is a very good question," Bhaja said, laughing. "Something went wrong with the surgery? It was never done?" She shrugged. "I'm certain the Emir is frantically checking all his eunuchs now, whatever else is going on. This man has quit the guards, obviously, but he was the one who allowed Chedar into the sanctum."

"The Emir should be after *him,* not Wararni."

"Yes. I hope the statements by Osora and Kaila will clear Wararni," Bhaja said. "Tarub has dared the Emir's ire by buying the concubines and freeing them, and now by hiring the men as guards for her household."

"Once your Wararni is cleared, I would like to focus on Darras's murder. We still think Malik must have killed himself, at least that is the ruling."

Pai nodded again. "Yes, I've made little progress on finding the killer of Darras, as yet." He cleared his throat. "But what do you think about the wedding?"

Bhaja rubbed her forehead. Pai was not usually so determined; the big wedding must be important to him. Or, more likely, to his Zetian. "I will think about it. Perhaps my mother would help; she loves planning parties."

"Would Tarub help?"

"Well, she might, but she has nothing to do with Wararni. It would feel wrong to just add him and Zetian to the other two couples."

"Please think about asking her about it; they are all three mixed up in this together, through no fault of Wararni. He was accused of what Chedar and the other man did with those ladies."

Bhaja smiled, realizing he was right. The concubines, who were now Tarub's housemaids and their lovers, had caused Wararni's problems. Her sponsor might be more amenable to a big wedding than she'd realized.

"We could have it here in the courtyard," Pai suggested.

Bhaja looked up to see his wide-eyed look as he assessed the courtyard as a venue. “I will see what Tarub has planned. It’s certain the Emir is not going to allow them to have the wedding ceremony in his gardens, as most Qurtuba couples do.”

On her way to visit Tarub, Bhaja ran into Javed, the mild judge’s brother. He was the one who had determined Malik’s suicide, which was now becoming more and more doubtful, to Bhaja’s thinking. Did he still hold to that belief?

She introduced herself politely to Javed after they gave each other formal greetings. “I think I might have information for you to consider, although I have not been able to verify all of it yet.”

“What information? About what?” Javed said, smoothing his mustache.

Bhaja bit her lip. Maybe she should have talked to Hathus directly before carrying what amounted to gossip to Javed.

“Well?” Javed said, a stern tone in his voice.

Bhaja decided to begin with the one fact that even Lylah had verified. “Malik al Jamal and Hathus min Alshamal contended with one another even as children, did you know?”

Javed sniffed. “I might have heard something about that. But that was long ago.”

“It was, but their rivalry continued more recently after Malik returned from al-Jazair.”

One slightly graying eyebrow lifted. “Indeed?”

“And many Qurtuban citizens have heard the two of them arguing.”

“Yes?” He seemed quite interested, now.

“The two men both courted Lylah, and Malik was upset that Lylah married Hathus.”

“So...Hathus min Alshamal might have murdered Malik?”

“I was wondering if that was worth considering.”

Javed smiled a crooked smile. “I thank you for this information, Bhaja of the Library,” he said.

Bhaja rather liked that title. She smiled at him and then they walked their separate ways.

16. Wash and Where

The pirates were in retreat, scrambling for their boats. *Bhaja speared the captain's leg and her squad swarmed over the fallen commander. The battle would have been over, except a rogue wave knocked everyone onto the sand. In the watery chaos, the pirates captured Bhaja. Pai didn't hesitate. He rode his bull into the pack of brigands and carried Bhaja to safety.*

"Bhaja, I've got you!" Pai assured his pillow.

"Are you dreaming?" Zetian asked.

He looked around the atrium. *No beach. No pirates. No bulls.* "Yes, just a dream."

He had slept late. Zetian had already prepared a breakfast of melon, bread, and tea. Wet clothes from the spilled kettle that had saved Wararni were everywhere. She rinsed each piece in warm water, wrang it out, and hung it wherever she could find space.

"Thank you for washing those muddy rags. Do you need any help?"

"I can take care of it." She examined a pair of worn-out pants and rubbed the material between two fingers and threw the garment into the tub to be washed again. "I was the one who decided to dump everything onto the dirt floor."

"Yes. That was very clever. You distracted the guards. Wararni owes his freedom to you." She tossed another clean robe back onto the pile of dirty ones.

"Are you sure you have to wash those things again?"

"When I taught you how to make fine paper, I emphasized the importance of clean fibers. Even a little grit will spoil the page."

"I recall. I'm happy to be making fine paper like they do in al-Qin."

She smiled. "And I'm pleased to not be in the Emir's hareem."

While Pai swept the mosaic floor in the shop, he sensed something was amiss. Zetian wasn't singing.

"Is something wrong?" he questioned.

She dropped a pile of dirty laundry into a kettle of warm water. "I'm thinking about Wararni," she said while stirring the pot. "Malik's house is so far away. Sometimes Wararni is too brave. He doesn't take care of himself."

She studied a freshly rinsed robe before hanging it over an empty kettle to dry. "Pai, don't you worry about your friend Sayyida alone with her brother's corpse?"

"I'm going to Malik's house to assist Sayyida with her brother's funeral." Pai answered and added, "I'll also check that Wararni is safe. I'll make sure everyone is all right."

Zetian brightened. "Good! You can go as soon as I pack a breakfast for him. I'm sure he is hungry."

Pai walked through the familiar streets of the medina, happy to be in Qurtuba. Even though he'd had many friends with him, he'd found Osuna to be foreign. He understood why few people traveled. Familiar places comforted him. He didn't fear getting lost. He knew where to find—a warm feeling enclosed him—anything he needed. He saw no reason to return to Osuna and couldn't imagine ever leaving al-Andalus. He wondered why Darras and Malik had roamed so far and so often.

He looked at the sack Zetian had prepared and thought of the crowd that had visited the villa in Osuna. Many people had collected to share fond remembrances of Darras and eat. Pai imagined a similar crowd at Malik's villa. Malik was a more important person in Qurtuba than Darras was in Osuna. The food Zetian had prepared wouldn't be sufficient.

He went to the souk and looked for something that could be eaten today or saved for later. Also, something that didn't need preparation. He scanned the different offerings: raisins, cherries, carrots, and more. There were so many choices. *It's good to live in Qurtuba.* He couldn't decide until he spied the fresh fruit lady from Ronda. "Peace be with you."

"And with you also, Pai," she responded smiling at his familiar face.

"What brings you all the way to Qurtuba?"

"The harvest was bountiful." She patted her donkey. "We had too much to sell in Ronda." She pointed to three large stacks of apples in front of her.

Pai selected the smallest stack. "I'd like to buy all these." He handed her a gold dinar.

She gave him a questioning look, as if to say, *I don't see any servants with you. What will you do with all those apples?*

He looked at her donkey. "Could you deliver them to Malik al Jamal's home?"

"My grandson is running around the market enjoying all the exciting sights and sounds. I will get him and the donkey to take the apples to you."

He gave her a handful of copper coins. "Thank you. You can give these to your grandson."

Pai exited the souk pleased that he'd purchased enough food until he smelled roasting chicken. *Chicken would go well with the apples.* The savory aroma came from the kosher butcher. *Isn't the shop closed for the Jewish holy day?* The mouth-watering odors drew him to investigate.

Inside the kosher shop, he found a Muslim woman standing over a large brazier. He greeted her and wondered aloud, "I expected the shop to be closed."

"I am not Jewish. The butcher started the fire and prepared the chickens before sunset. I stay here until the next sunset."

Pai wondered aloud, "Isn't that a long time to be awake?"

She laughed. "We closed the shop so I could sleep until morning prayers." She took a knife and pierced several pieces filling the air with a delicious scent. "Would you care to purchase something?" She helpfully added, "They are also halal for our Muslim customers."

Pai's mouth watered. "Do you have someone who can deliver them? I am going to Malik al Jamal's house."

She backed away from Pai. "His house is haram, and I am the only one here."

"What about that boy the butcher recently hired?"

The woman frowned. "Raviv? No. Never. He's Jewish. And even if he wasn't observing his holy day, he's afraid of Malik. I've heard him talk."

"I'm not going to leave without some tasty chicken." Pai held open the sack that Zetian had given him to carry Wararni's breakfast. "Do you think you can fit two in here?"

Using a rag to protect her fingers, she stuffed the hot meat atop whatever Zetian had prepared.

"Thank you." Pai handed her two silver coins.

Holding the hot, greasy sack away from his robe, he took the short walk to Malik's lane.

Pai had expected a crowd at Malik's house like at the Osuna villa for Darras's funeral, but the path through the exclusive neighborhood was deserted. Pai entered through the open door. The stench of death overpowered the roasted chicken. He looked around the reception room. Little had changed since yesterday. The tea sat on the brazier, but the fire had gone out and the tea no longer steamed. The melon had turned soft and brown. His basket of dates sat untouched.

He walked into the pantry. The two servants were reading the Quran. He respectfully interrupted them. "As-Salaam-Alaikum."

They jumped up, "Wa-Alaikum-Assalaam."

Pai passed the sack of food to the woman.

She took it and turned to the young boy. "Go find Sayyida. Tell her we have a visitor."

Pai didn't want to stay near Malik's body, so he followed the boy into the atrium where the air was fresher. The boy went to the sleeping rooms in the back.

Shortly, the boy returned with Sayyida. "I am so glad to see you," she exclaimed. "I have something to show you."

Before Pai replied, Wararni also appeared in the atrium. "Good morning Pai! I am hiding here just like you told me."

"No, you're not!" Pai corrected. "You're in the atrium where anyone can see you."

Wararni looked offended. "I checked before I came out." He looked down at his feet like a remorseful child.

"There's food. Zetian packed something just for you."

Wararni cheered up at the mention of Zetian's name.

"Get something to eat and hide yourself."

Wararni ran into the pantry and returned with both hands full of chicken, bread, a bitter orange, a long carrot, and some raisins. He again reminded Pai of a child, but a joyous one this time.

Pai followed Sayyida to her brother's body, neatly wrapped in a white shroud. She fumed, "He should have been buried by now, except for that awful pronouncement by Javed."

Pai nodded. "The Ronda fruit lady's grandson will be here soon with his donkey. Would you like us to carry your brother outside the city wall for burial?" He expected her to be happy with this. Instead, the idea just irritated her.

"Don't make any more suggestions until you see what I have to show you!" was her indignant response.

He pursed his lips and waited.

She gently unwrapped the shroud. "Malik will go to the mosque for a proper burial service."

Pai had so many questions, but after her sharp warning, he remained silent.

"Look at this." She opened the shroud and pointed to a deep stab wound in the middle of her brother's chest. Since Malik had been washed, the red slit was conspicuous among his chest hairs. Pai could easily have fit a gold dinar in the opening. He whispered, "So, not suicide."

Sayyida echoed his conclusion with force and anger. "I told Javed my brother wouldn't kill himself. I told him!"

Pai scanned the part of Malik's body Sayyida had uncovered. He was surprised to see the scars. "Your brother has been in many fights. He had a difficult life."

Sayyida softened. "It seems that you're right. I had no idea."

Pai lightly touched her hand to acknowledge her gentler tone.

To his disappointment, he saw Wararni lurking in the atrium. "Wararni! Why are you out here?"

The Emir's shamed guard didn't make any excuses this time. He retreated to a sleeping room.

Sayyida angrily snapped the shroud and rewrapped her brother. "Javed won't change his decision whatever I tell him. I've met men like him before. They don't listen to women."

"I'll make him reconsider," Pai assured her, recognizing the truth in her complaint.

"Not Javed! He'll never revise anything, and even if we could get Judge Javan involved, he'll always support his idiot brother."

"We could get Abbas," Pai offered.

"Abbas would agree that it wasn't suicide, but he wouldn't fight Javed or go to the Emir."

"You're right, but I will find a way."

Sayyida challenged, "How will you do it?"

Pai couldn't answer that question. "I'll go talk to Javed. I'm sure I'll think of something."

As Pai went to find Javed, something poked into his chest. *The knife!* He still had the knife he'd picked up yesterday and hidden in his secret pocket. *This wasn't just a strange knife anymore. It was a murder weapon! Why hadn't he noticed it when he'd put on his robe this morning?* He tucked it into his belt.

The guards made Pai wait outside when they went to summon Javed. While he waited, he made some rules. *Do not irritate Javed. Do not mention Sayyida.*

When Javed appeared, Pai treated him with more respect than he deserved. Pai bowed and placed his palms against his knees. "As-Salaam-Alaikum."

Javed did not reply. He just harrumphed.

Pai continued his campaign to placate Javan's idiot brother. "I noticed something that confused me. Could you please take a look so I may benefit from your wisdom and knowledge?"

Javed relaxed. "Let's see what you've found."

Pai kept a stone face while thinking, *I have him.* "I don't have it here. We have to return to Malik's house."

Javed grumbled. "Can't you figure this out yourself? I don't want to enter the haram house."

Pai bowed again. "This is a mystery to me. I need your experience and intelligence."

Javed marched out the door followed by two guards. "Hurry. I am a busy man."

Pai ran ahead of the procession with a big smile. When he entered Malik's house, he saw Sayyida standing at her brother's side, arms crossed over her chest and scowling.

He signaled her to leave the room.

She shook her head, "No."

Javed and his two guards pushed the door open and Pai signaled with more urgency. He breathed a sigh when she ran for the atrium.

"Welcome Javed," Pai said with yet another bow. "Look at this, so unexpected and hidden." Pai moved the shroud with exaggerated difficulty. "What do you think this is?" He pointed to the obviously fatal wound.

Javed played his part in this face-saving act. He made sounds of thinking and walked around the corpse to view it from different angles. "That is strange. It looks like he was stabbed after he slit his wrists."

Pai could hear Sayyida gasping in the atrium and hoped she would stay out of sight.

Javed finally proclaimed. "Malik al Jamal unsuccessfully attempted suicide and then someone murdered him. He can be taken to the mosque."

Pai didn't argue with this crazy explanation and waited to see if the pompous fool would make any further pronouncements. As Pai expected, Javed took charge. He turned to his guards. "Go back to the sleeping rooms and bring a pallet to carry Malik al Jamal to the Mosque."

Oh no, Pai feared they'd find Wararni.

Before the men could go off on their mission, Sayyida entered and feigned surprise. "Oh, Javed. I didn't realize you were here." Pai suspected she was stalling to give Wararni time to hide. She greeted Javed as an honored guest.

Javed smiled.

She opened her eyes wide and asked, "Is there anything I can do to assist you?"

"Yes, we are taking Malik al Jamal to the mosque. We need a pallet to transport him. Can you fetch one for us?"

Pai noticed that he hadn't asked her permission to take her brother, but hoped she'd leave well enough alone. She didn't immediately reply, confirming Pai's suspicion of her displeasure.

At that point, Wararni walked into the room carrying a narrow bed. He looked at Sayyida, "I brought this for you." Pai could tell from her eyes, that she was surprised to see Wararni. Wararni looked startled like he didn't expect to see so many people. When he saw the guards, he froze with his mouth ajar.

Pai felt like time had stopped. *Why couldn't Wararni have obeyed and stayed out of sight?* Everything happened at once.

Javed stared at Wararni, blinked, and shouted, "Get him!"

Malik's servants gasped as they watched the conflict from their hideout in the pantry. Sayyida joined them.

The guards ran for Wararni.

Wararni threw the bed at them.

The guards tripped over the bed with a crash.

Wararni ran.

The guards got up, unsheathed their swords, and pursued the fugitive.

Pai, Sayyida, and Javed all stared as the three fighters wrestled.

When time resumed, Pai saw Wararni tied and in custody.

Javed stood at the door. "We will take Wararni to the barracks. The captain already has orders for his punishment, signed by the Emir. Someone will return to transport Malik al Jamal to the mosque."

Pai looked on in disbelief. He'd promised Zetian he'd protect Wararni. What was he going to tell her now? At least, Malik would get a proper burial and Sayyida was happy.

Pai joined Sayyida and waited outside, away from the stench of death. He asked, "Do you think he believes that your brother tried to commit suicide?"

"Of course not, but those men never admit when they are wrong."

"What men?" Pai asked.

Sayyida scoffed, "All men, but especially those with power, from the citadel or the mosque."

"I try to admit when I am wrong." He thought for someone else to include. "Abbas ibn Firnas is a scientist. They always admit when they are wrong. Being wrong makes scientists happy."

She scoffed. "That is why neither of you will ever have a position of power." Another harrumph. "You're a shopkeeper and always will be."

Being a shopkeeper is not bad, Pai decided. Before he could respond to Sayyida, Javed appeared. Pai whispered, "He returned quickly. Let's try not to offend him."

Sayyida opened the door. "I had better say goodbye to my brother before he's taken away." She disappeared inside the house.

Pai deplored the way women were ignored. He took out the murder weapon for a closer examination. It had some strange writing on the handle. The inscription had to be an important clue to the murderer. He didn't show it to Javed. He'd give it to Bhaja because she'd recognize the writing.

Javed waited outside in the fresh air while his servants went to fetch the body. Pai turned to him and said, "Hathus min Alshamal murdered Malik al Jamal."

Javed gave Pai a sly smile. "Tell me, my son, what makes you say that?"

The jovial tone was suspicious, but Pai didn't let that deter him. "Every time someone mentioned Malik, Hathus got angry."

Javed's voice changed like he was talking to a small child. "Really? Is that enough to accuse someone of murder?"

Pai bit his tongue. *You accused Malik of suicide on much less.*

Javed chided him, "You know, young Pai, you sound like Hathus during his testimony yesterday. You should be careful. You don't want to sound like him."

Pai surmised that Javed knew more than he was saying. "What do *you* think?"

Javed puffed out his chest and clasped his hands behind his back. "When you have an important position as I do—"

Pai held his breath to avoid laughing. *You have no position. You're not even a shopkeeper. If you weren't the judge's brother, you'd be nobody.*

"—you'd realize how important it was not to jump to conclusions. You and Hathus made the same mistake."

Javed paused and stroked his beard imitating the wise men in the mosque.

"Yesterday I did my own investigation. Hathus has been charged with murder and is in custody. That is how responsible people behave."

"Hathus has been arrested?" Pai gasped.

"I just told you he was."

Pai hadn't been as clever with Javed as he thought. Javed already had changed his mind about the suicide. *Being lucky is as good as being smart.*

Pai congratulated Javed on his *investigation* while marveling how someone so incompetent had managed to do the right thing and be so smug about it. *Surely someone smarter must have pointed him in the correct direction.*

The moment Javed and Malik's body disappeared around the corner, Pai turned to Sayyida, "Bhaja and Tarub are meeting with the Emir. I must tell them of Wararni's capture."

Pai took off at top speed, his robes flapping behind him. His memory of the medina map guided him. He ran down the narrow paths, turning each time his route approached the main streets avoiding the most popular lanes until he was certain he'd passed Javed and his men hauling the pallet containing Malik's corpse. Then he sprinted the final approach to the citadel where he found Bhaja and Tarub and informed them of Wararni's capture and imminent punishment

Following Saturday afternoon prayers Pai left Bhaja and Traub to clear Wararni's name. He exited the medina through the river gate and walked downstream to the barracks. Two guards, both in leather armor and armed with swords and shields, protected the entrance.

"I am here for Wararni."

"Why would anyone want to visit that disgraced and condemned scoundrel?" the dark-haired guard asked with a laugh.

"I am his friend."

The redheaded guard mocked Pai, "I didn't think he had any friends."

The other guard added, "You know that nobody liked him?"

Pai had had enough. He stepped closer to the two men ignoring that they were a head taller than he was. "He is condemned and allowed a friend. Move aside."

Pai's chest pounded and he found it difficult to breathe, but his gamble worked. They moved apart and let him enter.

This was Pai's first visit to the barracks. He looked around like he was preparing to create a map. To his right were several long buildings. *Sleeping quarters.* To his left, overlooking the wall with a view of the river, was a two-story building. *Captain's residence.*

Ahead of him, a column of men marched in pairs, all wearing similar white robes and embroidered caps. The men on the left had leather baldrics over their right shoulders holding a short sword on their left. The men on the other side were reflections like from a lake on a calm day.

Pai had heard that the hareem guards were hired to be half right-handed and half left-handed to be better prepared for any intruder. This was the first time he'd seen that for himself.

They marched into a large building. *That's it. That's where Wararni would receive his punishment.* He followed them in.

The men lined up facing the front of the hall.

Seated, facing them, was Wararni. His arms and legs were bound to a chair, and a small shroud covered his lap. Pai had shown up to support his friend. Wararni's eyes brightened when he spied Pai. Pai waved and Wararni raised a finger in response. Pai reflected that even though he was just a shopkeeper, he could still be a friend. Everyone needed friends.

On the right was a doctor equipped with bandages and healing balms. In front of the doctor was a small brazier with red hot coals and three metal cauterizing tools.

On the left was a man wearing a black keffiyeh and robes with a small knife that he was sharpening with a grey stone.

The three figures left no question as to what would happen this afternoon.

Pai was the only extra person in the room.

Soon the Captain entered. "As-Salaam-Alaikum," he greeted the assembly.

The guards in formation answered with a single voice, "Wa-Alaikum-Assalaam."

"You are here today to witness the penalty for violating the hareem."

The guards stood motionless. Bhaja and Tarub were getting a ruling to save Wararni. But where were they? Pai crossed himself and said a small prayer for a miracle to save Zetian's fiancé.

"One last detail. Is anyone willing to offer mercy for your compatriot?"

Pai examined the formation. Not a single person budged. If Pai had questioned Wararni's story of the guards' dislike for him, this final act of cruelty proved its veracity.

Pai couldn't save Wararni, but he could offer mercy. He'd never performed the mercy maneuver, but if none of the experienced guards would do it, he would.

The Captain asked again, “You all worked together. Is anyone willing to offer mercy?”

The response was the same.

Pai looked back to the entrance, willing Bhaja to appear, but the door didn’t move. He spoke up, “I will do it.”

The Captain nodded and Pai took his place behind Wararni. He’d seen this done before, but never attempted it himself.

He moved slowly, flicking his eyes up to check the entrance, but Bhaja did not appear. He put his injured arm around Wararni’s neck and used it to grab his good arm. With his good hand, he pushed Wararni’s head forward. Wararni choked and Pai dropped his arms.

He backed away, fearing he’d done it wrong.

Wararni shouted. “That was fine. Don’t stop. Please. Do it!”

Pai wrapped his arms again around Wararni’s neck and pushed. When Wararni choked, he kept pushing. Soon Wararni went limp.

The guards applauded Pai’s successful effort.

The man dressed in black removed the shroud with his sharpened knife. The crowd when silent when he delicately raised Wararni’s limp member to uncover the part of Wararni’s anatomy destined for removal.

17. SENTENCE OR SOLACE

It was the Muslim holy day, Friday. Tarub threw down the note and cursed to the point that even the lady's usual companions were embarrassed. Bhaja pulled out her small bag of coins to pay the messenger, but Tarub waved her off and handed the now-blushing young man a coin.

"Tell the Judge we will appear as commanded," Tarub said. The young man left, already running as he exited the villa's courtyard gate.

"Is this a ploy by the Emir to get his hands on the ladies and guards?" the older of Tarub's ladies wondered.

"That is what worries me." She looked at Bhaja. "Your brother has training as a guard, doesn't he?" At Bhaja's confused nod, Tarub grinned. It was not a nice grin. "Can you please ask him to come quickly, along with any guard-trained men who have *never* been Emir's guards? I want to have plenty of neutral assistance, in case the Emir has some plan to seize what belongs to me."

Bhaja thought it might be prudent to offer those men some incentive. "Lady, can I encourage them with a generous—"

Tarub interrupted her with a wave of her heavily-jeweled hand. For a moment, Bhaja wondered how much all those rings weighed; Tarub wore two or three on each finger. Tarub said, "Give this to Yusuf and tell him there will be one for each man he brings!"

Bhaja stood frozen a moment. Tarub held out a small gold coin. It was small, but it was *gold!* She reached out and took the coin. "I will do so," she said.

"Please let him know this could be dangerous. The Emir's pride has been badly damaged. If he and his men attempt to seize my people, we will fight."

Raising her gaze from the coin to Tarub's face, Bhaja nodded. "I will tell him. Anything else?"

Tarub's teeth worried her lips as she thought. "You have a good scribe working at the Library, not Naomi, the Christian man from the Abbey?"

Bhaja knew she had introduced him to Tarub, but then, the woman probably met many low-level workers. Why would she remember all their names? "Isador, yes," she said.

"Please bring him along as well, to record for us exactly what the Emir's judge does and says, and what reaction, if any, the Emir has.

This just looks too much like a trap, and I want to be prepared. If I have to spread news of the Emir seizing private property or freed slaves because of his own personal grudge, I want an exact record of how and when this happened to share with the people of Qurtuba."

Bhaja saw the older of Tarub's two ladies lean over and whisper in Tarub's ear.

"Yes," Tarub said. She looked at Bhaja. "Please also bring Pai and anyone he can think of who can testify as to Wararni's innocence in the matter. I wish we had already had the ceremony to wed these two couples, but I will announce that they will be married on Sunday."

A perfect opportunity, Bhaja thought. "I wished to ask if Zetian and Wararni might join the wedding."

Tarub grimaced. "That's going to complicate things. I can't hold the wedding here, if a free man and his slave wife are going to join the ceremony. Plus, there's no place big enough unless we have it in the central square. Or...possibly...the old abbey. Yet another reason to bring your Isador along."

"Pai suggested having the wedding in the Library courtyard. It's big enough and quite lovely."

"Hmm. Let me consider that. It does have the distinction of being part of my Library, without being my home."

"And Pai was thinking he needed to free Zetian, as long as she promises to stay in Qurtuba and work in his shop."

"I'm not so sure that is a good idea." Tarub scowled. "She could decide to give the secret of paper to others, and Pai and I both would lose a great income." She shook her head. "No, he cannot do that, in any event. He does not own her; I do."

"If we can save Wararni, she would be forever grateful. He is the father of her child, and they do love one another very much."

Tarub sighed. "Let us get Wararni free before we think about weddings and freeing slaves," she said.

Saturday morning, Bhaja dressed carefully in nice but plain robes, braided her hair, and pinned it to her head like a circlet, then covered it with a plain white—*and innocent*—headscarf.

Tarub had asked that none of the group try to appear over-dressed, simply clean and plain. She wanted them all to use their best manners, to do everything properly, but not to abase themselves before the Emir. They were ordinary citizens of Qurtuba, and needed to behave accordingly.

Bhaja went by the Library and picked up Isador while Yusuf went to pick up the other men he had hired. Meanwhile, Tarub planned to arrive at the citadel with four of her own house guards, the two couples who would testify, and an old man that Bhaja remembered had once been an Emir's judge. Not the current Emir, of course, but his father the second Emir Abd al Rahman, who had wed Tarub. This old man was their own legal expert, who would ensure Emir Muhammad's judge closely followed the Law.

The Emir was not beyond stretching the meaning and administration of the Law to suit himself and his purposes, but his judge should not be so swayed.

Osora and Kaila, Chedar and the not-eunuch along with Tarub and her entourage were waiting on the citadel steps as Bhaja arrived with Isador, and Yusuf came from the other direction with four other men.

All of Yusuf's group were well-armed; some wore leather armor, and one even had a chain shirt, in the manner of the Gauls. The group bristled with spears and swords. One had a bow, another a shield and hammer. They looked quite intimidating to Bhaja, but would the Emir find them a threat? Together with Tarub's four men, they made only nine warriors against the two dozen the Emir could field, if he chose.

But that wasn't the point, Bhaja realized. Tarub was making a statement: she was warning the Emir she had right on her side and was not afraid to stand behind that claim. But Bhaja did also wonder if the *judge's* opinion would be at all swayed by any of this display. He would read a different message from the arrival of the well-armed group than the Emir would, that seemed certain. And dangerous. It was not the Emir's decision they needed to fear, it was the judge's.

They entered the citadel.

The judge that Emir Muhammad had appointed to this task was Kabos, of course. The judge who interpreted Islamic Law in the most conservative, strict manner, and who dispensed sentences that verged on cruel, to the minds of many of Qurtuba's citizens.

The Emir began by claiming his right to castrate Chedar, and the former "eunuch" guard, and also Wararni, for violating the sanctity of the hareem.

Tarub's judge countered, "Since they no longer work at the citadel, the Emir has no hold on them; they are her employees, now and thus no longer can do any damage to the hareem.

Surprising everyone, Kabos concurred with this. "It is the Law," he said.

Of course, Emir Muhammad scowled. He might have just lost his chance for vengeance against Chedar and the not-eunuch and the former concubines.

Next to Bhaja, Isador wrote furiously on page after page of Pai's fine paper. Isador had brought a kind of portable writing table that hung from his lean shoulders with one edge braced against his waist. It made a firm enough surface for him to keep writing the record, but the whole thing was rather awkward, and Bhaja had not left enough room between herself and Isador on the bench. She kept being poked, alternatively by the writing table or by Isador's elbow.

There was a short silence while the Emir's own scribe wrote as quickly as Isador did.

Bhaja took advantage of the short break to stand up, earning the Emir's glare. "Wararni has never violated the hareem. His case should be considered separately."

"It will be, when he is apprehended." the Emir said. He turned and addressed Chedar, the not-eunuch, Osora, and Kaila. "You are in the service of Tarub. You no longer have any business with me or this citadel. If any of the four of you set foot here ever again, for any reason, I shall have you beheaded. Is that clear?"

Bhaja felt everyone relax. Despite the death sentence, it was a good outcome. It should be easy for the four to avoid going to the citadel, they merely had to obey the law. Bhaja was less certain Chedar would be able to hold to this than the others would, but it seemed he had no choice. He was going to be married soon, and he must become more dependable or face Tarub's wrath or the Emir's doom.

They weren't finished yet, though.

Now Kabos spoke, "However, in the matter of Wararni, the circumstances and application of the law are different." He held up a page upon which he had written several sentences. Bhaja was just a little too far away to read them, but Kabos explained what was written. "At the time of the breach of the hareem, Wararni was a member of the Emir's guard, and still is, though he has been banned from the citadel."

"He had nothing to do with this," Tarub spoke for the first time. Bhaja was a little surprised she had spoken for Wararni, who was not one of her employees. She had expected Tarub to say nothing about Wararni, only to protect her own four miscreants. But of course, someone had to introduce the testimony of those four about Wararni's non-involvement.

There was a great deal of back and forth between Tarub's judge and Kabos, with quotations from the Quran, the hadiths, and previous judgments, with regard for who could testify, and whether that testimony could implicate themselves or not. Because, of course, by stating Wararni had not broken the sanctity of the hareem, they had to admit that Chedar and the not-eunuch had.

This brought up the Emir's ire again.

Then Bhaja heard the creak of the great hall's door. She turned and saw Pai was looking into the room through the partially opened door.

Finally Kabos stood up. The room went silent. The Emir remained seated, but raised one eyebrow, looking at his judge.

"I will consider this matter of Wararni, and the full applications of the Law to the matter of the testimony of these former slaves and employees of the Emir," Kabos said.

Pai pushed the door completely open and rushed into the great hall, panting and out of breath. "Wararni has been found and arrested, and has been taken to the barracks for punishment. Please we must clear him before an innocent man is punished beyond all repair." He found where the others were sitting and squeezed himself down between Bhaja and Isador, who stood up and moved back against the wall. Bhaja supposed that was better, now Isador had all the room he needed to carry his table and record events. She grasped Pai's hand and squeezed it.

Tarub's judge had risen and gone to Kabos's side. The two men spoke together in low voices; the Emir eyed them with growing impatience, if his expression told the truth of his feelings.

At last the two judges sat down. Just as the Emir was about to speak, Pai jumped to his feet and gave a short bow of respect. "Wararni's punishment is scheduled for this afternoon. May we have a delay until Judge Kabos has finished his interpretation?" he asked.

"No," the Emir said.

Kabos looked at him, but did not contradict.

This did not seem promising. *Please write fast!* Bhaja thought at Kabos.

Then she bowed her head and thought of the Emir. *Please do not punish the wrong person just because you have been cheated of your revenge against those who insulted you*, she mentally "sent" to the Emir, as if her thoughts could have any effect upon the actions of either man at all.

"We are finished, here," the Emir said. He stood up, turned, and exited the great hall through the small door behind his table.

“I think we should sit inside the citadel until Kabos is finished,” Pai said.

“I will definitely go back and wait by his door,” Bhaja said. “But first, we must sustain ourselves.”

“There is something I need to tell you,” Pai announced. “Not about all this,” he waved a hand, “but about Malik.”

“First, we eat,” Bhaja said. “I did not have time for breakfast, and I will not be able to hear Kabos’s pronouncement over the growling of my stomach.”

Pai laughed; it was strained but at least he had heard her and reacted. That was better than the strange, cold silence that he had borne the last few times she had met with him.

They walked out of the citadel, toward the food vendors on the main road that went past the Library. “Curry or skewers?” Pai asked.

“Skewers,” Bhaja said. “The old man’s curries are just too hot for my taste.”

Pai nodded.

“While you get lunch, I will go in and speak to Isador,” Bhaja said. The man had practically raced back to the Library by himself, to have time and quiet to finish writing his record of events as Tarub had asked.

“He will probably be hungry also. I will get enough for everyone.”

“Thank you,” she said.

When they finished eating and had washed up, Pai reached under his robes to get something from his belt.

Bhaja’s heart stopped for a moment, but then Pai withdrew a knife. The handle was polished wood, the blade a hand’s width in length. “From Malik’s house. I think it must be the murder knife, since Malik would have nothing like this,” he said. “Can you read the writing, here?” He showed her some Hebrew lettering that had been carved into the handle.

“I’m not fluent in Hebrew writing, but I do know those symbols. It means kosher.”

Pai met her eyes. “Perhaps we should show it to Naomi?”

Bhaja licked her lips. “I hate to think she or her son is involved in this, but it doesn’t seem like Ezra the butcher would have anything to do with Malik beyond selling him meat, so I doubt the knife would be his.”

Pai rushed off. “Please try to clear Wararni before it is too late. I will do my best to delay his punishment.”

Bhaja sighed. “It’s in Kabos’s hands. Insha'Allah.” She knew Pai was anxious for Zetian’s fiancé but rushing the judge would only damage Wararni’s chances.

After Pai had gone off, Bhaja entered the Library, washed up and said mid-day prayers.

Then she showed Naomi the knife.

“Is this yours?” she asked bluntly.

Naomi looked at it, but shook her head. “It is not mine. I use the widow’s knife, which has a different handle style,” she shook her head again. “I don’t recognize that one.”

Bhaja tended to believe Naomi. After all, the woman had been with her at Tarub’s villa during that stormy night when Malik was murdered. She could not have done it.

Hathus still seemed a likely suspect and Javed had arrested him for the deed. But Bhaja was not so sure about Raviv. This knife made Ezra a suspect as well, unless he had proof he had been somewhere else that night, because she was fairly certain this must be one of his knives. But what reason would Ezra have to murder the man? Even Lylah might be a suspect, perhaps planting the knife to divert suspicion away from herself.

Bhaja decided to say nothing of the knife, because it pointed in too many directions, raising too many possibilities to make a judgment about.

Indeed, she had more pressing business, to go and make her presence known to Kabos, that she was waiting for the papers to clear Zetian’s paramour.

Taking far more time than Bhaja found believable, Kabos wrote out his judgment to clear Wararni. She had sat and watched him for a long time, now. Afternoon prayers had come and gone long since.

Bhaja wanted to go in and grab the judge’s hand and push it along. What could be taking so long?

She knew somewhere in the barracks complex, Wararni was being prepared for castration. She could only stop it with the judgment, *this* judgment that Kabos was so carefully taking his time on.

It began to look to her like the Emir wanted his revenge in some way, any way at all, even though he knew Wararni was innocent of all the charges. She wondered if perhaps the Emir had told Kabos to stall until it was too late.

Perhaps this was his way at getting back at Tarub, not realizing Tarub didn't care about the man, that he was Bhaja and Pai's friend —and problem. Hurting Wararni would not hurt Tarub, though Bhaja knew the woman well enough by now to know she would be disturbed by this childish vengeance scheme, if scheme it was.

Finally she stood up and walked from the waiting area at the side of the office toward Judge Kabos's desk. An alarmed servant made as if to cut her off, but her scowl overwhelmed the woman's determination to stop her.

She walked until she had to stop at the desk.

Judge Kabos looked up, pen in hand, surrounded by papers.

"What is it?"

"You know what it is. Why the delay in writing a simple judgment? Are you and the Emir determined to see an innocent man harmed?"

Kabos actually looked alarmed. "What would make you say that?"

"His punishment—you know, the castration that was set as his punishment, even though he is innocent—was scheduled for some time this afternoon. You are stalling."

"No, no," he said. "No. This is actually complicated and required some research."

"Sir, I do not mean to overstep my position, but you should know the consequences if Wararni is castrated. He and his wife-to-be will most likely run away from Qurtuba, if this is how they can expect to be treated here." She swallowed and cleared her throat. "That will be the end of the production of the fine paper you are so profligately using. Is that your true desire?"

A deep frown wrinkled Kabos's forehead. "This paper is from Pai of Qurtuba's shop. How is this affected by Wararni the guard?"

"Paper from Pai's shop is made by the woman Zetian. Zetian and Wararni are engaged to be married. The ceremony is scheduled for Sunday, with the others. How do you think that's going to go, if Wararni's sentence is carried out? What do you think I and many others will say if an *innocent man* is treated this way?"

She paused to take a deep breath, assessing his stubbornness in the matter. She said in a loud, steady voice: "Here is what I think: I think the citadel will have no more fine paper, and the Emir will have no more men who want to be guards. His hareem and household will have to be protected by slaves, because no whole, free man would dare to come work here after this."

Kabos's frown deepened with every sentence that Bhaja said.

She still did not know if the Emir had directed Kabos to stall, but her words had definitely made an impact. Kabos yelled for a servant, who ran over; the judge then directed the man to keep his quills filled with ink.

Then Kabos set back to work writing furiously, reaching periodically for a filled and ready quill, and before his candle lamp burned even a small finger-width, he blotted the last paper he had written on with a felted wool pad, stacked the several pages neatly, and placed the stack into a folio.

Handing the folio to Bhaja he said, "Guard Leto! Take this woman to the barracks, to the physician's judgment room, *immediately!*"

But Bhaja didn't wait for the assigned escort. She ran from the room. She ran from the citadel, dodging the many people who still awaited the Emir's afternoon session. Most of these would not see him, Bhaja realized. It was too late in the day.

Maybe too late for Wararni.

She ran to the western gate of the citadel's courtyard, passed through into the formal gardens that were the Emir's first wife's city beautification project. She did not have time to admire any of the woman's work as she raced toward the small gate into the military compound. She glanced to see she had been joined by a guard—Leto, perhaps? —who raced steadily beside her.

"Straight ahead after the gate," he gasped as he signaled the guards at the door to let them pass. The guards made way, and the two runners did not even pause as they raced through into the dusty military grounds of the city.

Sweating heavily now, Bhaja held the folio away from her chest; it would not do to make the ink run.

They made dust rise as they ran across the field and toward a building that was presumably their goal.

The door banged against the wall, making everyone inside jump as Bhaja and the guard entered.

"Stop!" Bhaja yelled.

A man holding a very thin, sharp knife bent over Wararni, who was bound to an unusual-looking commode. The doctor looked fierce; behind Wararni, Pai looked frightened.

"This document is Judge Kabos's findings which clear this man of all wrongdoing!" she said. "There *is no sentence* to carry out!"

At the Guard Leto's urging, Bhaja handed the judgment folio over to a man dressed in grey robes. That man took the folio and scanned the pages. Then he looked up from the folio, alarmed, to meet Bhaja's steady gaze.

"Free this man," he said, and Wararni, who had been unconscious before, now let out a single, relieved whimper as they cut the ropes binding him. The man with the cutting knife backed away.

"Please leave the compound now," the grey-robed man said, "and do not return!" He glanced around the room. "There are men here who may feel compelled to follow through with their own version of justice!"

Bhaja and Pai helped Wararni to his feet, and then did as the man said, leaving the physician, grey-robes, and Guard Leto behind at the door. They passed through the garrison gate. With much relief, they entered the gardens and walked toward the tower of Tarub's Library, visible beyond the trees and trellised vines of the garden.

Bhaja noticed Wararni's shaky legs. The trembling built until the man shook all over. She and Pai guided him to a bench where he fell more than sat down.

"You are safe now," she murmured.

"My privates still have not had time to figure that out," the man said.

There was enough fire in the response that Bhaja, despite her deep embarrassment, knew Wararni would be fine.

"Think of your wedding," she suggested.

"I *am!*" was his response, and Pai laughed.

18. BOYS WILL BE BOYS

Bhaja took charge of Zetian for her wedding's eve. Wararni disappeared for his last night as a single man with the other fiancés. Pai slept alone. Even with the bright light of an almost full moon, he rested soundly and woke up full of energy.

After a quick breakfast, he briskly traversed the medina, through the central market and out the huge wooden doors of the western gate. He crossed himself when passing the Cemetery of Amir where Malik had already been buried. Cutting through an apricot orchard, he helped himself to a ripe fruit, wiping the juice from his mouth before entering the small chapel nestled among the ruined buildings of the abbey.

He chose a vacant pew in the back, crossed himself again, and waited. Single file, the abbey residents, monks and priests, filed into the chapel and took seats in the front. When all had settled, a small bell was rung, two young boys walked up to the alter carrying censers followed by the priest who wore a white robe embroidered with an ornate cross. Pai noted the stark contrast with the simple black or brown robes worn by the others.

Everyone stood up at the start of Sunday Mass. Pai heard someone arrive late and looked across the narrow aisle. To his surprise, Lylah, a Muslim, had joined the worship.

Pai's attendance at Sunday Mass was sporadic, but he found the ritual comforting. He stood, knelt, and sat following the lead of the darkly clothed men in the front rows. The rhythms of the Latin were relaxing even though he didn't understand. Pai felt a sense of Christian community. Clearly, some, mostly women, attended regularly. After all, Sunday Mass was just once a week, compared to the five times a day observed by the Muslims.

At the end of the service, he lined up for the bread and wine. He noticed that Lylah stayed back, but everyone else came forward. *What was she doing here?*

Pai caught up to her in the apricot orchard. "Lylah. Welcome."

She turned around appearing surprised and maybe frightened to be recognized. "Oh, Pai. I didn't expect to see you here." She stopped moving and her voice softened. "I was hoping to be by myself."

"You could hardly be alone at Sunday Mass."

She smiled. "Pai you've always been a sweet innocent. I think that is one of the reasons Bhaja likes you."

Bhaja likes me? Here was someone else who thought he and Bhaja were special friends. *So many see Bhaja and me together. I must speak to her soon without letting anything else delay me.*

"Did you enjoy the service? Do you find it confusing?" Pai wondered.

Lylah picked up a ripe apricot and headed toward the western gate. "I've been to many services at that chapel. Hathus often took me and he attended Friday prayers at the mosque. He would have been here this morning had he not been locked away. We are a mixed marriage, you know."

Bhaja again came to his mind. She was a Muslim like Lylah, and he was a Christian like Hathus. "Yes, I often wonder how that might work."

Lylah gave him a motherly look. "Don't worry Pai. It was harder when I wed Hathus. We were one of the first. You'll find so many other challenges. Religion won't be your problem."

Lylah had just confessed deeper concerns. *Other challenges.* Proud Hathus might have been difficult. *Many found him so.* But Pai supposed she referred to something else. He guessed, "It must be hard for him to be locked up in the citadel."

"Yes. I'm not surprised it came to this."

She wants to talk. "The Emir suggested that Hathus and Malik fought as children," he prompted her.

"The Emir never gets anything straight."

"Really?"

"Malik was a delicate child, soft and timid. He never fought with anyone. Hathus teased him, calling him a little girl, and telling him he should be wearing a headscarf instead of a keffiyeh."

Children can be so foolish. There's little difference between a keffiyeh and a headscarf.

Pai couldn't conceive of anyone teasing Malik. He only knew him as tough and aggressive. "He seems different now."

Lylah's eyes moved to the right and up into the trees. "Things changed when we were in our teens and our parents thought of marriage. Both boys pursued me."

Pai easily pictured Lylah as a pretty young girl.

"My mother wanted me to marry Malik. He came from a Muslim family, but my father said he was too weak to be a good husband."

Pai was grateful that he and Bhaja were older and didn't have family involved in their choices. "Is that how you ended up with Hathus?"

"Not at first. Malik's father agreed. Malik was sent to live with his Berber relations in al-Jazair. They were fighters and would toughen him up. I was to marry him when he returned."

"That worked. Malik is not soft or weak. Why didn't you marry him?"

Lylah's voice became somber. "He was gone a long time. Ten years. I couldn't wait. Even my parents grew tired. They didn't protest when I married Hathus, a Christian, but, obviously, they are happy that Abdallah studies at the mosque and might become an imam."

"Was Hathus jealous when Malik returned?"

"Oh yes," she replied emphatically. "The new Malik was tougher and still interested in me, and now I've lost them both. Malik is dead and Hathus is imprisoned."

When they reached the western gate, Lylah took the path that went to the citadel, while Pai went to the central market and back to Malik's house. Something told him that he'd missed a clue on his previous visits.

When he arrived, Pai saw the servant's son and some friends playing marbles in front of the open door. "Is anyone in the house?"

The boy looked up. "Just my mother. She is cleaning."

Pai looked inside. The food had been cleared. The pillows were stacked in the corner. The tracks of the visitors had been swept away. The stench of death was gone.

Malik's servant greeted him, "Good day, Pai. Can I help you?"

"I'd just like to look around."

She paused a moment as if wondering if she should object. "Let me know if you need anything." She returned to the pantry where Pai could see steam gently rising from a tub of washing.

He searched the atrium in an orderly pattern, first following the border of flowers. Then he examined each palm tree. So much had happened in the al Jamal villa, there had to be more clues yet to be uncovered. But it wasn't under the palm trees. He made a closer examination of the fountains, but the efficient servant had removed any clues that might have been left by the murderer.

Next, he visited the sleeping rooms. These had not been touched. The first room had been used by Wararni. Pai could see where his muddy clothes had dirtied the bed and he had littered the floors with apple cores, chicken bones, and breadcrumbs—much to the benefit of the local ants. Three thick tracks led to the outside walls. The room was a mess, but it contained nothing useful.

The middle room belonged to Sayyida. Her boxes and sacks lined one wall—some still waiting to be unpacked. A wooden chest carved with Arabic calligraphy stood proudly at the foot of her bed. Opposite, a line of pillows in oranges and yellows were stacked against the headboard. An orange cloth covered the expanse between.

He opened the unlocked chest and searched inside—something he wouldn't have done if he weren't looking for a murderer. It contained some robes and undergarments, an extra pair of sandals, and at the very bottom, he found a pouch of silver and copper coins. Certainly, such a modest amount didn't provide a reason for murder.

The last room belonged to Malik. His bed was also untouched. *Had he not slept in the bed the night of his murder, or had the efficient servant put everything back in order?* At the foot of the bed sat a wooden chest similar to the one in Sayyida's room. This one was locked, but with the aid of a knife, he forced it open. The dagger with the jewel-encrusted hilt lay on top in easy view. He'd never forget the weapon that had cut his arm. Next to it, also not hidden, was a pouch of gold dinars similar to the one Darras carried. The murderer hadn't robbed Malik.

Against the longest wall hung a great number of fine robes. He methodically patted each robe checking for hidden pockets. He didn't find any, but as he pushed the robes against the wall, the hem of one robe, a yellow one with embroidered interlocking squares, was pulled up. He looked down and saw something—Darras's bag, fine embroidery, soft leather handles, and silver buckles. There certainly wasn't another like it in al-Andalus.

Pai checked it. He found the fancy clothes he expected, but no coins. Perhaps Malik had taken the money. He also found a leather sack of white powder. He tasted it. *Chalk. Heartburn.* Abbas had said Darras had tumor disease; this confirmed it. At the very bottom was a scrap of parchment with two names written: Naomi and Gwafa. Pai knew Naomi but the other name was a mystery. Regardless, the bag proved Malik had murdered Darras just like Hathus had said. Hathus had been incarcerated by mistake!

But why? Pai was pleased to find the murderer of Bhaja's friend. He'd let the Emir and his judges figure out the *why*. That mystery might never be solved. Regardless, Darras would receive justice.

Pai had had enough dealing with Javed. He turned the other direction when he left Malik's house with the incriminating bag. He'd go straight to the Emir this time.

He hadn't gone far from Malik's villa when he saw Sayyida dressed in black accompanied by an imam. The imam had a long beard and a wrinkled face. Now that Malik had been exonerated, Sayyida was being treated with honor in place of the widow Malik didn't have. Both of them walked with bowed heads. The imam recited prayers in a soft voice.

When they came close, Sayyida looked up, "Good day Pai. Where did you find Darras's bag?"

Pai responded to Sayyida while watching the holy man. "It was hidden in your brother's room."

Sayyida didn't look surprised. "The last time I saw it was at Abbas ibn Firnas's home in Ronda. I wonder how it got to Qurtuba."

Pai had already figured this out. "Malik brought it here after he murdered Darras. Darras's money is missing, but the bag is still valuable evidence. I'm taking it to the Emir."

The imam spoke up. "Have you shown it to Judge Javan? He will know what to do."

Pai could hear the frustration in Sayyida's voice when she protested, "The judge has been ignoring my brother's death. He only sends us to his brother Javed."

The imam backed away and motioned Pai to continue his journey. "The Emir will summon a judge if needed."

Then he turned to Sayyida. "What will happen to this fine house in Qurtuba?" The imam paused and stroked his grey beard. "I remember when Malik was born. No one expected him to leave Ronda, even after his father acquired this fine villa." After another pause, he smiled at Sayyida, "Your brother never wed, so it belongs to you."

Sayyida properly corrected him. "And my mother."

Pai thought: *She'd already escaped Ronda with her room in this villa. But now she had a permanent residence in Qurtuba: an entire villa that was hers, her new home.*

"Will your mother move to Qurtuba?" the imam queried.

"Oh no! My mother has lived all her life in Ronda. She is happy in the valley. As she grew up on the mesa, she admired that beautiful farm. She often talked about how glad she was to marry my father and move there."

The imam moved closer to Sayyida and spoke warmly. "I know Malik owed a substantial amount in taxes. You would be blessed if

Malik's property went to the mosque and we would arrange with the Emir and provide you with an allowance."

Pai didn't want this holy man to cheat Sayyida out of her dream. He prompted her, "I thought you'd live in the villa."

Sayyida looked into the imam's eyes and showed Pai she could take care of herself. "I supervised the farm and we always paid our taxes. I'm sure I can administer this property and take care of those taxes also. I don't need the mosque to be my caretaker."

The imam looked surprised and changed the subject. "Insha'Allah. I wonder who killed your brother."

Sayyida looked down and clasped her hands. "Since he returned from Ifriqa, he has been so rough. I fear that many people were glad to see him gone. You saw how few attended his funeral."

The imam nodded. "Insha'Allah."

Pai heard the call for afternoon prayers. It was too late to go to the citadel. Pai held the extravagant bag tightly against his chest and headed back to his shop confident that the mosque wouldn't take advantage of his friend. He'd bring the bag to the citadel on another day.

19. Happy Day, Heartfelt Night

Late Saturday night, Bhaja was still scrambling to find items that would dress up the Library courtyard for the triple wedding. Her mother's help had been invaluable. Astonishing her, even Yusuf had contributed, climbing into the attic storage space of their house to dig out some ribbon their mother remembered being up there. He hadn't even grumbled about the dust that continued to float off as Bhaja unwrapped the old apron that had covered the spool of ribbon. Several ribbons, in fact, in all the colors of the rainbow.

"Do you want me to roast some chickens, or something?" Mother asked.

"Thank you, Mother, but Tarub is taking care of the food. What I most need is—"

"Sleep?" Yusuf suggested. He clutched a pillow to his chest and stuck his thumb in his mouth, like a child.

Even their mother laughed at that.

Ignoring his antics, Bhaja went on, "I will buy flowers in the morning. We have ribbons, and I have some plain cloth for table coverings and to cover the rough wood of the temporary pavilion. I have you—" she pointed to her brother—"and your friends to play some music for entertainment afterward—"

"Won't the imam object to that, Bhaja?" Mother tilted her head, thinking about it.

"No, I asked him. There's no music in the ceremonial part, but afterward, he thinks it will be fine. People can eat, or walk through the courtyard, or sit on the benches—Tarub has extra benches being delivered tonight."

"If they don't like music, they can just leave," Yusuf said, "though they'll miss our lively and lovely melodies!"

"Not too bawdy, Yusuf. These are mixed marriages, so it would be easy to offend one group or another."

"Yes, I talked to Xarq and his friend, and we have a short but nice list of music planned. Charming paeans to nature and love."

"Thank you so much," Bhaja went and hugged him, the scrap-cloth-stuffed pillow still clutched to his chest between them.

She thought a moment, "Then the only thing remaining is a gift from us to Wararni and Zetian, and something much smaller for the other two couples."

"I was thinking a pair of nice candles for each of the other two, but I have no idea about Wararni and Zetian. It should be more substantial than candles, but we don't have much money put away for things like this," Mother said.

"Yes, the candles are perfect. Other household things will be supplied by Tarub, but they won't need a lot, since they will be joining the staff at her villa. But the same isn't true for Zetian and Wararni."

"Will they get their own house?" Yusuf asked.

"I think Pai plans for them to use the extra room behind the paper shop. That works until the baby is born, at least."

"Baby," Mother said, tapping her lips with a forefinger. "I have a nice basket I bought long ago, hoping for you or your brother to use for your own firstborn."

"Oh," Bhaja said. "That's not going to be happening for either of us any time soon."

Yusuf rolled his eyes, but Mother didn't see it.

Bhaja made a face at him and thought about gifts. "I think a basket would be perfect. I will fill it with a nice linen towel, a bottle of bathing oil—and I noticed Zetian using an old broken comb on her hair. A new one of those with all its teeth would be perfect."

"I can get that at the souk tomorrow morning," Mother said.

"Maybe one more item for Wararni, and that should be enough." She bit her lip. "I don't know what he would need or like. I wish Pai was here; I would ask him."

"That sounds nice, Bhaja," Mother said. "Basket, towel, oil, comb. Perhaps that is enough."

"She's a slave," Yusuf said, frowning. "Is that too generous a gift?"

"I would think a slave needs even more than a free bride might," Bhaja said, shaking her head at her brother's notion.

Yusuf frowned even more. "I suppose," he said.

"Will Tarub free her?" Mother asked.

"I don't know. Perhaps as a wedding gift? But I know she desires to keep control of the paper, and thus the papermaker, so I am not certain what Tarub might do."

"Mmm," Mother said. "She should be freed. She will make Tarub's paper out of gratitude."

"Or she'll light out for al-Qin without a moment's regret," Yusuf said. "That's what I'd do: head for home!"

"Perhaps her home was not so pleasant," Bhaja said. "Her parents sold her, never caring that she would be taken far away from them. At least Wararni cares what happens to her."

"That's good," Mother said. "With Wararni as her husband, and Pai as her boss, she should have a decent life even if Tarub chooses not to free her."

Bhaja wasn't so sure she agreed with that, but she said nothing.

A light mist covered the riverside portion of the medina the next morning. That meant the day would not be so hot, a welcome turn of the weather for the weddings.

Wararni came by very early that morning, asking what time he and Zetian should arrive, but Bhaja had no certain answer for him. The details of the actual ceremony were up to Tarub, and to the cleric or imam found to perform them. "Before mid-day prayers," was Bhaja's advice to Wararni.

She and her mother strung ribbons, hanging some from the trees in coils, making bows and streamers. She covered the tables and the temporary pavilion. It didn't look too bad, though Bhaja definitely wished the nicer, permanent one Tarub had designed was already installed.

The boy she had hired showed up with his cart half-filled with wildflowers, cut fresh from the fields that morning. Bhaja paid the boy, adding an extra coin as thanks for his efforts to arrive early and with fresh flowers. He'd found sunflowers, daisies, lupin, wild peas, wild roses, and snowballs—all were trimmed and placed in ewers or bowls of water on the tables. They tied ribbons around a few of the sturdier sunflowers and hung those among the lower branches of the leafy trees. Bhaja made four small bouquets she wrapped with ribbon and tied to each leg of the pavilion. The ribbons and bright flowers gave the courtyard a very festive look.

A carriage arrived with Tarub, Kaila and Osora, and one of Tarub's personal handmaids. Bhaja bit her lip. Tarub only brought that girl on days when she felt unwell; the girl was a wizard with massage that helped Tarub stay on her feet. Bhaja could see from Tarub's tightened lips and eyes that she was already in pain.

"When did you plan for the ceremony to take place?" she asked after greeting her patron.

Tarub's face softened as she met Bhaja's gaze. "I told the cleric and imam to be here immediately after mid-day prayers. But I see you are almost ready now."

"We arrived early; I was worried about getting everything done in time." Bhaja smiled and introduced her mother, whom Tarub had never met until now and the two women wandered off together discussing the wording of the ceremony. "The simpler, the better," was Tarub's opinion, but they were out of earshot by the time her mother spoke.

It would be interesting to see what the two religious had to say as they performed three different mixed marriages: Christian Chedar with Muslim Kaila. Unknown-religion not-eunuch and Christian Osora. And Muslim Wararni with al-Qin Zetian. Was Zetian Buddhist? She didn't know.

Pai arrived, Zetian and Wararni with him, both dressed in nice clothes, Zetian's pregnancy now a mound that showed beneath her yellow, green, and orange gown. Wararni solicitously seated her at one of the tables and helped her raise her feet. "Her ankles get swollen," Wararni explained.

Behind the couple, she saw Lylah arrive. She'd come in a wagon that had rolled carpets in it, no doubt from the shop of her husband. Hathus's carpets were known even as far away as Gades, on the southern coast. People traveled from all over al-Andalus to Qurtuba to find just what they wanted at his showroom.

Lylah approached. She wore the long cotton tunic and baggy linen pants of the worker class rather than one of her lovely robe and over robe costumes. "Hathus is still in jail, but he asked me to bring these to you."

Bhaja frantically searched her memory. Had she asked for carpets? She did not remember speaking to either Hathus or Lylah, but perhaps Tarub had.

"You will want the bigger one for the officiants to stand on," Lylah said as they walked toward the wagon full of rugs. "The smaller ones can be scattered around for prayers, or for people to sit on and eat, later."

"Thank you so much, Lylah. These are wonderful."

The woman smiled. "It was my suggestion, but once made, Hathus was eager to send these."

When Bhaja saw the size of the bigger one to go beneath the officiants, she waved Pai and Wararni over. "Please help us carry this," she asked. They did so, and once the big one was in place, each of them took an armful of the smaller prayer-sized rugs and placed them randomly around the courtyard. Bhaja made sure several of them were placed in the nooks where plants and flowers made private-seeming bowers as well as more out in the open and facing qibla.

"I will return for these late today," Lylah said.

"You are welcome to join us for the celebrations if you wish," Bhaja said.

"Thank you. After I visit Hathus I will try to come by."

Bhaja waved as Lylah sat on the seat and the driver flicked the reins. The horses tugged the wagon into motion and Lylah disappeared among the shops and houses of the medina.

Bhaja turned to Pai.

He looked handsome in his new green and cream robes. She smiled at him, then realized she was still wearing her work dress, which was definitely neither clean nor nice enough for a wedding.

"I am going to lock the Library while I change clothes," she said to him. "I'll be right back." Then she ran into the Library and did that. Naomi stayed within to help her, while Isador, of course, was not there on a Sunday, so she had sufficient privacy.

She had planned days ago to wear her lotus-blossom necklace and had chosen lavender and rose robes accordingly. When she saw the colors in daylight she was immediately unhappy with the scarf she had selected; it was altogether too peachy, the wrong shade of pink.

"Oh, I wish I had known," Naomi said. "I have a beautiful lavender headscarf from the things Tarub sent. It would go perfectly with your robe."

Bhaja went to the cupboard where she had put spare work gowns and scarves and rummaged around. She pulled out a white silk scarf. "With purple ribbon to tie this on, white will be fine," she said, and Naomi agreed. Bhaja reopened the Library and went to steal one of the purple streamers they'd hung on a lemon tree earlier. It was just the right length.

She noticed Tarub out by the street, speaking to a man who usually set up a food cart on the road beside the citadel. Her mother and Tarub seemed to be arguing with the man. She walked over to see if she could be of help.

"He cannot get beef for skewers," Tarub said, flinging her hands out. "We *cannot* serve pork, so that leaves just chicken!"

"But that's fine, isn't it?" Bhaja asked, and her mother, at least, nodded agreement. "He is bringing lemon-baked fish, too," Mother said.

"I have chopped beef for stuffed grape leaves," the man offered. I can have thirty or forty ready in plenty of time."

"Oh, all right. That will have to do," Tarub said. Bhaja was surprised the woman seemed so cross. Originally, it had sounded like Tarub had been planning a small, simple affair. That she was now missing the skewered beef and was so upset about it, did not seem small or simple to Bhaja. "You will still have the lentils and chickpeas and flatbread?" Tarub asked.

"Yes, yes, Lady, of course," he said. "I go now and finish preparing all." The man went off to wherever his kitchen was, presumably to return later with his items for the feast.

"Well, we have many different kinds of fruit coming," Tarub said.

"So that will be ample, don't you think?" Bhaja said, trying to soothe troubled waters.

Tarub took a deep breath. "I realized after I planned things that this would be so close to the citadel, the Emir will certainly have people watching. It is my intent to show him how the people in my household are treated. Which is to say, very unlike how his are!"

By now Pai had walked up to the group and heard Tarub's last comment. He smiled. "I'm glad no one had to be emasculated." He grinned his quirked grin. "So messy."

Bhaja laughed, although Tarub and her own mother didn't seem to think it was very funny. She decided she didn't care, giving Pai a wink. His eyes sparkled with suppressed humor.

One of the religious arrived then. By his garb, Bhaja guessed it must be the Christian cleric. He spoke with Tarub, the two conversing as they walked away from the others.

"Can we talk?" Pai asked.

"I will go change to my nice clothes now," Bhaja's mother said, leaving them alone.

"Of course," Bhaja said, answering them both.

"Can you show me the lock?" Mother asked.

Bhaja did not particularly want to try explaining the complicated thing. She particularly *did* want time to talk to Pai.

"Naomi can do it, Mama," she said. Pai reached for her hand, and she clasped his. She smiled at her mother who nodded and disappeared into the Library. A moment later, the big door swung closed, so Bhaja and Pai walked away.

Pai gave her his sweetest smile. "I have been wanting to have time to tell you—" he began.

"Pai! My friend!" Chedar yelled from across the courtyard. "Can you help me tie this?" He held out a ridiculously long headscarf and looked at Pai hopefully.

Bhaja sighed. "Perhaps later," she suggested and Pai nodded.

The ceremony was indeed simple, and surprisingly short, given there were three couples to be wed, and that there were two officiants to do so in a way appropriate for several religions.

The Christian man spoke first, admonishing the couples to love, honor, and protect one another. Then the Muslim imam talked about The Prophet's delight for weddings, and that Allah required the partners to respect one another and to be faithful and helpful to one another.

Then each pair stepped forward to sign their specific marriage contract, which in each case included a slightly different statement about the money or gifts each husband would give his bride. In the case of Wararni and Zetian there was also a short statement that he acknowledged and would provide for their child.

By this time, the various food and drink vendors were arriving and placing the products of their kitchens on the biggest table in the courtyard.

Bhaja saw pink, orange, yellow, and blue fruit juices, stacks of pears and oranges, and clusters of grapes, watermelon slices, and plates of dates—sugared, plain, and stuffed with almonds. Fresh figs, dried peaches and apricots, and shelled pistachio nuts were intermingled with platters of garlic-baked eggplant, honey-glazed carrots topped with candied jasmine flowers, and grated radish and other condiments. A separate table held the promised stuffed grape leaves, roasted chickens, lemon-infused fish, and numerous spiced and sauced legumes, saffron rice, and anise-baked squash.

The mere scents of all the foods made Bhaja dizzy; she could not imagine even tasting every dish. She decided to be very selective, putting on her plate to share with Pai a little chicken, some of the squash and lentils and chickpeas. She remembered he liked rice, particularly saffron rice, and added a spoonful of that. She decided to treat the fruits as dessert and would come back later for those.

She caught Pai's eye, and he said a few last words to Zetian and Wararni before joining her at a small bench toward the outside edge of the courtyard. While they weren't that far from the next benches and tables, foliage screened them, giving the illusion of privacy.

"Now," Bhaja said to him, placing their plate between them on the bench, "perhaps we can talk."

"I want to say I think about you often, Bhaja. At all times of the days and nights of my life. I want to tell you of my growing love, and that I hope you feel the same, or that you might someday—"

She put a hand on his wrist. He stopped speaking and gazed into her eyes. "I do feel the same, Pai." He opened his mouth, but she forestalled him with one more statement. "I feel I have known you forever."

His eyes widened. "That's the other thing I wish to tell you," he said. "I have dreams about you all the time. About us, about being in another time and place with you," a tiny frown dimpled his forehead, "except it is you, but *not* you."

"A different face, with different eyes," Bhaja said, eyes slitted as she re-imagined her own visions. "But with *you* looking out from those eyes." She quirked her lips. "Although when I say this aloud, it sounds—"

"It sounds impossible, like dreams do—"

"Or visions," she put in.

He dipped his head. "Or visions. In a place by the sea."

"A temple with fat round columns," she said, "and smooth marble or sometimes colorful mosaic floors."

"Sunshine, grapes and olives in the fields," he said.

"And us, holding hands in that sunshine."

"In love."

Bhaja felt bumps rise on her arms, as if a chill wind had swept past them. She had been coming to believe her visions were real, that they *depicted something real,* not just her fantasies. And now for Pai to tell her of his own dreams, that were the same as her visions....

How could they not be true?

Ignoring the plate of food, Bhaja's hands dropped to twine together in her lap. "We are told by some that we have lived before, that we are reborn each time we die—"

"Until we learn perfection," Pai said, nodding.

"But I have not heard of two people meeting again, together," she said.

"It has happened *now,*" Pai said, voice firm, "to us."

"How could this be!?"

Pai waved a hand, meaning the courtyard and the people in it, and ended with his hand flattened against his chest. "Today reminded me that marriage is the deepest mystery. Or more exactly, that love is."

"I have no doubt that it is love that has bound us together, but...but wouldn't you think other couples have loved deeply enough to have met again later?"

Pai nodded.

"Yet we do not hear about that, not nearly so much as rebirth in general."

Pai tilted his head, eyes distant. Then he focused back on her. "It may be that they have spoken of it, but people did not believe. People may have thought such couples were crazy, or infested with demons or such."

"There are more and more places for people to be reborn. Perhaps they cannot so easily find one another?"

"And how long does it take, for each rebirthing?" he wondered. "Perhaps a few too many years separate them."

"Listen to us," Bhaja said at last. "We speak more of what we do not know than what we do."

"I know that I love you," Pai said. His smile was so sweet, his words so simple, that Bhaja felt tears slip down her cheeks.

Nearly everyone had gone home by the time Lylah returned for the rugs.

Bhaja was still feeling a rosy glow from the realization that she and Pai shared love, and a past together. She watched for long moments as Lylah began rolling up the smaller rugs, then she realized with a start that she needed to help the woman!

She met Lylah at the wagon, setting down her own small pile of rolled rugs next to the ones Lylah had just placed.

"Did the weddings go well, then?" Lylah asked.

"They did. Everything was just perfect. Thank you so much for your thoughtfulness; the rugs made everyone feel more welcome."

"You are most welcome," Lylah said. "I support Tarub's efforts for those women, and for the weddings."

"I am happy for them, though I do wish she had freed Zetian, as I thought she might do."

"Oh, I had thought Zetian was already a free woman, that she had chosen Qurtuba and Wararni for herself."

"She did choose Wararni," Bhaja said, nodding. "But no, she was sold in a faraway city and brought here for the hareem. Then Tarub found out about her papermaking skills and snatched her before the Emir could hide her away."

"I try to be sensible about the way our city is run, but I wish the Emir would do away with that terrible slave market," Lylah said. She scowled as she brushed back a tendril of hair that had escaped her headscarf.

Without speaking of it, the two went to the big rug and rolled it up, standing at either side. "Are all the men gone?"

Bhaja nodded. "Pai is supposed to be back later, but—" she caught sight of Naomi talking with Raviv at the door to the Library. "Oh, there's Raviv." She waved him over, and Naomi came with him, apparently realizing it would take all of them to lift that rug onto the wagon.

Bhaja felt like she had pulled a muscle, by the time they'd heaved the heavy thing up unto the wagon bed. She leaned against the sideboard and pressed her hand against the pain.

"Are you all right?" Raviv asked.

Bhaja looked up and met his eyes with a crooked grin. "I'll live," she said, "though that was heavier than it had any right to be."

They thanked Raviv, who went on his way, leaving Naomi to return to the Library and her work, and Bhaja and Lylah to finish picking up rugs.

"A good day," Bhaja said as they stacked the last of the small rugs on top. "Three weddings, great food, no fights."

Lylah laughed. "You were expecting fights?"

"Well I wasn't certain the various religious people were going to get along. Sometimes they are so certain that they each have the only right answer..." She ran out of words about the same time she realized she probably shouldn't be criticizing religion in front of Lylah. On the other hand, who better to ask about a mixed marriage? "How do you and Hathus do together?"

"We agreed at the beginning of our marriage to each keep our own beliefs. We serve the One God, even though we do it differently."

"God is God," Bhaja said.

"Exactly," Lylah agreed. "I pray my way, he prays his. Sometimes I join him for his Sunday services, but I understand very little of what the mass is about."

"Isn't it held in Latin?"

"Yes, so I literally don't know what the priest is saying. But Hathus has the same problem whenever he attends Friday prayers; even though he speaks perfect Arabic, he doesn't know a hadith from a psalm."

"But it doesn't seem to cause any problems for you in your marriage."

"No, that's not our problem."

Bhaja didn't know how to address that statement. Should she ask?

But Lylah went on to explain. "Every marriage has problems, of course," she said. "You are two people from different families trying to create your own family, and there are going to be things you disagree on."

"Of course," Bhaja said, hitching her hip up onto the edge of the driver's bench to take some of her weight off her feet. It had been a busy day.

"But Hathus wasn't my first choice, and that has been a thorn in his side since the very beginning."

"He is jealous?"

"He wanted to marry me from the time we first met. But back then, I had been promised to Malik al Jamal, and we planned to be wed as soon as he returned from al-Jazair, where his parents sent him for military training."

"I heard he was a gentle, kind man."

"Too gentle, in his father's opinion. It turned out he did not return for more than ten years. I told his parents I would wait, but then when year after year passed and he did not return, I began to think he never would. I returned his engagement gifts after the sixth year of waiting, and agreed to marry Hathus, who had never stopped courting me."

"Your parents agreed?"

"While a Christian rug merchant wasn't looked upon with as much favor as a Muslim landowner, the fact that Hathus was there and Malik wasn't became important. I was heading towards thirty years old and unmarried, which didn't look good."

"Mmm," Bhaja said, knowing the same status. Oh! She was going to tell her mother about herself and Pai, that would make Mama so happy!

"And I was lonely," Lylah went on, unaware of Bhaja's happiness, or its reason. "I married Hathus more because he was there, than because I loved him."

"I see. And Hathus knows this?"

"He's aware, though we do not speak of it." Lylah sighed deeply. "So things were fine for a while, and then Malik came back." She shook her head, looking down at the ground. "He came back, but he didn't come back the same."

"He was different," Bhaja said.

"He even looked different!" Lylah said. "His arms were solid muscle, his hands rough and hard, his skin darkened by the sun and dried by the desert wind. He came to see me the day he came back, asking about our engagement." She glanced up at Bhaja and shook her head. "Of course he was disappointed that I had tired of waiting. I told him I had wed Hathus, and he actually laughed, which I thought wasn't very nice. I don't know why, but even though he was so different after ten years, I still was attracted to him. My blood warmed when I looked at him."

Bhaja reached a hand out and touched the other woman's shoulder when she realized that Lylah now had tears running down her face, her beautiful dark eyes reflecting her inner pain.

“Even though I was married and thirty, I was drawn to him. I must have let that attraction show, because he—” Lylah choked and gave a little cry as she cleared her throat. She reached for Bhaja’s hand, and Bhaja took it in her own, offering whatever small comfort it could be to the sobbing woman.

“Somehow he had the idea I still loved him, and that I still wanted him. I was only attracted, I wasn’t desirous of a liaison between us, but he seemed to think he had rights to me and to my body.”

“Oh, Lylah, did he take you against your will?”

Like an angry child, Lylah’s fists mashed her tears dry and she lifted her head. “Abdallah was the result, so it wasn’t all horrible. And Hathus thinks Abdallah is his, so, please—"

“Of course I would not say anything, Lylah. Do not worry about that.”

She wouldn’t say anything, but she could still be angry about men who took what wasn’t theirs. What made them think they had the right?

She sighed and comforted Lylah as best she could.

She knew she hadn’t liked Malik the first time she met him.

Was it because she could sense that about him? That he was the kind of man who just took what he wanted, without caring about the damage he did? As if he was more important than everyone else around him?

She was profoundly glad Pai was a different sort of man.

20. OVERSTEP AND OVERHEAR

Pai dreamt of a ship with a single square sail. *Men lined both sides with their oars raised in preparation to embark on a long voyage. He and Bhaja stood next to a tent erected for their wedding night and waved farewell to her family. The ship pulled away to the cacophony of people cheering, drums, flutes, and lyres. Then the tidal wave rose over the top of the mast...*

He sat up unshaken by the vision. Instead, he recalled sitting with Bhaja amongst the flowers at Zetian's wedding. Bhaja had had the same memories of a time long ago when they were lovers, and now they were together again.

Zetian and Wararni had not left the storeroom he'd prepared for them—at least until the baby came. Nothing could spoil Pai's good mood. He rushed through his morning chores and wrote *closed* on one of his best leaves of paper. He nailed the page to the door and ran off to the souk.

"I couldn't wait to see you again," Pai exclaimed as he entered the Library with his arms full of fruit.

Isador, Naomi, and Bhaja looked up from their work. Bhaja smiled, but upon seeing the fruit, exclaimed. "Take that outside. No food in the Library."

"I have brought enough for everyone," he announced as he returned to the courtyard.

"I am so glad you're here, dear Pai," she added in a cheerful voice. "I'll be right out."

"Take your time," he replied, adding, "dear Bhaja." He was her *dear Pai* and she was his *dear Bhaja*.

He returned to the fountain and displayed the fruit along the wall.

Except for a few drooping flowers tied high in the trees, the courtyard had returned to normal. Soon Bhaja appeared with the others. Isador and Naomi each selected a piece of fruit and moved away to give the couple some privacy.

Pai and Bhaja peeled oranges and fed each other. The bitter Qurtuba oranges had never tasted so sweet. He looked at her and whispered, "You have the most extraordinary dark gold eyes."

She moved closer to him, close enough that their shoulders touched. Smiling, she said, "Why, thank you."

He held her hand but after some people around the courtyard stared, he let go. Yesterday was different with the weddings and flowers. Pai blushed, “Yes, eyes are beautiful, little artistic miracles.”

She laughed. “I know you are good at noticing details, Pai, I've seen it in your maps. Tell me about what you have seen regarding eyes.”

Pai thought. “Zetian has the darkest eyes. They are solid black, all one color.”

“Well, you work with her every day, I guess you would notice. How about someone else?”

Pai searched his memory. Sayyida had lovely brown eyes, and Tarub had exquisite green ones, but he didn’t want to mention another lady. Finally, he remembered the best example. “Here’s something strange. Lylah’s son Abdallah has unique brown eyes with golden flecks.”

“Tell me, eye expert, is that so rare?”

“Well yes. Neither of us nor anyone in your family has such eyes. I can think of no one else, except Malik, who has the same eyes, not even his sister. Certainly not Lylah nor Hathus.”

Bhaja stared at the Library in the distance, like she was thinking about something.

“Did you know Lylah and Malik were almost married before he was sent to Ifriqa?” Pai mused. “Can you imagine that Abdallah could be Malik’s son? Lylah had been married to Hathus for years, but she didn’t become pregnant until Malik returned.”

He had said enough. He took a bite from an apricot. After the orange segments, the golden fruit was too sweet. He chewed slowly until Bhaja responded. “You might be right.”

Pai took a deep breath and told what he’d been thinking, speaking quickly to get it all out. “If Abdallah’s parents are Lylah and Malik, two Muslims, and Malik is dead, then Abdallah is Malik’s male heir, so he will inherit Malik’s villa. Being the son of a rug merchant is good, but being a landowner is better. We should go to the Emir and help the boy get his rightful inheritance.” He took another big breath and paused.

“No, never! Hathus believes the boy is his. The boy doesn’t need Malik’s land. He needs two parents. Your idea will destroy a happy marriage.”

“How happy could she be if she went with Malik?”

“That was ten years ago,” Bhaja reminded him before she went back to work. Pai collected the remaining fruit.

As he passed between the citadel and the mosque, his chest swelled with pride at the majestic beauty of Qurtuba. He had never been to Rome or Baghdad, but he doubted they could be grander. The sun shone off the sparkling white walls and now with Bhaja, his life was perfect.

He thought of all the mixed marriages in Qurtuba and wondered if there had ever been such an accepting place. A white cloud passed in front of the sun and brought a moment of darkness reminding Pai of Hathus locked away. *He'd like these fruits.* Pai had no idea what they fed the prisoners, but certainly, it wasn't broiled lamb skewers and ripe apricots. Pai went out the city gate and followed the river down to the barracks complex.

"I've brought these for you." Pai handed the fruits to Hathus who wore the same robe as the day he was arrested. After sleeping in it for many nights, it didn't appear as fine. A few days in the jail had transformed Hathus from a proud merchant to a poor laborer who might repair the roads or dig channels for the waterworks. Hathus didn't seem concerned about his appearance as he chewed a big bite of apricot and peeled an orange.

Hathus offered a piece of peeled orange to the empty space beside him. His arm hung suspended in the air and he muttered, "Abdullah... Where are you?" Pai's heart ached for this father who was missing his son. Bhaja had said Abdallah needed two parents. Hathus also needed his son. Pai shivered at the idea of Hathus being convicted of murder.

Pai wondered if someone else had murdered Malik. He asked, "Why were you so angry with Malik?"

Hathus didn't respond.

Pai gave it another try. "Have you ever noticed Abdallah's remarkable eyes?"

Hathus stood up and threw his apricot pit across the tiny cell. It bounced off the grey wall leaving a tiny wet spot. "Those eyes!" he screamed. "Every time I hug my son, I see Malik's eyes staring back at me!"

Pai let the man continue.

"How do you think that feels? The man raped my wife and walked free. He sits on the Emir's council! I'm sure everyone laughs at me."

Pai ventured, "I could understand if you murdered him."

"Murder him? Murder Malik? This happened ten years ago. If I wanted to murder him, I'd have done it long ago!"

"Why didn't you?"

"I am a good Christian. *Do not be overcome by evil but overcome evil with good!*" He sat down and buried his face in his hands. In between deep sobs, he whimpered, "Malik was a trained fighter. He might have murdered Darras. I am a rug merchant; I don't even butcher my own meat!"

Pai took the man's hands as tears made muddy tracks down his cheeks. "Maybe something good can come from this."

The man choked.

"Malik died without a child. Abdallah is his heir."

"You're right!" Hathus choked and wiped his tears with his dirty robe. "If I never leave this jail alive, who will take care of Lylah and Abdallah?"

Pai prompted him, "If Abdallah inherited, they wouldn't go hungry."

Another cough. The man hugged Pai. "My friend. Can you go to the Emir for me? I can't have him imagining I am benefitting from my wife's sinful behavior."

Pai noticed that he'd stopped accusing Malik of rape and instead accused Lylah of adultery. Pai ignored those ten-year-old details. "I will go to the Emir and bring you some good news and more fruit tomorrow."

After Pai met with the Emir, he headed to the Library. Pai hadn't expected to see Lylah and Bhaja exiting the mosque. Bhaja tilted her head and spoke softly into Lylah's headscarf. Lylah gave Bhaja her rapt attention, eyes wide, rarely blinking. Pai rushed over to give them his good news.

Bhaja noticed him and called out, "We are going to eat, would you like to join us?"

Pai smiled. "Shall I get skewers for everyone?"

The two women nodded and soon they all sat on the fountain wall with grilled vegetables and rice.

"Hathus asked me to speak to the Emir," Pai said, without mentioning his role in the decision. Both women stopped eating. Lylah crossed her arms and furrowed her brow. Bhaja tilted her head and frowned. Pai was undaunted. "When I spoke to the Emir, I told him, 'Hathus couldn't have murdered Malik.'"

The two women continued to look unhappy.

"The Emir understood. He said, 'I know Hathus. He's my friend. I do not believe he is a murderer, but judge Kabos has the case. I can't intervene.'"

Lylah closed her eyes, but Bhaja pursed her lips in his direction as if to say, *I asked you to stay out of this*.

He rushed ahead with his good news. “I told him that Abdallah was Malik’s son.” Pai stared at the Library towering over the courtyard, avoiding Bhaja. “He declared Abdallah as Malik’s heir.” He looked to Lylah with a big smile and explained, “Your son will receive Malik’s property and you will administer everything until he is fifteen. Isn’t that wonderful?”

Lylah didn’t return his excitement, but her arms dropped to her sides and she let out a long breath. “This was a secret that has been killing me and my family. It was going to come out eventually.”

Bhaja put her hand on Lylah’s shoulder. “Everyone had already figured that out. At least you and your son will not starve.”

Pai had expected a warmer response, but he accepted that even after ten years, Abdallah’s paternity was still a difficult issue.

“Abdallah studies at the mosque every day. He hoped to become an imam, but with his father in jail he’s had to grow up.” Lylah closed her eyes. “At nine years old, he works in the showroom and keeps the accounts. He is a clever boy, but he’s had to miss some of his studies.”

Pai encouraged Lylah. “With his inheritance, he can continue his classes.”

Lylah moved away from Pai and leaned against Bhaja, “I’d rather have Hathus. Abdallah needs his father. A boy his age should be in a school, not a shop.”

“Mama!” shouted Abdallah coming from the mosque. “No more studies today. Let’s go open the showroom.”

Lylah and Abdallah walked off together. Pai imagined his happy face when she gave him the good news.

Pai was left with Bhaja. “Would you have preferred I didn’t speak to the Emir?”

She sighed and placed her hand on his shoulder. "I wish you would take the time to consider the ways your words will affect things before you speak. Hathus now looks more guilty. Lylah's reputation is ruined. Abdallah may be rich, but his parents are now doomed in society.”

Pai met her eyes. “I still think I helped.”

Bhaja bit her lip. “Someday we may have our own children. Do we want something like this to happen to us? Money is not the most important thing."

Before Pai could respond, she returned to the Library and closed the door.

Pai thought, *Money is the best recipe for happiness*, but also, *Bhaja is right*. He shouldn't have worried so much about Abdallah's inheritance. He was a shopkeeper and he'd never be rich like Darras or Malik or Hathus, but two of those men were dead and the third was in jail. Even though his job was to boil old clothes and his atrium smelled bad, Bhaja had still agreed to marry him.

Pai smelled spicy chicken and purchased a meal for Hathus sitting alone in jail. Thanks to Pai, his son would be able to continue his studies. Balancing the hot food on a bread circle, he took the shortcut through the citadel's courtyard escorted by a grey and black striped cat.

"This is for my friend in the jail."

The cat replied with a long meow.

He leaned down to pet her. She arched her back, and he could feel her bony ribs against his hand. "You poor skinny kitty, you need this food more than my well-fed friend."

He settled down on a stone bench leaning against the citadel wall. The cat went back on her haunches with her two front legs perfectly straight. She had white paws, which she washed. Pai gave her one of the chicken pieces. She purred loudly as she leisurely licked the welcome meal.

Pai enjoyed the gardens installed by the Emir's first wife. With the cat occupied, small birds approached and sang in the orange trees.

"When were you going to tell me about the harlot's affair?" shouted an angry voice.

"I didn't think it had anything to do with your case," was the loud response.

Pai moved closer to the citadel and placed his ear against the wall. The Emir and Judge Kabos were arguing on the other side.

Pai had never heard anyone talk back to the Emir, but Kabos said, "You are not a judge, not an imam, you have not studied the Quran and the hadiths as I have."

Pai waited for the Emir to put Kabos in his place, to chastise him for his insolent manner. Instead, the Emir replied, "Insha'Allah."

Kabos continued. "Do not make pronouncements on matters of the Law."

The two men on the other side of the wall stopped shouting. Pai heard enough to determine that Hathus would be called to the citadel later today. He dropped the rest of the chicken for the cat, tossed the bread a safe distance away for the birds, and ran as fast as he could to warn Bhaja and Lylah.

When the Emir took his seat on his purple cushion high on the dais, Judge Kabos was standing at his side. Pai looked around until he saw two guards holding Hathus still wearing the same dirty clothes from days ago. Pai looked up on the balcony to catch a glimpse of Bhaja and Lylah.

Judge Kabos frowned at the Emir as if to say, *Stay out of this.* The Emir nodded and waved to the guards. They marched Hathus to the front.

Kabos began with a warning against perjury and bearing false witness. "Hathus, even though you are a Christian, you must answer truthfully."

Hathus responded as if he were a Muslim. "Allahu Akbar."

"I have learned that you knew that your wife had a child with Malik al Jamal."

The audience gasped and the hall filled with shocked whispers. Hathus bowed his head avoiding the women in the balcony. His shoulders slumped and the robes he'd been sleeping in looked even shabbier.

Kabos spoke louder. "Hathus min Alshamal. Give us your answer!"

Hathus whispered, "Yes."

Kabos repeated the full accusation even louder this time.

"Yes, Judge Kabos. That is true."

Kabos waited until the hall was quiet and he had everyone's attention. He looked at his audience, stepped forward, and spoke softly. Everyone had to pay close attention to hear. "We have two serious transgressions, adultery and murder."

When he said murder, Hathus sobbed.

Pai shivered. Hathus hadn't murdered Malik! He waited for the Emir to intervene, but the Emir sat motionless and silent with a stone face.

Pai shouted, "No! Malik was a soldier and Hathus was a shopkeeper. It isn't possible!"

The audience came to life. The room filled with susurrations. A few shouted "Not Hathus!" while others answered with, "Jealous murderer!"

The Emir signaled a guard with a long horn. The sound echoed off the walls and order was restored.

Kabos acted like the disturbance hadn't occurred. "I have studied the Quran and hadiths for many years. I am prepared to announce my judgment."

He smiled at the Emir.

"For the crime of adultery, I apply the principle of Diya, financial compensation, against Malik al Jamal. Abdallah min Alshamal will henceforth be known as Abdallah al Jamal and he will inherit all of Malik al Jamal's properties. Allahu Akbar."

Everyone, from the Emir on his throne to the women in the balcony echoed, "Allahu Akbar."

Kabos paused again for silence and continued. "For the crime of murder, I apply the principle of Qisas, retribution in kind. For the murder of Malik al Jamal, I order Hathus min Alshamal to be beheaded."

The ululating from the balcony reverberated through the hall.

Kabos shouted, "Allahu Akbar," but only a few echoed him.

Pai still believed that Hathus hadn't murdered Malik, but also regretted not listening to Bhaja. His day would have been better if he had spent it boiling old rags and selling maps instead of visiting the jail and meeting with Hathus's soon-to-be widow. He prayed for a miracle.

Judge Kabos led the procession to the military compound followed by the two guards dragging Hathus. Two additional guards escorted the tearful, keening Lylah preventing her from approaching her husband. Pai walked alone. Neither Bhaja nor the Emir was present.

When they all arrived at the oak stump stained black from previous executions, Hathus was held down with a guard holding each arm and two on each leg. He couldn't move. A guard applied a blindfold and a muscular soldier appeared with a steel ax.

Lylah shouted, "No! No!" Pai prayed. He felt responsible. *Why did this happen? Why had he found Malik's corpse? Why had he taken the knife? Why had he noticed the golden flecks in Abdallah's eyes? Why had he told the Emir about Malik and Lylah?*

The executioner raised the ax and the sun reflected off the polished blade. A horn sounded and everyone looked to Judge Kabos, Allah's Protector.

The judge's deep voice echoed off the compound walls, "Allahu Akbar."

"Stop!" shouted Pai and he ran to grab the ax before it could drop onto Hathus's neck. The guards and witnesses gasped. He looked at

Kabos's angry face remembering Bhaja's exhortation to "consider the ways your words will affect things before you speak." *Too late,* he realized.

Kabos broke the stunned silence, "What is the meaning of this? I ignored your earlier outburst, but now you risk joining your friend."

Pai didn't release the ax. "I have evidence. I must testify. Doesn't your Quran say, *Do not conceal testimony, for whoever conceals it, his heart is indeed sinful*?"

Kabos smiled, "You know the surahs well for a Christian."

Pai bowed and put his hands on his knees glad that he'd remembered the Emir saying that.

Kabos spoke in a gentle voice. "Tell everyone your evidence Pai of Qurtuba."

This calm demeanor surprised and encouraged Pai. Judge Kabos, Allah's Protector, usually responded harshly whenever he was interrupted. He'd been known to execute anyone foolish enough to question his judgment. As Pai had heard through the citadel wall, not even the Emir dared to challenge the judge.

But the judge's face had softened. Fortunately for Pai, new evidence appeared to be an acceptable justification to interrupt a beheading. Despite his fearsome reputation, Kabos cared about justice. Pai looked at the judge with new respect.

Standing tall, Pai spoke with a strong voice. "The knife! Malik was murdered with a Jewish knife."

In a fatherly tone, Kabos asked, "The knife? Where is this knife?"

"Bhaja has it."

"Bhaja?" Kabos looked angry again. "Hathus's sentence will be delayed until I can examine the *Jewish* knife." Kabos turned to the guard. "Return Hathus to the jail and find Bhaja." He turned around and marched back to the citadel.

Lylah hugged and kissed her husband until he was taken away. Then she hugged and kissed Pai.

Pai didn't need to be rich or powerful. He'd gotten Abdallah his inheritance and now he'd saved Hathus's neck.

21. Unknown Unknowns

Pai's shop seemed smaller with the newlyweds sharing the space. Still, he enjoyed seeing the happy couple when he awoke. Wararni distracted Zetian with hugs and lovers' chats. Each meal became a romantic ritual of feeding each other.

"Zetian, we received a request for more paper from the judges. All these murders and weddings have been good for business. Our stockroom is empty."

"I will start a new batch." Zetian stoked the fire and filled the kettle with water.

Wararni put his arms around her expanded baby waist.

She slapped his hands. "You are not helping. I can't carry the water like that."

He leaned down and kissed her bare neck.

"Stop that!" She scolded and shrugged her shoulder to deter him. "Do I have to send you away?"

He just switched to the other side.

She dropped the kettle, spilling the water.

"Wararni, my love, you are impossible. Now you refill the kettle and put it on the fire."

He laughed and made an exaggerated bow. "Yes, my princess!"

Zetian went to the pile of old clothes and selected pieces for Wararni to tear into strips before throwing them into the hot water.

Wararni shouted to Pai who was in the shop selling maps, "See how helpful I am!"

Pai just laughed, pleased to see how well they got along together. He had felt proud for his part in getting these two together.

With Wararni and Zetian occupied in the atrium, Pai relived his glorious flight over the Ronda valley—*That map could be popular with all the excitement about the treasure*—but one copy had been stolen and the other was far away ensconced in a Roman wall. He took out one of the last pieces of paper and began to draw a third copy. He started with the edge of the Ronda mesa and the twisted path of the Wadi al-Laban as it ran down the gorge, through Sayyida's fields, and into the burnt olive groves that now belonged to Abdallah al Jamal.

His pleasant reverie was interrupted when Sayyida walked in. She was the last person he expected to see. He worried about his old friend, now that she'd lost the family's villa to her brother's illegitimate son. "Where did you sleep last night? In the street? Under the bridge?"

"Of course not," She scoffed. "I asked Lylah to let me stay in my room, but she refused. Fortunately, Bhaja offered me a place in the Library. Isador was happy to spend the night with his friends at the Abbey."

"I should have expected Bhaja wouldn't let you sleep under the bridge. Did you come here for breakfast? I can get you some tea and bread."

"I ate in the Library courtyard." She looked into the atrium where Wararni and Zetian were tearing rags and exchanging kisses. Pai followed her when she stepped outside. She spoke quietly even though the street was deserted. "Pai, thanks to you Wararni was not castrated and Hathus was not beheaded. Now I need you to help me."

Pai opened his small stable. "Do you want to borrow my donkey to return to Ronda?"

"No!" she exclaimed. "I'm not leaving Qurtuba."

"How can you stay without a place to sleep?"

"Judge Kabos should never have given Malik's villa to Abdallah."

"Do you think I can challenge the judge again? I'm not even a follower of the prophet."

"He made a basic error, but I can't do anything about it because I am a woman. I need a man to speak at the Emir's gathering."

"You want me to question Judge Kabos? Do you know how dangerous that is?" Pai couldn't believe this.

"You saved Hathus. I'll tell you what to say."

He'd done enough. He did not want to get involved with whatever Sayyida had in mind. He walked back to his shop prepared to go inside and bolt the door before she could follow.

"Bhaja said you would be the best one to do this," she pleaded.

If Bhaja had recommended him, he reconsidered. "What do you want me to say?"

"My mother is a primary heir and can't be excluded. Judge Kabos can't give the villa to Abdallah!"

Pai understood her. Even non-Muslims knew about primary heirs: parents and children. Recently a father tried to disinherit his daughter for marrying against his wishes. Everyone had heard how she was a primary heir, and he couldn't do it. When he died, she received half of his wealth. Still, Pai didn't want to offend Judge Kabos who seemed to be looking for someone to castrate or behead. With the judge's wishes thwarted, he might be willing to vent his frustration on Pai.

Pai had an idea. “Instead of going to the Emir, let’s go to Lylah and strike a compromise that doesn’t involve the judge.”

Sayyida thought for a short while. “If you will go with me, we can try to reason with Lylah.”

“Good. Let’s go. I want to stop at the souk to buy a gift for Lylah and Abdallah first.”

Sayyida looked unhappy. “I’d prefer to get a sugarcane stalk to beat her but we can do this your way.”

Pai wondered if he should allow Sayyida to go with him.

“However,” she said. “If she doesn’t agree, you have to speak to the Emir.”

He still didn’t want to confront the Emir, but the time to argue had passed. Together the two of them took the path that led to the central market to purchase gifts. They soon arrived at the villa that had belonged to Malik carrying Pai’s purchases.

Pai handed Lylah a robe of silk from al-Qin and Abdallah a small sack of brightly colored marbles from Venice.

Lylah turned to her son, “Mind your manners, Say thank you to Pai and fetch him a glass of tea.”

All eyes were on Pai, as the two women did their best to ignore each other. Malik’s, now Abdallah’s villa, was little changed. The room where a short while ago he’d expected breakfast with Sayyida and Malik, where Sayyida had washed her brother’s body, still held the same low table and rich cushions. When his tea came, Pai began. “In the excitement, the principle of primary heirs was forgotten.”

Sayyida’s face opened up with a big smile, while Lylah pulled her son close and frowned.

“Rather than go back to Judge Kabos, Protector of Allah, Sayyida is here to offer you a compromise.” Pai paused to let Lylah absorb her predicament. She was a Muslim and had to be familiar with primary heirs.

“If you will return the villa to Malik’s mother, Sayyida will guarantee an allowance for Abdallah to continue his education.”

“No! Never!” Lylah shouted. She grabbed the tea from Pai, spilling the hot liquid on both of them. “Get out of my house.” Lylah pushed Sayyida so hard that she slammed into the closed door.

Pai opened the door and accompanied Sayyida outside.

Sayyida, who had been silent, now shouted. “I will see you in front of the judge! You will regret this.”

Pai still didn’t want to confront Judge Kabos. “Perhaps we should go back.”

“I will not grovel before that woman!”

Pai thought of a compromise. "You want to live in Qurtuba. What if she lets you keep your room? Wouldn't that be enough?"

Sayyida pursed her lips and muttered, "I will show her." She turned to Pai, "I haven't told you everything. I was trying to be nice because of the innocent child."

Pai listened to her story and agreed to present her case directly to Judge Kabos.

"Let's go to the Great Mosque for noon prayers. Judge Kabos prays there five times a day."

Sayyida didn't move. "If he is there, I won't be able to speak to him. Men and women are separated."

"Let's hope he is there. I want to meet him outside. I don't want to confront him during the Emir's audience."

"You're right. I should have thought of that. Wait by the men's entrance. I'll wave to you if I see him." She disappeared into the Mosque.

Sayyida waved and Pai studied the few men who had attended noon prayers on a Tuesday. The judge appeared studying a page of ornate calligraphy he held in both hands. Pai proudly saw it was written on paper from his shop. *A good omen,* he thought.

When he approached the judge, Sayyida was at his side. "As-Salaam-Alaikum Judge Kabos."

The judge muttered, "Wa-Alaikum-Assalaam," without raising his head.

"Judge Kabos." Pai put his hands on his knees and bowed. "I am only a Christian, but I try to follow the Prophet's Way."

The judge stopped walking.

"I was wondering, why did Abdallah receive all of Malik's possessions. Isn't Malik's mother a primary heir?"

Now Kabos smiled. "I can explain that to you. You haven't studied the hadiths as I have, so you aren't expected to understand. My decree had nothing to do with inheritance. The diya—" Kabos interrupted himself. "You understand that diya is financial compensation, don't you?"

Pai nodded.

"Because of diya, Abdallah received Malik's possessions before Malik died. Therefore, Malik left no estate. There was nothing for the primary heirs to inherit."

Pai felt a bit silly not to have thought of this, but he was glad to see Kabos in a better mood. He bowed again, "I understand."

The judge headed for the citadel.

Pai ran around him to block his way. He didn't wish to shout, and he certainly wouldn't touch the judge.

The judge stopped before crashing into Pai, who began, "When Sayyida washed her brother's body, she discovered—"

"Haram!" The judge scowled at Sayyida. "Women should not prepare the bodies of men."

Sayyida bowed her head and remained silent.

Pai didn't want to discuss funeral practices, so he jumped to the end of his story, "The person who we all thought was Malik al Jamal was an impostor."

"What?"

"Sayyida discovered that the man was not circumcised." Pai didn't need to explain that all Muslims were circumcised.

Kabos shouted, "Did you see this yourself?"

Pai shook his head no.

"Well, that's the end. I will not exhume the body, and never accept the word of an unmarried woman on such a topic. She can't know what she is talking about!"

Sayyida whispered, "The imam."

Pai thought, *the imam?*

As if he'd been summoned, the imam appeared walking to the food vendors. Sayyida ran to him.

Pai figured it out. *The imam!*

When Sayyida returned, the imam testified about the funeral, confirming that the body buried in Malik's grave had not been circumcised. He finished with, "I performed the ritual on baby Malik almost forty years ago. The man living in Malik's villa was not Malik. Allahu Akbar."

Judge Kabos stroked his beard. "I must not be hasty. I will consider this carefully." In a softer voice, he said, "So Abdallah shares no blood with the al Jamal family."

Pai turned to the judge, "I found Darras's bag in Malik's room. Well, not Malik, but the person pretending to be Malik for the last ten years. Darras's money was missing."

Kabos said, "That is Judge Javan's case," and walked off.

Pai entered the great hall amid a cacophony of shouts and gasps from the crowd and keening from the balcony. The Emir sat on his purple throne. Beside him stood Judge Kabos with a solemn frown showing through his grey beard. On the other side of the Emir, guards surrounded a group of prisoners.

When Pai saw the people being held, he also gasped. Abdallah concealed himself behind his mother and Lylah hid her face in her headscarf. Pai's heart ached for the nine-year-old boy. The Emir shouldn't have allowed a child to be dragged in front of this crowd.

The judge gave a quick look to the Emir who responded with pursed lips and a small nod. "Hathus min Alshamal, step forward to testify."

Two guards pulled Hathus, still in his dirty robes, before the judge.

"Did you allow your wife to lie with Malik al Jamal and then murder him so your son would inherit his fortune?"

The man fell to his knees. "No! Never, no."

Pai's eyes were drawn to the nine-year-old boy forced to stand before all these people and watch the judge disgrace his father and mother. This was the Protector of Allah that Pai expected and feared. Pai pursed his lips, remembering Bhaja's advice and willing his mouth to remain shut. *No child should hear such accusations.*

Kabos looked back at the Emir and showed his teeth in an evil smile before addressing Hathus. "I believe your declaration of innocence. You didn't murder Malik," he paused and waiting for the audience to stop chattering before continuing, "and your wife never shared Malik's bed."

After releasing Wararni and delaying Hathus's execution, Pai had thought the judge's harsh reputation was undeserved. Pai had begun to like him. But Pai guessed what was coming next.

"I believe Abdallah is your son. There was no rape, no affair. You just made up the story to get Malik's wealth."

Now the room went silent. Would Lylah contradict the judge and admit to adultery? Would Hathus insist that Malik raped his wife?"

Pai cringed wondering what the judge would say next. What further indignation would be heaped on Hathus's family?

"If Lylah had been with Malik, she would have known he was an impostor. That man wasn't even a Muslim. He'd never been circumcised!"

Lylah couldn't have known he wasn't circumcised, Pai thought, but he didn't interrupt the angry judge.

"Your family conspired to cheat the al Jamal family. Abdallah min Alshamal gets nothing from the al Jamal fortune."

Pai couldn't believe that the judge included Abdallah as part of the conspiracy. *The judge should protect the innocent child!*

The judge's final surprise ended the proceedings. "The citadel will hold the villa until we can determine Malik's whereabouts. He may still be alive."

The guard escorted Hathus back to jail. His family followed, trying to touch Hathus to comfort him.

Back at the Library, Bhaja and Sayyida were still distressed about the proceedings. "Why was the judge so cruel?" shouted Bhaja. "Poor Lylah couldn't say anything. It would have been too much for her to admit she had an affair with Malik, or whoever that was, in front of all those people. But the silence made her appear to be a liar and a cheat."

"The judge trapped her. No matter what she did, she'd appear guilty," agreed Pai.

"And what was the judge saying about circumcision?" asked Sayyida. "Is it true that Lylah should have noticed that?"

The two women looked to Pai. "Chedar says it's false, an old wives' tale. In the time of passion, it is difficult to tell if the man is circumcised or not."

Bhaja said, "I feel sorry for her, all alone with a small child and her husband still in jail. We should find her."

"I expect she is waiting outside the gates of the barracks," said Pai.

"I don't think anyone is going to sleep in the villa tonight. Can I spend another night in the Library?" asked a somber Sayyida.

"That's a good idea. The Library is big enough for you, Lylah, and Abdallah," responded Bhaja.

Pai added, "You offered to provide an education allowance for Abdallah if you got the villa. I think you should honor that. It might cheer up the woman who's been so publicly abused by *Allah's Protector.*"

Sayyida agreed and they went to buy some dinner and find Lylah.

"Lylah! Abdallah!" Pai called. "We've brought you some food."

They sat together in the citadel garden. The grey and black striped cat returned. This time Abdallah was the one to share his chicken with the hungry animals. The cat rubbed against the boy's legs and purred loudly. Pai's heart rejoiced to see the boy smile.

Sayyida took the boy to explore among the orange trees. "Let's look for ripe fruit fallen to the ground. You can tell me about your studies at the mosque."

The boy gave his mother a hug. "That man was mean," he said in a strong voice before going off with Sayyida to collect oranges.

With the boy on the other side of the garden, Bhaja spoke to Lylah, "I'm sorry the judge treated you so badly."

Lylah sobbed, "It was awful with Abdallah standing there seeing and hearing everything. I was mortified with no idea what to do."

Bhaja moved closer to Lylah and asked in a low voice, "What really happened ten years ago?"

Lylah spoke slowly. "When Malik returned—I thought he was Malik. He was so attentive. Hathus had become more interested in rugs than me. We had tea at the villa. We walked along the river."

She sobbed. "One evening, when Hathus was away buying rugs, Malik invited me for a meal at his villa. I felt safe with his servants always there."

Pai looked to Bhaja, wondering if he should leave. Bhaja ignored Pai but put her arm around Lylah.

"What happened next you ask." Tears dripped down Lylah's cheeks. "The servants were gone. When I tried to leave, he forced me! What could I do? I had gone to his villa. I was trapped."

Pai tried to imagine what Lylah should have done. He considered her accusing Malik of rape but realized that no one would believe her, a married woman alone with a man who was not her husband. He considered her going to Hathus. That wouldn't have helped either. In the end, he saw the truth. She *was* trapped. He didn't know what to say. Besides, he realized this wasn't a time to interrupt the two women.

"Just like Judge Kabos this afternoon. Powerful men are the worst. Someday we'll stop them," Bhaja said.

Lylah echoed, "Someday."

Pai was embarrassed to be a man, but at least he wasn't powerful. He was glad that he was just a shopkeeper.

22. The Judiciary Versus Jews

Bhaja stood up from her stool and stretched. Sometimes she got so intent on her translations she forgot to move. Behind her, Isador dropped a scroll, then several more items fell to the floor. She turned and saw he'd spilled some ink and was frantically sweeping papyrus, parchment, and paper from his table before the ink got them.

She picked up a rag from her own desk and tossed it to him to mop up the ink, then bent to pick up the spilled documents.

At that moment a noisy commotion at the door told her they had a visitor, or more than one. She stood up, arms full of various writings, and saw a pair of the Emir's guards. *What on earth?*

"Which of you is Bhaja?" the bigger of the two men asked.

"I am."

"You are summoned before Judge Kabos to testify in the case of Hathus min Alshamal."

"Oh," Bhaja said. She put the scrolls and folios in her arms onto one of the worktables, removed the rags from her fingertips that she used to protect them from ink stains, and went to wash her hands.

Naomi had already gone to the citadel to observe Hathus's case being handled by Judge Kabos. Bhaja didn't know if the woman had also been called as a witness, or if she had chosen to go on her own; she had simply asked for the morning off so she could watch the proceedings. Bhaja worried about Hathus, but she worried about Naomi as well.

She dried her hands and left the Library in Isador's care as she went out with the guards.

The guards seated Bhaja in a room filled with men. Naomi, along with any other women who watched, was upstairs, behind a carved wood screen in the gallery. Bhaja felt her face reddening as she received stares from several of the men.

"This is the woman named Bhaja," one of the guards announced to Kabos, the judge.

"Stand before me," the judge said.

Bhaja stood up and stepped forward, wondering if she was supposed to remove her shoes, or bow. Then she remembered watching other people who had been called before a judge, and they had simply stood there. She did the same, while he looked her up and down intently.

"You are Bhaja of the Library?" Kabos asked.

"Yes."

"It has been made clear to me that you have in your possession a Jewish knife that was found near the body of the man we have known as Malik in his home."

"I have a knife; I believe it was from Malik's house."

"I was told it is Jewish in origin," the judge said.

"It has a mark on it that means 'kosher,' yes," Bhaja replied.

"Why have you kept this a secret?"

Her cheeks flamed as she said, "I am so sorry. I had forgotten about it."

"Do you have this knife with you now?"

"No, I put it in the Library safe."

"Why?"

"At the time, I was uncertain what it was. But I thought it might be important, so I kept it."

"The knife that murdered Malik al Jamal! You kept it secret to protect your Jewish friend!" Kabos said, scowling.

"I'm sorry, Most Beloved of Allah, but as I stated, I had completely forgotten about it. I had weddings to plan as well as my ordinary work to continue, and it slipped my mind."

"You were willing to let Christian Hathus die in order to protect a Jew! That is why it 'slipped your mind'!"

Bhaja shook her head, feeling her skin go numb with fright. She stared at the floor, thinking. Why was Kabos so emphatic about a Jewish murderer? Was he simply bigoted? Or did the knife indeed mean she had, however inadvertently, protected a Jewish perpetrator?

"Did the Jews pay you to 'forget' about the murder knife?"

"What?" She shook her head. "No one paid me anything. I am an ordinary person, who simply forgot I had something which has now obviously become important." She looked up at him. "Anyone, Muslim, Christian, or Jew, can pick up a knife and use it." She stilled her body's attempts to tremble and met the judge's eyes. She must impress upon him that she was telling the truth. But that might be difficult if he was determined to accuse a Jew.

She had one more fact to lay before him. "The only Jew I have occasion to work with is Naomi. But I know Naomi did not murder Malik, for she was with me at Tarub the Learned's villa the night of the big storm and the murder."

The judge was silent a moment, looking her up and down again. Bhaja dared not look up at the women's gallery. Was Naomi there? Had she heard the judge's antisemitic remarks? Allah weep, what would she think of Muslim law proceedings with that kind of prejudice seeming more important than the law itself?

"And will Tarub the Learned confirm that you and the Jewess Naomi spent all of that night at her villa?

"Yes." Bhaja knew Kabos probably did not like Tarub or her Library, the same way the Emir did not. But the man also knew that Tarub would not lie, if questioned.

The judge referred to some papers on the table before him, then shook his head. He turned to the pair of guards at the door. "Go arrest the Jewess Naomi and send word to free Hathus." He turned back to Bhaja. "The knife clearly implicates a Jew, if there is a kosher mark on it. If it wasn't your Naomi, she will know who it was."

"But why would she murder Malik? She had no reason to do so!" But then she remembered how Naomi had paled and run from the Library when Malik had burst in to bully Darras. There was history between them, that was clear.

"Who else would have a kosher knife?" the judge asked, leaning forward. "Perhaps the son of Naomi, who works with the butcher Ezra?" He leaned back and sniffed. "Unless you contend that Ezra himself did it."

How did he know Naomi had a son? Worse, he had somehow been informed that Raviv worked for Ezra—Ezra the butcher who had lots of knives marked *kosher*. Bhaja shook her head, temporizing. "There are many people who might use a kosher knife," she said. "I don't even know Ezra; why would I implicate him?"

"So it is Raviv?"

"No!" Naomi's hoarse voice cried from the gallery above. "He did not do it!" The screen behind which the women sat was pushed aside and revealed Naomi standing there, looking very distraught. She glared at Kabos.

"How can you say Raviv did not do it?" the judge asked in a harsh voice.

"Because it was me!" Naomi gasped and went on. "I...I snuck out of Tarub's house while everyone was sleeping!"

The judge raised an eyebrow, and Bhaja looked away from him and back to Naomi. Could this have happened?

Naomi would not meet her eyes.

"I—I had brought the knife with me in case we had to go home late at night alone," Naomi said. "But we stayed at the villa. I got up and went out. I stole a horse from Tarub's stables! I rode to Malik al Jamal's house and I stabbed him!"

The room erupted with voices commenting, arguing, or agreeing with these statements. "She could have done that," some said. "That's absurd," others said.

"Though I am not surprised," Judge Kabos said, "I do wonder why?"

"I cannot say," Naomi said. By this time she appeared to have herself under control, her story—her *false* story, Bhaja knew—well in hand.

"I am a very light sleeper," Bhaja said over the continuing noise in the room. "I would have wakened had she left the room."

Judge Kabos glanced at her, but then returned his attention to Naomi. "It is just as I suspected," he murmured.

"Murderer!" someone shrieked from the gallery, out of sight behind the other half of the screen. "You killed my brother!"

Sayyida, Bhaja realized. That was Sayyida's voice.

What was she doing here?

"Silence!!" Kabos cried, jumping to his feet and pounding on the table so hard with his fists that the papers jumped. His voice and the pounding carried, and the room became silent.

"Arrest that despicable woman," Kabos said, pointing to Naomi. "For the murder of Malik al Jamal."

As the guards rushed to do so, other guards poured into the room, chasing everyone out. Bhaja saw Kabos leave via a hidden door in the wood paneling behind his table before she was encouraged to leave by the guards wielding pikes in a very unfriendly way.

Heart pounding, Bhaja exited the citadel, her mind wobbling between either trying to believe Naomi's confession, or to find more evidence that it was false. She sent a runner to Tarub, to tell her what had occurred, and that Bhaja believed Naomi was innocent. The murder had occurred the night the two of them had stayed at Tarub's to avoid the storm. The storm, and the terrible wind which blew the heavy rains sideways.

Bhaja remembered watching Naomi dress in the morning. None of the woman's things had been wet. Silk dried fast, but linen undergarments didn't.

Naomi had not gone out in the night as she had claimed.

Bhaja arrived back at the Library in time to pray, then went out and bought herself and Isador their midday meal from the usual street vendor, along with some fruit she would bring to Naomi later. She spoke with Isador while they ate, explaining what had occurred at the hearing about not-Malik al Jamal's murder.

"She would never have done such a thing!" Isador exclaimed.

"I agree. Nevertheless, that is what she confessed."

"Do you have more evidence that it could not have been Naomi that did it? I thought this man Hathus was accused."

"He was. But wrongly, especially if the fatal wound was made with a *kosher* blade."

"There is no reason to suppose only Jews could have a kosher knife!" Isador shook his head. "While it is true I have not known her long, I believe Naomi to be a woman of strong faith. It would go against all she believes to have killed a man. What reason did she give?"

"None," Bhaja said. "I intend to visit her and find out."

Isador nodded. "I hope you can discover why she is trying to take the blame for this. I am quite fond of her."

Bhaja gave him a gentle smile. "As am I."

Isador returned to the Library. She could see him through the open door as he washed his hands, then crossed himself and said a short prayer. Once he had gone back to his worktable, she closed her eyes and leaned her head on her hands, thinking the whole murder scenario through.

At first, Javed had claimed it was suicide, because of the long slashes on Malik's wrists. It became known the man needed money to pay his past taxes—perhaps he had despaired? But no, when the body was washed, a deep wound had been discovered in his chest. A heart wound, but with no blood on the robes or the floor around the body.

So, he had been killed, then dressed in a clean robe, and placed with the knife, in his atrium. There had been no blood around the body or indeed, anywhere in the house, according to Pai who had been there early the following morning. The suicide had been staged.

She realized that meant that of course, the murder had occurred elsewhere, not in Malik's house. Somewhere else. Somewhere where a sudden quantity of blood would not be noticeable?

She abandoned that thought for the time being, focusing back on who *not*-Malik could be, and pondering how to find the real Malik—for wouldn't that man, the real Malik al Jamal, have returned to take up his business and residence—if he still lived?

Bhaja copied Pai's excellent idea of bringing fresh fruit to the jail. Naomi might not feel like eating, but the oranges would keep. Even the early quince fruits might last for several days.

Then she realized that if the fruit lasted so long that meant Naomi would not have been cleared of the murder. She must hope

Naomi was cleared by then. The woman could give the wretched fruit to someone else as she left.

Bhaja made her way past the barracks of the military compound.

Pausing at each guard station to explain her business, she gradually made her way to the chamber where Naomi was held. The big door had a tiny window covered by a metal screen. The guard looked through it and then opened the heavy slide bolt. Once Bhaja went inside, she heard the door slam and the bolt slide shut again.

Naomi was sitting on a built-in stone bench, hands clenched, staring at the musty hay on the floor.

She glanced up as Bhaja approached.

"I am so sorry this is how I repay all your kindnesses," Naomi said.

Bhaja handed her the fruit, then sat down beside her.

"Did you know that Isador cares for you?" she asked, watching Naomi's face closely. Even in the dim light of the small chamber, she could see Naomi's sadness. Naomi stared at the floor, saying nothing about Isador, or in her own defense.

"I know you made a false confession," Bhaja said, blunt in her effort to shock the woman into confessing her lie.

Naomi looked up sharply. "You need to mind your own business!" Bhaja saw tears spring in the woman's eyes. "You have been kind to me, but this is not your concern!"

"Tell me why it *isn't* my concern, Naomi."

"There is more to the story than you know."

"I am *trying* to know, Naomi. Tell me."

She could almost see Naomi gathering her courage. Eventually the accused woman spoke. She told a long, hard tale.

Naomi's revelations gave Bhaja a real shock. Life as a woman could be so ugly. The only good thing about it, Bhaja thought, was it explained a few puzzling things. It was a vivid, rough thread in the 'Doings of Malik al Jamal' tapestry.

She watched as the older woman peeled one of the oranges.

"So we know Malik was even worse a man than I first thought," Bhaja said.

Naomi would not look up from the fruit. Bhaja could barely make out the sad woman's faint voice, "Not Malik, Gwafa."

"I will do my best for you, Naomi."

Silence was her reply.

When she returned to the Library, the last thing Bhaja was interested in was translating some moldy papyrus. Her mind just refused to focus on it. She gave up in disgust and went outside.

The sun on the courtyard was warm, but a gentle breeze cooled her just enough to make the day perfect. She thought about perfection, and the ways Allah created such simple beauty. He had taught humanity many ways to copy that beauty of nature. He had gifted some men and some women with special skills to honor that beauty.

She sat in a similar courtyard, the sun and a similar breeze wafting the scent of jasmine to her nose. The building around the courtyard was shaped like a horse's hoof, the courtyard cupped in the arc. She turned to the open end and saw a short distance away a single, magnificent tree, surrounded by a low stone wall. The Lady Tree, she thought. Then, as happens in dreams, *she was suddenly elsewhere. A workshop...her father's workshop.*

He glanced up and greeted her with a warm smile. Here was a good man. He sat on a bench before a long table covered with tools, bits of metal, and a spool of gold wire.

He snipped bits of wire, and using tools and heat, he created tiny perfectly round beads that he let cool, then set into a necklace. The central pendant of the necklace was a lotus blossom.

Her *necklace!*

She abruptly came awake at the sound of measured boot treads. Soldiers marched up to her through the courtyard. No, not soldiers, she saw. Guards from the Emir's citadel. A half-dozen or so.

"You will give us the murder knife," the soldier wearing a gilded belt said, voice stern.

"Oh," Bhaja replied, still groggy from her nap, and her dream of the other place. She blinked and stood up, thinking about all those boots clomping into her clean Library. "Please wait out here, I will get it from the Library safe."

Gilded-belt gave a short nod, and all the guards remained standing in formation behind him as Bhaja rushed into the coolness of the Library. It felt so much like a sanctuary, she sighed.

Isador looked up from his table and watched as she bent before the safe. When she glanced at him before opening the lock, he was back at work, long lashes screening his eyes as he gazed at the words he wrote, quill scratching on the fine paper.

She retrieved the knife and locked the safe back up again. She returned to the courtyard and handed the knife, hilt first, to the gilded-belt guard. He took it from her gently, careful she wasn't cut by the blade as he accepted it from her hand.

Then the guards about-faced and marched back toward the citadel. It was peculiar the Emir had sent so many, simply to retrieve a knife.

Bhaja watched them go, feeling as if they carried Naomi's doom with them, thanks to her and Pai. Why had he given her the knife? How had she managed to forget about it? She licked her lips, feeling complicit.

She slipped out of her shoes at the portico of her mother's house. "Hello, Mama, I am home."

Her mother looked up from the stove, face flushed from the heat of the oven, where Bhaja could smell fresh bread baking, and the stovetop, where Basmati rice from al-Hind steamed. The aromatic pan was enriched with bits of lamb as her mother cut leftover roast from the bone and added it.

Bhaja's stomach growled so loud her mother heard it and laughed.

"Please wash for dinner. Yusuf will not be joining us tonight; he has a job."

Bhaja nodded and went to wash. She sat down just as her mother placed two plates of lamb and rice on the table.

"The bread will be for later. It took longer to rise than I expected, so the baking started late."

"Thank you, Mama."

Her mother smiled and took a bite. "Oh," she said, swallowing, "I keep forgetting to tell you I sent pots and pans and some utensils over to Pai's for Zetian."

"Oh, thank you. I know she will be so grateful."

"And how was your day?"

"To be honest, I would rather hear about yours," Bhaja said, a wistful tone to her voice.

"My day is never exciting," Mother said. "Just garden work, and some laundry and cooking. I mended Yusuf's oldest tunic."

Bhaja smiled. "That is just what I want to hear about, Mama. Something normal and nice."

Her mother's eyes met hers, query clear in them. But Mama had years of experience with her offspring. Rather than ask Bhaja uncomfortable questions, she filled her daughter's ears with news of vegetables and herbs. Just what Bhaja needed to hear.

23. SECRETS FOR SECURITY

Early the next morning, Bhaja again sat beside Naomi in the jail cell.

"Naomi, I understand about Gwafa." She gave the woman a small, tight smile. "But can you solve this mystery for me? Can you explain now why you confessed to a murder you didn't commit?" Bhaja had her own idea about Naomi's confession, but it would be helpful to hear what the woman had to say.

But Naomi said nothing, abruptly shaking her head. Bhaja could see the woman's hands tremble as she held an orange segment, her fingers picking unsteadily at the white filaments on it. But she did not eat it.

Bhaja could not help but think that if Naomi even opened her mouth, something she did not want to say might come out.

Their eyes met and Bhaja sighed and tried again, rephrasing her question, but to the same result. Naomi couldn't or wouldn't explain.

Bhaja returned to the Library and refocused. She must now concentrate on her work. She had established the new categories of Alchemy and Mathematics, and must decide whether Astronomy was a branch of Mathematics or the other way 'round. Or should they be separate?

She glanced at the stack of Astronomical writings, and then at the shelf where many texts on Mathematics were already stored.

Separate, she decided. If nothing else, the shelf count worked out better that way. She hated having to assign a whole empty shelf to just three folios or scrolls in hopes there would later be more. If there were ultimately only those three examples of a topic, they should be combined with something else. But there were many more than three Astronomy texts.

Within each topic, she had decided to sort the volumes alphabetically by author. Unfortunately, that left a pile of "Unknown" and "Anonymous" to be included in every case. She decided to call them all *Anonymous,* and put them toward the front of each category. Perhaps eventually they would discover the author. Often such things were mentioned by another writer, or referenced in a compendium about the topic.

It was good to have something to distract herself with—never mind that it was her job, and Tarub was counting on her to organize the Library. Having her best worker confess to murder was very disruptive to the whole process.

She looked at the two chests from Darras's villa that hadn't even been opened yet. She had enough to do for the next *year,* even with Isador and Naomi's help. She decided to speak with Tarub to see how long the woman intended to fund the extra helpers. Of course, that was assuming that Naomi was cleared of the murder and could continue working.

She would have to do something about that, but Naomi had asked her not to. She gritted her teeth and stared a moment at Isador. Maybe it was selfish, but Naomi had been such a huge help in the Library that Bhaja could not imagine letting the woman sacrifice herself.

A citadel guard arrived, with word that Judge Kabos had instructed Bhaja to be present for the judgment and sentencing of Naomi. She would leave for the citadel immediately after midday prayers. Tarub the Learned had also been "invited" to attend, the guard informed her.

She found herself getting angry again as she remembered the harsh cruelty of Judge Kabos. How could the man be called "Protector of Allah" when he was so obviously prejudiced against Jews, and women in general?

Perhaps his wife was a harpy. Or maybe he had no wife; that might make such a man grouchy and mean.

Well, despite Naomi's request that Bhaja stay out of the affair, she had no choice now. Judge Kabos had actually helped by ordering her to attend.

Now she would add Tarub's confirmation that Naomi had spent the night of the murder at the villa, and Bhaja could tell the court about the lack of wet clothes, indicating Naomi could not have gone out.

If all that failed, she might have to break her promise to Naomi. She went to the butcher shop and picked up Raviv, who had also been asked to attend, being the accused's son.

The son that apparently Naomi thought might have murdered Gwafa, hence her pre-emptive "confession."

She and Raviv left Ezra's butcher shop, walking toward the citadel. They passed Hathus and Lylah's rug shop, with its piles of patterned glory.

They passed the pawnshop. She noticed the shop window display was sparse. Bhaja took that to mean times were good; people did not need to sell their valuables for quick cash.

Raviv glanced at the shop. “Do we need a bribe?”

“No,” Bhaja said. “No, we have an alibi, bribes are not needed.” She hoped those words were true.

Raviv looked uncertain.

When they arrived at the citadel entry, Bhaja glanced at Naomi’s son. “Best wash your hands,” she said.

He looked at his hands, where a few streaks of dried blood showed. He washed his hands at the fountain and adjusted his robes to hide the small dark red mark on his under robe. Bhaja looked him over and nodded.

She checked her own clothing, knowing she would be seated in the center of Kabos’s courtroom, because she would be giving evidence. Everyone would be looking at her, so she especially wanted her appearance to be orderly and demure.

Bhaja seated herself on a floor pillow in the middle of the room, while Raviv was escorted to the front, immediately facing Judge Kabos’s chair. After a moment, Abbas ibn Firnas sat down beside her, removing his beard from where it caught in his belt. He patted it, like he would a cat, then turned and grinned at her. She tried to smile back.

She felt as though all the weight of the trial had settled upon her. How had it become her job to clear Naomi of Gwafa’s murder? Part of the reason was Naomi’s lie; part was the pure selfish desire to free a woman whose work she treasured. At least Abbas was here. The old man would testify about the state of Gwafa’s body. It occurred to her that Pai should be here, as well. And indeed, she later noticed he had come in and sat behind her.

Then the judge came in, his beautiful robes swishing around him, a sheaf of papers—mostly Pai’s fine paper, Bhaja noticed—clutched in one hand, and a glass of cooling tea in the other. He sat on the dais pillow and placed papers and tea on the small low table beside him.

He said, “We have heard the confession of the woman Naomi in the matter of the murder of Malik al Jamal. Or, more properly, not-Malik al Jamal.

“Two individuals have claimed this confession to be a lie, and today will testify regarding an alibi for the time of the murder: Tarub the Learned, and Bhaja the librarian.

“I now call Tarub the Learned to confirm or deny this alibi.”

From behind her, Bhaja heard, then saw Tarub rise and move forward to face the judge.

"I hosted a party the night of the big storm, which was the night of the murder. Among other guests, Bhaja and Naomi were at my villa," Tarub said.

"And the woman Naomi remained for the night?"

"Yes. Bhaja did as well, since they had arrived together. The storm was bad, their hired transportation did not show up, and it was late. So, I invited both Bhaja and Naomi to spend the night."

"Was Naomi there in the morning?"

"Yes, she was."

"She claims she rode one of your horses to the al Jamal villa and there murdered him. Is this so?"

"I did not see her leave. I have no idea who killed the man pretending to be Malik. I presume she spent the entire night in the suite I have set aside for female guests.

She cleared her throat. "I know none of my horses had been ridden that night because my stable boy said they were all dry and rested the next morning, with clean hooves. None had been out in the storm. Therefore, I cannot see how Naomi's confession could be true."

The judge grunted, consulted a piece of paper on the side table, then nodded at Tarub. "That will be all, Learned. Thank you."

Tarub gave Bhaja a grim smile as she passed, returning to her seat.

"Next, I call on Bhaja the librarian to answer my questions."

Bhaja stood up. She did not move forward, because Raviv blocked her way, sitting directly in front of her. Beside her, she heard Abbas ibn Firnas clear his throat. She glanced at him. He gave her a nod, his usual bright-eyed smile dimmed somewhat, but he clearly was trying to encourage her.

"You told my guard you have further evidence that Naomi the Jewess did not leave Tarub's villa that night?"

"Yes," Bhaja said. "As most of you recall, the storm that night was exceedingly violent, with strong winds, hail, and lightning and thunder." Around her, she could see heads nodding as others remembered the storm. "First, as I stated before, I am a light sleeper, and was awakened several times by the thunder and the sounds of the wind. Every time I woke, I saw Naomi was still in the room with me, asleep on her bed."

Judge Kabos nodded, waiting for new evidence.

"In the morning, I saw Naomi get dressed." She could feel her cheeks flame as she told the audience of mostly older men these intimate details. "None of her garments were wet, nor even damp. If she had gone out into the storm during the night, she would have been drenched."

"Her robes were fancy for a party," Kabos said. "Everyone knows silk dries quickly."

"Silk robes dry quickly," Bhaja agreed, "but linen undergarments do not." Her face flushed again; she could feel it.

But she saw many heads around her nod agreement. They'd all had the experience of damp linen.

"If she had gone into the storm and gotten soaking wet, her linens would never have had time to dry. Therefore, she didn't go out."

"Or," Judge Kabos said dismissively, "she did not wear...her own clothes."

Bhaja gritted her teeth. He was determined to discredit any piece of evidence in Naomi's favor. Clearly he had already made up his mind.

Well, she wasn't finished yet.

"The Quran allows the family to be compensated, with the rule of Diya, in place of execution. We should prudently locate not-Malik's family to see if they will accept compensation, rather than vengeance against Naomi!"

"That might indeed be prudent, if we had any idea who not-Malik really was," Kabos said with a grimace.

"Then permit me to tell a story, Most Blessed of Allah, that will explain some of this."

The judge raised an eyebrow, paused a dramatic moment, then nodded his permission.

"Twenty years ago, in the town of Tiaret, in the Mahgreb of Ifriqa, the real Malik al Jamal arrived for military training as his father had intended."

The judge waved a hand in a circle, prompting her to hurry up. "That was a long time ago."

"It was, Most Blessed, but it is significant." She licked her lips and went on: "Somewhere there or nearby, a man named Gwafa found and murdered Malik al Jamal, then robbed him of all he possessed. This theft included stealing his name and his history and family.

"Shortly afterwards, Gwafa not-Malik met young Naomi, and tried to woo her. But Naomi was not interested in the man. First he was not Jewish, and second, he was pushy. He was, in fact, a bully.

"Infuriated by her refusal, he forced himself upon her."

"You say he raped Naomi?" the judge asked, blunt in both tone and words.

"He did. And then he abandoned her, returned to Qurtuba, and acting as Malik, he took over the al Jamal trading business and villa. There are many people, some of whom have already testified in this matter of Malik's death, that will tell you that when Malik returned from Ifriqa he was a different person.

Again, heads nodded in the audience, among them Hathus and Lylah and Pai.

"Since that had been the entire purpose of sending him to Ifriqa for military training, Malik's parents accepted the imposter, who was indeed rough and tough, not the gentle kind son they had sent off. Then Malik's father died, and his mother retired to their home near Ronda, leaving Gwafa entirely in charge of the business and their city villa."

"His sister, Sayyida, has stated he has gone on hajj five times. We can presume this was to seek absolution for the murder of the real Malik, and for his rapes of both Naomi and Lylah, and who knows how many other women."

Judge Kabos shook his head at this. "This is gossip. We have testimony for two rapes only, and neither Malik nor this not-Malik, Gwafa, can be here to answer those accusations, since they are dead. This is not evidence of innocence." He sniffed. "In fact, it seems to me, it is further proof that Naomi killed him, in revenge."

"Gwafa was a murderer and a multiple rapist. Darras of Osuna had made plans to murder the man in revenge for his treatment of Naomi. Darras was a witness to Naomi's despair and humiliation."

"Since Darras of Osuna is also dead, he also cannot testify."

"I have here the rough plans Darras was considering." Bhaja held up a vermin-chewed piece of parchment with writing on it.

The judge signaled his aide, who rose and stepped forward, taking the page from Bhaja and handing it to Kabos. Kabos looked it over for a moment, then shook his head. "There is no proof this was even written by Darras—"

"I can show you his handwriting in the many papers of his I have for the Library," Bhaja countered. "This matches that writing."

Kabos glared at her now, probably because she had interrupted him, but also because he disagreed. "This is still no evidence that Naomi did not kill Gwafa."

"It shows how evil a man Gwafa was, that even a sweet soul like Darras would think of ridding the world of him. Gwafa killed Malik, stole his life and his living, raped at least two women, and probably murdered Darras as well. I ask for mercy for Naomi. Even if she did murder him, *which she did not*, it would have been a balancing of the scales of justice!"

But Kabos was shaking his head. He stood up. "No. This Jewess *murdered* a Muslim man! I have all the proof I need! She will be beheaded in the morning, that is my final word."

In front of her, Bhaja could see Raviv's fists clench as he murmured, "No." Then he jumped to his feet and shouted, "No! I killed Gwafa! My mother lies to protect me!"

The judge did not seem at all prepared for this turn of events. He stood there with his mouth open for several seconds before clenching his teeth. Then he sat down, lips tight together. "Explain," he said.

"I was in the butcher shop, closing up for the night, before going into my cubby to sleep. It was dark. There was a noise in the back. At first I thought it might be Ezra, coming back for something he had forgotten. Then I glimpsed the face of the man who had snuck in through the back door. It was Gwafa. A man whom my mother feared above all others. She had told me my father's name was Gwafa, but—" he shook his head, an agonized moan escaping his lips, "not how he *became* my father. That he had taken her against her will, I did not know until just now."

He turned and glanced around the room, then back to Kabos. Bhaja could see the tension in Raviv's back. "I wanted to *know* my father, to learn of him and from him. I didn't want to kill him! But...he came at me with a long dagger in one hand, a sword in the other.

"Gwafa shouted at me, but I could not understand him. Then he said, 'You know who I am, don't you?' and I said, 'I think you are my father.'"

Raviv raised his hands in a shrug. "Then I don't know what happened. It was as if a riding whip had hit a fractious stallion. He went berserk." He pulled his robe away from his body, showing the judge something Bhaja could not see. "I didn't understand at first that he was trying to kill me. He stabbed me, thus," he let his robe fall closed, and Bhaja realized he had shown Kabos a wound.

"So then I grabbed up the first weapon thing I could find, one of Ezra's short, sharp kosher knives, to defend myself." She could hear tears in his voice as he went on, "We exchanged a number of blows, there in the dark among the hanging meat. I don't think any of our blades touched flesh, even though he fought so fiercely and fast, I truly thought I would be dead soon. I did manage to knock the dagger from his off-hand. With the sword, in among the meat, I think it was difficult for him to get a long swing at me. I managed to stab him with the knife I held. I thought I was aiming for his sword arm." Raviv was staring at the floor now, recalling each bit of memory about the fight. "Then, he fell.

"I was so shaken it took me several moments to re-light the lamp. Then I saw I had given Gwafa a death wound. I saw the life leave his eyes." The muscles in his neck tensed. "I did not know what to do. How could I explain this? I would have to reveal my mother's suffering to explain why Gwafa and I were there, doing that. I think he might have meant to scare me into silence, but our fight went far beyond fright.

"I took the sword from his hand and hid it." He fumbled in his robes again, baring a belt with a scabbard and long sword. He drew the sword awkwardly, nearly hitting himself in the jaw with the hilt. "This sword."

"That is the al Jamal family sword!" Sayyida's voice cried from behind the women's screen."

The judge scowled up at the gallery. "If it is, it will be returned to you," Kabos very nearly growled. He looked back at Raviv. "Then what?" he asked.

"Then I took the butcher's cart and horse, loaded the body into it, and drove it to the al Jamal villa. There I dragged the body inside, washed away the blood, and redressed Gwafa's body in clean robes. Then I used his dagger to cut his wrists. I tried to make it look like he had killed himself. I left the dagger in his hand, and left the body in the atrium, all out of sight of his servants who were preparing morning meal. Then I went back to the shop. I tore the bloody robes into scrap rags, put the stained portions into the stable slop to rot, and then washed every drop of blood from the floor, the cart, and myself, and tried to pretend nothing had happened."

Bhaja stood up. "You can see his mother confessed to try and save him, for we all know a mother's love for her child is the strongest love of all."

Were those actual tears she saw in Kabos's eyes?

Abbas ibn Firnas stood up, so Bhaja hastily sat back down. "That story coincides well with what Pai and I discovered on the body," ibn Firnas said. "We were sorely puzzled how there could be so little blood from the wrist cuts if this was a suicide. These events that Raviv has described are verified by everything we saw."

Now there was silence in the courtroom as Kabos deliberated. He allowed everyone to remain in the courtroom as he glanced through the papers he had carried in.

Then he cleared his throat and stood up.

“The killing of Gwafa was in self-defense,” he said, and it was as if the entire room heaved a sigh of relief. “There is no judgment against Raviv, since it was not murder, but an accidental killing as a result of defending himself. The woman Naomi is to be freed, although I issue a caution against lying to the Emir’s judges.”

Naomi, silent all this time, and under guard at the side of the room, issued a stiff smile.

“The scales of justice are in balance,” Kabos said. “There will be no direct compensation of Diya to the al Jamal family, because the murderer himself has been murdered. I will ensure some portion of the trading business is settled on the family, after taxes are paid.”

Bhaja stood up with everyone else as the judge left the courtroom through his little door at the back. Everything she had thought about Judge Kabos had been wrenched awry.

And everything she and her friends had worked for and hoped for had come true. There wasn’t a much better result to be had than that. Well, that was not entirely true. As she and Pai and Abbas walked out the door, she could see Hathus min Alshamal shaking his head, a cruel scowl on his face. She shrugged internally. He should be happy, he and his had been cleared entirely of any wrongdoing.

Naomi, released by the guards, ran towards her son and threw her arms around him. Raviv hugged her, looking over her shoulder to Bhaja’s little group, a teary smile thanking her for her great help. It all had mattered. It all had made a difference.

Bhaja grasped Pai’s hand and swung around to face him, planting a big kiss right on his astonished face.

24. Now or Never

Pai placed new pages to dry in the sun, while Zetian stirred another batch over the fire, and Wararni tore old cotton robes into narrow strips. Pai observed the happy couple. "Live your life like Darras. Make people happy while you're here and sad when you're gone."

"Not like Gwafa. No one attended his funeral," said Wararni.

Zetian gave her paddle a strong stroke. "I agree with my husband. No one lost tears for him, but I'm sad for Raviv. He only defended himself, but it still must hurt to kill another person. I could never imagine doing it."

Pai hung up the last piece of paper. "Enough sad thoughts, tonight is the harvest full moon celebration—a time to be thankful!"

"I'm thankful for my friends and to be married," shouted Wararni throwing up a colorful cloud of cotton scraps.

Zetian put down her paddle and stood on her toes to kiss her new husband. "Me too, my love."

Pai smiled at the happy pair and gave silent thanks that he and Bhaja would soon be united like the couple in his dreams.

Everyone in Pai's shop slept late after the harvest moon celebration, so they were still eating their breakfast of fruit and bread when Bhaja arrived holding up a piece of Pai's paper. "Look what I've found!"

Pai felt a rapid pounding in his chest. It was the map, his original map! "That's wonderful. Where did you find it?"

"It was mixed with a stack of loose parchments in a trunk from Darras of Osuna."

Pai studied the map. "This map shows the treasure to be exactly where I discovered Darras's dead body."

"A corpse is no treasure," said Wararni. Zetian poked her elbow against his hip to stop him from saying any more.

Pai continued. "There was no treasure there."

Bhaja asked softly, "Could your map have been wrong?"

"I did draw that map during a night of fitful sleep. I could have confused my true memories with my dreams."

"So is the treasure forever lost?" queried Zetian.

"I don't know," Pai admitted, "But the real mystery is how did the map get mixed up with those parchments?"

Wararni asked, "Was it in those boxes we brought from Osuna?"

Bhaja nodded. "When we were in Osuna, Darras was already dead, and Gwafa was nowhere around. I doubt the culprit was Abbas so that only leaves Sayyida."

Pai looked at Bhaja in disbelief, "How can you suggest Sayyida had the map?"

"We have *Peri Hermeneias* by the Greek Aristotle in the Library. His *logic* suggests Sayyida had the map," Bhaja said firmly.

Pai didn't want to believe that his childhood friend was involved in Darras's murder. He changed the subject. "There is a second map that I drew with a clear head during the light of day. Perhaps it is correct. It is hidden in Ronda. I'll go retrieve it."

"Good idea," Bhaja said without repeating her accusation of Sayyida.

Almost a week later, Pai entered Ronda still thinking about Aristotle's logic. Had Sayyida stolen the map? Did she murder Darras? He immediately visited the farm to investigate.

To the side of the villa, he noticed the remains of the glider, many pieces of bamboo, some broken and some not, a few silk ropes, and torn scraps of silk cloth. *I will ask Abbas if I can have the silk to make paper,* he thought. The original glider had included goose feathers, but none of those remained.

He spied one of the workers who had retrieved him from the Wadi al-Laban. "Can you show me where the glider crashed?"

"Just follow me," was the cheerful reply.

He went around the building and through the paddock. The horses ignored them as they made their way to the river. He searched the crash location and found a few feathers and some more silk rope. The worker collected some apples and carrots for the horses.

While the worker gave the horses their treats, Pai pondered Bhaja's logic. He pointed to a large white horse that looked familiar. "Who rides that horse?"

"No one. That is not one of our horses."

Darras's white stallion, Pai realized. He now recalled seeing Darras's horse when he returned to retrieve the treasure.

Pai flashed back to hanging from Abbas ibn Firnas's glider. *Darras had mounted his horse with its long mane glistening in the bright sun and waved. "I must ride to Qurtuba today."*

At the end of the flight, Pai had passed through the same paddock as today. *Was Darras's horse there the first time?* Pai looked at the horses. The white horse had not been there. Darras had returned to Qurtuba as he'd said.

He looked at each horse thinking that they were hiding an important clue. He took some carrots from the worker and offered them to the horses. "Tell me. What am I missing?" He recalled standing in wet clothes, and Sayyida offering, "You're welcome to stay overnight with the workers."

He looked again into the paddock. There had been another horse! Malik's grey mount with its distinctive white blaze that looked like the minaret of the Great Mosque. Sayyida had hidden that Malik had been visiting! That's why she didn't invite Pai into the house.

He still didn't want to believe his childhood friend had murdered Darras. He'd seen enough and returned to the mesa following the same path he climbed on the day of the glider crash.

When he reached the Roman ruins, he was greeted by the same stray cats, one black and one striped, both with white feet. "My apologies but I have not brought you any treats." With that, the two scampered away. Either they'd understood his words, or they could not smell any meat on him.

He pried the loose stone from the wall and retrieved the second map. He unrolled it and, as he had hoped, it was different from the first one. *I've found the real treasure map.* He put the map in a hidden pocket in his robe, but immediately removed it. He held the map in his hand, not willing to entrust it to a pocket. He didn't want to lose it.

The two cats returned with a dead snake. He stroked them and scratched between their ears and by their tails. They purred loudly. "Thank you for your kind present, but I am not hungry. You'll have to eat that."

Eventually, the cats tired of his attention and settled down to eat their prey. Pai headed back to Qurtuba.

In a few days, Pai arrived in Osuna. Qusayma greeted him, "Welcome back. I will prepare you a meal and you must stay in my villa for the night."

"Thank you. I appreciate spending a night among friends."

"My stable hand will take your horse and care for it. You both must be tired."

Pai still had the map in his hand.

He recalled the scene last time he'd been in Osuna. The trunks and Wararni were piled in Bhaja's wagon. Sayyida's wagon that had carried Darras from Ronda to Osuna followed, carrying sacks that Sayyida was moving from the farm to her room in Malik's villa.

Sayyida had so many sacks. Pai wondered if one of those sacks had contained Darras's fancy travel bag, the one with the leather handle and silver buckles. He speculated that Sayyida had placed the bag in Malik's room. Maybe Bhaja's logic was right. Why had he ever doubted her? He'd known Sayyida since childhood, but Bhaja was forever and for all time.

On the road back to Qurtuba he put all the pieces together but remembered Bhaja's admonition, "Consider the ways your words will affect things before you speak." Now that he and Bhaja were together, he endeavored to not disappoint her again.

He thought about Sayyida, how she'd lost her brother. She had suffered enough. Then he thought of Hathus and Naomi, how they'd spent time in jail and narrowly escaped execution. No one was looking for Darras's murderer. He decided it would be better to say nothing.

A week later Pai attended the Emir's audience even though the meeting had become dull now that the mystery of Gwafa was settled.

The Emir announced, "My hareem has petitioned me to include a woman on my council. I learned from my father that one should never ignore the women of the hareem."

The men in the audience were silent, but a murmur of whispers and some laughter was heard from the balcony.

"Since Sayyida al Jamal is now a major landowner, I appoint her to the council to replace the position illegally held by Gwafa impersonating her brother. This honors her brother who was viciously murdered long ago."

The Emir turned to the back wall and the secret door opened. He held out his hand and Sayyida entered the room in robes of flowing silks. As she advanced, the only sound was the chimes of the many gold bangles on her wrists and ankles.

When she reached the Emir, Hathus shouted, "No! Never!" At first, Pai thought, *Hathus just wants the position for himself.* But then the crowd exploded. The screen in the balcony slid open and Pai could see Bhaja and Tarub. He couldn't tell whether they were applauding the recognition of a woman or jeering the choice of Sayyida.

The Quran and the hadiths must have been divided because Judge Javan supported the decision, while Judge Kabos stood silent.

Pai looked at Sayyida dressed in finery and standing proudly. He couldn't remain quiet any longer. He walked to the front of the room. In a soft voice, he said, "Before you do this, let me tell you what happened to Darras."

After a cacophony of shushes, the room waited in silence. Only the birds singing in the garden could be heard.

He looked to Sayyida, the only woman among the men below the balcony. She hung her head.

"Darras's fate was determined in Ronda when he offered to split the treasure with Sayyida. She agreed, but this was not why she murdered him."

The crowd gasped. No one had suspected her of murder. She gave Pai an angry look.

He took a deep breath. "Before Darras returned to Qurtuba, he told her how Gwafa had raped Naomi and then murdered Sayyida's brother. Darras wanted to avenge Naomi's rape before he died of the tumor disease. He enlisted Sayyida's help with the double enticements of treasure and justice for her brother."

The crowd whispered among themselves speculating on what Pai would reveal next.

"This plan survived until Gwafa, still pretending to be Malik, arrived. He rarely visited Ronda, but there he was, waiting at the farm after Darras departed."

The birds were again heard singing.

"Sayyida was torn. Should she believe her brother, or Darras with his outlandish story of rape, murder, treasure, and impersonation? At her first opportunity, she told the story to Gwafa, thinking he was her brother. Gwafa denied everything and said they needed to kill Darras." He paused for the crowd to consider Sayyida's dilemma.

"She didn't know who to believe. Both men wanted to murder the other. She wanted to leave the farm. Either way, her wish would be granted. Darras promised her treasure. Gwafa promised her a home in Qurtuba. How could she decide?"

The birds continued to sing as everyone waited for what came next.

"She had stolen the map from me. When Darras returned from Qurtuba, she went with him to recover the treasure.

"But, there was no treasure! With that, she decided that Darras was the liar and Gwafa was telling the truth. Darras's fate was settled. She killed him and made arrangements to move into Malik's villa in Qurtuba."

Now Sayyida keened and wailed, "No! No!" She ran at Pai and pummeled him with both fists. "This is all your fault!"

Pai covered his face with his arms, while the crowd gasped.

Sayyida didn't let up. She beat Pai, shouting, "Your map was wrong, wasn't it? You tricked me!"

The crowd took her fury for a confession and began shouting, "Murderer!"

The Emir signaled his guards, and they took her away. When the crowd settled, he proclaimed, "In the matter of Sayyida, Judge Javan will decide her fate." He rubbed his jaw, making his beard dance. "Now I have a dilemma. I won't have a murderer on my council, but I must honor my promise to the women of the hareem."

He looked up to the balcony. Pai imagined him considering Tarub the Learned, but she was already too powerful. Surely, she was the example Emir Muhammad's father used when warning him about the power of the hareem.

Lylah also stood prominently against the railing. Everyone knew Hathus desired a position on the council, but choosing Lylah would not satisfy him, nor would others in the city respect that choice.

The Emir said, "I appoint someone who we can all respect and who has worked hard for the good of Qurtuba...Bhaja the librarian at Tarub's Library."

Pai cheered louder than anyone. Before Bhaja responded, she looked to Tarub. Tarub gave her a small smile that might have only been seen by Bhaja and Pai.

Bhaja replied in a clear voice. "I accept."

The crowd's agreement drowned out the few remaining dissenters. Pai looked at Hathus with his glum face. Men like Hathus were like the Romans; their time had passed. In the future, Muslims and Christians might marry and women would share in the governance of free cities everywhere, putting an end to men like Hathus and Kabos. The year 880 was a momentous one that would be celebrated into the next century.

When he met Bhaja and Tarub outside the citadel, all three of them couldn't stop smiling.

Pai couldn't contain his enthusiasm. He turned to Bhaja, "We should hurry to get married and have children. This is a wonderful time for everyone."

Bhaja glanced at Tarub, then met Pai's eyes. “Does this mean you intend to share the work of raising the children?”

How much work is it? Pai wondered.

25. RESOLUTIONS AND RESOLVE

"Come to dinner and meet my mother," Bhaja said with a teasing grin at Pai."

"Oh," said Pai. "So soon?"

"What? You expect to court me before you even meet my mother?"

"No, no. It's just that I've already met your brother, who doesn't seem to like me much. I had hoped to secure his approval before venturing on to your mother."

"Do not worry. Mother is much more agreeable than Yusuf. He thinks he should be my boss, that he should replace Papa and be the man of the house, even though he is younger than me. Mother is more practical."

Pai muttered, "We should also discuss our opinions on money, and housing and many other things—"

"Are you saying you don't want to court me, after being in such a rush?"

Now Pai seemed distraught. Bhaja saw his face fall, his forehead wrinkle in worry, and his eyes flash and jump around as they did when he was upset.

She hurried to reassure him. "It's fine, Pai. I am only teasing you a little. But it *is* time to meet my mother. Your opinions of each other will help us decide how and what to do after we are wed."

"I, oh, um, of course."

"Tomorrow evening," Bhaja suggested. "Right after sunset prayers." She tilted her head and smiled at him. His face relaxed and he looked more like his usual self-sufficient, exuberant self. "Will that do?"

"Of course," Pai said, smiling back at her.

"You've been practicing!" Bhaja exclaimed.

Pai laughed and used his barjyn to stab and pick up a piece of the tender roast lamb. He popped it in his mouth and chewed, grinning.

The scents of rosemary and sage floated above the table. Mama had made a fancy meal in Pai's honor.

"Well, I am almost as good as you now are," Bhaja said, demonstrating. She had been practicing at home, to her mother's exasperation.

"What need have we of these things?" Mother had said, her stubborn face well in place. But, to Bhaja's surprise, Yusuf had supported his sister rather than his mother.

"If you want to look like a sophisticated city person, you need to use them. Even the Emir's guards have all learned, Mother."

Their mother had shaken her head and refused the barjyn Yusuf had offered her.

But Pai obviously sensed what was the coming thing. He had not refused to learn, as he now demonstrated.

"Ibn Firnas is the one who insisted we practice," Pai said. "Zetian uses her sticks, but even she has tried the barjyn and found it useful. You can hold your meat with the barjyn in one hand and cut it with the knife in the other."

"I've always thought taking dainty bites from a piece of meat on the end of a knife was manners enough," Mother said. "But I can see your point, if you wish to be pretentious. It still seems silly to me."

"Mother!" Yusuf cried, "don't be backward!"

Their mother grinned and pulled a silver-tined barjyn out of her pocket and began eating with it.

"Ahhh!" Yusuf said. "You were being silly."

"My son is an Emir's guard, and my daughter is on the Emir's council. Their mother cannot be the only person in Qurtuba who doesn't have any manners!" Her declaration was said with sparkling eyes and a quirked mouth, but Bhaja heard the truth among the joking: their mother was proud of them and would not risk embarrassing either of her children.

"Very nice," Pai said watching Mother's skill.

"Speaking of manners and Qurtuba," Bhaja said. "And before I forget," she glanced around the table. Only Pai's eyes were on her, though both Yusuf and Mother seemed to be listening. "Tarub the Learned has decided to sponsor a Picnic in the Fields, and a Treasure Dig Party."

"In Ronda?" Pai wondered.

"The fields that belonged to the al Jamal family, below Ronda, yes," Bhaja said.

"We are all invited, of course, along with Zetian and Wararni, and Naomi and Isador, and Abbas ibn Firnas."

"No," Pai said. "Someone needs to watch the shop."

"And the Library," Bhaja said in agreement. "She will leave a pair of her guards at each place for safety while we are gone. She is bringing many of her servants and guards, and a huge tent, and plans to make a big adventure out of it."

"What if the treasure isn't... "

"Isn't there?" Yusuf suggested.

"Or isn't a treasure," Pai said. "We know Darras's letter from the Pope was fake. Maybe the treasure is too."

Bhaja shrugged. "That isn't the point; it's the picnic, the party and a fun outing." She glanced at her mother. "You are welcome at Sayyida's mother's house, Mama, where you can sleep comfortably in a real bed. The al Jamal heir is now solely the mother, and she would welcome some company, so Tarub says."

"Oh. That would be nice." Mother blinked as she thought a moment. "I should bring a small gift for her house."

"Maybe. But yourself is the best thing to bring. She is lonely. A woman's perspective and friendship would be a fine gift to her."

"Yes, but also flowers. Or fruit," mother said. She was clearly determined to bring a guest gift.

"She has plenty of fruit, there's orchards on the property," Bhaja said.

"And wildflowers in the fields," Pai added.

"Oh, then that is perfect. I will bring her one of the glassblower's fine vases to put those flowers in," Mother said. She met Bhaja's eyes. "When is this grand event?"

"In three weeks. Tarub wants plenty of time to plan it and fill out her invitation list." Bhaja couldn't keep the laughter out of her voice. "She is considering inviting Judge Kabos!"

Pai joined her in laughter. "Maybe that will mend his sour face!"

"So, Isador and Naomi, you are both invited to this event as well," Bhaja said, after explaining Tarub's party plans to the other librarians the next day. "Two of her own guards will stay in the Library, and two more in Pai's shop, so everyone can come."

Bhaja saw Isador meet Naomi's eyes, and the priest grinned. "Sounds like fun," he said.

Bhaja was fairly certain there was something building between those two. Perhaps only a good friendship, perhaps more.

For the first time in quite a while, she saw a sparkle in Naomi's eyes. "Is this casual dress? Or given Tarub, are we supposed to be fancy?"

"*Picnic outdoor wear* was what she told me," Bhaja explained. "We could even wear loose trousers, but will want our headscarves still, for the sun is fierce."

Naomi nodded.

Bhaja stood between the two, and now looked down at Isador's worktable. He had a larger than average sheet of Pai's fine paper on his slanted table, and had begun writing a verse from the Bible, in a large decorative Arabic script toward the top of the page.

"I mean to add the same or a similar quotation from each of the Quran and the Torah or other writings from each faith. They can be our artwork on the walls between sets of shelves and over the doors."

"Will you add colors, do you think?" Bhaja asked, still examining the lovely page.

Naomi leaned over to look, too.

"I plan to, unless you think it a grievous waste of inks."

"No," Bhaja said. "Use them." She nodded confirmation of her words. "We celebrate the written word, here, and these are a beautiful example of the treasures that can be found in our texts."

"I've been working on them as a break from translating and copying," Isador said. "A change of pace helps me refocus on our real work."

"This is beautiful," Bhaja said. "You are well-versed in the teachings of other religions," she went on, "Is that a normal thing to study at the Abbey?"

Isador looked embarrassed. "No," he said. "I am one of the few priests in al-Andalus who is willing to perform mixed marriages, so I have studied the books of other faiths. Besides, most of the monks and priests at our Abbey are there on retreat, to study and pray, or for their retirement in old age. They don't perform weddings at all."

"The...um...head person at the Catholic church in the Christian district...does he not perform weddings?"

"He does. But only Christian to Christian. Which means, of course, Roman Catholic to Roman Catholic. He will not even marry a Byzantine Catholic to a Roman one, believing, perhaps with some good reason, there will be friction regarding religion in the marriage."

"I am curious," Naomi said, "why you will perform mixed weddings, then, yet others will not? Would there not be more friction with two different religions?"

Here Isador paused what he had been doing and stood silent in thought for a moment. "I think it has to do with the rigidity of our beliefs about the *intent of the words* in our religious texts. I have found in the Bible and the Quran—and probably will in the Torah, though I have not studied it as closely—contradictions within the texts themselves. Particularly between the Gospels and the older sections of the Bible. Once I saw apparently contradictory passages in my own religion's Book, I began to look for them in others.

"So, after some study, I chose the more liberal applications of law and principles, while other priests are more conservative."

"Who is right?" Bhaja wondered. She had heard similar discussions among imams and judges in her time working at the Mosque, and several times scholars had sought evidence from the library there to back up conflicting points.

"Both?" Isador suggested. "There are several places where the Bible says that religious leaders can and must sometimes use their own judgment to interpret a story to fit in local situations. There has never been an al-Andalus before. We are learning how to live together in peace, which I believe needs common sense and an open mind."

Bhaja continued to work on the scroll she was translating for a few moments. Then she lost her focus on the Latin, and entertained thoughts about marriage between her and Pai.

What a discovery! The very copyist she had hired for the Library was a person who could perform their marriage ceremony, something she had been worried about. Of course, that was if Pai agreed. And if he indeed asked her to marry him, or perhaps she would ask him. She stared at the page before her, unseeing, as she drifted back to a vision of *a high mountain wedding, and a flower-decorated bull stepping delicately between the guests.*

She heard a noise, a quill snapped, a low-voiced curse.

She refocused, returned to the Qurtuba Library, and finished the scroll. Then she turned to the trunk she had pulled it from and noticed it was now empty. "Oh! We are now on the last of Darras's trunks! Another thing to celebrate!"

The day was sunny and heading toward very hot. Perfect so far for their grand picnic, though the hard work of the Treasure Dig might need to be postponed until after the heat of the day. There were few trees to shade them, and those that had survived the wildfire were thin and mostly leafless.

Bhaja wore light cotton robes and was enjoying the breeze that helped cool her from the gilt sunlight that poured down.

Under a canopy held by four of her guards, Tarub reclined on a stool with an adjustable back. The contraption looked odd, but had been easily unfolded and appeared comfortable. Bhaja grinned at

Tarub's almost magical ability to find people to construct such new things for her. Abbas had probably designed it.

The canopy was an old idea, but the way it unfolded and could be staked into the ground was new, as was the big tent Tarub had had constructed for everyone to sleep in. As soon as the workers finished driving the stakes in the ground, the guards affixed the poles that held up the tightly woven canvas, and then the canopy over Tarub's head stood by itself. Tarub waved Bhaja into the shade with her.

Bhaja immediately felt cooler. Working so many hours indoors in the dimmer light of the Library had spoiled her ability to spend much time in the sun. Even her skin had gotten paler, she noticed.

Beneath a much larger canopy and atop a clean large canvas floor, The Learned's kitchen crew was preparing the early afternoon meal, and some, no doubt, were already working on the evening feast. Bhaja could see a man with what looked like blacksmith's arms kneading dough.

Tarub made an exclamation and Bhaja turned to see Qusayma and her husband arrive. As they dismounted, Tarub's stable hands ran up to unload their gear and take the horses away. They led the animals to the temporary rope-and-stake corral where Bhaja could see Yusuf still showing off his new charger. Bhaja and her mother had pooled their savings to buy him the big black—of which he was extremely proud, extolling the horse's virtues to anyone who would listen.

Qusayma approached the canopy and the women underneath it, carrying an umbrella of stretched linen to shade herself. The servants carried the box of fresh vegetables they had brought over to the cooks.

Bhaja was fairly certain everyone who had accepted Tarub's invitation had now arrived.

Before they had left Qurtuba, the Emir had judged the treasure on the al Jamal lands should belong to Darras and his remaining family—which of course meant only Qusayma and her offspring—thus the woman would inherit whatever the group managed to dig up today. The fields themselves belonged to Sayyida and Malik's mother, along with the bungalow Bhaja's mother would sleep in tonight. The two women had seemed to enjoy talking to one another, so Bhaja was glad for that bit of company for both of them.

Pai was presently out of sight, rechecking landmarks against his map. The *correct* version of his map, he had been eager to point out, not the one Sayyida had used to wrongly conclude Darras to be a fraud.

Bhaja sat down on the canvas rug and leaned back on her elbows, watching as Judge Kabos walked up to Tarub. Everyone had been surprised when the man accepted Tarub's invitation. Today he had been a perfect gentleman, even apologizing to Naomi for considering her a suspect in the murder of the supposed Malik.

Bhaja was still not certain the Judge could be considered a friend, but aside from his intense, nearly rabid belief in and knowledge of the Law, he seemed to be a sensible man. Maybe even a kind one. And most notably, one who was interested in Tarub. Who could have guessed? Well aware, Tarub flirted with him. Bhaja had to hope their intensity didn't flare up and burn them both.

She turned to the east, shading her eyes, which gave her a view through the orchard on that side of the party site. Two figures were walking toward the tent and canopies. Pai and Abbas, in animated conversation if the movement of the old man's hands was any indication.

As they approached, Pai flashed his bright smile at her, and she could not help but smile back. His enthusiasm was infectious.

"I have staked out the location of the treasure to the best of my ability," he said as he sat down beside her. "We'll begin digging right after mid-day prayers and our meal, both of which should happen soon." He used a corner of his robe to wipe perspiration from his forehead and eyes. "Or," he went on, "we may wait until it is cooler."

"Yes, I think that is becoming more and more the right option," Bhaja said.

On her chair, reclined like a queen, Tarub nodded her approval of this plan.

Heading towards sunset the air cooled down. With the sun lowering closer to the western hills, the light was less bright as well as less hot. Pai picked up a shovel from the pile beside Tarub's tent.

"Aha!" Judge Kabos said, "Time to dig!" He suited action to words and picked out a shovel as well. Soon he was joined by Yusuf, Isador and Naomi, Qusayma and her husband, and a couple of Tarub's guards. Wararni chose to sit out the work beside Zetian, who had been suffering in the heat.

"I have my own heater," Zetian said, patting her rounded belly. They stayed behind along with Tarub's cooks as the rest of the group trailed after Pai and Abbas.

Pai's stakes quickly became visible as they moved through the remains of burnt bushes and grasses. Tarub's aide set up her folding stool under the sole tree, an olive that still had half its leaves.

Bhaja stayed close to Pai as he waved his shovel indicating where they were to dig. He pushed his shovel into the packed soil, scooped up what he had loosened and tossed the dirt and ashes and rocks to the side.

Soon the group had the treasure surrounded, but the digging was slow going. It had been a while since there had been any rain, and the soil in this field had "always been full of clay," Bhaja remembered Sayyida saying.

She spent a brief moment feeling sorry for Sayyida, for the woman's circumstances that had set up her desire to be free. But Darras had been a good and kind man, and helpful to Bhaja. She did not think she would ever forgive Sayyida for his murder. Darras had not been in Sayyida's way, he had been trying to help.

She shook her head, feeling anger build. But no. That wasn't what she was going to think about today. Today was a day for happiness.

The treasure was buried surprisingly shallow in Bhaja's consideration. About an arm's length of soil and rock and dead plant matter covered the top of an urn made, apparently, of rock. Several more were discovered, made of what ibn Firnas described as marble, and then smaller ones of plainer stone.

"I think this is a Roman funerary site," Abbas ibn Firnas said, scratching his chin and then rubbing his nose.

"Ha!" Judge Kabos chortled. "So we have dug through ashes to find ashes!"

A few of the others found the irony funny as well, though most, including Pai, looked disappointed.

Abbas bent down and looked at the first marble urn. "No, I think this one is definitely porphyry. The ash is useless, of course, but the marble itself has some fair value."

Pai carefully used his shovel to loosen the remaining soil around the porphyry urn, as Abbas brushed it away with his hands.

"Yes," he said as more of the reddish-pink urn was uncovered. "Definitely. And this one looks like fine white alabaster."

The more enthusiastic among the group continued to dig, loosening and removing urns, of which there were about a dozen.

Yusuf, having little appreciation for someone's remains who had been dead five hundred years, dumped over the clay pot he had unearthed. Glints of gold lay among the ashes. He brushed the ash away, and they were able to identify two gold Roman coins.

Abbas glanced at Qusayma who had been leaning over looking at the coins in fascination. "You will probably receive a higher return from a historian and collector than from a goldsmith if you choose to sell these," he advised her.

She nodded.

With Yusuf having found something of some value, the others also removed the various pots from the ground and emptied them.

Laughing, they each claimed to have found the best treasure: A pair of highly patinated copper earrings; a broken chain of fine gold; more coins, mostly silver; another pair of earrings, gold this time; some unidentifiable copper lumps; and so on.

When all was dug loose and emptied, Qusayma's total treasure consisted of: Five gold Roman coins, three pairs of silver earrings, two pairs of still-lovely gold ones, and the worthless copper pair. Two chain necklaces, one silver, one gold; a silver buckle including its prong (which are usually missing, Abbas said); five silver bangles and one gold; and a dozen rings of silver and gold and enamel, and all of varying sizes; likewise a batch of hairpins in all mediums and styles; and last but not least an assortment of daggers, knives, and bits of stuff that Abbas said had probably decorated scabbards. Plus the alabaster and porphyry urns, of which there were two each.

Qusayma immediately claimed all of the bangles, sliding them onto her arms alongside the two she already wore. When she saw Bhaja looking at the gold earrings with rosy pink enamel flowers, she said, "Oh, please take those if you like them, Bhaja. I really have small use for such things."

Bhaja glanced up at the young woman, wide-eyed. "If you are certain?" at Qusayma's nod, Bhaja smiled and said, "They will look so nice with my heirloom necklace."

"These are an heirloom, too!" Pai joked. "Saved here by some Roman hero's wife."

Wondering if she should feel bad about wearing a dead woman's earrings, she immediately laughed at herself. What was her lotus blossom necklace but a dead woman's? That was how things became heirlooms, after all.

"So there was some treasure," Tarub said with a crooked grin.

"Please help yourself to a piece or two of jewelry," Qusayma invited everyone around her. "I cannot use it all."

Tarub picked a silver hairpin with an interesting design.

Pai took a small gold ring. Neither Abbas nor Kabos took anything.

"If I may," Yusuf asked, holding up a small but heavy silver ring. Qusayma nodded. Yusuf smiled, polishing the ring against his robes. Bhaja eyed him and he flushed, but said nothing as he placed the ring carefully in a hidden pocket. He clearly had someone in mind to give it to, but Bhaja let him keep his secret—for now. "Thank you, Qusayma," he said, and others chorused their thanks.

She smiled, pleased to be able to be generous.

The stars were brilliant against the cloudless sky.

Bhaja and Pai lay side by side on a blanket some distance away from Tarub's tents and canopies.

"The stars were the same in my dream place," Pai said.

"Oh, I think I never saw them in any of my visions," Bhaja said, feeling a little sad she had missed that. "It was always daytime, or I was indoors."

"You need to get out more," Pai observed.

"Thank goodness for the courtyard at the Library," Bhaja said, agreeing.

"But I like how the arrangements of stars do not change shape," Pai continued. "The sky looks like the same sky, no matter how our love might travel through time."

Bhaja sighed, still staring at the stars.

She felt Pai stir beside her. He took a sip of water from his bota. He stayed sitting up and opened his arms wide. Bhaja looked at him. He spoke:

"The blades of grass are burnt
but not destroyed by prairie fires.
when spring winds blow,
they bring it back to life.

"A poem among others Zetian has told me." He sat all the way up and turned to face her. "Just like the grass, our love might appear to die, but it returns, reborn in us. Love is forever."

"Yes," Bhaja said.

"My dreams make sense. The lady I love in my dream came back to life like those blades of grass."

She nodded, watching him closely.

"My love is eternal," Pai said. "Bhaja, please say yours is as well."

"Yes," she said. "I believe it is."

"Will you marry me?"

"Yes, of course," she said. "I will always marry you."

TO THE READER

Please accept the authors' gratitude for finding and reading our book.

We are independent authors and appreciate how difficult it is to select our book from the flood of offerings. As independent authors, we are significantly dependent on reader-to-reader recommendations.

If you enjoyed our novel and wish to support independent writers, we would appreciate any posts on social media, and especially an all-important Amazon review.

You might also be interested in **The Two Pearls: An international science mystery of climate change. (Pandemic Mysteries #3)**

Reader's praise for Pandemic Mysteries: "Kudos to you for weaving in a good story with accurate biological and cultural detail."

Available from most online booksellers. ISBN: 978-0963175588

https://amzn.to/2BiELpR

Thank you.
J. and D.R.

References

Anderson, Glaire D., Concubines, Eunuchs, and Patronage in Early Islamic Cordoba, in Therese Martin, ed., *Reassessing the Roles of Women as 'Makers' of Medieval Art and Architecture*, (2012) Brill, Boston, ISBN 978-9004-22828-3, pp. 633-670.

Ayoub, Mahmoud M., (2013) *Islam: Faith and History*, Oneworld Publications, London.

Campo, Juan Eduardo, (2009), Encyclopedia of Islam, 2009, Facts on File, Inc., New York, NY.

Christys, Ann, (2001) Cordoba in the 'Vita vel Passio Argenteae' in Mayke de Jong, Franz Theuws and Carine von Rhijn (eds.) *Topographies of Power in the Early Middle Ages: The Transformation of the Roman World 6*, Leiden Boston: Brill pp.119-136.

Christys, Ann, (2006) *Muslims and Christians in Umayyad Cordoba: the formation of a tolerant society?* retrieved from Academia.edu.

Fernandez-Morera, Dario, (2018) The Myth of the Andalusian Paradise, ISI Books, Wilmington, Delaware.

Garcia, Jorge Alonso, (1987) La Ciudad del Castillo, Bobastro-Tacarona-Ronda, Grafsur, S.A.L., Armilla, Granada.

Guenther, Sebastian, (2020) Education, general up to 1500 for *The Encyclopedia of Islam* retrieved from academia.edu.

Helou, Anissa, (2018) Feast, Food of the Islamic World, Harper Collins Ecco, New York.

Herrero, B. and L. Santos, (2009) Medicinal plants of traditional use in Castilla y Leon in Acta Horticulturae, January 2009.

James, David, (2012) A History of Early Al-Andalus, The Akhbar majmua, Routledge, London and New York.

Lane-Poole, Stanley, (2018) The Story of Moors in Spain, OK Publishing, Musaicum Books, e-book.

Lewicka, Paulina B., (2005) *Restaurants, Inns and Taverns That Never Were: Some Reflections on Public Consumption in Medieval Cairo*. in Journal of the Economic and Social History of the Orient, vol. 48, no. 1, pp. 40–91.

Martinez-Moreno, F. and E. Igartua, L. Solís, (2017). *Barley Types and Varieties in Spain: A Historical Overview* in Ciencia e Investigación Agraria. 44. pp. 12-23.

Menocal, Maria Rosa, (2002) The Ornament of the World: How Muslims, Jews and Christians Created a Culture of Tolerance in Medieval Spain, Warner Books Hachette Book Group, New York.

Moreti, Juan Jose, (1838) Historia de L.M.N.Y.M.L. Ciudad de Ronda, reprinted by Forgotten Books, 2018, London.

Rezvi, Ruhul, (2020) *History Development and Famous Historians of Abbasid*, Bholanath College, Dhubri, India, retrieved from academia.edu.

Robinson, Majied, (2013) *Prosopographical Approaches to the Nasab Tradition: a Study of Marriage and Concubinage in the Tribe of Muḥammad, 500-750 CE*, Ph.D. Dissertation, The University of Edinburgh.

Rouighi, Ramzi, (2011) *The Berbers of the Arabs*, Studia Islamica, nouvelle édition/new series, 1, pp. 67-101.

Ruthven, Malise, and Azim Nanji, (2004) Historical Atlas of Islam, Harvard University Press, Cambridge, MA.

Scott, Charles Rochfort, (2013) Excursions in the Mountains of Ronda and Granada, Project Gutenberg, e-book.

Toral-Niehoff, Isabel, (2018) *Writing for the Caliphate: The Unique Necklace by Ibn ʿAbd Rabbih*, The Journal of Middle East Medievalists, 26, 80-95.

EXCERPT FROM SURAMARTI SAGA BOOK 1

The Murders, The Mosque continued the adventures of Bhaja and Pai which began in **Kitane, Bull Jumper: Courting and Catastrophe in the Bronze Age** (Suramarti Saga Book 1)

Available on Amazon [https://amzn.to/2SkWZKt] and from most online booksellers. ISBN: 978-0963175564

Reader's praise for Kitane, Bull Jumper: "You really captured the feel of the landscape and brought the Minoan civilization alive."

EXCERPT

SCENE 1 — KITANE AT SURAMARTI

The bull whuffed then trotted toward Kitane. She reached her hand out and scritched the base of each ear. She had to stand on her toes to reach. Enosidas then tossed his head, ready to work out.

Kit gave his head a pat, then turned and trotted in a big circle, side by side with the bull. When they had good momentum built, she reversed, running in the opposite direction, getting ready for her leap. Then she heard the roar and felt the shaking of another earthquake. She and the bull both stopped, waiting it out. Sometimes the quakes were quick; sometimes they kept going, as this one did. It felt like the ground beneath their feet was heaving, like some monster was trying to hatch out of it. Then it settled, the noise diminishing, the ground lying back down, still.

She heard the braying of donkeys and saw two animals running wildly toward them. She patted Enosidas' head, then ran toward the donkeys, arms waving. It would not do to have them spook the bull—he'd stayed calm so far. The donkeys' wide white eyes saw her. They changed direction, running down the hill toward the Tylissos fields.

"Which is probably where they belong, anyway," she muttered. Jura needed to get his animals under control. Weren't they supposed to be penned up?

Frowning as she thought about it, Kit moved downhill toward Tylissos. Jura's pack animals were kept in a pen with a good solid fence. Normally donkeys did not panic any more than any other animals. Was something wrong at Tylissos villa? She glanced back and saw Enosidas browsing on the sweet new grass coming up after the recent rains. He should be fine. She walked toward the neighboring villa, thinking about Jura.

He had been wooing her for months now. He compared well with her other suitors, except for his stiff disposition. The man seemed made of stone he was so rigid. She kept hoping she would catch him in a softer mood, but that hadn't happened yet. He was her mother's pick, and he would be a good match. But. She sighed. Was there always a "but?" Wasn't there one perfect man among her choices?

In truth, it wasn't only the choice of suitor that was the problem. The direst problem was the bulls. If she or Eno ever made a mistake and lost the competition, he would be sacrificed at the end of the "celebration."

She shuddered, just thinking about it.

This "tradition" was simply wrong. No trained bull should ever be slaughtered, no matter how badly they lost, how poorly they showed. She did not believe such a sacrifice could ever honor Jasasara, the Goddess of life whom they honored with the bull jumping.

At Tylissos, the steward directed a crew of atomai, bringing saws and axes to cut up the big tree that had fallen into the donkey pen. No wonder the animals had been terrified. One donkey lay pinned and squealing beneath the weight of the ancient plane tree that had crashed down upon it.

As she approached, Kit saw the steward bend down and cut its throat with a sharp bronze blade. The squealing stopped. Jura ran into the pen from the small Tylissos stable, a blade in his hand, a moment too late to do the deed. He and the steward conversed, then Jura spotted Kitane walking toward them down the hill.

"I am so sorry for your loss," Kit said, nodding toward both the tree and the donkey.

"Potidas is still so angry," Jura said.

"I am asking the Goddess to intervene," Kit said. "I am asking my sister for her blessing for all Keftiu. Whatever has angered Potidas, She may be able to intercede for Her people."

Jura nodded. "I honor Potidas each morning, in the traditional way."

"That is good, Jura. It is good." But is it enough? Kitane wondered, looking at the destruction.

The sun flowed warm over her shoulders as Kitane admired the new courtyard they'd built around the

goddess tree. Her family had long intended to enclose the ancient tamarisk tree and create a small shrine here behind Suramarti villa. Now it was done. She stepped forward, under the tree.

The dappled sunlight the tree let through felt softer, as though the tree had gentled it, making it kind. She eyed the bench her cousin had carved from the dead goddess tree at Zakros. The costly wood had been smoothed and oiled and then left in its natural shape on a stone platform carved to hold the wood. Kit wandered over to look at it, and to compare the wood with the living bark of the tree that shaded it.

"Such a waste of resources," Jura said, walking into the courtyard on sandaled feet. "The money spent on that wood could have paid for the entire new wing of your home."

Kit eyed him over her shoulder with distaste. "Even if you think so, the living tree should still be honored with bare feet!"

Jura looked down at his sandals, retreated to the small gate, and slipped his footwear off, placing them outside the gate beside his dog, who had better manners than its master. Re-entering the courtyard in his now bare feet, he essayed a smile at her. "Sorry," he said, seeming to address Kit more than the Goddess with his apology.

Kitane continued to scowl, her peaceful enjoyment of the new enclosure now broken by this stone of a man. It wasn't as if Jura was poor, either, he just was a natural conservative when it came to spending—even when it was for the Goddess or the Temple. Or rather, his mother was, and Jura was too much a traditionalist to try to change that.

She could think of nothing to say to him. She looked back at the tree, brought her clenched hand to her forehead with respect, and backed out of the enclosure. She turned and walked rapidly toward the new wing of the Suramarti villa, abandoning Jura and the tree together.

Her mother's sister and family had recently fled from Akrotiri, which the priestesses said was no longer safe. The new wing had been built to house them here at Suramarti, and it had created another kind of courtyard, sheltered on three sides, filled with flowers and trees and a small fountain. The small rectangular garden was protected on one side by the new wing, on the other side by the old wing, and topped by the original cross-corridor with a shrine and a long wall pierced by doors and windows—the polythyron—for celebrating the Goddess.

With six sleeping rooms, three workshops, and a plumbed toilet per wing, the villa was now huge.

She walked through the corridor of the new wing into the dining hall where the family was gathered. Everyone was here except her brother Diwoki—at sea in his trade ship, and sister Sakusna—also at sea, with the trader Tros.

Halima, Diwoki's wife from Kmt, far to the south, and her two little children were a dark accent among the bronzy-skinned Keftiu. Kit reached out a hand and clasped Halima's slender one. As graceful and agile as she was, Kit always felt chunky next to the tall, slim Kmt woman. They embraced, and Kit explained how the ceremony would work for the benefit of her sister-in-law.

Kit's eldest sister, the Priestess Qazipatima, had come from the Knossos Temple to bless the villa's new wing. Kit smiled to see her little sister Biaja following Qazi rather like a little bald duckling waddling after its mama. Bee was an initiate at the Temple, learning what the school there had to teach.

Her mother, father, aunt, and cousins filled the space along with several neighboring telestai, including Jura. She nodded at Jura, then grasped her cousin and friend Isari's hand. The three young women, Halima, Kitane, and Isari, watched as Qazi and Bee walked around the room, making sure everything was in place for the ceremony.

"Everything looks so beautiful," Isari murmured.

"The rooms are lovely," Halima said, her accent clipped and charming.

"The Goddess has truly blessed us," Kit said softly.

They all filed through the lustral basin one by one, removing and stacking their sandals, and cleansing their bare feet with the herbs and leaves in the bottom of the basin. Kit had helped gather them that morning. The greens released a delicious aroma of bay and thyme and rosemary as they were crushed. Formally, each person saluted Qazipatima, fisted hand to forehead, as they entered the ceremony room on cleansed bare feet.

Qazipatima the priestess would transform into an incarnation of the Goddess before she made the blessing. Kit tried not to burst with false pride at the sight of her beautiful sister honoring the Goddess Jasasara and blessing their lovely villa. It was due to Jasasara, not to her mother or father or her sisters or any of the Suramarti families, that they had such a beautiful home. Kit knew that pride was one of her personal failings, and she worked on conquering it every day.

Beside her, Isari sighed and Halima stood a silent shadow. They faced the first door and window combination. One novice priestess who had come with Qazipatima oversaw opening the door and window shutters of the polythyron at the correct times. Another initiate, probably her sister Biaja, would light and extinguish the lamps, so that the appropriate sections of the frescoes would be illuminated as the ceremony proceeded from west to east. At peace, Kit smiled and prepared to celebrate Jasasara's blessing.

After the family and guests finished eating and the ceremony was complete, the younger people dispersed. Halima went to her rooms to care for her infant daughter and chase after her son who had just discovered running.

Kit invited Isari to come out to the field to watch her practice. Isari was suffering from displacement, loss of her regular routine after the abrupt move her family had made. Much had been left behind when they escaped Akrotiri. The earthquakes were so large that they had been felt on Keftiu. Priestesses at Thera had sent strong warnings to all their people on that island. Earthquakes and steam warned of the Goddess' anger. Now Isari was on Keftiu with nothing to do.

"Take Isari around with you," Okune, Kit's mother had said. Okune had welcomed the refugees, but expected them to help at Suramarti. "Let her see what is available here for her. She could set herself up in one of the new workshops, perhaps."

"What is she going to do for tools and supplies?" Kit asked.

"Her father should be here soon with all that he could carry on the last family boat," Okune said, frowning with concern. "Until then, I suppose she could borrow from us, or perhaps from Jura's family."

Kit automatically scowled at the mention of Jura.

Her mother went on, "She could follow you around until then, perhaps help groom Enosidas?" At Kit's even deeper scowl, she hurriedly added, "Or perhaps they could use help at the Temple; she can go with you to the ceremony at the end of the week."

"Yes, all right. I'm happy to have her with me. But no one touches Enosidas but me. He *is* a bull, mama, not a pet for all to play with!"

"Of course," Okune had said, lips quirking.

Still scowling, Kitane went to find her cousin.

"I don't understand," Isari said as they walked to Kit's practice field. "I don't have to marry until I find the perfect match. Is your family rule so different from ours?"

"You don't have three sisters," Kit said. "That's the difference. Mama made sure we all understood that a long time ago. By age seventeen we have to be married, or the estate passes along to the next youngest sister. Qazi and Sakusna both chose not to marry—Qazi for the Goddess, Sakusna for trade."

Isari shivered. "She sails with that pirate Tros."

"He's not a pirate!" Kit looked at her cousin in shock. How could Isari believe such nonsense? Perhaps her mother was feeding her stupid stories—or Kit's own mother was. "He's a powerful trader. And rich." She thought about Tros, his strong, angular face, his dark-lashed deep green eyes. "I have thought about choosing him."

Isari looked at her, disbelief clear in her features. "*Tros!?* Oh, Kitane. *Oh.*"

Kit flinched. Now even her cousin was going to become involved in her choice of husband? It felt as if there was pressure coming from all sides. Then she thought of her father, who had said nothing at all about husbands or suitors or choices. She felt as if she had been hugged by the quiet, kind man. Perhaps she should spend more of her time with him, who did not pressure, did not judge her.

With a sigh, Kit turned and signaled Enosidas to catch up. The big animal had stopped to chew on his favorite snack bush. Kit watched carefully to make sure he did not get into the nearby oleander that made him so irritable. He—and she—needed to be perfect for the ceremony.

"Try to think of Tros as his own person, not as the wild man your mother has obviously described," she said. She hated to be short with Isari, but really. The prejudice she showed when she had never even met the man was a disgrace.

Isari shrugged. "Everyone says so, not just mother. But if you like him, I will try to also. He's probably better than Jura, who is just as big a statue as you said."

"Mother is looking at his wealth, his villa, his proximity. I don't think she's ever looked at the man himself. Oh! So rigid, so...umgh!"

Her cousin laughed.

"Oh! Remind me on the way home to show you where the best clay dig is."

"Yes, I want to get started, my hands are bored," Isari said with a smile.

They stopped walking at the top of a hill amidst wild grasses and small shrubs. This was Kit and Enosidas' practice field. From here they could see far down the slopes to the distant, blue Middle Sea, the jumble of stone and clay roofs of the Temple at Knossos, tiny so far away in the East and partly hidden by laurel and pine trees.

"I think it would be best if you sat here. I usually take him in a circle around this hillock. We won't run up here because of the stones, and they make a nice seat."

Isari nodded and lifted her pale blue linen robe up enough not to pull as she sat down. Kit tugged her own robe off over her head, leaving her torso and legs bare, just the tightly woven wool loincloth covering her, held up by the wide firm belt that fitted around her waist. She took off her necklace with its seal on a leather thong and set it on top of her robe. Isari patted the robe and watched as Kit stretched out briefly, then asked Enosidas to begin trotting in a circle.

Kit moved alongside him for a bit, loosening up her muscles some more, then she paused, turned, and ran the other way so that she and the bull were on a collision course. As they neared one another, Eno lowered his head and sped up a bit. She leaped, placing her palms firmly on the broad plane of his forehead, letting the momentum of her leap carry her feet over her head and the bull's. She landed facing backward, the soles of her feet firm and flat on Eno's back. She pounced forward, still using the momentum from her first leap and the bull's speed, placing her palms on his rump as she flipped off his back onto the ground, momentum still propelling her forward in a trot away from Eno and then around to meet him again.

After a few leaps, Kit fed Eno a handful of the oats she kept stashed in a sack among the stones, then stretched out again, and let Eno rest between the practice runs.

Isari walked over to where Kit was catching her breath. “Wow cousin, I never saw bull jumping like that on Thera. Our jumpers always grabbed the bull's horns. The bull did all the work tossing the jumper to the animal's back. Your way looks harder, but more dramatic. Is it dangerous?”

"There are many styles of jumping. I found when I used the horns, I always over-jumped. I landed on Eno's rump without room to push off for my final flip. I imagine it has something to do with the jumper's size and the bull's strength.”

Isari shook her head. “I thought all jumpers did the same tricks.”

“No, the most dangerous part of bull jumping is the many falls and injuries while figuring out the best method for the team. It's one reason no one ever tries a different bull once the camaraderie between the jumper and bull develops."

Isari watched, eyes wide, as Kitane and Enosidas performed the maneuver over and over again. Two leaps, two flips, two landings. For the ceremony, with thousands of people watching and the terrible penalty for losing, they needed to be perfect.

Scene 2 — Jura at Tylissos

Jura relived his childhood as he walked through the ancient olive trees to the highest point of the Tylissos villa. He entered the sanctuary and could recall his father's voice.

"Young Jura, the goddess Jasasara planted this olive tree when she granted your mother's family this land." He had raised Jura to touch the double-axe. "We call this a 'labrys' and it honors Jasasara." Next to Jasasara's monument, the horns of consecration towered over young Jura. "When you look up at the twin pylons, imagine the horns of the god Potidas' Bull."

The horns of consecration no longer towered over him and these early memories filled Jura with gratitude to be living in this time of peace and prosperity. Even when his little brother Ukan was born and Jura felt abandoned, he could find solace in the sanctuary. Jura upheld the traditions of his mother, and his mother's mother, with pride and honor.

His assistants filled the bull's head rhyton with wine and placed two baskets of small terracotta cups at his feet. The preparations for the morning ritual were complete. The atomai, all given time off for the ceremony, lined up to receive their portion of wine to honor Potidas, god of earth, sea, and the underworld.

Before the ceremony began, the earth shuddered, the baskets of cups rattled, and the atomai fell to or sat down on the ground. Jura reached for the nearby horns of consecration for balance and stood strong as a third pylon. He never skipped an opportunity to praise the gods. "Do not be afraid. Get up, arise. Potidas protects you in his sanctuary." They followed his example, though arising cautiously.

Jura was a telestai, a landowner. As a child, he walked with his father and looked for broken bricks, crushed stones, and pottery shards.

"Father. Look at that! What is it?

"Jura, you know. That is from an earthquake that collapsed an old building. All our villas and temples rest on the ruins of previous ones. The telestai always rebuild bigger and better after earthquakes."

Jura did not fear earthquakes.

The line of people moved quickly, each picking up a cup and receiving the portion of wine Jura offered. After refilling the rhyton several times, fifty supplicants stood around the horns of consecration. Before the ceremony started, Jura addressed the gathering. "Welcome, atomai of Tylissos. Together we protect and bless Keftiu."

He raised his cup and turned to face the priestess along with the others.

A priestess originally from Mount Ida, dressed in a purple robe with a gold belt and matching gold circlet, pronounced the invocation. Each person took a sip of wine, anointed the horns with the remainder, and smashed their cup.

One more earth tremble, stronger than the rest, knocked over a basket of cups and ended the observance. Still, Jura had honored Potidas as custom required. He knew the God approved.

He drank one extra cup of wine and smashed it for the many telestai and atomai who neglected their responsibilities. The gods had inflicted the recent spate of earthquakes because the people of Keftiu had forsaken their traditions. Good times had brought lax observances of these important rituals.

Later in the day, he searched his family's storerooms for a gift to bring Okune, something appropriate for the mother of the woman he wished to marry. Today he selected a pitcher, painted with graceful blue dolphins. He knew that both Okune and her daughter Kitane favored dolphins, and the Keftiu artists had portrayed them so well they almost looked like they were alive and leaping in the waves.

He filled the pitcher with his special olive-blossom honey and sealed it with beeswax. He strapped it to his back for the short walk to the Suramarti villa. That family was the oldest and most revered in the area. Some said that they had settled here even before the gods chose Knossos for the temple site.

"Thank you for the lovely pitcher and your fine honey." Okune handed the round-bottom pitcher to a servant and took Jura's hand. "Walk with me and tell me what is on your mind."

Even though tradition said Kitane would make her own choice, everyone knew Okune was in charge. Okune had already broken tradition by demanding her daughters marry by seventeen or forgo their inheritance. Two daughters had already lost their chance. Jura had to please both Okune and Kitane if he wanted to marry Kitane, and Kitane's seventeenth birthday was closer every day.

They walked through the vineyard. He began, "Every day I come to visit Kitane, but she is always busy. Yesterday she rebuked me for not removing my shoes, then ran away. Before that, she sat with her ladies spinning. Another day she worked with her father, Radamitu, in his goldsmithing workshop."

When Okune didn't reply, he thought she didn't believe him. Then he recalled, "Once she was baking pita. She walked around the saj, constantly turning each piece of bread with a long wooden spatula. Each time a loud clang interrupted our conversation."

Okune kept walking in silence.

After waiting to see if she would respond, he continued. "Sometimes I think she is avoiding me. I can never get her alone to talk about us and our future. My father says I must talk to her uninterrupted."

Okune nodded. "Your father is correct. Even though I support the match, you know the ultimate decision is with Kit."

She said it was Kit's decision but without Okune's endorsement, his chances were small. He took her comment as an indication that while he was her choice, he was not Kit's.

Discouraged, he looked at the ground. "I don't know what to do. I have followed the Keftiu way. I am here every day. I bring gifts, some of which she accepts. Still whenever I am around, she is busy. My younger brother Ukan, who is in training at Knossos, just laughs at me. I am sure he talks to her sister Biaja in Knossos and they laugh together."

Her mother took a deep breath as if she felt talking to her future son-in-law was tedious. She let out the breath and spoke slowly, as if to a child. "Every morning she walks by herself to our sanctuary in the hills." Okune pointed toward a hill covered in olive trees, but he didn't look up. He knew the place well. He had lived next to the Suramarti villa all his life.

When Jura's first facial hair sprouted under his nose, his father walked with him up to the sanctuary. Under the ancient olive tree, he explained, "Your sister Eluwari will inherit Tylissos." He then put his arm around his son, "Radamitu and I expect you will marry Kitane and move to Suramarti."

Jura did not reply. Even at that immature age, he understood that such decisions belonged to the women.

He had never expected so many difficulties courting Kitane. He explained to Okune that custom demanded he honor Potidas each morning to help calm the earthquakes, something others were neglecting. "I'm certain that these critical ceremonies are getting smaller and fewer. I dare not stop now."

Okune nodded. "Good, thank you."

That short answer told Jura to try something else. "Thank you for your suggestion. For one day, I will have my steward organize the ceremony. I will be there tomorrow morning."

"Without your shoes," Okune said with a quirk of her lips.

Jura couldn't believe that these women kept complaining about his shoes when they had not fulfilled their responsibility of daily rituals to entreat Potidas to save Keftiu from the earthquakes. Of course, Kitane's extraordinary bull jumping also pleased Potidas and helped. Nothing at Suramarti was simple.

"Yes," Jura said. "Without my shoes."

SCENE 3 — BIAJA AT KNOSSOS

Biaja rubbed at her scalp again. The barber had scraped a little too closely that morning, and cut her. She tried to rub it gently, so as to not start it bleeding again, but it stung and itched. Had he put something in it? She crept out of the prayer room on her hands and knees and went to the apothecary.

“A small pot of beeswax, please?”

“For what purpose, Initiate Biaja?”

Wordlessly, Bee turned her head and pointed at the cut.

“My, that is a bad scrape. Did you annoy the barber?” the woman said, turning toward a shelf on her right.

“I did not,” she said. “Not that I know.” Perhaps he was drunk the night before, she thought.

“Perhaps he was too rushed.”

Biaja shrugged and accepted the tiny bowl.

“Chamomile flowers in that, for soothing. That should help.”

“Thank you.” She immediately scooped up some of the soft scented wax with her fingertips. She set the bowl down, pulled the back hair lock out of the way and spread on the ointment. Immediately, the sore patch on her head felt better. She gently spread another scoop over the area, then took the bowl and walked to her dormitory. She placed the beeswax on the little table of cosmetics on the wall opposite the six sleeping mats, where all the initiates had their hairbrushes and other personal things.

She stopped to admire one of the other girl's hairbrush, with bristles made from boar whiskers, or some such thing, that had come from very far away. It was made near the land of the stone circles, which her brother the trader had talked about. She wondered what other treasures they might have in that land, where such a wonderful brush was made. Such faraway places always sounded like intriguing mysteries to her. She sighed and set the hairbrush back down in its place.

She was stepping out into the hallway to head back to the prayer session when she saw the klawiphoros heading her way. She flinched, trying to hide when there was nowhere to hide.

How did they ever get initiates to stay and become priestesses when they were exposed to someone like this woman? The klawiphoros was in charge of the initiates; it was her job to keep track of the young women and ensure they exhibited proper behavior. But no one called her by her title. Everyone called her the Aurochs instead, even the Priestess Qazipatima, Biaja's eldest sister.

Biaja ducked her head as she passed the old woman, but she did not get away so easily. The Aurochs grabbed her by the upper arm and pulled so that Bee came to a stop sideways. Then the Aurochs leaned forward and spoke in her ear.

"This. Is. Prayer. Time," she said in a heavy whisper.

Bee bowed and kept silent, as was proper. Of course, she knew it was prayer time. But it did not honor the Goddess to have blood dripping everywhere from improperly shaved heads. She turned her face away from the Aurochs, to show the back of her scalp, now glistening with beeswax.

"Oh, such a deadly wound," the Aurochs said. "I see it has been treated. Get back to the business of prayer. One-mark extra service duty tomorrow morning."

Biaja bowed again, still silent. Inside, she seethed. This was not her fault. It was not her doing that the barber made a mess of her head! The unblessed *barber* should have to clean for an extra mark!

Nopine commiserated with Biaja over the extra work.

"She is so strict. I wonder if she is just unhappy?" Nopine said.

Bee set down Nopine's hairbrush and began braiding her friend's hair. "I don't know. I mentioned it to Qazipatima and she seemed surprised."

"You are so lucky your sister is here to watch over you."

"Actually, I believe that is part of the problem. Maybe the Aurochs thinks I expect special privileges or something."

"But you don't, Bee. I make a lot more mistakes than you do," Nopine said, handing Biaja the ribbons to tie off her braid. Bee wished she could have hair again. She would not be a full initiate for another half-year. Then she could let her hair grow out. Nopine's had been growing for two years now. It actually looked like hair, instead of one front and one back lock pasted on to a bare head.

Biaja shook out the ribbon strips of fine linen and aligned them to each other before tying them onto the ends of Nopine's heavy hair. Even after two years, Nopine's braids were frizzy from all different hair lengths—the ends escaping and looking rough.

"Qazi said, 'That is not the Goddess' Way.'" Biaja shook her head. "Then she said something about aching bones, and walked away. I really hope she doesn't talk to the Aurochs, or I'll be in even more trouble. I should never have said anything to her."

"It will be all right, Bee. I'm sure the priestesses keep an eye on things, to be certain they are fair."

"I am pretty sure this *is* the Aurochs being 'fair,'" Biaja said, sarcasm weighting her tone.

Nopine went on to the classroom where she was studying writing and reading and accounting.

Bee went and got a rough pitcher of warm water and a scrub brush. She put some lye from the pithos full of cleaning solution into her pitcher and took it into the Preparatory Room.

She'd worn her oldest robe, but now she tied the skirt up with her tight belt and got down on her bare knees. They'd heal better than the robe would. She scrubbed the floor of the lustral basin, thinking about robes. Qazi had been wearing a beautiful purple over-gown when they'd spoken the previous evening. For the ceremonies she had been doing all day as priestess, Qazi had tied on one of her two flounced long aprons and had worn a matching headdress. The colorful traditional outfit was the only thing Bee looked forward to—if she ever got that far in the Temple.

She dunked the scrub brush back into the pitcher of lye-softened water and scrubbed each stone of the steps with care.

Qazi was already so beautiful, and when she donned the formal clothing of a full priestess she became quite intimidating, both because of her position, and her beauty. It was no wonder the guasileus begged Qazi to attend when he must entertain foreign dignitaries. She was impressive and carried the Goddess in an aura of sheer feminine power. Her Presence helped all Keftiu.

Biaja sighed. Even Sakusna was prettier than she and Kit were. It was as if the Goddess had run out of beauty by the time she got to the two younger girls. Kitane was graceful and agile. Bee didn't know what she herself was yet. She liked to think she had lovely blue-black hair and interesting green eyes. But so far, no man had even looked at her, much less shown interest in courting—because Kitane must marry first. If she was going to at all.

Biaja shook her head. She could not make up her mind between wanting Kit to marry Jura so that she herself would not have to, and wanting Kit to not marry at all so she could inherit.

Owning and running an estate did not seem so bad. She liked the idea of having the resources of an entire villa at her disposal. But it would be at the cost of marrying Jura. She felt a fair amount of sympathy for her next-oldest sister. In truth, no one seemed to want to marry Jura. If Kit married him—which she must do soon or lose her right to inherit—then Bee could choose among the many other young men available. She went down the list geographically: closest to Suramarti was Tylissos where Jura lived, along with his younger brother Ukan. The younger brother was funny and kind—and well on his way to becoming the village drunk. He would not do for Biaja.

Then there was the young man from Amnisos, the port below Knossos. What was his name? He was cute, but foolish. Maybe he would improve with age.

She went and dumped the dirty water from her pitcher down the drain, made her way to the rainwater cistern by the kitchens and refilled it. She splashed lye into the water with a wooden scoop and used a stick of firewood to stir it. She returned to the Preparatory Rooms and, turning the corner, ran full into the Aurochs. Sudsy, caustic lye-water splashed over both of them.

The Aurochs was speechless. Then the woman snatched Biaja's robe loose from her belt and used the skirt to wipe her own legs and feet dry. Biaja set down the pitcher and tried to help.

"Stop it, you stupid girl! You are only making things worse!"

Bee froze like a mouse in the shadow of a hawk.

When the older woman was dry enough not to drip, she glared at Biaja, then turned to walk out of the room. Just before she went through the door, she turned back, scowling, and said, "There is a load of goods that must be taken to the shrine at Mount Ida. That will be your job tomorrow. You may take one donkey to carry the goods. You will, yourself, walk. I expect you back before the end of the following day. Use this time to think about what you are doing, who you are becoming, initiate."

"But—" her hands flew up to cover her traitorous mouth too late to prevent the escape of the single word.

Eyebrow raised, the Aurochs went on, and "I expect you to help the priestesses there to store away the votive cups and tablets."

Biaja bowed. She stared at the Aurochs' back as the woman swept from the room.

So much for being able to join Nopine at the initiate's ceremony tomorrow.

Scene 4 — Tros on the Middle Sea

The open sky and bright midday sun provided no warning for the afternoon winds. The waves washed into Tros' ships, soaking the oarsmen. He could taste the salty sea foam that filled the air. He raised his triangular signal pennant and spun it around. "Left. Left! Turn left into the waves."

The oars on the left side, totaling three hands, rowed in reverse and the three hands of oars on the right side pulled forward.

"Archers, don't just stand there. Help them."

The archers squeezed in beside the oarsmen. The two smaller boats, with only a hand of oars on each side, followed his lead.

"Good. Now bail. The rest of you bail!"

The nighttime oarsmen, who had been sleeping amidst the cargo, jumped up, grabbing pottery and baskets, and bailed the ships. The bare-chested men, soaking wet and covered in salty spray, sweated and grunted as they battled against the sea.

Tros kept careful watch, for the ships threatened to sink into the angry water as the waves grew larger. "Bail! Faster!"

He took a mental inventory of the cargo in his care. The cheapest, heaviest cargo would go first. However, he was an experienced captain, the best sailor in the Middle Sea. This storm would not frighten him into foolish action. He knew his men. The danger gave them energy and strength.

He had the foresight to take on an extra load of bronze-gold. It didn't bring as great a profit as the scarcer bronze-silver, but the extra weight kept his ships stable in rough seas. Regardless, this would be the first to go, if the gods demanded a sacrifice.

With sunset, the winds exhausted themselves, and Tros had not needed to throw any cargo overboard. By dark, the wind had stopped and they were victorious. Tros had once again demonstrated his expertise as the ships' captain. The crew knew he was the best.

This reputation went beyond his home in the Hellene territories, all the way to the island of the major trading families—Keftiu. Several months ago, one of the strongest trading groups had partnered with Tros. Their representative, Sakusna, now occupied the captain's tent at the front of the ship.

Tros hadn't wanted a woman on his ship, but in the end, he had made the family pay dearly for her passage. The fee had been enough to replace the worn woolen sails with shiny new linen ones.

Only the best ships had linen sails, and this showed everyone that Tros was the best.

He smiled to himself when the Suramarti seal stamped the agreement. Beyond the prestigious partnership, he had bigger plans. He intended to marry Sakusna's sister, Kitane.

With the evening calm, Tros' little fleet returned to their easterly heading on the final portion of the many-months journey. They had visited the great island of Alashiya for bronze-silver which they had traded for cypress lumber from the Hittite empire on the eastern shore of the Middle Sea, and for gold, ebony, and ivory from the Pharaoh of Kmt. In Kmt, Sakusna also traded Keftiu palms for date palms. They completed the circle back to Alashiya for more bronze-silver, and on to Arzawa for resin before returning to the Archipelago.

This had been a profitable voyage. Now they headed back to Keftiu and the grand port of Amnisos. When Tros agreed to the voyage, his hope of a union with Kitane had prevented him from negotiating too hard. Tros could still feel the attraction of her athletic form, and her tantalizing odor, a combination of sweat, grass, and her bull.

During the long expedition, the situation changed. The gods expressed their displeasure with the Keftiu outpost on the island of Thera. The volcano at the center of Thera, known as Kaimeni Island, spit steam and ash. The god Potidas shook Thera, Keftiu, and the entire Archipelago. Everyone abandoned Thera. Others refused to even sail through the Archipelago. He was not afraid, and if Sakusna had not demanded her strange concept of fair-trading practices, he could have made a good profit. He regretted his alliance, but the thought of the lithe Kitane kept him going. *If Sakusna had not been on board... If Kitane had not been so tempting...*

While it was still dark, Tros scanned the night sky for the big and little *Double Axes* to locate the star of the *Great Bull*, the North Star. Once he confirmed his ship's course, he looked to the east.

The *Triton* was rising in the east. Next would be the *Dolphin* with the sun. Tros had not slept. Even though the wind was calm and the sky cloudless, the god Potidas had stirred the sea all night. Tros had pointed the ships into the angry waves, but still the crew had not slept, bailing all night.

Tros was a young captain. He'd only lived four hands of summers. From an early age, he had sailed with his father, over his mother's objections. She kept him home during short days of the stormy season and prayed to Jasasara the rest of the time when heavy winds could interrupt even the nicest days. His parents fought over this constantly. In the end, Tros sailed during some winter storms and stayed home from some peaceful summer voyages.

Fate and his mother made him miss the journey that was hit by an unexpected summer tempest. His father's ship had not returned. His mother urged him to stay ashore and manage the family bronze-silver mines, but he demanded to sail in his father's memory. Now, also in his father's footsteps, he intended to marry a Keftiu girl and bring her to the Hellene territories.

The boy at the top of the single mast shouted, "Ship!" Tros wasn't a pirate, but every ship at sea was an opportunity for profit, profit he didn't have to share with Sakusna's organization. Information, trade, and salvage could all benefit the better crew and captain, and Tros was the best.

Tros curled his fingers into a small opening and peered through it to better view the target. It was a solitary ship, sailing the Middle Sea alone. No experienced captains went out with just a single ship. Small planks lashed together marked the ship as cheaply made. Tros sensed many possibilities.

"At stations, boys. Row hard. Approach with all speed. Archers take your places."

Tros rushed to the raised platform at the front to assess the situation. In the dim dawn light, he tripped into the captain's tent that shared the observation deck.

"Tros! Tros! Goddess curse you! What are you doing running around before the sun?"

That would be Sakusna. Tros had to remind himself that she was the Suramarti representative and Kitane's older sister. He put up with her imperiousness because her cooperation would help to convince the Suramarti matriarch that he was a suitable match for Kitane. More than once, he'd considered abandoning this annoying sister. As a last resort, he planned to have the lovely Kitane hide in the tent and sail away without her family's approval.

They neared the foundering ship, and an old woman shouted across the waves, "Greetings, we claim the right of the goddess for assistance at sea."

Sakusna immediately responded, "I am of the Suramarti family. Have no fear, the goddess brings you comfort and security."

Tros clenched his fists and assessed the situation. The approaching ship had oars totaling less than two hands on a side compared to his superior three hands of oars, plus his smaller boats. Their wool sail, which they should have furled in this weather, had been through too many storms. The rising sun shone through the tattered edges and holes eaten by rats. The ship held too many passengers and not enough cargo. It rocked precariously. Only the mercy of Potidas kept it afloat.

"Rowers, stow your oars." Tros looked away from the sad ship to Sakusna. He shook his fist, "Do not forget this is *my* ship. You are just a passenger. You do not speak for the captain."

She turned to Tros and replied in a steady voice, "I speak for the goddess."

He thought, *you and your goddess can join this sorry ship. Potidas can take you to his underwater home.*

Scene 5 — Paian at Knossos South Entrance

Paian had traveled across the sea to Knossos, the grandest temple in all the world. He was born in a settlement far to the north dedicated to the Hellene goddess Athena. At first, Knossos bewildered him with so many rooms and stairs. He thought the Keftiu who built it to be gods. Later he found the peaceful and orderly Keftiu society even more unbelievable than the Temple.

He could still hear his father, "Never venture outside our walls."

When he grew big enough to carry his own sword and shield, the advice changed, "Paian, always stay with your patrol group, never go off alone."

Still he could explore more than the girls, who were never to leave the village. Since he'd arrived in Keftiu, he'd not had an occasion to even unpack his sword or shield. Even without venturing beyond the temple walls, he observed and interviewed, writing a history of his visit to the exotic land of Keftiu, complete with sketches and a map.

Today he received shipments from the peaceful countryside. Men and women walked for days to deliver goods to the Temple with little concern for their own safety. The well-traveled paths presented negligible risk from man or beast. He waited in the south house. To pass the time, he took a piece of damp clay from a leather pouch that hung from his waist. He flattened it into a miniature tablet, inscribed a short poem, and hid it on a high shelf to dry.

Bull jumper of grace and agility
You inspire my admiration, my awe,
My love.

Due to today's festival, many people streamed over the ravine across the wide viaduct. Beyond the rolling hills to the south and west, he could see the sacred peaks of Mount Ida. He hoped someday to visit the holy sanctuary, but he still worried that such a journey would be dangerous without an armed escort.

Initiation Day, he thought. Groups of boys and groups of girls, all with shaved heads, walked through the South Entrance, chatting nervously. Most wore undyed wool, uncut cloth, wrapped around their youthful bodies and tied with coarse ropes. The rare robe dyed green or blue stood out in the mass of grey wool and olive skin. Many wore bracelets. Some girls wore small earrings and pendants with blue or green stones sparkling in the morning sun.

He searched the crowd for seal stones. Even in far-away Athens, he had heard of the Keftiu seals. For the entire world, seals indicated a people of organization. He tied his seal around his wrist with a leather cord. He had traveled to Knossos carrying a block of red marble, smaller than his fist, just for this purpose. Of course, he'd waited for his arrival to get it carved, as the most accomplished sculptors were in the Knossos workshops.

The seal stones marked the children of the telestai landowners or other important people, including scribes like himself. He silently thanked his mother for insisting he learn to read and write. Athens might be dangerous, but the people of Athens valued writing more than temples and gold. He thought proudly, *so many Athenians can read and write they do not need seals.*

The writing of his home differed from Knossos Temple writing, but there was enough in common and he picked it up quickly. Often, he wrote the same thing twice to keep in practice with both forms.

Behind the heads of the initiates, he spied a line of donkeys. He walked down the road to meet them, noting that none in this group wore a seal stone.

He greeted them with, "Welcome pilgrims. Blessings of the Goddess Jasasara upon you." Taxpayers would have been a more accurate salutation, but pilgrims sounded nicer, politer. Besides, he didn't know the Keftiu word for taxpayer.

The leader, no older than the boys and girls attending the festival, replied, "Blessings to you also, scribe Paian, from across the sea."

She recognized him. This was not the first delivery he received from her. He looked again and blushed in embarrassment at not recognizing her. "Goddess' greetings and blessings to you Maza, good friend."

She replied, "The Goddess may bring blessings, but the God Potidas shakes the ground terrifying the children and animals."

She added, "Do you have another poem you want delivered to the bull jumper?"

He worried that she remembered too much. "No poem today."

Paian felt nervous speaking to Maza. She belonged to the worker class, atomai. Since he could read and write, he was an elite on Keftiu where the atomai and telestai led separate lives. Back home all those living within the village walls were equal. They lived or died by the efforts of the group. This was something the Keftiu could learn from the people of Athens.

He thought of himself as an outsider in this strange place. He belonged with neither the atomai nor the telestai. He could read and write, but he didn't own land. Back home his mother had a school where all could learn their letters. Something else the Keftiu could learn. He found the situation awkward and confusing, but he tried to remain neutral, to be a friend to all.

He led Maza and the donkey train away from the initiates. "Because of a festival today, we cannot use the South Entrance. We must go around to the west."

She kicked a rock.

"I'll bring you as close as possible before we need to carry them..." He looked at the line of donkeys. They were laden with cloth sacks, so not olive oil, or wine. They could have brought ceramic clay, or wool for weaving, or plaster for frescos, or herbs for dying. Knossos required so much from the countryside.

It was none of those. The odor answered his question.

"...carry the onions to the storerooms."

She gave him a faint smile. "I trust you, Hellene Paian, to be fair."

They tied the donkey train in the west courtyard and carried the onions. Paian carried a sack on the first trip as a friendly gesture. Everyone else made several trips. As with all routes through Knossos, the halls turned many times, like a maze, until they reached the long repository corridor.

They emptied their sacks into waiting pithoi, the large ceramic storage jars which could easily have held a couple of those initiates marching to the festival.

Each time they filled a pithos, he secured it with a string and a wedge of clay from his pouch and imprinted the seal with his stone. He also made Maza a duplicate seal for her receipt.

She filled one sack with clay receipts and another with the empty sacks. He walked them out and watched until they disappeared at the bottom of the ravine where they'd water their animals for the return trip, to somewhere....

Back in the south house, he retrieved his poem. He wrapped it in a grape leaf and sealed it like a pithos. With Maza gone, he'd have to find another courier, but that was safer for the secrecy of his plan. He put it in his pouch along with his remaining supply of clay.

In the middle of the day, someone came to relieve him, and he went to the Central Court. The festival would certainly have food, and the seal stone around his wrist would gain him entrance and the privilege for a bowl of barley in olive oil with some bread or pistachios.

As he ate, he looked across the crowd for someone who could deliver his poem to the bull jumper, someone that lived or worked along the path to Mount Ida. He collected his courage and asked one of the initiates, "Do you go to Mount Ida often? Can you deliver my poem to the bull jumper who lives on that path?"

The girl ignored him and walked away. He turned to another and repeated his query adding, "Please. I am from across the Middle Sea and have never been out of the temple."

She looked at him. He gave her a crooked smile.

The girl pointed across the hall. "That is Biaja. She might help you."

"The one with the shiny black seal stone around her neck?" he asked.

"That's the one," she said and ran off to catch up with her friends.

When Paian left Athens, tears ran down his mother's face as she hugged him. She whispered in his ear, "Your father wants to you learn Keftiu writing. He sees the days when we might go to war with one another, and we will benefit if we can intercept and read their orders."

He held his mother, "You know I am a good student. I will learn to read and write Keftiu. I will even write a story of my travels, twice, with both letters."

She did not let go, "You have not asked me what I want? Why do I let my son travel so far away?"

"What can I do for my mother?"

"You can bring home a Keftiu bride. They are the brightest and strongest. A Keftiu bride will be the best partner for you."

"Yes mother, so you've told me. I will not forget."

Paian searched for a Keftiu wife. His first choice was the graceful bull jumper. He watched the girl with the black stone as he walked around the large room, tightly grasping the small clay tablet wrapped in a grape leaf.

"Blessings of Jasasara, lovely Biaja."

She turned to him, first with a smile, but when she didn't recognize him, a small frown. "Who are you?"

He ignored her lack of return blessings. He thrust the package toward her, "Here. For the bull jumper that lives on the path to Mount Ida. Would you carry it there for me?"

She paused as if she would not take it, but finally did. She smiled as if there was some private joke here.

"Lucky for you, I am off to Mount Ida soon. I can carry the tablet, but I cannot assure she will read it."

He retreated, walking backward, embarrassed, but hoping the bull jumper would receive the tablet as he intended. Maza had delivered a couple of poems, but he'd not received any replies. Women of Athens loved poems; Keftiu women were different. He found this hard to understand.

The afternoon deliveries distracted him from his quest for a bride. The first shipment included many sacks of plaster. The plaster came from a nearby gypsum quarry. He knew some gypsum came in blocks of different shapes and sizes, but the quarriers cooked much of the gypsum to make plaster that the Keftiu used to cover their walls.

He directed the donkeys laden with plaster to the west courtyard. They had a longer trek to carry the plaster up two levels of stairs to the throne room. The new throne room had a beautifully carved throne made of gypsum. The walls were white. He watched the artists carve lines in the plaster. He could see plants and animals taking shape. Baskets of black, red, yellow, and blue pigments awaited the next step.

Acknowledgments and Credits

Many people and organizations (knowingly and not) contributed to this work of fiction. Acknowledgment here does not imply an endorsement, review, or even knowledge, of this book.

We must mention these two, Zoomie and Moshi, who still believe this book is about cats.

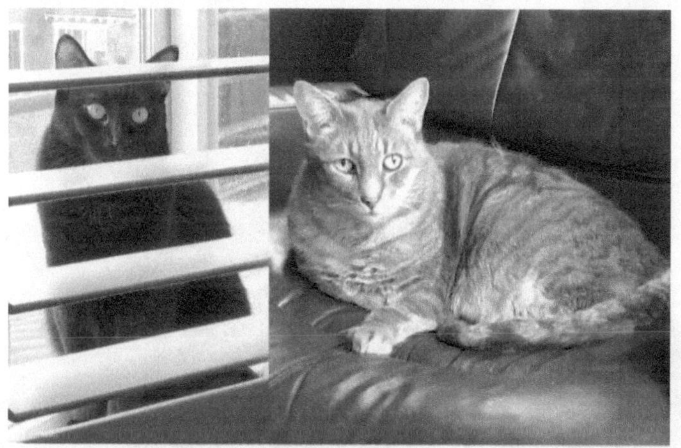

Special thanks

Thanks to the advanced readers who are responsible for the improvements from the earlier versions and have nothing to do with the remaining issues.

Chapter graphics

Mosque by VectorIconSet10 from the Noun Project 1743661
Spa by Creative Design from the Noun Project 2528450
Writing by Template from the Noun Project 2873092

About the Authors

The authors grew up outside San Francisco and New York City before meeting in Salt Lake City. J. raised three wonderful children while founding Omega Cat Press and making time to publish poems and short stories. D.R. researched Silicon Valley startups. Today they live in Southern California with their two cats. They enjoy international travel (when possible), reading, and writing, and gathering a different perspective from the magical minds of their grandchildren.

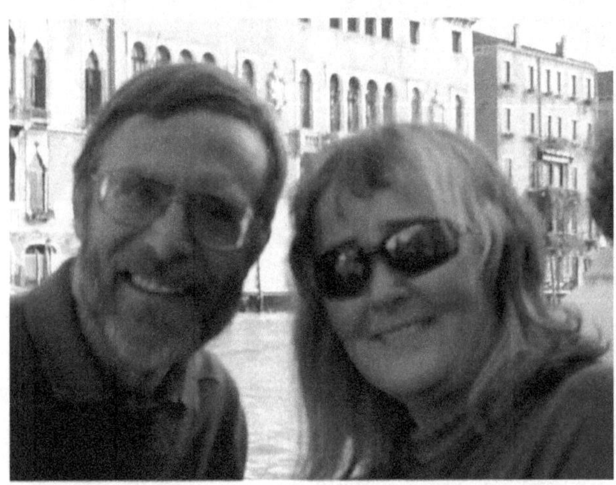

www.ingramcontent.com/pod-product-compliance
Lightning Source LLC
Chambersburg PA
CBHW020312200626
46814CB00006BA/2214

* 9 7 8 1 9 5 4 2 2 5 0 0 8 *